STOLEN MIDNIGHTS

ALSO BY KATHERINE QUINN

THE MISTLAND SERIES

To Kill a Shadow

To Shatter the Night

The Golden Huntress

STOLEN MIDNIGHTS

KATHERINE QUINN

DELACORTE PRESS

Delacorte Press
An imprint of Random House Children's Books
A division of Penguin Random House LLC
1745 Broadway, New York, NY 10019
penguinrandomhouse.com
rhcbooks.com

Editor: Alison Romig
Cover Designer: Casey Moses
Interior Designer: Jinna Shin
Production Editor: Colleen Fellingham
Managing Editor: Tamar Schwartz
Production Manager: Shameiza Ally

Library of Congress Cataloging-in-Publication Data is available upon request.
ISBN 979-8-217-11721-5 (trade) — ISBN 979-8-217-11723-9 (ebook)

The text of this book is set in 11-point Dante MT Pro.

Manufactured in China
10 9 8 7 6 5 4 3 2

The authorized representative in the EU for product safety and compliance is Penguin Random House Ireland, Morrison Chambers, 32 Nassau Street, Dublin D02 YH68, Ireland, https://eu-contact.penguin.ie.

TO THE DREAMERS, THE REBELS,
AND THE REVOLUTIONARIES IN PINK—

RISE UP.

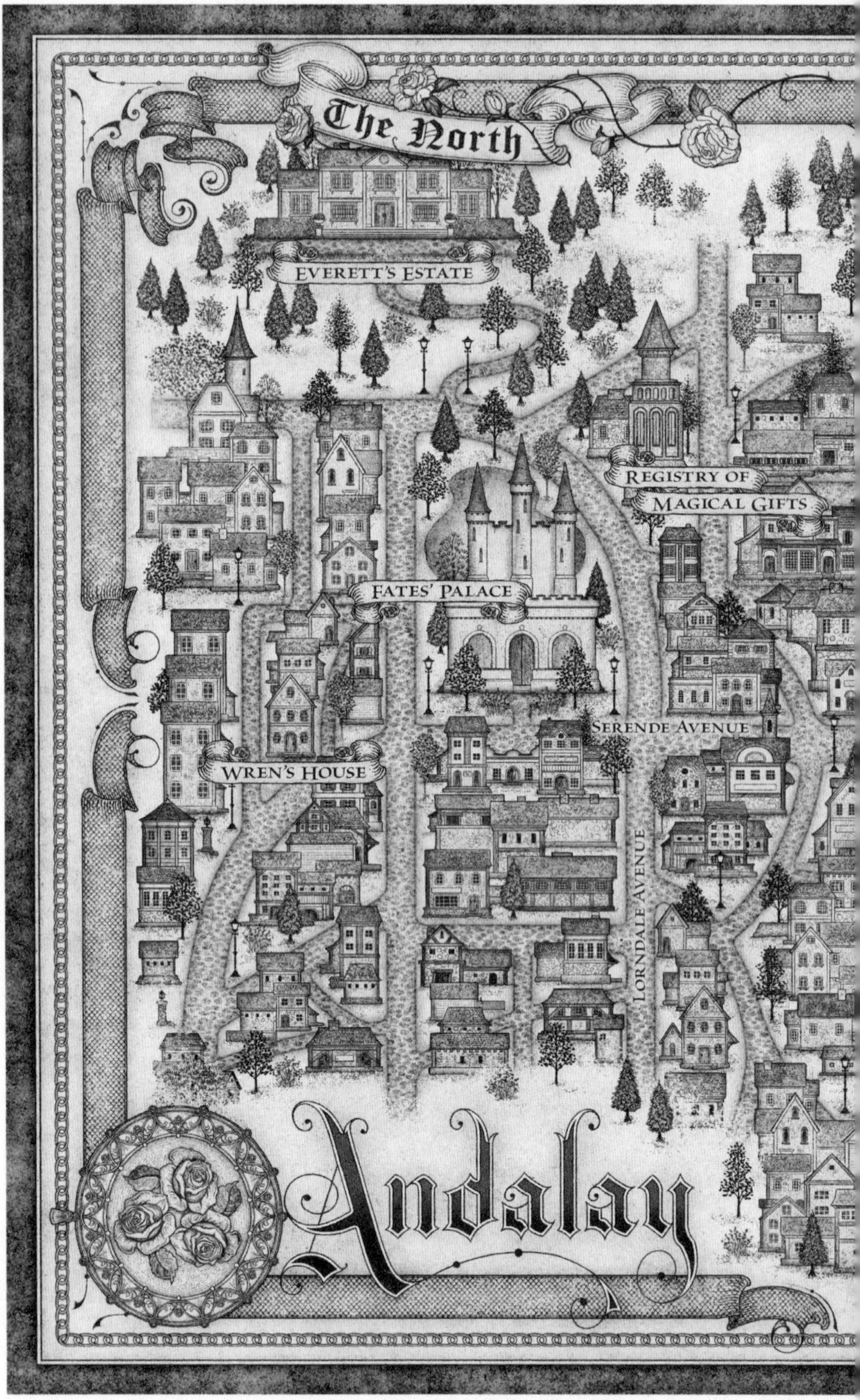

The North

Everett's Estate

Registry of Magical Gifts

Fates' Palace

Serende Avenue

Wren's House

Lorndale Avenue

Andalay

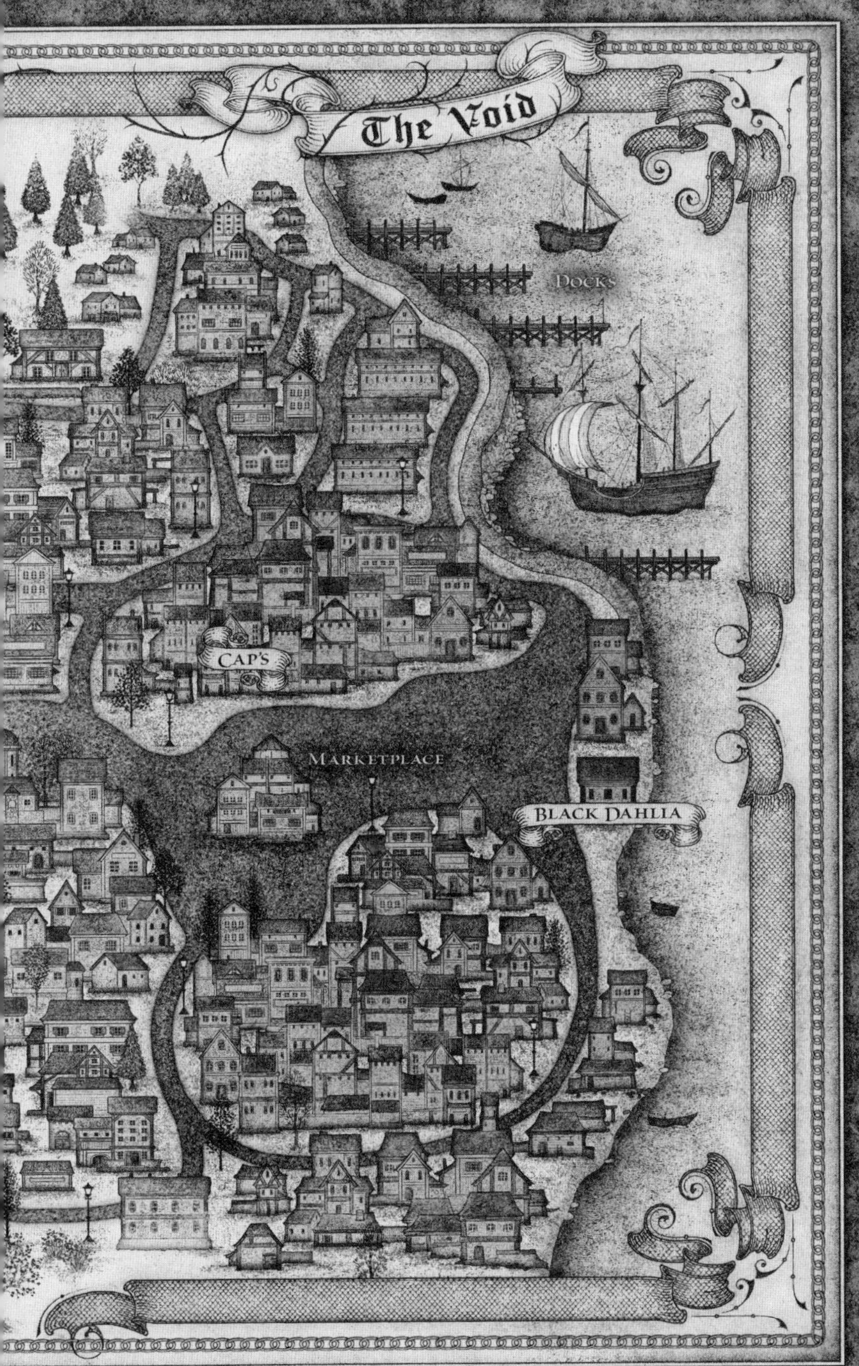
The Void
Docks
Cap's
Marketplace
Black Dahlia

CHAPTER ONE

WREN

Magic is in our blood. It is our birthright.
—AURILIAN DECREE

When the clock chimed midnight on an Aurilian's eighteenth birthday, a remarkable and utterly beguiling event would occur.

For the blessed—deemed such by the almighty Fates—a *gift* would be delivered.

It could be a tarnished pair of earrings or a plain silk ribbon. A polished pocket watch might appear, a mottled hand mirror, an empty picture frame. Yet these were no ordinary gifts; not the unimpressive celebratory trinkets they seemed to be.

They were born of *magic*. Gifted to the most faithful and highest-ranking members of Aurilian society in the capital city of Andalay by the three Fates that walked among us—Dawn, Day, and Dusk—and presented by their loyal onyx hounds in a simple blue box.

On my walks through the market with Mother I'd linger to gaze upon the three towers belonging to the Fates' palace. My heart leapt at the sight of the crystalline spires and dusty-pink marble, how those walls reminded me of clouds settling below a summer sunset sky. The Fates were untouchable behind their fortress in the heart of the north, yet our world spun around them, their ethereal home a reminder to trust in their guidance.

Tonight, I would finally join my father, mother, and sister; the Hayes family had never *not* received a gift, and soon, it was expected I'd assume my rightful place among my powerful family.

I paced before the ornate grandfather clock in our parlor, my heavy pale pink skirts swishing about my feet. The luxurious satin produced a grating sound with each step, but I couldn't stop; my time was almost here.

I prayed that one day I'd be fortunate like my mother. Not only did she receive her gift, but she was one of the rare few *spoken* to by a Fate. On her thirtieth birthday, the elusive Dusk had pulled her aside during a grand party. They spoke for but a minute, and while many harassed her for details after Dusk departed, Mother remained adamant that the words were for her, and for her alone to know. She hadn't even told Father.

A shiver ran down my spine at the thought of being alone with one of the ancient beings whose magic coursed throughout the realm; through each flower to every gust of wind.

Maybe I'd get lucky too, though the thought intimidated me.

Eighteen. Whether or not I would be favored like my mother, I was still turning eighteen at midnight, and my magic would arrive. *I* would arrive.

I had to maintain faith that all my years of prayer and loyalty hadn't gone unnoticed.

"Settle down, Wren," Father barked from his brocade armchair, a glass of brandy cradled in his palms. His bushy gray mustache wrinkled as I ignored him, shooting off for the other side of the room. I eyed our ancestors' portraits hanging on the forest-green walls and scowled at the way their serious faces were forever frozen in disappointment.

An entire line of Hayeses that I had to live up to. Favorites of the Fates, society argued. *Blessed.*

"One more minute," I mumbled, sneaking an impatient glance at my mother, Lenore, who looked appallingly bored sprawled across the velvet chaise. She, too, held a glass of liquor in her dainty hands, her fingers covered in rings of rubies and diamonds. She was elegant, my mother, stunning in a way no one had likened me to. The only trait I possessed of hers was her eye color, which was a bright turquoise shade that had been the admiration of her earlier suitors before my father, Cameron Hayes, had swept her off her feet. While her hair was bright and golden, mine was a deeper caramel color and, she complained, was incessantly tangled and wild. My nose wasn't upturned and effortlessly regal like hers, and my lips weren't half as full and lush. I'd heard the petty gossipers whispering away during our dinner parties, murmuring what a shame it was that I didn't possess her delicate beauty.

But there were much greater things to achieve in life than idle beauty. And I liked my reflection just fine.

Father grumbled, the shine of his magicked pen catching the glint of the firelight. That fountain pen held immense power, a way to convince the recipients of his letters of almost anything.

The gift of persuasion. It was the reason we lived in our three-story brick mansion in the swanky center of Andalay—the capital of Aurilia—and the reason he was the entrusted Representative of Ward One. With a simple vial of ink, he swayed politicians and society members alike, his words captured on paper more potent than any partisan speech. Or the actual king in the western lands, for that matter. Not that the royals had much authority in the east.

I envied such an ability. The control—how wonderfully devious Father must feel being able to hold such influence with the flick of a wrist. True freedom—that's what it represented, and after a lifetime of boredom and pretending to be the perfect well-bred daughter, I desired any and all excuses to be exceptional. To be *me* . . . but without constraints.

Mother, on the other hand, had been granted a pair of cornflower-blue silk slippers. She barely wore them—the prize kept on a high shelf in her armoire. They weren't as impressive as Father's pen, but when she chose to don them for the season's exclusive events, she rivaled any professional dancer on the floor. Once upon a time, she'd been renowned, a famed performer who was welcome in any fine theater or hall. As the years wore on, society had inevitably shifted its focus to the young and spry; bright new faces that people admired from afar. I didn't think she'd ever gotten over being pushed off the stage.

A small part of me felt sorrow for her. If she hadn't been so aloof, so prickly, that part might've been larger. Maybe we'd be closer once I became blessed . . . I had to hope. Our relationship couldn't get any *more* strained.

"Miss me?"

Callie swept into the room on light feet, her long, curled black hair swinging at her waist as she swayed her hips. My older sister by two years was a sight—a rare beauty—and my closest confidante.

I wanted to run into her arms.

"Always," I admitted with a playful eye roll, not breaking stride during my ceaseless march across the parlor.

"Don't sass me, little bird." Callie fell into a chair beside Father, her blue dress crinkling with the movement. She made a point to touch her simple silver earrings, a brow raised.

Her gift. With those earrings alone, she owned the ability to control people's emotions, sometimes bringing out the deepest, most buried feelings within her targets.

A glorious gift if I'd ever seen one. Father had been over the moon when she received her magic.

I, however, had been her victim many times in the past, especially when she wanted the last word in an argument. She had since ceased to use her influence on me unless requested—like when my nerves buzzed in my chest like angry bees. But it was a rare occasion when I asked for her to turn her steely gaze upon me, her finger pressed against the enchanted metal.

"Don't threaten me, Callie, or I'll use my new gift on *you,*" I warned, a proud smirk lifting my lips. Yes, perhaps she'd get a taste of her own medicine.

Callie laughed, the sound airy and unbothered. "Oh, sister. Let's wait to threaten each other until *after* you get your gift, eh?"

I gave her a withering look. One she returned.

Without Callie, I swore I'd die of boredom.

"Thirty seconds, little bird," she mused, drawing my attention back to the clock.

I swallowed a curse. I was seconds from wearing down the wooden planks of the parlor floor, which would be a shame, as it had been polished that morning. The clock would chime and then the front door would mysteriously open, and one of the Fates' beloved hounds would come barreling in, my gift bared between his sharp teeth.

"Cameron, please tell her to cease all this . . . movement," Mother commanded, idly waving a hand. Some of her brandy sloshed over the rim and onto her overly bright red dress. "She's giving me a headache." She turned to Callie as if for support. My sister didn't indulge her, staring into the hearth instead with a smirk on her face.

I sighed. I was always giving Mother a headache.

"That would be the drink, my dear," Father replied, straining to keep his smile hidden. "And we all know she won't stop until—"

The first gong sounded.

I went utterly still, the breath knocked from my lungs. Excitement slithered up my spine, the kind that preceded a life-changing moment.

Midnight approached.

My parents paused their bickering as the bells echoed throughout the firelit room like a death knell. All eyes fell to the clock, to its teasing hands.

What would I get? I wondered, heat flushing my cheeks. Would it be an elusive pocket watch that controlled time? Or perhaps a mirror that rendered one invisible?

I was dreaming far too big, but I couldn't help it. The miraculous objects circulating through our kingdom had always fascinated me; how the people the Fates blessed were given a shred of otherworldly wonder.

Four bells.

Sweat banded across my brow like pesky drops of rain. I hastily swiped them away, some of my hair falling into my face in the process and sticking to the damp. Fruitlessly, I blew at the wayward strands, but they simply fell right back into my eyes.

Seven.

Fates, I wanted to scream. To release the pent-up energy swirling through my veins. My dress suddenly became too heavy. My corset too tight. I typically never wore them unless Mother demanded, but this evening was special and I had wanted to dress for the occasion. I thoroughly regretted my choice.

Nine.

It was happening . . . my chance to break out from under my father's and mother's thumbs and gain the respect of my sister and my peers. A way to belong. To break out of the gilded prison surrounding me—

Eleven.

The final gong rent the air, its echoes sending pinpricks down my spine. *Midnight.*

I twisted about the room, waiting for the scratching of paws on the wood flooring, searching for the black hound encased in shadows sent by the three most formidable beings in our realm.

Any second now . . .

No footsteps. No scratching. No twist of the lock opening.

All I heard was a silence so loud, it stung. A silence and the haunting echoes of my desperate exhales.

"Where is the hound?" I heard myself saying, though I couldn't feel my lips moving.

A sharp stab of ice pierced my chest when the echoes of the clock's chimes eventually ceased. When that wretched silence reigned over the parlor in its truest form.

"Where is it!" I was yelling now, uncaring that I sounded like a petulant child. "It's supposed to arrive at exactly midnight, right?" I raced to the clock as if it were a foe, running my hands over its worn sides. "Is it broken? Off by a few minutes?"

It had to be broken. That was the only explanation. Not once in all of our family history had a Hayes *not* received a gift on time.

Whirling around, I came face to face with Father, his lips slashed in a thin line. My eyes prickled, tears begging to be freed. His stony features told a story all their own, and I had a suspicion I wouldn't care for the tale.

"What? What is it?" I asked, breathless, feeling like I'd die should another second pass. I was panicking, I was aware of this, but . . . but this was the only opportunity I'd secure to gain respect, to step out from my family's shadow and be my own woman. Someone society regarded as an equal because I'd been given a divine token of great honor.

I supposed I expected the world in the form of this gift. A silly notion, a desperate hope to be *more.*

From my periphery, Mother stood and gently placed her glass upon the side table. She, too, joined my father, and her attention roamed the room subtly, a slight twitch forcing her lips downward. True emotion shone in her eyes for the first time in years as she glanced out of the parlor toward the front door. It was locked and secured.

No.

I stepped backward, my spine hitting the wall with too much force. A painful puff of air left me, and Callie hissed audibly, her face contorted in grief.

Panic surged, a humming in my ears drowning out all sound. I didn't realize I was running until Callie's face vanished entirely and the warmth from the parlor evaporated. In the hallway, I glowered at the ornate front door, willing it to open. To hear the baying of the hound.

Silence.

"Wren," Callie started, standing behind me, her voice a whisper. "It's all right, maybe—" The humming drowned her words out. I couldn't stand there a second longer. Couldn't stand there as they all judged or pitied me. Because . . . I'd been overlooked. Deemed unworthy.

Grabbing my skirts, I raced in the opposite direction of the door, my mother's muffled voice calling my name while I darted down the corridor and beyond the empty kitchen, the doors leading to the garden in my sights.

The brisk night air of Andalay struck me in a startling blast, the chill drifting across my warm skin like a thousand pinpricks. Callie called out to me now, begging me to return, but I delved deeper into the mess of enchanting pink and amber roses that had grown wild.

Fireflies flitted about, and I angrily swatted them out of my way, repressing the memories of my youth when Callie and I would bottle them up in hopes of stealing their light.

It's a mistake, I repeated as I reached the end of the garden, now facing the thick hedges blocking off our mansion from the main streets of Andalay.

Perhaps I hadn't waited long enough, or maybe it had been delivered and I'd been too busy fretting to see it. But Father had explained that I would be drawn to the item like it was a piece of myself. A piece of my very soul.

I'd felt no such connection in the parlor. Not in the entire house. Not even in this wretched garden of brazen blooms.

Just . . . emptiness.

I dropped to my knees, the dampness of the earth seeping through my skirts and undoubtedly staining them forever. Lifting my chin to the sky, a heat of anger washed over me.

Hadn't I been devoted enough? Good enough? I was the only one in my family who'd pored over the books of the Fates and their gifts. It was me who visited Day's temple every first day of spring, offering a bouquet of freshly clipped canary-yellow roses and creamy lace. Me who thanked the Fates each night before bed and prayed that Dusk would keep the deceased safe. Me who greeted each morning with a smile and a prayer to Dawn. I'd gone as far as commissioning a statue of my favorite Fate, Day, to stand before our home. A symbol of light and peace.

It hadn't been enough.

Glowering at the moon, I clenched my hands into fists, my lungs working to get in air.

A soft trickle of chords sounded from somewhere in the distance, some sort of music escaping a magical instrument. The fireflies flickered a resplendent blue in response, pulsating with the ethereal light.

It could've been ten minutes or an hour, but broad hands eventually grasped my shoulders. I smelled brandy and musk—Father.

Silently, he urged me to my feet, my knees trembling.

I'd never felt so small. So weak.

Step by step, we wandered through the garden and back into the warmth of our home. Callie stood by the threshold, the corners of her bright green eyes narrowing as she wrung her hands. She didn't speak to me.

The rest was a blur as Father led me to my bedroom on the second story. He didn't utter a single word during the entirety of the walk, and somehow, that made it all worse.

The pity. The quiet shame.

The moment my bed was within reach, I tumbled unceremoniously onto the fresh white coverlet, grasping it in angry fists.

My heart hammered as my father paused above me. There were no tender words offered or kind condolences. No determined promises to discover why I'd been forsaken. Just the jarring click of the door shutting a minute later.

I was the first Hayes in all of our history who hadn't been blessed.

Now I'd be seen as nothing but a curse.

Chapter Two

Damien

The Fates' gift weighed heavily in my pocket.

It would fetch a decent price, and I might haggle for a higher amount with my client for my troubles—I'd been hiding alongside the edge of the representative's fine town house on the northern side of Andalay for *hours.* A guard patrolled the streets, but with a flick of my wrist, I took advantage of the gift I'd been given on my own eighteenth birthday a year ago.

Concealed by the prickly hedges, I watched through the window as that insipid young woman paced. She couldn't sit still, much to her parents' and older sister's dismay, and her rosy cheeks got redder and redder as the seconds ticked by.

She was a bright thing, full of hope and light, and with nothing better to do, I'd studied her, taking in her pink gown and flowing sleeves, the neckline a tad low by society's standards. Or perhaps she had moved and tugged at her garment so often that it had shifted. Either way, I'd been captivated by her anxiety. The way she displayed emotions so easily and without concern.

I bet she'd never experienced a hardship in her blessed little life.

As the daughter of Representative Hayes of Ward One, she possessed riches beyond my wildest imagination. It helped that they were blessed by the Fates themselves—much like most high-ranking lords and their children. With each new generation, a dog came to the Hayeses' home, and without a doubt, Wren would follow in her ancestors' footsteps.

Lucky, was what she was. The rich and powerful got all the magic, while the people of the Void got nothing. The Fates claimed they gave out their trinkets based on faithfulness, but that also was a falsehood. I knew plenty of the faithful in the south, and none of their children received gifts. No, they were smart, the Fates, gifting those who paid for their opulent palace and did their bidding with charmed tokens.

I shouldn't have magic in my own hands, but that mystery—why I of all people in the Void had received a gift from the Fates—had never been solved. And not due to my lack of trying.

My eyes found hers through the glass, and for a moment, my chest squeezed, convinced she had spotted me. Fates, they were blue, even from this distance and with the glass between us. My heart pounded, but thankfully, she darted off to the right, wringing her hands as she babbled, her rosy lips moving a mile a minute.

I sighed in relief.

Even if I took her gift, she'd be fine, likely married off to some wealthy lord. Her ruthless father would arrange for it, surely. Hayes wasn't one to be trifled with; he had that damned pen that could change history itself—

Including making the Void and those without gifts second-class citizens. My people could barely afford food, let alone a roof over their heads, and that man had signed into law every act that made it more difficult for us in the south to secure proper work. I bet he'd even had a hand in the mysterious disappearances of the southern people over the last few years. Politicians like Hayes took out anyone who tried to fight the criminal laws they shoved into our faces. He was nothing but a gangster.

I doubted the bastard's younger daughter was any different.

Wren. That was her name. I kept forgetting, as it was far from important.

All that mattered was that when that clock struck midnight, I'd be ready—

And ready I was.

On cue, the black hound trotted down the walkway, one of the Fate's dutiful messengers. Clutched between his sharpened teeth was a simple blue box tied with a yellow ribbon. *Wren's gift.*

With my enchanted mirror in my pocket, I crept from my hiding place, my other hand reaching for the fresh scrap of meat I'd snagged from the butcher's shop on the way over.

The beast sniffed the air but continued, ever dutiful.

Here, boy. I tossed the scrap before him, mere steps from the Hayeses' home. This time, he paused, and it was a long enough pause for me to seize the box he carried, though some of the elegant ribbon had frayed from the pull of his teeth.

The dog abandoned the meat, a whining filling the air as he searched for the valuable package . . . which I'd slipped into my jacket pocket, nice and safe. I cringed thinking of the animal's warm saliva coating the box, but the price outweighed my personal distaste.

Despite the local lads not knowing how I became so exceptional at general deception and thievery, they nicknamed me the Ghost for a reason: I could break in and out of a home while the victim stood in the same room—with or without my mirror. I was a criminal, and a well sought-after one at that. Even before I miraculously received a Fate's gift last year.

I'd been shocked beyond belief when the hound had stood over my worn mattress, the oil in my lamp long gone and my closet of a room cast in darkness. Dropping it gently on my chest, the beast had turned and trotted away, leaving the door open and me stock-still with my jaw dropped. Even with hatred for the Fates burning away in my heart, I'd opened the package with care, a small jolt working up my arm when I brushed over the cold metal of the mirror.

That moment changed everything, and not just my *trade,* but how I viewed the world. When all of my searches as to why I'd been blessed led nowhere, I'd given up, silently forming a plan to get what I needed.

Invisibility. A rarity—even among high society. Hell, I didn't know why a man like me had been favored by the Fates, but I sure as shite wasn't about to broadcast it. If anyone knew, they'd string me up or kill me and steal the mirror for themselves.

Good thing I liked to be left alone . . . and people thought me a cutthroat. I didn't correct them.

I smiled as I made my way down the sidewalk and away from the frantic hound, who sniffed the ground, his small whimpers growing louder. The potent scent of the meat overwhelmed his senses; divine dog or not, he was just as susceptible to temptation as any average mutt.

Whistling a soft tune, I took in the neighborhood for signs of movement. Of course, at this hour there wasn't a peep. This side of town was all fixed up nicely, not a stone out of place. Each town house was pristine, constructed of brick and shrouded with lush ivy. Arched windows peeked out, some decorated with painted glass and depictions of the Fates. It all felt too perfect; like a picture painted by some fanciful artist with rose-colored glasses.

Good riddance.

All of Aurilia's crooked lords, ladies, and politicians resided here, pretending to be upstanding citizens. It was laughable, really, when in reality, the blood of innocents painted their delicate, uncallused hands. Even if they weren't directly involved with the city's one-sided regulations aimed at making the rich richer, they were complicit.

A mile passed before I reached into my trouser pocket, fumbling around for the small oval mirror I never took off me. I slept with the damn thing. With care, I held it to my face. Only its surface showed the truth, and I beamed at my reflection, overlooking the smudges marring my tan skin and the grime greasing my black hair.

Fates above. Taking her gift had been far too easy. The fact that it belonged to Hayes's daughter made the prize in my pocket all the more satisfying. Maybe I should do this more often—steal from the rich like some fabled hero. I liked the idea of that. Except I'd keep all the winnings next time.

With a final peek at myself—followed by a gleeful wink—I snapped the lid closed and placed it in my left jacket pocket, a sigh escaping when it settled right over my heart.

Thank you, old friend.

Too bad Wren Hayes would never experience the pleasure of owning magic. She had enough as it was.

I whistled all the way back to the dim streets of the Void, my shoulders losing more of their tension the dirtier the stones beneath my scuffed boots became. I passed by a couple of Missing posters, recognizing one woman as Tilly. She used to work at the laundry a few months ago but then vanished into thin air. Rumor was, she'd run off with a lover, but I'd never seen her with anyone before her disappearance.

Her grayed poster fluttered, seconds from being ripped away completely by a harsh wind. That was how it felt living here—one step away from ruin.

I shook off thoughts of Tilly and all the other posters I'd spotted on my walk. Some familiar faces, others strangers with bad luck.

Time to sell off whatever silly bauble Wren Hayes had received. There was a fool reckless enough to schedule a meeting with me in the dark this evening, and maybe I'd take a souvenir from them, too, after the transaction. I hadn't seen their face the first time we met, as they'd insisted upon wearing a ridiculous cloak with a low hood and hid in their carriage, but I'd suspected they were someone important when they sent their bodyguard to do the negotiating. They wanted a gift, and they'd get it, and I'd save up my new coins and get out of this hellhole. I didn't care who they were or why they wanted a gift. That wasn't my business.

I turned down Sulley Street, on my way to the predetermined meeting spot, when I had the sudden urge to see the damned thing for myself. What kind of present might the princess of Ward One get?

The buyer had specifically asked for it to remain untouched, but fuck that. I put my neck on the line for this.

Carefully undoing the flimsy ribbon, I lifted the box's top.

Sheltered inside a nest of yellow rose petals lay a simple silver locket. I frowned, reaching inside and turning it over, searching for any clue or symbol as to its powers. I found none.

Unease prickled down my back. I shouldn't have opened it, but now that I had . . .

Pulling out the delicate locket and its thin chain, I once more flipped it over, finding nothing exceptional. I supposed that was true with all gifts, mine included. "Let's take a closer look." I pried open the clasp, wondering what image the locket concealed, if any.

The two sides fell open and all the air rushed from my lungs.

Shite.

The night tilted on its head.

I *should* have continued to my buyer, but I found myself instinctively whirling around, my feet picking up into a run as I bolted in the opposite direction from Sulley Street, away from my client, and away from the darkest parts of the Void.

I didn't cease running until I'd stormed through the Broken Wing Tavern and climbed the stairs leading to the dimly lit room I rented above. I slammed the door and locked all four locks behind me, muffling the raucous laughter and lively music carried up from below.

Uncharacteristically shaken, I slumped to the floor, my heartbeat pounding against my ribs. With trembling hands, I clutched the locket, eager to confirm that my eyes hadn't played a trick on me after all.

There was indeed a photograph inside . . .

And it was of *me.*

Chapter Three

Wren

Dawn, Day, and Dusk; these are the Fates.
Most, though, pray to the Fate of Day, as she symbolizes our present, and represents the hope of each new day.
—*Origin of the Fates*, Chapter One

One Week Later

I'd been forced to attend the opening party of the new season.

"If you hide away, they'll talk, and our family doesn't need any more of that," Mother had chastised from the threshold of my room days before. She'd hung a gown on my mirror and departed without a word, leaving only a slight chill in the air. I swore that woman was made of ice; she thrived in the winter months. I shuddered thinking of all the animals butchered to create those fine furs she wore.

Callie, on the other hand, knew me better. Every morning, sweets greeted me on my nightstand. Decadent milk chocolates and sugary pastries that I inhaled beneath the covers. My sister understood not to pester me, especially now, but she showed her love and concern in other ways. I considered myself blessed in that respect; to have a sibling who actually cared. These last few days, I'd had the urge to ask her to use her gift on me—to make me feel calm, indifferent, carefree . . . yet I wouldn't. It felt wrong not to endure the truth of myself. That I wasn't who I believed. Maybe it was penance for my thoughts, for while I went to the temples of the Fates, my mind often drifted elsewhere. As people prayed before the statues, I'd think of the lands I hadn't ventured to—the west and its jagged mountains, and the far north with snow so persistent, it remained all year. And that was just our continent.

I desired to see it all.

Which was why I believed I was being punished.

My gloomy routine stretched on for days—me holed up beneath my blankets as I mourned the loss of something I never had but always craved. Since I could remember, I'd studiously watched Father with his pen, writing to representatives and lords and ladies. He told me he would change the world for the better, and I yearned for such an ability. To be viewed as more than some silly girl whose only ambition was to entice a partner into marriage.

Our society wasn't kind to women. Anne Langston held a representative seat, but it was due to her obscene riches. In most cases, if we were given a magical object greater than a man's, we were sold off to the highest bidder as a wife. I never wanted that. My plan, however naïve, was to remain unattached, using my new magic for *myself* and myself alone. Love wasn't something I coveted, and my parents were hardly examples of an ideal marriage. Often, I wondered if they'd ever loved each other to start with.

Marriage simply wasn't for me. I refused.

Yet if I was to be magicless and live beneath my father's roof, I'd have to attend the tedious ball and stand alongside my family with a feigned smile. Until I discovered how to change my destiny, that was. And all of those minutes spent hiding from the world provided me with an idea—

I would seek out the Fates themselves and ask if there'd been some error. I'd get on my knees and beg if I had to. If I hadn't been so desperate, I would've laughed at the very notion of knocking at their palace walls. You didn't request to see the Fates. *They* summoned you, if you were lucky.

What is there to lose? Making a fool of myself hardly seemed important, especially since I had no plans to marry, and the worst that would happen would be a few days of petty gossip.

Besides, I was a *Hayes*. A devout one; for the most part. There was a high chance that something treacherous had occurred. Perhaps a lost hound. A thief. An incorrectly recorded birthday.

Something.

These thoughts were all that kept me going. Kept me hoping.

It was the evening of the ball and I stood in nothing but my undergarments. With a sigh, I snagged the dress Mother selected from the hanger and eyed the many buttons curving along the back. I cringed.

"Callie?" I called. Her room was next to mine, and the walls were vexingly thin.

Footsteps pattered before my door creaked open, revealing an already dressed Callie. She wore a gown the color of red wine, the deep shade enhancing her stunning black hair, which she'd left down, the ends reaching the small of her back.

Her green eyes flashed. "You're up." She shuffled closer, a hesitant smile creasing the corners of her mouth.

"I'm not some injured predator," I insisted, waving my hand. "You don't need to approach me like I'm going to bite."

At my teasing, her face smoothed, and she closed the gap between us.

"Need help?" I nodded, and she grabbed the dress from my outstretched hands. "You know, *I* actually selected this gown for you," she said proudly, a small smile tilting her lips. She motioned for me to turn around. "I saw it at the modiste and it reminded me of the night sky. Of the stars you love so much."

A bit of warmth blazed in my chest, melting some of the ice. Maybe her magic had inadvertently seeped into me, not that it felt terrible, and she *was* wearing her earrings tonight. "It's stunning," I admitted, raising my hands for her to slide it over my head. She danced me around like I'd become a living doll, brushing the full skirt down and fixing the off-the-shoulder tulle straps into place.

"Of course it is. I picked it out." She beamed when she spun me around, both her hands on my arms. "We all know I have impeccable taste. You're lucky to have me for a sister. Fates know what you'd end up wearing if left on your own." She gave a mock shudder.

I rolled my eyes. "So full of yourself, Callie." I tapped her nose and she wrinkled it in affront. "That's why Father has plans for you."

I wasn't daft. I'd noticed how they both stole away to his study, and once, I dared to eavesdrop on a conversation when the door had been left ajar. He was teaching her about the ward. About the budget and tedious rules, and which influential members of society could be manipulated. Callie was his protégée.

Her face sobered. "We both know being a woman and a representative is nearly impossible. I hear what they say about me. That they think Father is wasting his time." Her eyes narrowed as if she could hear the petty gossipers now. "I just want what Father has, Wren. A chance to help the ward. To be . . . respected."

Respected as a ward representative. As a powerful woman in command.

It shouldn't be an impossible feat, and yet it was, in our world.

Now I felt like an ass for bringing it up. Callie was ambitious. Like me, she desired to be *more,* and I couldn't fault her for striving for her goal. Especially since her cunning mind deserved a spot on the council.

"I didn't mean to sound cruel," I said with a sigh. I had a tendency to speak without thought, and I was particularly irritated this evening. "If anyone can overcome those obstacles, Callie, it's you. I'm just cross about tonight. Mother and her threats are the only reasons I'm even going."

I watched her throat bob with emotion. "Thank you, *baby* sister," she replied with a smirk. She knew I despised it when she called me that. "I'll try to make you proud one day. And who the hell knows? Maybe I'll surprise everyone." Callie tilted her chin toward the vanity, her features hardening as if she were about to command an army. "Now, we must do something about that rats' nest of hair."

I expected pain would ensue.

It took ages, but eventually, Callie swept my long hair into an effortless updo, some strands meticulously left down to frame my face. After applying some rouge, lipstick, and kohl eyeliner, she deemed me appropriate.

"Callie! Wren!" Father called from downstairs, urging us to hurry.

My sister scoffed at Father's brusque tone. "Time to face the music." She made for the door, leaving me just enough time to grab my letter opener and slip it deep into the neckline of my gown. High society might dress in fine clothes and possess titles, but they often believed their names allowed them to touch what they shouldn't, and I'd grown sick of their hubris.

I'd be prepared this time if one of them decided their hand belonged on my backside. *Again.* One could never be too careful.

With one final glance at my reflection, I left my room and padded down the stairs. My parents and sister had already headed for the open door and the waiting carriage, and I hurried to keep pace.

Outside, my dress shone in an entirely new light. Shimmering beneath the nearly full moon, the off-the-shoulder cobalt number dripped with sparkling crystals resembling falling stars.

"Wren, the ball will be over by the time you make it to the carriage!" Mother barked, and I ceased admiring the dress to join them inside. Callie *did* have excellent taste.

The ride was bumpy and painfully stifled, although Mother continuously fixed the strands of my updo whenever they fell out of place. "Can't have a daughter of mine looking like she ran through a rosebush," she scolded, her eyes sharply focused as she fixed me up. I sat through her prodding, accustomed to it after so many years. Of course, Lenore Hayes dazzled to perfection in a green dress, gorgeous and heavenly as always. She would die before her lipstick smudged.

I loved her, I did, but she was often detached in a way that reminded me of an empty husk of a woman. Perhaps you had to be when everyone's eyes were constantly on you. I wanted to know her, the real her beneath the collected façade, but I suspected she'd played this role all her life and wasn't sure how to turn on her humanity again. It was one of the many reasons I'd grown bitter about the northerners. How easily they judged, how easily they could turn their backs on so-called friends.

They played a game I was too exhausted, and possibly frightened, to play.

Father clasped my arm as we exited our carriage, Callie on his other side. With wide eyes, I took in the grand mansion belonging to the Lovetts, who owned half of Aurilia's weapons industry. Father and Lord Lovett were close, and I suspected they'd sneak away to the study for most of the night.

"Smile," Mother whispered, her voice low and dulcet. Her mask was fully in place.

Canting my chin, I gazed at the three-story building covered in winding ivy, the arched windows shining with welcoming light from the party roaring inside. It was a fine brick home, elegant in a way that hinted of taste and old money. The Lovetts were not exclusively in the shipping business, but noble members of society as well. They were the perfect family to host the first soiree of what would be a summer of extravagant gatherings. I'd likely have to be dragged to each and every one—

Unless the Fates accepted my request, and my desperate hope of discovering a mistake was realized.

Doubtful.

My knees shook and sweat ran down my spine. However welcoming the Lovetts would be, others wouldn't be so kind. One thing I loathed more than our society's inability to recognize women as the fierce creatures they were, was attention. It made my skin prickle and my cheeks flush. These uptight bastards had the vexing power to make me feel as if every move I made were the wrong one. Maybe they simply enjoyed watching others wither beneath their assessing gazes, like it awarded them more satisfaction than any magical item could.

Thanks to Callie and her blunt approach to our world, I'd learned such lessons early.

I sucked in the last bit of fresh air and eyed the stone pathway leading to the massive entry, the stained glass of the door casting dancing rainbows across the incoming guests, all proudly exhibiting their excessive finery.

"Keep your chin up and smile," Father murmured tersely into

my ear. He tugged me from Mother's grip, and instantly, his warmth seeped into me, making me feel more stable, less nauseous at the glowers I suspected I'd find within the mansion. "A Hayes doesn't bend or bow," he added, leaning back to wink at me. I softened at the twinkle in his eye, which rarely made an appearance. It used to . . . back when I was a child and he hadn't grown into his full might yet.

I returned his wink, wishing with all my heart he'd become the gentle and carefree man he used to be, if only for a night. But wishing would be useless.

My lips, which had been cemented into a frown for the past week, tugged up rigidly at the sides. If Father had to work with the ruthless representatives of the various wards of our city, then I could walk into this party and pretend, like I always had before. I could smile and act as if I weren't shattered and broken inside. As if I weren't some useless cretin no one would dare get close to.

It was fine.

I didn't care for many people anyway.

Fates. If I told myself that lie one more damned time, I would lose my mind.

One step at a time. One breath at a time. Smile.

I held my head high as Father had instructed, and while my chin quivered and my palms grew clammy beneath my long white gloves, I didn't pause, didn't hesitate, when I walked over the threshold and into a magnificent hall captured straight out of a whimsical dream.

Gauzy ivory drapes fluttered between sconces of polished silver, and copper keys of varying designs were strung above the towering foyer. A gasp left me as we strolled past the entry and into the lavish ballroom beyond. Actual trees had been uprooted and placed in every corner, their branches dipping low and their leaves painted vibrant colors. From their mighty limbs, diamonds glistened, and elegant scraps of folded parchment tied with green satin ribbons swayed in an invisible wind that smelled of spun sugar.

Unable to quell my curiosity, and momentarily forgetting *not* to make a spectacle of myself, I broke free from Callie and my parents and wandered over to one of the majestic trees. Gently, I reached for one of the rolled-up papers, my heart thudding with curious excitement. In gilded script were five words:

Seek the magic you cannot see.

I cocked my head at the vague and slightly silly message.

"They're meant to be *mysterious.*"

I turned to the unfamiliar voice. A young woman wearing an emerald dress stood to my right, her brown skin shimmering from some glittering lotion and her lids painted a bold pink. She smiled, her light brown eyes friendly enough.

"I suppose it goes with the theme?" I said, twisting to appraise the rest of the room. Indeed, the Lovetts' home had been transformed into a fairy-tale forest, and flowers of every shade adorned the walls, while lush green ivy encircled the blooms. Crystal glasses dyed a pretty pink were being passed around by black-suited waiters, and the liquid inside called my name.

Fates, I could use some courage. Maybe two or three glasses of it.

"Ruby," the woman said, thrusting out her hand, a silver signet ring glistening in the ethereal lighting.

I startled for a moment, surprised I hadn't seen her before, but I instinctively held out my hand in welcome. "Wren."

Her grip was firm, much more so than I was expecting, and I noted the roughened feel of calluses on her ungloved hands.

Before I could ponder it further, Ruby whirled to the closest waiter and snagged two glasses, relinquishing one to me. "I have a feeling you'll need this," she whispered, her attention cast ahead. I followed her stare as my stomach churned.

Lovely.

My new friend had been correct in her assumption. Every pair of eyes in the room flitted my way before being hastily averted. They were far from subtle. Now that reality had settled in, I perceived my name on their lips as well.

It occurred to me that this would be a rather long evening.

Is it too early to bolt?

Across the ballroom were the usual young women I socialized with; all daughters of lords or representatives. Father approved of them as "acceptable" friends, and without a choice, I made do with their tedious conversation and gossip. If not, I would've been trapped in the town house all day.

This evening, the ones who owned gifts wore them proudly, and I spotted Cecile stroking the red ribbon tied to her sweeping pink dress. It had the ability to transform her into a vision of perfection, the ribbon imparting physical beauty. She adored it, but I was greedy and wanted more than to look pretty for people I hardly cared for. That might have made me sound self-righteous and all sorts of stuck-up, but they were my true thoughts, and at least I wasn't sharing them out loud.

Danielle, Cecile's cousin, smiled at Lilly as she touched the woman's drink, the sapphire ring on her brown finger refilling the cup. Her gift was interesting, able to fill what was once empty; from drinks to plates of food or dried-out fountains in a garden. Danielle was the kindest of the group, and the one I gravitated toward during our afternoon strolls. She wasn't as unforgiving as the others, and her smile could light up a room. Though such a smile was rare.

Cecile lifted her nose when she caught me staring, and quickly ushered her friends onto the dance floor. Danielle shot me a quick look but trailed after Cecile, helpless. If she stayed, she, too, would be cast aside.

Their absence didn't stop the sharp stab of hurt that shot through me as I watched their retreating forms. Here I'd believed they'd at least *speak* with me. We'd been acquaintances for most of our lives.

How quickly they deemed me *less than*.

I scolded myself, knowing I should've prepared for such a reaction. I'd witnessed such things before with other ladies of society, never believing it would happen to me.

Fool.

Fates, even the young nobles avoided my gaze, not one daring to step close enough to be seen as taking an interest. In their eyes, courting me would lower their own worth.

I swallowed thickly and turned my head to the band, pretending the sting of betrayal wasn't present. A lively tune had begun, played by a stout musician with a trimmed mustache. He lifted his violin, and instantly, I understood that it was magicked as well, for the notes he emitted were accompanied by other sounds that could not possibly have been created by one instrument alone.

Magic was everywhere.

I was instantly jealous. No, beyond jealous. Sad, hurt, pissed—you name it, I felt it. All of those emotions stirred within me like a poisonous brew.

The glass in my hand suddenly felt too heavy, but I had an easy fix. I chugged the contents in one go, uncaring if my mother, who was currently surrounded by admirers, glared at me in distaste. She could simmer for the rest of the night for all I cared. She had dragged me here, after all.

"Whoa, slow down," Ruby admonished with a giggle. I had nearly forgotten her entirely. "Though I did find that impressive," she added with a raised brow.

With the drink warming my belly, I gave her a wry smile. "Oh, I most definitely am going to need another one of those."

I lost sight of Ruby sometime around ten when she slipped away to the powder room.

With everyone murmuring my name, and with the horde of nobles glancing down their noses whenever I passed, I decided to sneak away to the Lovetts' famous gardens. I couldn't take the scrutiny anymore, and plants and flowers blessedly didn't have the ability to glare.

On most days, I considered myself a fairly optimistic person—within reason—but . . . it was too much. Those narrowed eyes. The disgust and confusion when they spoke my name alongside my family's honored one. Shamefully, my father was working the room to cast me in a better light, and falling short. And he was *beloved*.

It seemed that I'd ruined not only my life but his as well.

The Lovetts had commissioned a breathtaking fountain beyond the veranda, the size of it akin to the downstairs of my home. Water spouted from spigots at timed intervals, and tiny lights turned the leaves a mellow sky-blue shade. I sighed, striding over to one of the many benches positioned off the path where you could take in the view.

Rich green plants and blossoms curved around a cushioned eggshell-colored settee; a place lovers might find themselves on nights like this one.

I watched the cascade of water, losing myself in its soothing noise, numbly shoving aside the cruel world that awaited me inside the mansion. Out here, in the quiet, I drifted, my thoughts turning less frantic, less anxious. Clouds swept across the moon, and little light shone down from the heavens. Surprisingly, I took comfort in the dark; it was where secrets could be shared . . . though *I* felt like a secret I wished I had the answer to.

Soon, I promised. *You'll request an audience with the Fates tomorrow and—*

"I can't believe he brought her."

I jerked upward from my relaxed position, the silence and peace I'd experienced forgotten. I recognized that voice. Unfortunately.

Lord Allen. He visited Father often, mostly protesting to keep the working class from entering our side of town to find work. Those living in the "Void"—the southern portion of Andalay I'd been forbidden to visit—didn't possess gifts, and they relied on steady occupation to keep food on the table.

Yet Allen didn't pay his employees a living wage, and I knew this because Father had drunkenly told me one evening. My chest had ached when he spoke about the south as if it were a plague on the land, its people, too. At times, I willingly played the fool when it came to Father and his dealings. I hardly wanted to know if he was connected to such heinous people and their beliefs . . . but the older I became, the harder it was to pretend Father was the same man I believed—or wanted—him to be.

"He's trying to brush it off, Allen. What would you do if your daughter ruined your family line?" A scoff, and then, "She may not be as beautiful as her mother, but he could easily marry her off."

I didn't recognize the new voice, but his words heated my blood. Warmth suffused my cheeks, and I clenched my hands into fists. How many damned times did I need to be compared to her? On top of that, all I was good for now was marriage; to be a wife and mother. Not that they weren't admirable jobs, but it wasn't what *I* wanted.

I yearned to expose myself, to leap from my hidden alcove and confront Lord Allen and his lackey, and pray that their cheeks darkened with the embarrassment of being caught. My nails bit hard into my palms. I wouldn't do a damned thing. I *couldn't*.

My grief and rage grew as their heavy footsteps passed, and I curved to the side, half of my body practically shoved into the nearest bush to avoid detection. Very dignified of a lady, of course.

Soon my parents would search for me, which meant I had to once again lift my chin and smile, and gracefully walk past a bunch of snakes who scorned me for no righteous reason.

Get it over with.

The longer I sat here ruminating over my misfortune, the longer I'd have to stay at this hellish ball. Grumbling a curse, I rose and stepped beyond the alcove—

And immediately bumped into the rather hard chest of Lord Everett Sinclair.

Liquid spilled everywhere, wetting my skin as the scent of whiskey stole from the floral fragrance of the garden. Everett bit back an ungentlemanly curse and brushed at his fine sapphire velvet jacket before lifting his striking blue eyes to mine.

Fates.

"I'm so sorry!" I hurried to say, eager to avoid this interaction. Mother, on the other hand, would've been thrilled; well, not by my clumsiness. "I wasn't watching where I was going." *Obviously.*

Everett was three years my senior and quite handsome, one of the *many* suitors Mother had pointed out to me months prior. Her scheming would be all for naught after this little display. I hoped.

Everett swept a hand down his once-pristine white shirt, his stunning silver wristwatch catching the light of the weak moon, the mother-of-pearl face shimmering. Before he could speak, his mouth barely having opened, a waiter rushed by, a fresh towel hanging from his arm.

"Sir!" called the waiter, a towering man with unkempt black hair and the coldest gray eyes I'd ever beheld. "Let me assist you."

Leave it to the Lovetts to arrange for waiters and assistants to be hidden in every nook and cranny.

I stepped aside as the waiter meticulously attended to the spill, mumbling apologies here and there, when really, it was me who'd caused the mess. Everett shifted closer to the man as he awkwardly patted the waiter in what I took as gratitude. But his eyes stared deeply into mine, making me adjust my footing while crossing and uncrossing my arms. I didn't care for the attention, and certainly not the kind of attention he was so openly displaying.

I immediately began to formulate my excuses to leave.

Everett spoke first.

"Wren Hayes." His voice was smooth like silk, and when my name sounded from his lips I understood why many found him alluring. "I've been meaning to seek you out all evening, yet it seems you've been hiding out in the garden among the flowers. Though you yourself are reminiscent of one tonight." The corners of his mouth quirked up.

I could've sworn I heard the waiter muffle a choked scoff. I resisted the urge to join him.

"I needed the fresh air," I answered smoothly, ignoring the sickly-sweet compliment. All I desired was loose clothing and the comfort of my bed and my book—which had just gotten to the good part. "Perhaps at the next party we'll meet and there will be more time."

"But—"

"All done, my lord," the overzealous waiter thankfully interrupted, stepping back with a curt nod. I looked at the waiter then, taking in the shadows that played across his sharp cheekbones and highlighted the corners of his full, curving lips.

"Thank you," Everett said stiffly, not sparing a glance at the man who'd assisted him.

But I did.

I watched as he hurried down the pathway—in the *opposite* direction from the house.

"I was hoping for one dance, but I suppose I can be patient," Everett said as he lifted his arm and ran his hand through his dark blond hair, a boyish smile playing on his lips.

My heart skipped a beat when I noticed it . . . or the *lack* of it.

His silver watch—

It was gone.

I whirled to where the waiter had taken off. The man must've stolen it—he'd been all too quick to "help," taking his time to run that cloth up and down Everett's suit. The slick bastard had pinched it right before our eyes. I wasn't sure what came over me; perhaps it was the need to escape or the heat building inside my chest, a small voice telling me to give chase—

I took off in the direction the waiter had taken, starting a jog that soon turned into a run. I was impervious to the fact that Everett called my name or that I sprinted through a garden in a ball gown—an act that would cause my mother to faint.

The gardens were vast, but I caught glimpses of black hair glimmering in low light just ahead of me beside a bed of yellow roses. The sight would vanish altogether a blink later. I frowned, confused, but kept racing forward, determined to retrieve Everett's watch.

Soon the waiter's silhouette came into full view, the end of the path nearing. A looming wrought iron fence surrounded the Lovetts' land, with no gate in sight.

No escape, I pondered gleefully.

The man before me was quick, and each time I blinked, he seemed to flicker. It had to be a trick of the dark night. It didn't matter. I was equally fast and more determined.

I was positive that Everett had the means to replace such a fine watch without issue, but I'd been beaten down so many times since my birthday that I needed a win. *Something.*

With the last of my waning strength, I lunged, colliding with the muscles and heat of the thief as I shoved him to the ground.

He let out a crude, accented curse as we rolled, me fighting to pin him down. Most of my hair had fallen out of its updo, and I heard the harsh rips of my dress. I didn't care. I'd become some sort of vengeful warrior, someone I didn't recognize . . . but a thrill ran from the crown of my head to my toes.

We came to a halt, the waiter landing on top, his weight pressing me farther into the soil. Both of us panted, soaked in mud and plastered with dried leaves.

"What the fuck are you doing?" the thief barked, his dark eyes glinting with silver flecks and malice. He stared down upon me with indignation, having the audacity to act affronted as he swiped his hair out of his face—which was more handsome than I wished to admit. His bronze skin seemed to glow all on its own, and his cutting cheekbones were severe and dangerous; an invitation to temptation. But it was those eyes that captured me . . . so cold, outlined in black—yet there were traces of light, like tiny stars dancing across his stony irises.

His attractive face would have no effect on me. Some of the most treacherous things in this world were disguised behind a mask of beauty.

My chest heaved as I met his trenchant gaze. I didn't bend. I was a Hayes, after all.

"You stole his watch," I accused, another thrill running down my back. "And I'm here to get it back."

He scoffed before lowering himself to whisper in my ear, his heated breath causing me to shiver. *Escape,* my inner voice begged. I ignored it.

"Let's see you take it from me."

Chapter Four

Damien

Wren Hayes had *tackled* me to the ground.

Fates above, I had not expected the princess of Ward One to chase after me in a voluminous ball gown, let alone wrestle me in the mud. Then again, I supposed even *I* would do damn near anything to get away from the pompous prick who'd cornered her. He looked like sleep personified.

Below me, Wren's caramel hair spread around her like a halo, the color somehow shining in the dimness. And her eyes . . . I hadn't had the chance to see them up close before, but the turquoise specks swimming in the greenish blue appeared too stunning to be real. If she weren't the daughter of Cameron Hayes, I might've found her attractive. *Might* being the key word. But it was the sheer look of rage painting her features that stole my attention.

"I will not *take* it from you," she snapped, the bite in her tone unexpected. "You will hand it over. *Now.*"

I sneered at her request, making a show of glancing down her frame where she was currently trapped below me. Wren lifted an unimpressed blond brow, clearly unfazed by my blatant attempt to intimidate. If anything, her eyes turned sharper, the colors that ignited the night growing more pronounced.

This couldn't be the same anxious woman who'd paced in her parlor on her eighteenth birthday, all rosy cheeks and anxious energy. She'd been the embodiment of bright pink and wildflowers and spring. This creature, on the other hand, her lips set in a thin line and her eyes narrowed into catlike slits, was a thing to be reckoned with.

My twisted mind rather enjoyed it.

I cocked my head, ignoring the way her body felt against mine. How her heat seeped into my bones. My thighs digging into her generous curves . . .

Focus. She's the enemy.

I grinned, fully utilizing the smile that typically set others on edge. The one where my canines poked into my bottom lip. "You're awfully confident given the fact that I'm—"

Something cold pressed against my ribs. *Well, shite.* I didn't need to look to gather it could pierce some decent holes into my flesh.

Whatever this little rabbit had planned piqued my curiosity. A rather difficult thing to do—even if my life might have been on the line. Eh, what was a little tangle without the threat of death?

Smile set in place, I sought the source of the metal, finding a bronze letter opener poking into my side. Impressive, really; a princess with a weapon and fire in her eyes.

My stare lifted, pleased when I discovered a smirk plastered across her face. One that silently screamed she wasn't to be trifled with, even by the likes of me. And I so loved a challenge. Wren Hayes should know better than to engage in fights with criminals.

"I don't have a knife, but maybe this could do some damage," she taunted, and for the first time in ages my smile became genuine.

"Do you always carry a *letter opener* to balls?" I winced when she pressed harder.

Note: If lacking a weapon, a letter opener will suffice.

"You never know when some prick might get handsy," Wren retorted, glaring daggers. There was a hardness in her stare that told me she'd encountered something of the sort before. At the thought, a rush of unexpected ire shot into my veins, and my grin vanished. Wren, unfazed by my expression, added, "Or when you might need to catch a thief."

If only she were aware of what I'd stolen from *her.*

A brief pang of guilt throbbed like an open wound. The locket was safely on my person, tucked away in my waiter's jacket. I hadn't sold it to the buyer like I'd intended, my picture thwarting my plans. My connection was a mystery I hadn't solved. I didn't like mysteries.

Sleep had evaded me since I'd pilfered it, and I argued with myself over and over that it meant nothing. That my picture slipped inside the casing was a flimsy coincidence. An error. The man a look-alike, even.

I would pawn the damned thing when I pawned the snobbish lord's watch. The original buyer had lost their chance. Or more like, I didn't wish to give them a chance to gut me after I wasted their time.

"Well?" Wren asked, lifting her chin. Her full lips were pursed, her eyes defiant. "Get off me and hand it over. Or I can test out this letter opener on your ribs."

My breath caught as she lifted her head, exposing the elegant curve of her neck. I cursed. This was the woman whose gift supposedly—because, yes, I was still in denial—contained my damned photo. She was the daughter of the man I loathed most. Our meeting tonight had to be the Fates playing some sort of wretched trick on me.

Perhaps that was why my mirror hadn't worked as well during my escape—and the entire week before—my gift of invisibility flickering in and out. I hadn't considered the reason until it was lying beneath me, soft and warm and full of rage.

Wren.

I'd never put much stock in the Fates or in them watching us mere mortals, but I imagined that if they *did* watch us, the proof of my magic disappearing lay before my eyes. They were pissed.

The letter opener jabbed at my side.

"Fates, sunshine, that hurt."

"Good," she snapped, right before thrusting it deeper. "And don't call me that."

"But you're so *charming* and—"

I yelped as she kneed me in the groin and shoved me off. Scooting back, she scowled at where I clutched myself, my teeth grinding together while I writhed on the ground.

Through squinting eyes, I caught the little wretch beaming, clearly enjoying herself. She'd made her cut, and the burn lacing my side made me forget why I'd been impressed with her to begin with.

"Damien!"

I groaned at the sound of Ruby's voice from the other side of the fence. Her timing, as always, was awful.

"You're late," she called out again, right before coming face to face with Wren and me on the other side. Her lips parted in an O at what she found. "Fates! Did Hayes's daughter just knock you on your ass?" Ruby snickered, a small snort escaping. She clapped her hands slowly three times. "Bravo, Wren."

"You!" Wren sprang to her feet, her sparkling gown a mess of leaves and snags. "You *know* this man?"

Ah. So they'd met inside at the ball and made friends. Lovely.

Ruby rolled her eyes. "*Know* is a rather familiar term. We . . . work together from time to time."

That was a very vague explanation of our relationship, but I didn't correct her. If I were a man with a more sensitive heart, I'd have been offended.

It didn't take Wren long to put the pieces together.

"As thieves, you mean," Wren accused, crossing her arms and pushing up her breasts. My traitorous eyes fell on her chest before I cursed again. I seemed to do a lot of cursing around Wren Hayes.

"I'm fine, thank you for asking, Ruby!" I bellowed, heat racing up and down my ribs. Wren had cut deep enough for me to bleed, but I doubted it required stitches. If it did, Ruby would make certain it left a scar. I avoided working with her on serious missions whenever possible—mainly because she tended to get sidetracked—but this party had been too good to pass up, and that silver watch . . . *whew,* it would feed us for a month, regardless of splitting the cost. However, now that I'd been *stabbed*—and kneed in the groin—I debated haggling for a larger percentage. All Ruby did was pick out the target, and then she would secure a buyer. A gift she came by naturally. She had the uncanny ability to know who could and couldn't be trusted.

"No one cares, Damien." Ruby cocked her head as she observed Wren, an odd expression crossing my companion's face. "At least someone put this deviant in his place. Cocky thing, isn't he?"

I was going to murder her. Slowly.

"He truly is," Wren agreed, softening ever so slightly as she dropped her arms. "How do you hold back from smacking him all the time?"

Ruby shrugged. "Sometimes I do. Very therapeutic, I might add."

Wren snorted, seeming to forget her rage for just a moment.

This little camaraderie of theirs had to stop. It was giving me a headache.

"Enough chitchat, we need to go." I made for the fence, preparing to start the climb, but a small hand grasped my arm.

"The watch," Wren demanded, ignoring Ruby altogether. "Don't make me stab you again." She held up the letter opener in warning, droplets of my darkened blood staining its sides.

I smirked. "You don't seem the type to make the final blow, and I like my chances."

With that, I scurried up the fence and out of her reach. She called out my name—familiar with it now, thanks to Ruby—and tried to follow, but her dress made it all but impossible. She growled out a curse I hadn't heard from someone of her standing. It sounded endearing more than threatening.

At the top of the fence, with my feet dangling off the sides, I peered down at Wren. My heart skipped a beat. "Until next time, sunshine," I taunted before hopping down and landing on my feet next to Ruby.

A win was a win, and this one tasted sweeter than the others.

Wren grasped the iron that separated us with her gloved hands and scowled. "You better hope not."

"Oh, don't tempt me, I enjoy threats," I called over my shoulder with a snicker. I caught a brief image of her; a seething mess now set on my destruction. My chest warmed at the image. It was rare that a person surprised me.

Ruby skipped along in her "borrowed" dress, the delicate hemline already ruined by her careless movements. "That's the woman you stole from a week ago? Fates, Damien, you're in trouble."

I didn't care for her telling me this; I already knew.

"And you were far too friendly with her," I grumbled. "Next thing I know, you'll be invited for tea."

"And I'd accept," Ruby answered cheerfully. "I'd never say no to tea and biscuits. Besides, I think I like her, and the fact that she had you on your ass—"

"Yes, yes." I cut her off. "I get it. You're probably angry you missed the show."

"Damn right."

I needed to remind myself not to work with Ruby again. But that would be a lie. We'd known each other for ten years now. I was stuck with her.

We walked in silence, Ruby occasionally humming to herself

while skipping here and there, her cheery disposition grating on my nerves. As she danced around the burly men and scowling women of the Void, I had the sudden urge to reach for the locket I'd kept on me since that fateful night. It felt too important to keep in my room, where anyone could break in. Then there was that odd pull of magic that kept me rubbing its smooth surface each night. I wanted to understand, and until I did, I kept it right beside my mirror—

I stopped in my tracks, ice trickling down my spine, my hand frozen in place inside my pocket.

It wasn't there.

It wasn't *fucking* there.

"What's wrong?" Ruby asked when I slowed, bumping into a few townspeople, who shot her vile gestures she ignored with the ease of someone who'd grown up in this dark place.

I checked my trousers and patted down my jacket, and all the while, uncharacteristic nerves caused my hands to tremble.

Gone. The locket was gone.

Either it had fallen out during our tussle and it was now back in Wren's possession . . . or someone at the party had stolen it from *me.*

Which didn't make sense, did it? I *never* lost things. Hell, my career depended on the trait. Besides, the pockets of my jacket were deep. Far too deep for the object to have simply fallen out.

Some thief at the party had taken what I'd claimed. With all the bodies moving around in there and all the commotion, it was the most reasonable answer. I couldn't have been the only criminal there, right?

A thought struck.

The waiters weren't the only ones in that room tonight. And the man who'd originally commissioned me to steal the gift? He could've been dancing before my eyes. He knew my face, while I'd been denied his.

I faced Ruby. "I don't believe I'm done with Wren Hayes after all."

Chapter Five

Wren

Dusk rarely ventures from the palace, but
when she does, it can only mean trouble.
—*The Darkest Fate,* Chapter Ten

I took five whole minutes of indulging myself by glowering down the street where Damien had melted into the shadows before I released the iron bars. I wanted to climb the damn fence and give chase, but it was far too late, and my corset was digging into my ribs painfully.

I supposed I didn't get my win for the evening after all.

Wretched dress.

"Wren!"

I turned at the voice of Lord Everett, who stumbled through the garden, his eyes wide and consumed with worry. I had the sudden urge to laugh. The higher society *would* deem a woman running through a garden frightful.

"Over here," I called, sighing. Picking up my tattered skirts, I walked toward the lord, assuming I appeared a mess and deciding not to care. It wasn't like I could magic myself into a respectable lady anyway, even on a good day.

"What in the Fates' names happened?" he asked, lifting his arms as if he planned to run his hands down my sides. He ended up dropping them and clenching them into fists, a muscle in his jaw twitching as he appraised my state. I had no doubt that twigs and leaves and other unseemly debris clung to me as well.

"The thief escaped," I admitted with a grimace, still sore over the entire thing. I wished I'd had the nerve to stab him a little harder. He wouldn't have *died,* and I could've been handing over the watch right that moment. Triumphant.

Everett huffed, his eyes sparkling. "I don't care about the thief, or a silly *watch,* for that matter, Wren. Look at you. You could've hurt yourself. Or he could've . . ." He trailed off, his tone deepening with worry. I frowned, taken aback by his genuine concern. I expected disdain, disgust, or even indifference, but he gazed upon me as if he sincerely cared.

In this duplicitous world of ours, such things mattered.

Maybe I'd been avoiding the wrong man after all.

My cheeks blazed against my wishes as I tilted my chin downward and took in the mess I'd become. Mud and leaves covered the dress of night and stars, and the hemline had been utterly ruined when I attempted to climb the fence. My updo was no longer, my hair falling about my shoulders, the strands tickling my skin.

The softest graze of fingers whispered over my bare shoulder, the touch warm and soothing. More soothing than I imagined it would be. When I met his stare, Everett cleared his throat, his eyes falling to where his fingers skimmed my collarbones.

"I know about you, Wren Hayes," he said, avoiding my eyes. "Not just who your father is, but . . ." He briefly shut his eyes before taking a deep breath as if to muster courage. "You've played the role of the perfect daughter well, and at every ball, I notice you. How you bend the rules, if only slightly." He chuckled, likely referring to my choices of necklines or hems. "Or when you put Cecile and her group in their place when their gossip turned vicious. I may not be an overly active member of society, but I observe, and I find I quite like you. Gift or not."

I swallowed thickly, taken aback by such an unexpected declaration. Everett had been watching me? I'd seen him briefly at events but assumed he was like all the others Callie warned me about. But what he just said . . . the brave admission sparked something warm in my chest, and tingles raced from where his fingers continued to run across my arms. I didn't shove him away like I could have. Like I usually would have.

I blamed the lingering adrenaline.

"I had no idea," I admitted, not sure what else to say. I was never one who went out on a limb to shine in social settings, mainly because it gave me hives, but he'd seen me all the same.

He laughed, the noise deep and like a rumble of thunder. "I didn't tell you all of that to make you uncomfortable. I just thought you should know." His ensuing smile lit up his entire face. "I don't particularly like to speak my mind, and rarely put myself in such positions"—he waved awkwardly in my direction with his free hand—"but . . . I'd like to get to know you better. Without all the eyes." He motioned behind him, to the ongoing gala.

What was there to say? Words were trapped in my throat, which grew tighter by the second. He would expect to court me, which led to marriage. I didn't wish for those things, even if I found his honesty attractive. Along with his face. Again, a shock.

"I—"

"You don't have to answer now," he interjected, seeming to read my mind. I sighed in relief. "Let's just get you out of this chill and home safe."

Fates, if any of the nosy gossipers caught the pair of us skulking in the far reaches of the Lovetts' garden, with me looking as if I'd rolled about on the ground, assumptions would surely be made.

Everett seemed to grasp this and gently took my hand. His voice was far steadier when he spoke. "We'll bring you out the back. Your carriage can pick you up outside the kitchens." He winced slightly, his bright features pinched. "No one will see. I'll make certain of it."

How very gentlemanly of him.

All right, perhaps that snarky thought was unwarranted. He *was* being a gentleman; I just probably needed a good bath and a good night's sleep.

"Thank you," I said, though my smile was strained. It was a task all by itself. I wasn't in a "kind" mood, and my temperament soured the second that thief bested me. I should spare Everett my wrath.

Nodding, he held out his arm, offering me the chance to slip mine through his. I did, but only because my knees were wobbly and my heart raced. As we walked in silence back through the gardens—Everett's stiff posture suggesting that nerves consumed him, which made me smile—I returned to *him*.

Damien.

He obviously wasn't from the northern side of Andalay, what with his distinct accent and crude curses and . . . well, his profession. Yes, being a thief would eliminate one from upper-class society. He had to belong to the southern side; what most called the Void. Which didn't make sense either.

The people there didn't receive gifts. They weren't blessed by the Fates, nor did the people worship the deities. I knew what I'd seen—Damien flickering in and out of existence, using *some* sort of magic. It had to be a gift, but how Damien acquired one was a mystery.

If Damien did live in the Void, then I knew little to nothing about his home other than that it belonged to the people Lord Allen swindled. But it wasn't as if I'd been allowed to venture there in the past, and if I brought up going there to Father or Mother, they'd likely laugh, thinking I jested.

Still, I ached to understand more.

Or, more accurately, I aimed to find this Damien and watch as his smirk fell when I cornered him. Learning about the Void would be a bonus. A way to take in the side of Andalay I hadn't been permitted to see. Now that I was without high-society friends watching my every movement, I might get the chance.

Foolish plans took shape, all of them ones that would land me in dire trouble. Nonetheless, the more a plan flourished, the more my heart skipped for an entirely different reason other than defeat.

Excitement. The emotion I was experiencing was true excitement.

"Just on the right side." I flinched when Everett spoke, so lost was I in my own scheming. He pointed with his free hand toward the Lovetts' mansion, specifically to a door off the main house and shrouded by ivy. No guests lingered there.

"Thank you, again," I said, turning to catch Everett's eye. The shock had worn off, and now, curiosity had replaced it. I sensed he brimmed with questions, but out of kindness, he kept them back.

Lucky me.

He opened the door, a blast of hot air wafting over my already heated cheeks. The kitchens. I smelled the rosemary and spices and a hint of sugary frosting that must have dotted the small cakes being passed around the ballroom. I cursed myself for not trying one of them sooner. Hopefully Callie snuck some home for me like she usually did.

Everett guided me beyond servers and cooks. The head chef barked orders at the workers, sweat pooling from his wrinkled brow.

I hated to admit I was grateful for Everett's presence now. The overwhelming clamor of the kitchen had my head spinning, and the heat caused my ears to burn.

And you didn't eat much today, I reminded myself. I'd been too nervous.

"Almost there," Everett promised softly, leaning close enough that his breath teased my unruly hair.

Maybe I'd misjudged him. I tended to do that often, especially with the suitors my mother selected. He could easily have gone straight for my parents and caused a scene, but instead, Everett helped me make my escape without fanfare.

Aside from his declaring his interest in me.

I'd deal with *that* later.

The door leading outside was in sight, and when the crisp evening air slid over my body like a sweet caress, I sighed loudly.

"I want to ask what occurred more than I want anything else," Everett whispered conspiratorially, a tinge of playfulness lightening his usually serious tone. "But I have a feeling it's not something you'd like to share. Must I be civil and respect that?" he asked, one corner of his lips quirking.

Able to think a little more clearly without the chaos and stifling heat of the kitchens, I smiled at him. "I would appreciate a little discretion," I replied. "And you are correct in your assumptions. However, one day I might relay the tale."

I likely wouldn't, but the lie made his grin widen. "Very well, then, Lady Wren. I will see you to your carriage and pray the day comes when I can hear of your harrowing evening."

Arm in arm we strolled to the line of waiting carriages and the bored drivers manning them. When William, our driver, spotted me, he jerked upright in his seat and straightened his crumpled brown coat. Flakes of pastry tumbled onto the cobblestones below.

"Can you please take Lady Wren home?" Everett asked. "She has a horrid headache."

William took one peek at me and I noticed the slight rise of his bushy graying brow. If he knew better, he'd understand that a headache was an excuse for something that typically *caused* headaches.

Nevertheless, he nodded. "I'll return for your parents once you're settled."

Thank the Fates.

I was being saved from the partygoers *and* my parents. I truly owed Everett a dance at the next event.

Everett helped me climb into the carriage, my hand in his. I imagined for *just a second* that it wouldn't be so bad being with someone like him. He had an outstanding reputation, and his gift rendered him a master with numbers. He kept the wiry glasses in his pocket with him at all times, never knowing when his assistance would be needed for some representative or anxious lord who'd had an evening of indulgence and worried for his estate.

"Good night, Lady Hayes," Everett said once I'd taken my seat. "I do hope to see you soon, though perhaps next time we'll leave out the garden escapades."

He was very much—and surprisingly—interested. Mother would be thrilled.

"Promise," I replied. "Thank you again." I'd spoken the words so many times tonight.

"It gave me an excuse to play hero. While the thief managed to get away, I got a chance to spend time in your company."

I hid my grimace well. It was a nice thing to say. A way of flirting. No matter the way it made me want to cringe. He might be nervous, I reminded myself, trying not to be cruel. Secretly, I wanted to ruffle his hair and see him break character. To uncover more beneath the façade.

Everett grinned as he shut the door gently, and the carriage heaved forward with a jolt.

Twenty minutes later, I stood safely inside my bedroom, attempting to rip off my dress. I'd dismissed our maid, Sarah, who'd gasped at my unseemly state before I shut my door.

Damn it all. I ripped at the already ruined fabric until I slid free. The remnants dropped to the wooden floor with a whoosh. My corset, on the other hand, proved harder to get out of, but I was nothing if not persistent.

Hair combed and changed into a fresh nightdress, I slid into bed and turned the knob of the lamp upon the nightstand.

In the voiceless dark, I didn't envision Lord Everett or his handsome, kind face. I pictured *him,* the thief. His sneer. That exasperating smirk. The way he'd assumed me incapable of inflicting harm.

I'd been underestimated my whole existence. That ended today.

In the morning, I planned to visit the Palace of the Fates, but my thoughts were set on gleaning more information about the thief and determining how to let him know that Wren Hayes was no witless damsel of Ward One.

I woke before dawn.

My parents and Callie had stumbled, *loudly,* into the house hours earlier. They should be well and truly asleep for most of the day. Judging by their late arrival, they hadn't missed me all that much at the ball.

Perfect.

Dressing in my finest to appease the Fates—an understated yellow satin number with a square neckline and short tulle sleeves—I grabbed my coat and crept down the stairs.

I avoided all the creaks I'd memorized over the years, but no one roamed the halls, and I made it downstairs unnoticed. Using the garden exit, the sun barely rising in the sky, I unlocked the gate with the brass key I'd snatched from the hook hanging in the kitchen.

Making sure to lock up behind me, I surveyed the glistening avenues of Andalay. The sunrise painted the streets in dreamlike shades of peaches, bright pinks, and dusty oranges, the colors dancing together as they illuminated the northern end and all its charmed brilliance.

Since we lived downtown, quaint, upscale shops surrounded our town house; some dedicated to fixing magical gifts, others simply boasting luxurious clothing and jewelry. The weary-eyed shop owners were only now making their way to open up for the day, flipping their Closed signs to Open.

Everywhere you looked, the upper-class merchants could be seen employing their gifts—from the realm's most prestigious bakers using magic-infused rolling pins to craft the freshest breads, to renowned seamstresses exercising their magicked needles, which didn't require a touch to sew luxurious garments. They might not be noble, but their esteemed professions got them invited to numerous balls and parties, and they were often spotted frequenting the same establishments as the elite.

I passed them all, my sights set on the dusty-rose palace and its three high towers. Hedged in on all sides, the entrance would be heavily guarded—and without a summons, I doubted they would see me. Not that I wouldn't try. Maybe they'd been waiting for me to visit them after I failed to receive my gift. Perhaps all of this time spent agonizing could've been averted if I'd only had the courage to leave home.

Please don't let it be denial. I'd spent too much time considering why I'd been neglected, and come up short. While that might make me seem cocky, I was adamant that I'd spent a lifetime worshipping the immortals as they requested. I'd always known what I wanted, and I had undoubtedly put in the effort.

A butterfly landed on my shoulder as I crossed the road to the palace entrance, its wings a vibrant pink and gold. "Wishing me luck?" I asked cheerfully, though a slight quiver remained persistent in my voice. It fluttered its wings in response. I smiled. "I'll take that as a good sign." The little creature tickled my cheeks before flying off and leaving me to face the Fates alone.

Two guards manned the front entrance, but looks were deceiving; there should be hundreds inside if what my father said stayed true. He'd been summoned a year before, and according to him, the Fates hadn't deigned to meet him in person—rather, they sent an attendant who had briefly questioned him on his ward's overall productiveness. The whole thing lasted twenty minutes. Though now that I thought about it, he'd been absent most of that day. Callie had been sick at home, unable to attend, but even she proved curious as to where he'd gone. Likely the office, but Father kept his secrets close to the chest.

A deep sound of protest worked up my throat as I sat there and made excuses not to move.

Just do it, Wren. Walk across the street and ask. What harm can come?

Well, what *more* harm could come?

My hands were slicked with sweat by the time I faced the first guard, an older man wearing the stiff Andalay jacket of deep blue threaded with golden stitches. He awarded me a cold once-over, reminding me of Mother.

"I am here to see the—the Fates. Spe-specifically, Day." I hated how my voice shook. It wasn't like the guard himself was Day; he was simply one of the immortals' lackeys.

The man's graying brows pinched together. "And you are?"

"Wren Hayes." I ground my teeth to keep my chin from wobbling. Anxiety hummed like bees through my chest, my heart a fluttering mess of uneven chords. When he opened his mouth, I assumed he'd turn me away or laugh, but then he paused. His head cocked to the side and went utterly still as if he listened to some imaginary voice. Abruptly, the guard stepped aside, his companion mirroring his comrade's actions.

"You are permitted entry to the Gardens of Dusk."

Dusk? No, surely he must've misheard me.

"But I said—"

"That is the only area where you are permitted . . . unless you'd like to turn around and return home?"

Dusk didn't frighten me. Not like she did some others. Yes, Dusk endured as the keeper of the dying and the dead, but she also guarded us in our older years. Saved us from pain. Supposedly, we saw her face when we took our last breaths, and her mere existence allowed the passage of souls to the afterworld. If she was the lone Fate willing to see me, then so be it. This would be my only chance.

I would see a Fate today. A *Fate.*

More sweat gathered on my brow, elation and fear mixing together to form a heady combination.

I stepped beyond the gate and past the two rigid guards. Instantly, the scent in the air transformed from the fresh pastries being baked in the city to an overwhelming aroma of gardenias; they were my nan's favorite before she died, and Callie and I had a fondness for them. The floral smell invaded my senses as I stood before the palace, seconds from meeting a divine being. I'd never felt so small. Insignificant.

Three pathways had been erected, the thick trees with lush green leaves making it all but impossible to walk straight toward the palace itself. The first pathway shimmered in golden light, jasmine blooms sprouting from the earth. Roses of yellow and pink covered the second path, much like the ones from my own garden. Dawn and Day. Those had to be the routes to their domains.

The last pathway lay shrouded, the air surrounding it shades darker than the others, like night itself warred to rule over the entrance. Surprise filled me when I noted vibrant red poppies springing from the soil; the flower of remembrance. Heart thumping in my ears, I headed for the darker of the three trails, tripping over my own feet as I went.

Breathe, I reminded myself. Such a difficult thing to do when fear overtook you. And yes, I was afraid now, but not of Dusk, just at being in the presence of something bigger than myself. Not many were permitted to see the Fates up close, and I'd hidden my shock when the guard allowed me to enter. Or I thought I had. I'd been told I was lousy at hiding my emotions by Callie many, *many* times. All right, she claimed my face might as well be an open book. I supposed I should work on that.

I continued ahead, focusing on admiring the bloodred poppies until the trail yawned open, revealing a circular garden. *You can do this,* I repeated over and over again, my little mantra dying like a song's ending when Dusk's garden loomed ahead.

Brilliant yet austere arched bridges painted ivory led over several perfectly round ponds of vibrant blue, the waters dense and still. The poppies grew like angry red walls around the perimeter, each flower swaying dreamily in the wind. My stare moved to the center of the scene, where a grand stone pavilion stood, its edges trenchant and menacing.

I found the garden of stone and red poppies eerily beautiful in its simplicity.

With my eyes on the pavilion, I walked across the first bridge, feeling like some lost heroine wandering into a wholly separate universe. My vision swam as light and dismal shadows flitted across my eyes, and I had to grasp the rail for support every now and again to right myself.

If such tricks were meant to deter me, the most feared Fate didn't know me at all.

By the third bridge, my sight had somewhat cleared, my eyes

having grown slightly accustomed to the wavering dance of night and day. I wished my nerves had calmed as well, but that proved an impossibility I didn't even hope for. Until I left the palace gates, my body would be buzzing, ready for flight. The Fates were all-consuming, while we mere mortals were just their playthings. Prey.

I didn't dare confuse my standing.

Stepping from the stone bridge, I hovered before the pavilion, carefully noting two cushioned chairs composed of black velvet set up to face each other. A simple oak table sat between them, the top boasting a silver serving dish and two cups of hot tea, the steam still swirling around the rims. Beside the cups lay a single folded piece of parchment, which, of course, I ached to open. I eyed the small initials *W.H.* scrawled in the center, and my curiosity rose to new heights.

Had she expected me?

Resisting the urge to rush for the paper painted with my initials, I took in the moment and smiled, thinking how ordinary sharing tea with Dusk would appear. Maybe it wouldn't be so frightening after all.

"Hello?" I called out hesitantly, searching for the immortal. No one emerged. "I was told by the guard to come here—"

The world spun on its axis the moment I took another step.

Red.

The exact color of the poppies, small droplets stained the pristine floor beyond the entrance of the pavilion. I'd nearly missed them, so taken with the entirety of the garden's splendor. Now they were all I saw. All I could smell and think of.

Clenching my fists, I dug my nails into my palms as I staggered closer, my heartbeat roaring in my ears.

This time, when I sucked in a deep inhale, a rush of stringent copper filled the air, the unmistakable scent of blood tainting the garden's natural aroma.

My knees nearly buckled, yet I continued on, inch by inch, watching in horror as the speckles grew in size; like the injury had grown worse. Around the table, behind the farthest chair, a *pool* of red glinted in the light. I clutched a hand to my mouth, my silent scream dying on my lips. Violent streaks broke up the puddle, marring the ivory flooring. It was as if something—or *someone*—had been dragged across all that red.

"Dusk?" I called, *needing* her to reply before I began hyperventilating. I scanned the pavilion, the paths, the garden. No one was in sight. No divine being.

The earlier panic caused me to stumble as it grew, the pounding in my head and ears like the warning beats of drums.

Something bad had happened here. It didn't take a genius to deduce that. But if the Fate had been hurt, that meant so much more than I could wrap my mind around. And if she *had* been attacked, was her assailant still here, watching me?

My throat closed, my breathing nothing but a wheeze. If the guards found me beside a pool of immortal blood . . .

I'd be the only suspect.

I jolted, jumping nearly a foot in the air when a discordant alarm blared. Soldiers. They would come storming into the garden, and they'd most assuredly accuse *me*. Hell, *I* would accuse me.

I wasn't thinking straight when I bolted to the table and snatched the single piece of folded paper with my initials. Wasn't thinking when I ran across the bridges and made it to the main path. But I didn't take it—guards would be swarming it at any second.

Instead, I shoved my way through the thick leaves and brittle branches, entering a world of darkness.

Shouts rang out behind me as I ran.

Chapter Six

Damien

The whiskey went down smooth.

The bartender, Cap—a former ship captain, and not so cleverly named by his tavern's patrons—shot me a dour look as I slammed the empty glass down on the wooden counter. He needed to mind his business, was what he needed to do. I might live above the Broken Wing Tavern thanks to him, but he wasn't my father. I didn't *know* my father. Or mother, for that matter. I'd been found outside the Void's orphanage as a baby. It didn't take a clever mind to deduce that my childhood hadn't been sunshine and sugar.

"Problem?" I confronted Cap, arching a brow.

He continued to wipe the same glass over and over. At this rate, it was the cleanest thing in this place. "Not if you don't cause a scene," he replied grimly.

Ah, yes. I couldn't fault the man there. The Broken Wing Tavern was where the exhausted and reckless men and women of the

Void ventured when the sun collapsed from the sky. A place where bets were placed and illegal fighting matches went on well into the early hours. If I had to recall any trouble caused by me, it would be a month ago, when I *might* have cheated at cards and *might* have caused a fight to ensue that broke some furniture. In my defense, the place needed some redecorating anyway.

"I'm just here to drink, nothing to worry about, old man." Cap's stare turned threatening. He didn't fool me, and while he was a tall man with more muscles than he knew what to do with, he certainly didn't frighten me. His weakness was sentimentality. The proof was his allowing a ruffian like me to live upstairs once the orphanage kicked me out. Cap knew what I did to gain coin and he didn't care as long as I kept the "scenes" to a minimum. Oh, and didn't steal in his bar; another mundane stipulation.

I still envisioned his face when he found me cold and shivering outside the tavern three years ago, half buried in snow. I'd failed that week, stealing just sparse bites here and there, but not enough coin for a warm room. Cap had growled a curse and grabbed my thin jacket to haul me to my feet.

"You gonna cause me trouble?" he'd asked. I'd shaken my head. "Will ya steal from me?" Another shake. "Then keep quiet and follow me. I can't have another dead body to deal with on my steps."

See? Sentimental.

But if not for him, I'd probably be one of the poor fools whose faces were plastered across the many Missing posters. Maybe some killer was on the loose, eager to slay the helpless. There'd been too many lost souls for it to be anything other than suspicious. Not that the men of the law cared.

A bang on the counter and the calling of Cap's name had him abandoning me to my woes; which truly weren't terrible, all things considered.

After Ruby had hounded me about Wren, I opened up about the locket and what it contained. I shouldn't have told her, but it felt good to get it out, and it also put an end to her pestering. As expected, she immediately told me to get off my arse and find the locket if it meant that much to me. I argued that it didn't, but the memory of my picture tucked away inside like a secret burned through my thoughts.

There were no such things as coincidences.

At least the pawnbroker we sold the watch to didn't give Ruby and me trouble. She knew him well, having used him for various other trades. Now I had coin to last the month and then some.

But the cursed locket . . .

I *should* be out there thinking of my next con.

My first rule: Always plan ahead. Life could, and would, deal you a bad hand, and things would easily go to shite.

Yet here I sat, on one of the many wobbly barstools in a dimly lit tavern falling apart by the second, already on my third glass of the cheapest whiskey Cap owned. Around me, the crowd cheered, some card game in the works, played by the predictable gamblers. Judging by the raucous shrieks, someone had just made a killing.

Since it was early yet, no music played, but when the day grew late, singers, guitarists, and other musicians would take to the rickety old stage and entertain the main room. Some patrons would dance. Others would simply drink and watch the revelry with drunken grins. But it was *alive,* all of it, and being surrounded by such riotous life typically lifted my spirits, even if I chose the role of onlooker.

Unfortunately, the promise of tonight's revelry did nothing to brighten my sour mood.

Not only did the locket consume me. Which was a problem. Wren Hayes didn't linger in my mind because I fancied her; she was spoiled and vexing, and utterly self-righteous. I should hate her. But—

The damned woman who'd threatened me with a fucking letter opener intrigued me, and it was a dangerous thing indeed to intrigue someone like me. I had no qualms about uncovering answers as to why my picture lay in her gift in any way I needed—and most of my methods veered on the side of criminal.

I shifted in my seat, hissing at the stinging reminder of where she'd carved into my side. She'd managed to score a decent strike, the cut deep, but nothing that slowed me down. My lips tugged up against my will, memories of her victorious smirk as she stabbed me, sending a burst of heat into my chest. Wild, that was what she was; wild and dogged. Stubborn.

And beautiful.

No. Wren probably used her beauty as a weapon of manipulation. Besides, I could have my pick of lovers, I told myself. People threw themselves at me when the hour turned late, and while I occasionally indulged, I more often than not went to my room alone. Wren captivated me because she was someone new . . . and someone from the other side of the city who'd managed to surprise me. I doubted that surprise would last once I discovered she was just like everyone else from the north.

I searched around the bar, itching for another drink, when shrill alarms pierced the air. Patrons grumbled and a few staggered to the door to see what had caused all the commotion and ruined their good time. The main doors were flung open, and the sirens blared loudly enough for me to want to cover my ears.

So much for my headache.

With my back to the door, I placed my head in my hands, willing away the noise. It wasn't until I heard the shouts a minute later that I deigned to lift my head.

"Dusk is missing!" Timothy, a regular at the Broken Wing, stumbled across the threshold, half dazed, his bleary hazel eyes wide as he rubbed at his balding head.

Words like *impossible* and *ridiculous* floated about, but an eerie chill brushed across my skin that hadn't been there before.

I leaned back, one elbow propped on the bar as Timothy relayed his short tale. The man appreciated being the center of attention, his lips straining not to smile.

Before I took another sip of my drink, a gust of wind blew through the bar. I halted, the scent overpowering the filth of the place.

Gardenias.

I only knew this because it was one of Ruby's favorite flowers, and she liked to occasionally wear them tucked into her curly brown hair. Those, or wilted yellow roses she stole from the northern gardens.

"How do you know this?" Cap demanded of Timothy, slapping his towel over his broad shoulder. The scent of the flowers drifted away as I turned my focus to Timothy, awaiting his reply.

He made a grand show of panting, and I refrained from rolling my eyes at the display. "The palace is in an uproar. Guards are everywhere, and I overheard one of them say blood covered Dusk's courtyard. That she's nowhere to be found. They're searching for some girl, they said. Some *highborn* girl from the north."

An unexpected wave of ice skittered down my back.

"Did they give a description?" I found myself asking, my words sounding like they came from far away. Or perhaps I'd reveled in the whiskey a little too much.

"All I know is she's got unusual blue eyes and long blond hair," Timothy revealed. "One of the commanders gave more of a description, but I didn't wait long enough to find out. I didn't trust them not to arrest me for being on the wrong side of town."

It was plausible. They harassed the people of the Void all the time for just walking the northern streets. As if not having a gift made them scum. Cursed.

My head spun as I took in Timothy's words, rolling them around.

Unusual blue eyes.

A highborn.

Blond hair.

Someone who would have the gall to request to see the Fates—

Like someone who hadn't received their gift and carried a letter opener as a weapon.

I didn't need a full description of the woman. My damned gut screamed at me, churning harder the longer I sat there, motionless. Fates, Wren would be foolish enough to go to the palace, that I knew without a doubt.

Clutching my head, I groaned.

Dusk had been taken, and they were searching for Wren Hayes. It had to be.

Without paying, I slunk off in the chaos of the ensuing arguments, Timothy surrounded by a horde of patrons eager for more information. Gossips, all of them.

Slipping past the gathering crowd, I grimaced as the unforgiving sun assaulted my senses. I'd forgotten it was morning. Far too early for whiskey, but to my credit, I had a long night, and I hadn't exactly slept.

While I didn't know much about the princess of Ward One, it didn't take a genius to grasp that she wasn't a killer. Wren could've murdered me with that blasted letter opener and she hadn't. She'd had two opportunities to do so, in fact.

The guards had to be mistaken about her involvement in the Fate's disappearance; she'd been in the wrong place at the wrong time.

Fuck me. Why am I heading north?

It could be someone else.

I wished I believed that.

My feet carried me swiftly through the throngs of the Void, past the smoky marketplace and the clamoring vendors boasting their weeks-old vegetables and questionable meats. Beyond the crumbling rusty-brown brick hovels people called homes. Farther from the polluted air that entered your lungs and made each breath a struggle. Every inch of this place was obscured by a layer of grime, dust, or filth. The city had turned its back on us all, and as a result, the Void lived up to its dismal name.

I couldn't risk using my mirror just yet, as it barely managed a few minutes the last time I opened it—which had been last night, when Wren threw off my usual confidence. The mirror remained safely tucked inside my jacket as I sauntered down the street, keeping to the shadows like I had before I'd turned nineteen. Old habits die hard.

When the distressed pavement turned into neat ivory cobblestones, I slowed my pace, keeping my head bowed as I entered the northern end. Timothy had been right about the soldiers; they were everywhere around the palace in the distance, and groups of them ventured off to nearby stores and other establishments, no doubt to search for the suspect or any other culprits who could've been involved.

Walking past a clothing store, some of its wares displayed on the walkway, I easily snagged a hat of expensive wool. It hid my eyes well, the owner too busy watching the soldiers inch closer to the shops to notice. It might've been a good thing that I still wore my jacket from the previous night, which gave the impression of decency, regardless of its belonging to a waiter. If you didn't look too close, it almost resembled something fit for a day's walk in the north.

Why the hell I indulged in this little escapade was beyond me. Sure, my mirror's magic waned, and yes, I suspected it had to do with stealing that fated locket, but I should be at the bar—half asleep and slumped over a generous glass that would make me forget.

Maybe I was simply a masochist and wanted to find out if Wren had retained the locket after our scuffle, or if my assumption that it had been stolen was correct. If the latter was the case, I would require a list of all the people who'd attended the party, including the staff. But I often got ahead of myself. First I needed to find where Wren Hayes had run off to.

Something told me I should've had one more glass of whiskey.

Chapter Seven

Wren

Each gift is specifically curated for its owner.
The gift grants their greatest wishes.
—*Aurilian History of Magical Objects,* Chapter Two

The thicket had done well to cover me in scratches and thoroughly ruin my dress. It was nothing but tatters now, and it didn't help my overall appearance that dirt caked my face.

It seemed I had a tendency as of late to destroy perfectly fine dresses and wear dirt as others wore expensive rouge.

Alarm bells rang from all sides as I fought the branches, scrambling to reach the wall. I lacked a plan for *after* I reached it, but I wasn't thinking clearly. *Obviously.*

They could very well believe I had something to do with all that blood.

Was Dusk missing? Hurt? *Dead?* Was I the main suspect? I'd

just been sent to her domain, and the guards had my full name, so it wouldn't be a stretch to make assumptions. Selfish of me to think of myself instead of Dusk; my mind raced on its own accord, images of a prison moving through my sight faster than bolts of lightning.

The parchment I'd snatched in those last frantic moments peeked out from my neckline, the coarse paper reminding me of its sharp edges with each step. I desperately wanted to reach inside, unfold it, and read its words, but time felt precious, and the forest I wandered through was dim.

It bore *my* initials. Like Dusk had been expecting me. *Or it could stand for something else entirely.* The immortal might've simply been writing to someone with the same initials.

Then why had I felt the all-consuming need to take it?

I cursed, using my favorite word, which pissed Mother off no end. *A lady shouldn't speak in such coarse language,* she would gasp, and I'd cover my smile with the back of my hand. Didn't she get it yet? I had no plans to be one of the ladies she knew. I had my own idea in mind—to leave Andalay.

My foot slipped beneath a root, sending me flying forward with an *oof.* I screeched as I went down. *Hard.* My hands flew to protect my face, but I already felt the sting of something prickly pressing into my cheek. I angled my chin upward.

The parchment rolled out during my fall, now inches from my grasp.

Damn it.

If I was going to be hunted by soldiers and likely hauled away for questioning, I might as well take a second to pry.

Still on the ground, covered in filth and mud, I extended my arm and snatched the note.

Dirt smudged the fine paper as I carefully unfolded the letter, my touch gentle even if it no longer mattered that it had been ruined. Dusk had *touched* this. In my heart, it felt sacred.

I sucked in a gasp and squinted down at the page.

Little bird,

Some gifts are crafted with an abundance of magic. Others, very little. The gift you were meant to receive is composed of my own magic. Dangerous magic I originally had no intention to give.

There are two roads. Two outcomes.

Black and blue. Blue and black. Two sides of the same cursed coin.

One ends in cruel bliss, the other, with a destiny fulfilled.

Black and blue. What color will you choose?

Robbed of your right, find one cunning and deceptive enough to secure it once more. A dark soul with green hopes. I've chosen well, already placed you in their path. Another, an ocean carrying the brutal truth.

Choose, little bird, or life will choose for you.

Destroy this as soon as you're done reading.

The bottom of the page lacked a signature, but Dusk had written this. To *me*. My father and mother had called me little bird since childhood because they claimed I was forever on the verge of flitting away, never able to sit still or cease daydreaming.

That last line, *Destroy this as soon as you're done reading,* weighed on my chest, an uneasy sensation crawling up my spine. She clearly had meant for this note to be seen by my eyes alone.

Which, again, made absolutely no sense, given who I was.

I panted, a mess on the ground, my face smeared with Fates knew what. The letter's warning, of dangerous magic and cruel bliss, of finding the person they'd placed in my path—someone who could help me retrieve what had been stolen. It made my head spin, an abundance of questions zipping across my mind without anyone to answer them.

Swallowing thickly, I shut my eyes, trying to center myself like my sister had taught me. *Three big breaths,* she'd say in that gentle voice of hers. *Nice and slow, that's it.*

Thinking of Callie made me wish she were here with me now. She'd know what to do. She was the brave sister. The one who'd made the monsters go away when we were little and I crawled into her bed at night.

Still, Dusk's demand haunted me, pressing me to locate the gift. Until then, I'd be unable to settle.

A dark soul with green hopes. I've chosen well, already placed you in their path.

A face popped into my head, but it couldn't be right.

Recalling Dusk's instructions, I reread the letter one more time before I took it in my hands and ripped it down the center. Then I ripped it again. I shredded the paper until my fingers burned and not a single piece remained larger than a square inch. Shoving the remains beneath the soil, I buried them, hoping the earth would swallow up the evidence. Dusk hadn't wished for anyone to read her letter. Just me.

A selfish thrill zipped through me.

"I *do* have a gift," I murmured to myself, easing up. Dirt slipped from my skirts, my arms caked in speckles of it. My body itched and the small cuts from my race through the trees stung, but I didn't care. "So where is it?"

I'd secretly feared it had been my own incompetence that prevented me from receiving a gift from the Fates, but something else, something—or *someone*—had gotten in the way. Had *stolen* my gift before I'd had a chance to claim it. Dusk decreed it powerful, and it had to be. It was created *by* her.

Elation mixed with my dread, my stomach nothing more than a twisting chaos of knots and tangled feelings.

My gut screamed at me to move, to hunt down the person Dusk mentioned. I would require someone cunning and cruel. Dangerous and deceitful. A person with a dark soul to find my gift.

And I couldn't banish the face that continued to linger in my head like an unwanted guest.

Shouts rent the air, the guards closing in.

There'd be no escape. What I could control, however, was going to them. Making it seem like I'd been just as much a victim as Dusk. It was the truth, after all. While I never should have run—as it made me appear guilty—the past couldn't be undone. Ruminating over it now, I could've laughed at myself for believing that *I* of all people had the prowess to scale that imposing palace wall. Hell, I couldn't even scale the Lovetts' *fence*.

With a sigh, I tilted my chin and turned in the direction of the shouting. On shaking limbs, I trudged through the woods, aiming for the guards, who'd likely arrest me.

Sometimes to win the game one had to surrender first. Father had told me that.

With the walls and forest surrounding me, the only way out of this was through.

"Help!" I called out, making my voice as frail as possible. Not a challenging task given the circumstances. "Please, somebody, help!"

I waited where I stood, tapping my foot impatiently. Not especially keen on being arrested, I desired to get the whole embarrassing debacle over with as soon as humanly possible. Father would hear about this and run to my aid, fervent to avoid further scandal.

Everything will be all right.

Ha. As if I truly believed that.

When the first soldier burst through the branches I allowed thick tears to slip free; a devious little trick I'd used several times to get what I wanted as a child. "Help," I rasped again, secretly thinking that Mother would be proud of my acting. I looked like nothing but a helpless, lost noblewoman. An inconvenience, if anything.

The soldier reached me just as three more came barreling into the space. Their hulking frames fenced me in on all sides like a cage crafted of muscle.

Before they grabbed me, I fluttered my lashes theatrically and rolled my eyes back. *This one is for you, Mother.* I forced myself to fall, my eyelids closing as if I'd fainted.

I wished I had. The ground was not kind to my limbs.

The men weren't gentle when they hauled me up and into their arms. They weren't gentle when they carried me back toward the palace exit, and they certainly didn't think of my well-being when they threw me into a waiting carriage. I landed roughly on the floor, my cheek pressed against a thin carpet. It smelled of the inside of shoes and other things I didn't want to think about.

I peeked open an eye some minutes later, finding the window above my head. I ground my teeth. We were headed to a brick building I'd passed by hundreds of times without worry.

The main guard station neared—or in other words, the place where they kept the criminals waiting to be interrogated or processed for the mines.

I closed my eyes before a real tear could fall.

Chapter Eight

Damien

I watched from across the street as they hauled Wren's unmoving body from a carriage and into the main guard station. Her fine dress, which once might've been a luminous yellow, was torn and muddied, and filth streaked her cheeks and brow.

The soldier carrying her had scooped her limp body into his arms, her head lolling back at an awkward angle. My teeth ground together at the way he handled her so roughly, not caring when he readjusted her, his big hands yanking and pulling without consideration. She'd either fainted or . . .

If she'd died, they wouldn't have taken her body here. This was where all the wickedness of the officers came out to play, their inner monsters impatient to interrogate their victims. If they believed Wren *was* the woman involved in Dusk's disappearance, they wouldn't hesitate to allow those monsters free rein.

I was familiar with how the guards treated their . . . suspects.

Caught once at age ten, they'd beaten me to a pulp in one of those dingy cells. Cells that I wouldn't even put a rat inside. After a week, they shoved me out onto the streets, hungrier than before I stole a peach from a local vendor. Back then I hadn't been as smooth. I learned quickly after that.

What would they do to the ward princess if they believed she'd been involved in Dusk's disappearance? Would her father help? Surely he would. I bet he was journeying here now.

I slunk farther into the alley between a bakery and a florist, using the shadows to hide while I lost sight of Wren and the bastard guards carrying her up the steep steps leading to the square brick station.

Logically, I should go. Return to the Void and go about my own damn business. Wren wasn't mine to worry about. I'd only stolen from her.

Then why weren't my feet moving?

Why did the idea of turning my back feel akin to betrayal? Loyalty was everything where I came from, but I owed her nothing.

I cursed my idiocy. Cursed and kicked the stone wall next to me. My secondhand boots were too thin, so I cursed again when sharp pain radiated up my calf. Unless you were kin or had made a vow, everyone in the Void understood the golden rule: Every man and woman for themselves if they got caught. Especially thieves or criminals like myself.

The one time I put myself on the line for someone, it had been for Ruby, and that had been an accident. We might've known each other since we were children, but after that incident, she deemed me her friend, not knowing that my attacking the lawman cornering her had to do with someone paying me to rough up the man, who owed a gambling debt.

I'd earned coin and a sarcastic shadow for the rest of my days.

Running my hand through my hair, I once again surveyed the building. Took in the cold bricks and repressed the unease clawing at my stomach. My thoughts slipped to the young boy I'd been, bruised and bloodied and frightened. Then it went to her.

Shite. I planned to do something very, very stupid.

Sneaking into the main guard station had been easy. No one was idiotic enough to break into hell—aside from me. *Getting out* might prove difficult, mainly if my mirror decided to play games.

Unlocking the compact, I slipped it into my jacket pocket, the usual tingle of magic buzzing through my system. Marching up the stairs, I strayed to the edges, avoiding the severe-looking guards, who probably needed a night of debauchery and drink, judging by their inability to show an ounce of human emotion. They were similar to the windup toy soldiers children played with.

When the double doors opened and a handful of patrolmen passed through, I slid in behind, careful to conceal the sound of my breathing.

Why are you doing this?

It was the tenth time I'd asked myself that same question.

From experience, I remembered that they kept the "interrogation" rooms in the basement. Below that existed a level I shivered to recall. The cells. If she'd been brought to the cells, Wren was royally screwed.

"Fucking brat made me carry her the entire way. I bet she was awake the whole time."

I turned to the left, finding a muscular guard leaning on the marble countertop placed at the center of the open room. He loomed over a seated man on the other side, whose eyes were wide with interest at the latest scandal. The mouthy guard set down a full cup of tea, steam rising from the top as he groused. "I bet Hayes will be here any second and spring the spoiled bitch before we get the chance to ask questions."

The hairs on my arms rose and my feet slowed to a halt. I stood before the stairwell door, prepared to go down to the basement undetected. But his words . . .

I might not like Wren Hayes, but his insult grated on me. No, it pissed me off. I could tell by the way my blood boiled, how my cheeks heated with fire. The reaction hadn't been expected, but it happened regardless.

Only *I* could insult Wren Hayes. She was mine to tease and provoke. Had been the moment she tackled me and stabbed me with a letter opener. Not that I would *ever* call her such a vile word. That was beneath me. I'd needle her with a little more creativity.

Taking advantage of my gift and praying its power held, I strode over to the bastard of a guard and flicked a wrist—knocking his tea all over his uniform.

He shrieked out a curse before jerking back, his lips contorting in pain as the scalding liquid drenched him.

I beamed, my steps lighter as I sauntered away, leaving the asshole cursing and rubbing at his uniform in confusion. That would be the highlight of my day.

Back at the stairwell, I waited until the coast cleared before opening the door just enough to slip through. I'd flickered a few times on the stairs, my mirror struggling to keep me hidden. My breathing grew ragged for this reason, my palms slick as I locked the door behind me. Hopefully, they hadn't taken Wren to the cells; that level required a key, and not many guards possessed one.

The steps led down in a straight line, the gas lamps hanging on the brick walls doing little to light the gloomy space. One misstep and I'd be left with a broken bone. It took a minute to get to the bottom, the door to the basement shrouded in shadows.

I hated that I was here. Memories of my fucking childhood rushed back—of the sneering guards who loved to kick hungry children. They took pleasure in roughing me up when I was unable to defend myself.

If not for my magic and the picture of me in the locket, I would have run in the opposite direction by this point. That magic seemed to be settling now. The flickering ceased, and I froze before the entrance to the interrogation ward, relieved. It just needed to keep me safe awhile longer.

Placing my ear on the cold metal door, I listened for the telltale patter of boots. A pair passed by, followed by the thudding of multiple boots, signaling a group of guards. To my surprise, and luck, they didn't open the door I currently leaned against. When everything went still, I chanced it all.

Like an idiot.

Pulling back on the handle, I peeked around the wooden frame, sighing when I found the hallway empty. Rows of locked doors, cracked tile, and sputtering lamps gave the basement an air of nearly tangible misery. I supposed that was the whole point; to intimidate and frighten.

Checking to make sure my pocket mirror continued to behave, I snuck down the hall, the buzz of magic growing stronger with each step. I'd yet to experience anything like it—the flare of power that rushed into my veins the closer I ventured down the corridor. Whatever was at play, it kept me safe, and I could question it when I wasn't neck-deep in a vipers' den.

Pausing every now and again by the doors, I listened for voices. By the time I crossed the fourth door off my list, one down the corridor blasted open with a bang. I shrank back, pressing my palms against the wall. A middle-aged guard, one with five obnoxiously polished stars decorating his blue velvet cuffs, stormed out, his face a mottled red.

"She knows more than she's letting on!" he barked at whoever stayed. I assumed Wren was present as well.

Now was my moment. As he screamed some more about the many ways they could "extract" information from her, I crept to the doorway and waited until he turned on a shiny heel and stormed away like a petulant child. Before the door closed entirely, I stole into the dingy room, bursting with the hum of magic, my invisibility firmly in place.

Wren Hayes sat in a tarnished metal chair in front of a chipped desk, her vibrant turquoise eyes giving away nothing. Even streaked in mud, she lifted her narrow chin, her hands placed delicately in her lap like a lady receiving tea service. Fates, she was good. An actress if I'd ever seen one—and that knowledge set me on edge, the hairs at my nape rising to attention. I expected her to be a good manipulator—all highborn leaders were, so of course, their offspring would be as well.

"Any other questions?" she asked as if bored, and only then did I realize we weren't alone. Standing in the far corner, another guard walked into the light, his arms crossed tightly against his broad chest.

"I still don't understand why you ran into the woods?" the second guard asked. "If you had just stayed there—"

"I already told you." She sighed dramatically before chewing on her lip. My focus lingered there, watching as she released the delicate flesh with her teeth. "I was fearful for my life. I glimpsed the blood and believed an assassin might be nearby. I ran. My instincts kicked in. Simple as that."

Her stare, so cold and emotionless, stayed firm, unyielding. If I'd been in the guard's shoes, I would've believed her. Since she and I had tangled in the past, I found it rather obvious that there was more she didn't share. This *act* of hers was proof of it.

I'd discover more later when I had her alone.

The guard, an older man with graying hair and dull gray-blue eyes, rubbed at his face. "It's hard for me to imagine you're a killer, Lady Hayes," he murmured. "Yet I've seen more unassuming killers than you before."

"If I'm a murderer then where's the body?"

"You could've had help," he argued.

"I don't associate with anyone aside from five ladies hand-selected by my mother, and my father can attest to my whereabouts at all times. I have a schedule to keep." She made a tired sound from deep in her throat. "Speaking of which, this whole thing"—she waved a hand about the room—"has likely thrown off my day. I'd planned to visit with my father's closest constituents this afternoon. I do believe they're discussing a bill that would increase the budget for Ward One's patrolmen." She arched a brow at him knowingly.

I leaned back and crossed my arms, staring at the woman across from me. So damned bold. So detached. Smooth. I wondered if her pulse raced. If the hands beneath the table were slicked with sweat.

I longed to find out. No one was that perfect. Especially since the two times I'd seen her up close, her emotions had been clear for all to see. The woman had no filter in my presence.

"Just . . . just stay here," the guard ordered, sounding exhausted as he made for the door. "I hear your father is on his way."

She nodded primly, releasing a faint noise of assent.

As soon as the door shut, I walked over to her and stood at her back. Wren slumped a little in her seat, releasing a groan. From this angle, I had a clear view below the table, and her hands were indeed wringing themselves. Wren had done well to hide her fear. I almost admired it.

Leaning forward, mere centimeters from her ear, I whispered, "Don't move."

Her entire body instantly went rigid, and I would've given a pretty coin to have seen the frightened look on her face.

"You," she said on a sigh.

Hmm . . . She recognized me by my voice alone. How endearing.

My lips accidentally brushed her skin, her scent filling my senses. "Yes, *me*." I couldn't help myself. I reached for a twig that had snagged in her hair and removed it, causing her to shudder. "First you stab me, then you're accused of either kidnapping or assassinating a Fate?" I tsked. "My, my, Wren. You've been up to a lot, haven't you, sunshine?"

She twisted her chin to the side, my lips inadvertently brushing her cheek. A snarl contorted her mouth as mine lingered, my body momentarily frozen. I repressed a shudder at the addictive smell of flowers wafting from her and inched back just enough so my lips weren't pressed against her soft skin.

"I told you not to call me that," she snapped.

"Why not?" I asked, smiling at how easily riled she was. Though she hadn't pulled away. Fates, her skin felt so damned silken and warm. Warm with anger, most likely. Unwelcome heat coiled in my chest, a flood of something I'd rather not name invading my body like a plague. I cleared my throat and said, "And here I assumed we were friends."

She choked on a laugh. "I wouldn't befriend you if my life depended on it. You're about as trustworthy as a venomous snake."

My smile lifted at the image. She wasn't wrong.

I plucked another bit of dirt from her hair, taking my time. Twirling the caramel strand around my finger, I spoke into her ear, thoroughly enjoying how much my nearness wreaked havoc on her. "I *do* like to bite."

Now she jerked back, her chest rapidly rising and falling. I full-on grinned, loving how her mask fell. Wren quickly tried to wrestle back her feeble control, but I'd already seen beneath her façade.

"*Friends* don't hide from one another." Her voice was tighter than a string set to snap. "Frightened, Damien?"

"Of you?" I snickered. "Not likely."

"Then what do you want?" she demanded, done playing our little game. Which I'd shockingly enjoyed, if only because I'd discovered that the tips of her ears burned red when I pushed her buttons. "Why are you here?"

Two very good questions.

"I'm here because we have unfinished business, Wren Hayes, and I wanted to make sure they didn't toss you in a cell before our business is concluded."

"What business?" she asked hesitantly.

"You took something from me last night." Well, something she *might* have taken back. I went out on a limb, though, going with the accusation first.

She scoffed and slipped a hand through her tangled hair, some speckles of dirt landing on my face. I scrubbed my hand down it, grimacing. She'd probably done that on purpose. "I am no thief. Unlike *some* people." That last part burned with spite.

I hated that I believed her. It would be so much easier if she had the locket.

Leaning away, I analyzed Wren's face, relishing the fact that she couldn't see me. Her jaw set in a firm line, her eyes hard. Everything about her posture screamed that she spoke the truth. A rare thing, to tell the truth in my world. More often than not, people hid behind lies like barricades, believing their words to be stronger than steel. Sometimes, they were.

She had no reason to deceive me. Not even with the fury swimming in her eyes.

Watching her, *seeing* her, set me on edge. I ground my teeth and brushed off the peculiar sensation working its way into my chest.

"Well, *someone* stole from me," I continued, attempting to regain the upper hand. "And I've decided that you're going to help me get it back." I circled her again, my hand trailing up her arm. I hadn't meant to touch her, but when she shuddered, my heart leapt. Wren Hayes was affected by me. And I could use that.

Perhaps it was for this reason that I bent down and gently took her hand in mine. She stifled a stunned noise as I placed a menacing kiss—a mere graze of my lips—on the back of her hand. Just like a gentleman. The next sound that left her wasn't one born of fear.

"This won't be the last time you see me, sunshine," I warned, dropping her hand. I took my time, inhaling the scent of citrus in her hair, on her skin. Savoring the way the highborn princess had retained her composure until the moment my skin greeted hers.

It was a powerful feeling.

"Is that a promise or a threat, Damien, because—"

The door banged open, interrupting whatever she'd planned to say. The older guard from earlier cocked his head at Wren, likely noticing the difference in her demeanor. Nevertheless, he said, "Your father is upstairs. Come."

She stood quickly, nearly knocking the chair to the side in the process. Her movements were rigid and her face emotionless once more, but then I glimpsed the twitch of her eye. The only indication that she wanted nothing more than to find and possibly strangle me.

Without a word, she strolled out of the room and shadowed the guard, not once gazing back or giving me the satisfaction of seeing her anger face to face.

The grin on my own face was pure triumph. But then I realized something—

Not once had my pocket mirror failed to work while close to Wren. No flickering. No moments when my connection wavered. If anything, the magic I sensed had heightened, and now . . .

As she walked away, that very power faded.

Mouthing a curse, I bolted after her, not willing to chance getting caught in the very hell I'd escaped years ago.

By the time I stormed out of the main guard station, holding on to my magic became difficult, much like flying a kite in a snowstorm. Before I materialized from thin air, I sprinted down the steps and into the same alley and its merciful shadows. My chest heaved as the magic wore off and my body reappeared, exhausted and drained.

It hadn't felt that way around *her.*

There was no question in my mind that Wren Hayes and I had been destined to meet. And without a doubt, our lives were now tied together in a way that would be impossible to unravel.

I'll see you soon, sunshine.

Chapter Nine

Wren

The Fates are immortal.
If there are no Fates in the realm, all magic shall perish.
—*Aurilian History of Magical Objects,* Chapter Ten

"What in all the Fates were you thinking?" Father's shout was a dagger to my eardrums, the headache throbbing between my eyes protesting each biting syllable.

We sat in our personal carriage, me wearing the scraps I'd been dragged into the main guard station in, and Father clad in his finest tweed suit. His bowler hat hung low over his eyes, but it didn't mask the furious storm raging behind them. Beside him, Callie fidgeted with her hands, not meeting my eyes. She'd been observing Father at work, so it was no surprise she was sitting in the carriage when the guard opened the door. Not that she could say or do anything to help me now. Father would admonish her if she used her gift to settle my nerves—he claimed such influence took away from the punishment—and he'd kill her if she used her power on him. But Fates, for once I wished for her gift on me, if only to cease the riotous nerves churning in my stomach.

Nerves that had nothing to do with my father.

"I wanted to ask about my gift, and the guards directed me to Dusk. I thought she might . . . help," I protested, leaning forward in my seat. I rarely spoke against Father, but he had to know I didn't just go barging in! I was invited.

Perhaps not *invited,* per se, but *allowed* to come inside the palace.

The northern side of Andalay passed by with the curtains sealed, and I jumped each time we hit a rut in the path. To say that I was on edge was an understatement.

Distantly, I heard shouts of people calling Dusk's name.

It appeared she had yet to be found.

"Foolish child," Father eventually grumbled, wiping his hands down his trousers. I swore I saw new wrinkles crease the corners of his eyes and his temples, weariness taking a toll on his body.

The insult stung, which had been its desired effect. He never used to call me names, not even when I was a rambunctious child who often destroyed his office by scattering my drawings across his desk. He'd laugh at the mess and scoop me into his arms, his eyes bright as he stared down at me.

All I'd ever craved was his approval. That joy in his eyes that shone whenever I pleased him.

Now his eyes were dull. Unnaturally so. It had to be more than lack of sleep, the tiny red veins sprouting from his once-vibrant green irises. Something bothered him of late, and not just the usual ward dealings. It made his temper shorter than usual.

Not that I didn't deserve *some* of his anger now.

"You know better," he continued, his face turning a dark shade of red. "The Fates summon *you,* not the other way around!" He bellowed each word, spittle flying from his mouth. I flinched as a droplet hit my cheek.

The man before me wasn't someone I recognized as my father, but he also wasn't wrong. I'd gone ahead and taken a chance on myself, and while it landed me in an interrogation room, I remained more upset about what happened *after* my visit than my decision to go.

Father didn't need to know that part. Didn't need to know about Damien breaking into the room, his hot breath brushing my skin as he demanded aid in whatever scheme he had planned.

And he accused *me* of stealing something from *him*. Laughable.

I'd get him to do my bidding in the end—the man wouldn't be able to resist silver.

"I'm sorry," I eventually whispered when Father's cheeks lightened a few hues, his rage waning. I intentionally bowed my head and prayed it appeased him, making him remember I was his daughter and not one of his ward lackeys. My chest ached more the longer silence reigned, and I added a quiet, "I was desperate."

I peeked through my lashes as Father took off his hat and ran his fingers through his dark hair, messing up some of the neatly combed strands. It looked like he wanted to pull them out. "It was beyond reckless. Beyond impulsive. If you weren't my daughter, they probably would've thrown you in a cell, do you understand that? Not many people leave those cells. I . . . I can't have a daughter of mine involved in such scandal, especially now . . ."

He trailed off, his eyes on the fluttering curtain. I wanted to ask what he meant by that last part, but I sealed my lips. It wasn't the time. Still, I tucked that tidbit into the back of my brain.

I glanced at Callie, whose throat visibly bobbed, but she, too, nodded glumly. She held my stare, silently conveying that I keep the peace. Agree with everything he requested.

A scandal in our family *would* be a nightmare. Father was the top dog, the leader of Ward *One*. His enemies—and there were likely many of them—would relish using his family to aid his downfall.

I broke contact with Callie, staring at my twisting hands. Sweat glistened on my palms, and I wiped them on my dress. That prison; the coldness of it, the sense that something horrid lingered just around the corner . . . I couldn't get my mind off it.

I'd gotten lucky; if Father hadn't been a Ward leader, those guards wouldn't have been as *pleasant*. My privilege had gotten me out of the situation, and my throat constricted imagining all the other souls who weren't as fortunate. Had they been given a fair trial?

The fact remained, however: I didn't know. And I *should*.

The epiphany struck like a slap to the face.

Here I'd been, breaking traditions and rules all for my own greed—and it *was* greed—while, on the way to the interrogation room, I'd witnessed a few chained prisoners being led below the basement to Fates knew where. I had been too focused on my act at the time, too scared for myself, but I'd spotted them seconds before the heavy doors shut. It had been a frail woman with a child, and a man with two swollen black eyes.

Before, I had assumed that the people who went into that building deserved such treatment, thinking they'd committed despicable crimes, but what if they had been in a situation like mine where they were in the wrong place at the wrong time?

"Wren?" Father waved his hand before my face. I must've zoned out.

"Yes, sorry." I rubbed at my eyes, hating that they watered. Me and my damned emotions.

His features turned to stone, any trace of the jovial Father I remembered from years ago a distant memory. I'd do *anything* to get him back. "You are not to leave the house for the next couple of weeks. No friends, no balls, and certainly no more visits with the Fates. Am I clear?"

"But Father, if she's not seen by society . . ." Callie started, only to be waved off. She met my eyes and winced.

"I understand," I conceded, nodding. I would do whatever I needed to be free of Father's scrutiny and out of this suffocating carriage. Later, I'd plan what to do with Dusk's instructions.

Dusk's note had been clear that I must find the certain someone she placed in my path to aid me. I had just the person in mind, and he'd found *me* first.

Since I wasn't in a position to journey to the Void, especially if Father amped up security around our home, I'd have to play the good daughter for now. I would place Dusk's instructions on hold and try to slip back into obscurity until they found the Fate.

If she was found.

Never in all of our history had something like this occurred.

The carriage ride continued in silence, and I gnawed at the inside of my cheek, pushing aside everything else, and simply studied my shoes. My bed sounded like heaven at the moment, and I desired nothing but to bathe and then hide beneath the covers for an eternity.

Father grumbled when he helped me out of the carriage outside our home, his grip on my arm firm as he led me quickly up the steps. He didn't need to tell me to go to my room for me to immediately head that way. There were no protests. Barely able to keep my chin lifted, I was done with the outside world for the day. For two weeks, apparently.

The second I shut the door behind me, all my mixed emotions flooded out in a torrent. I'd kept unruffled enough during the interview, doing my best to channel Mother and having observed years of her cold nature. It had been harder than I imagined, and I nearly broke dozens of times.

Then *he* had come, using a gift no inhabitant of the Void possessed, and hid himself, startling me half to death. I still wished for answers as to why he had that power. Maybe idle jealousy crept up on me, but my skin burned as I thought that a *thief* had magic and mine had been unjustly kept from me.

Without thinking, I lifted the back of my hand and placed it against my cheek, at the place where his warm lips had grazed my skin. It had been a challenge, if anything. He enjoyed the power of invisibility, of seeing me when I was metaphorically in the dark. I frowned, an unexpected surge of determination flooding my veins as I recalled how he'd whispered in my ear, his voice deep, like a lover's caress. How he'd touched my arm like he'd done it a thousand times. How I'd *shivered* beneath that touch. Never before had I been so affected by another person, let alone a simple graze of their fingers. My skin had felt hot to the touch. It *still* did.

Damien. The thief. A man with a dark soul, and one who'd assist me in locating Dusk's magic. If he insisted *I* help him find a stolen object, then *he* could do the same for me. We'd both win, even if I had to twist his arm to gain his assistance.

I sighed, shaking myself and the foolish notions of him and his shiver-inducing fingers from my head. It had been a physical reaction, nothing more. We had business to attend to, and I didn't plan to have anything to do with the bastard once this ordeal passed. Heading to my bath, I turned the faucet, waiting for the gas to heat the water.

Patience wasn't a virtue I possessed, but I'd toed the line today, and if I made one more mistake, two weeks would look like a gift in comparison.

Practically ripping off my ruined dress, I sank into the warm water and allowed it to consume me.

Two weeks. Two weeks of ruminating over endless possibilities. Weeks when I could plan . . .

Then would come the time to hunt.

By the second week, I'd become as restless as a lion in a cage.

Callie and Father went to his workplace, my sister often shooting me sympathetic looks before she obediently followed on his heels. She, too, knew what it meant to piss him off, and I didn't blame her for not wishing to be added to his list of disappointing daughters.

The only thing she kept me updated on was Dusk. Apparently her sisters sent out a realm-wide search party but had come up empty-handed. Callie said there was disquiet in the streets, and the faithful were at Dusk's temple praying every day and night.

She had to be alive, I reasoned. Surely Dawn and Day would've felt a severed connection if she'd been killed. Yes, they were immortal, but it was never clear if they could be killed by unknown forces.

It was the evening before my freedom when I decided to venture out of my room for a glass of water. It had to be around midnight, the house silent and eerie as I crept down the creaky stairs. I shuddered. The house itself was stunning, but at night far too many shadows seemed to reach out, itching to grab at me.

I practically skipped down the remaining steps and entered the kitchen. After quenching my thirst, I still found myself restless. Uneasy. Like I should be doing more than simply sitting in my room all day, silently plotting.

On edge, I decided to walk about the house, enjoying the blissful hush. If I was up already, I might as well take advantage of the freedom.

After turning on a lamp in the parlor, I walked past the haunting display of family portraits, observed the miniature marble statues my mother had shipped in from across the Aurilian realm, and flipped through some of the books left here from our library. Some hours had passed, enough for my eyes to grow heavy, and I sighed, believing it best to give sleep another try.

Before I reached the stairs, I heard it.

Well, heard *them.*

Father and Callie.

"I already told you that I needed you on Thursday, and you vanished. They were putting up a fight, and you know what they expect from us."

They?

I halted in my tracks before sliding around a corner, my heart hammering at my throat. The voices came from the foyer down the hall. Hopefully they hadn't seen me pass.

Something told me I should *not* be listening in on this conversation.

It didn't stop me.

Callie's voice came like a whisper, but I made out her words. "I was busy, as I've told you. But they can't continue to act in such a way. Word will spread."

A grunt, and then, "If you enjoy the way we live and would like to keep it that way, I'd suggest you get it done," Father warned. "Don't disappoint me. I already have another daughter who does."

Pain sliced at my chest, my eyes prickling. But I couldn't cry, not when heavy footsteps pounded the wooden floors, heading my way. Instead of running up the steps and causing each one of them to creak and give me away, I snuck into the kitchen and waited with bated breath. By the time the softer set of footsteps reached the stairs and commenced the climb, I relaxed. Slowly.

Father and Callie rarely argued. She was the perfect daughter and the child he'd wished for; cunning, smart, ambitious. Even if she had to contend with the misconceptions of being a woman in a man's world. Which she would—with a grin on her face as she vanquished them all. Nevertheless, I couldn't purge Father's threat from my mind. And I wasn't thinking of how he'd called me a disappointment. It had pierced my heart at the beginning, but that pain had waned, until all I recalled was *If you enjoy the way we live and would like to keep it that way, I'd suggest you get it done.*

What did he need Callie to do? She clearly didn't want to use her gift of influencing emotions on someone, or more than just *one* someone, by the way he spoke. They were up to something, some plan I wasn't privy to but would strive to uncover. As my sister, Callie's discomfort became my own.

When half an hour came and went, I garnered the courage to climb the stairs, noticing that Father's study door was closed. I ventured a guess that he'd locked it as well. He'd been adamant about carrying the key around his neck like his most prized possession. I sighed, twisting from the room of secrets, and shuffled half-heartedly to my chamber. The door shut softly behind me.

Sleep felt impossible now, but I wouldn't do myself any good by being exhausted, especially since I intended to uncover the true meaning of their conversation. Among other things . . .

I'd had two weeks to think, after all.

Soon, I'd be able to leave, and what Father or Mother didn't know wouldn't hurt them.

Fates, all that time in seclusion had been a blur of mind-numbing embroidery and rereading old books of lore in my room.

It had become a prison, my own little cell. Yet it had supplied me time to grieve, tame my anger, and more importantly, *plan*.

Mother hadn't summoned me once. I'd overheard her and Father arguing in the hall that first night after I'd been arrested, and she'd made it clear I was to be punished. "She'll learn," Mother insisted. "If her reputation ever rebounds, then we need to marry her off. *Quickly.*"

I'd seethed at the words, hiding behind my door, my fists clenched as heat erupted across my face. *Marry.* They wished to marry me off to avoid further humiliation. If I allowed this, I'd be forever trapped, shackled to someone for all eternity. The second I was able to leave, I knew where I'd go. Who I'd seek. If all went according to design, I'd find the thief and coerce him to help me hunt down my gift. Having become acquainted with the bastard, I'd resolved that my coercion would involve coin; lots of it.

I slept very little that night, tossing and turning, my dreams more like nightmares. Blood and tangled vines and endless forests.

I also dreamt about *him*.

Somehow, he was in the forest with me, his dark features steady and cold. Yet his ice-gray eyes couldn't conceal the oddest flecks of warmth in them. No matter how hard he tried to play the villain. Or perhaps he was a villain, and I was simply too naïve to accept it.

"I'm off," Mother announced to the room the next morning at breakfast. Father barely lifted his chin as she placed a chaste kiss on his cheek. "I'm having lunch with Lord Lovett's wife," she said with a smirk. "The woman is positively dull, but she knows all the good gossip."

I frowned at her, taking in her bright outfit. Apparently she'd gone to the modiste.

A pink tulle gown fitted her slender body, the bodice laced with black ribbons, a sleek white coat tucked over her arm for when the winds changed. On her feet were matching pink boots with satin ribbons, which were new as well. They weren't the ones I'd spotted ladies wearing this season, but it must be recent fashion.

As she passed, Mother patted my head—not in an affectionate way—before she leaned down to whisper into my ear. "Be good, Wren. The entire city is watching, and you have no idea how hard I'm working to restore our family name."

Ice skittered down my spine when she broke away, her heavy perfume smelling of gardenias and a hint of vanilla. It tasted like poison in my mouth.

Father shoved from his chair, jolting me. "I'm off too." He glanced at Callie. "Ready?" he asked, which earned him a nod. She stood, smoothing her gray dress, which I knew she loathed. Callie loved bright colors.

"Behave," Father commanded as they brushed past me and into the hall.

I swallowed thickly. I'd *try*, but . . . I had places to be today. A certain thief to harass. I suspected that wasn't exactly "behaving."

Gathering my nerves and steeling my spine, I stood, brushing out the wrinkles in my simplest dress—a navy blue with a modest skirt that flared slightly at my hips. Copper buttons ran down the small V of my neckline, and a few matching buttons decorated the cuffs of the long sleeves.

On my feet, I wore the scuffed brown lace-up boots I sported during hunting season when Father and I *used* to bond at our country home over the thrill of the chase. I had a decent aim with a rifle, but nothing compared to Mother; she could shoot the eye of a bird a hundred feet off the ground.

With my hair swept into a simple updo with plain copper pins, I decided I'd done my best to achieve my objective—to blend in. Before I left the dining room, I snatched a black cloak I'd brought down and flung it over my shoulders.

I could do this. I'd contemplated nothing else, imagining the second I tasted the air of freedom and took back what was rightfully mine. My first stop—Damien.

Slipping down the hall, I crept into the deathly quiet parlor, my heart hammering. The only person left in the house was Sarah, who, as a result of my father's obsessive need for privacy, served as both our maid and cook. I strained to catch her shuffling footsteps, sighing in relief when she eventually opened and shut the front door. She journeyed to the market in the afternoon like clockwork.

Instead of using the main entrance, I took to the garden, easing around the overflowing shrubbery and vibrant blooms until I reached the menacing wrought iron gate. Guiding the stolen key into the lock and twisting, I exited out onto our back street, making quick work of securing the gate.

A sigh of relief bubbled up my throat. Now to reach the southern side of Andalay. A place I'd never set foot before—easy, right?

I would've rolled my eyes at myself if I could.

Pulling my hood low over my head, concealing my dark blond curls, I strode down the avenue, turning left, rather than my usual right to the upscale boutiques and cafés I frequented. People milled about in groups, socializing and gossiping, their chatter following me long after I passed. Anxiety wormed its way into my belly, and my chest constricted when an acquaintance from my old circle paused, her flowing skirts swishing to a stop. I barreled past her, hoping she mistook me for a maid on an errand. My garments didn't scream Lady of Ward One.

With my heartbeat pounding in my ears, I swiftly turned right and onto the bustling Serende Avenue. Beyond the lower-end tailors and pastry shops and jewelers, the beginning of the Void awaited like a black shroud. I knocked into two people in my haste, my stare lowered to the ground; my peculiar irises might give me away if someone should look too closely.

Find the thief and obtain his aid. And yes, I'd brought my letter opener—I still didn't trust him. Its reassuring weight soothed me when the looks I received sent goose bumps rushing down my arms. It might've been paranoia, or I had every reason to worry, but something told me I already opened a door that would be impossible to shut.

Locating Damien in the Void had sounded easy in my head. Like he'd magically appear before my eyes the second I crossed the invisible boundary. In reality, it would be akin to searching the beach for one particular shell among hundreds.

Too late now, I thought, pushing ahead. I was here, out of the house after weeks of being treated like a child and locked away in my room. Weeks of pondering where Dusk had gone, and who, if anyone, had a part in her disappearance. But mostly, I reflected on the very things I shouldn't . . . like those stolen moments in the interrogation room that pestered me to no end.

A downside to being so sheltered was that it didn't take much to make my body react. How else could I explain it? I despised Damien and his smirking face. A face that begged to be smacked.

My gut told me that wasn't out of the realm of possibility in the near future.

The crowds thinned the closer I drew to the Void, the shopfronts boasting bars, laundries, butchers, and run-down secondhand clothing stores with smudged windows. Clutching at the ties of my cloak, I walked farther, deeper, until the very sun itself seemed to shudder and dim. The cobblestones beneath my feet vanished, replaced by crumbled black and gray stones, and the smells of fish and something nauseating filled the air. Shouts rang out, boisterous vendors selling wares from a modest market constructed of rotting wooden stalls. I lifted my head a little more, taking in the south and its foreignness.

Children wearing ragged clothing rushed by my skirt, giggling. A rail-thin girl patiently led an elderly woman down the street—her mother or grandmother, perhaps—helping her avoid bumping into one of the many men carrying navy blue satchels with red straps. I'd seen a few when I visited Father's offices, and recognized them as messengers. They were paid next to nothing, which was why the upperclassmen used them.

Above the chaotic market, women leaned out their windows,

hanging freshly laundered clothing, some chatting with their neighbors, others simply observing the bedlam. I ground my teeth, hating how the dwellings were stacked atop one another like too-heavy books, each one seemingly smaller than the last. How could people—no, families—live in such conditions? Surely, their health would be at risk, with the smell of smoke hanging in the air. I suspected it came from the Lovetts' weapons factory by the coast.

Bile rose in my throat. It wasn't disgust causing the reaction.

It was shame.

Not once had I considered venturing here. Not once had I asked Father about the living conditions I'd heard about through gossip. I couldn't blame anyone but myself for my ignorance.

I'd wished to please my father to the point that I'd done everything possible to deflect his temper, which bringing up the south would inevitably inflame.

Maybe I should finally realize I'd never gain his approval.

Or I shouldn't even want it at all.

These people were deemed less than, simply because they didn't have gifts. Well, except for Damien, which I'd question him about later *when* I caught him. The northerners despised the south, probably because it made them feel better about themselves. Important.

How very . . . pathetic.

It would be easier to forget about it all. To pretend I'd never come here and seen the too-thin bodies and the air clogged with gray smoke.

But pretending would just make me complicit.

There were things I could do, namely, speaking with my own flesh and blood. If I *could* help, then I should at the very least *try*. Or Callie could use whatever influence she'd earned and we could work together.

"Spare a coin?"

I stopped to peer down at a small child with grime streaking his face. He smiled wide, his teeth on full display. It was a genuine smile, and my heart tugged.

Slipping a hand into my pocket, I retrieved a silver coin and placed it in his waiting palm, wishing I could do more. His gaze widened. "You sure?" he asked, almost fearfully. I nodded hastily, expecting him to run off. Instead, he reached into his pocket and lifted a small trinket. Taking it from his hands, I beheld a miniature statue of Day, the sun at her back.

The boy broke into a run after I grasped the figurine. He had no coins, yet he gave me a gift. I couldn't picture anyone in the north doing such a selfless thing. Tucking the treasure into my pocket, I took in more of the forgotten south.

While the buildings needed work, and the people were skin and bones, I noticed interactions here and there—vendors selling below price to an exhausted mother, a man wearing overalls and a Lovett Factory patch across the middle sharing his lunch with a fellow worker. I took in the camaraderie, the unity.

Not that I didn't notice the darker side, which mainly consisted of obvious pickpockets and menacing men stalking the streets, a couple of them stumbling and clearly drunk.

My ears perked up every time I heard Dusk's name as I wandered the market, the people of the south just as eager for information as those in the north. They whispered behind their palms, eyes cast to the ground as if they'd get caught by the royal guards, a few of whom I spotted roaming the avenue.

I startled when raucous laughter filtered out from a pub a block ahead, along with a hint of music emanating from some sort of wooden instrument. My attention drifted to the swinging sign above: THE BROKEN WING TAVERN.

If I'd learned anything from the many books I read well into the night, pubs contained a plethora of information. I had a few coins left and I'd use them wisely. The bartender would be the first on my list; Damien looked like the type who enjoyed a decent drink.

Or five.

Picking up my skirt and lifting my chin, I entered the tavern.

Chapter Ten

Wren

They came from the sky and blessed
the earliest mortals with hope. Yet it was the tokens
they gifted that kept the people worshipping them.
—*Origin of the Fates*, Chapter Twenty

I was immediately thrown off-balance by how little light illuminated the space. Walking to the long wooden bar, I located an empty stool and took a hesitant seat as I swept my gaze over the dozens of tables and mismatched chairs arranged haphazardly in the main room. A stage stood front and center, a guitarist currently playing a lively tune, singing about some place called the Black Dahlia and its many . . . delights. Even during the daytime, people were half drunk and deep into their whiskey or ale, clapping as the man onstage finished his song and started another.

I'd never been to a pub before, I realized, and a sudden burst of adrenaline made my blood turn icy and then much too warm.

I prayed to all three Fates that I looked like I knew what I was doing, or that I'd been to a pub at least once. Judging by some of the curious—and somewhat menacing—stares directed my way, I suspected I'd failed.

"What can I get you, miss?"

A jittery huff left me as I turned around on the stool and came face to face with the burly man behind the bar. Eyes harder than stone, his lips curled into a cruel frown like he grasped that I didn't belong. I didn't, though a secret part of me wished I did, if only to experience some of the joy the other patrons displayed openly. They swore and danced and barked obscene jokes met by laughter; everything I'd been forbidden to do.

I might as well have stepped into a whole new universe.

"An . . . ale, please," I mumbled, fishing out a copper with Dusk's face stamped on the back and placing it on the bar top. He nodded and snatched a glass to fill up at the tap. Mercifully, neither my hands nor my voice had trembled. My acting talents were improving. I supposed my time in the interrogation room had paid off.

With a grimace, I remembered that I planned to weasel information out of this giant of a man. He looked the sort who would take pleasure in ripping my head off if I blinked wrong.

Inside, my heart beat like a fist against my rib cage, and sweat trickled down my spine. Such blind confidence I'd had when I made this plan. All bluster, all desperation. Actually sitting here, being in the Void, thinking I could find this deceptive cretin—it all felt idiotic. I was naïve to think I could—

"Wren?"

The familiar voice jolted me, the muscles in my neck and shoulders turning to stone.

Wiping the grimace from my lips, I plastered on what I hoped resembled a smile. Swiveling in my seat, I regarded the very last person I would ever have expected.

Everett.

So many vile curses shouted in my mind. If anyone had peeked inside my head, they'd have been aghast at the vulgarity. Or impressed by my vocabulary.

Gratefully, a foul word didn't escape, but the squeak that left me was somehow worse. It was all I could muster.

Everett chose a seat to my right as if he had countless times before, his demeanor relaxed and easy. My smile immediately strained upon seeing what he wore: simple trousers, a plain button-down, and none of his usual finery. Even his dark blond hair appeared like he raked his fingers through it rather than using a comb, and his chin sported a dusting of coarse stubble. He looked . . . different. Wild, somehow.

I hated that my heart gave a little leap when he leaned closer.

"What are you doing here?" His striking blue eyes scanned the room before turning back to me. Concern creased the corners of his mouth, a furrow marring his brow.

What was *I* doing here? Hell, I should be asking that question of him. He should be in some white-walled office with his stacks of notebooks and numbers. I wondered if he had his enchanted glasses on him, or if he'd taken the day to himself. But why here?

"Wren?" he pressed.

"I . . ." I what? *I want to hunt down the man who robbed you of your watch because the missing Fate wrote me a letter instructing me to retrieve my stolen gift containing dangerous magic? Oh, and she ordered me to locate this cunning and deceptive thief who might very well kill me.* Everett and I weren't *that* close.

"I needed some time away . . . away from—"

"From the north," he finished for me, nodding like he understood. "I heard what happened, Wren, I mean, my lady. I hope you're doing all right." Everett let out an awkward cough, his muscles tensing at his shoulders and pulling at his shirt. His body was much broader than I'd originally assumed when not hidden beneath a finely tailored suit, and my damned eyes lingered. Everett swallowed hard, barely maintaining eye contact. He had no idea how to act around me outside our usual surroundings. That much was clear.

I boldly placed a hand on his exposed arm and shook my head. "Please. It's just Wren. And I'm fine." When his stare landed where my hand curled around his muscular forearm, I immediately dropped it, my cheeks flaming. His seemed a little redder too.

I would've expected him to demand I take a carriage home. To leave the south and never speak of it again, but he didn't. Everett had been surprised, yes, but he'd immediately fallen into a seat to strike up a conversation. Not to judge or scold. He wished to talk, by the looks of it. That made me like him a little more, giving me hope that he wasn't like all the other brutes Mother paraded in front of me. And his attire? I found the roguish look suited him much better than the stuffy suits I'd seen him wear before. Maybe it was his *true* look. This, his true self.

"Wren," he whispered gently, seeming to taste the sound. "Are you here by yourself?"

I nodded, noting how his jaw clenched.

Obviously it had been foolish, but I wasn't going to enlist my parents. Or Callie; I would do my best to protect her from our father's temper. By some twist of destiny, I sat beside a lord I hadn't thought much of weeks before, and now, his welcoming smile relaxed the tension in my shoulders. He hadn't even asked if the rumors were true about my arrest. He just asked if I was *doing all right*.

Why did that make me feel . . . more? Was I that deprived of affection?

"I won't tell you it's dangerous here, especially on your own, but would you mind if I keep you company and walk you home afterward?" His smile broadened, becoming a breathtaking grin, and another beat skipped in my chest. "If you would take pity on me, it would make me feel better."

"Why are *you* here?" It flew from my lips, partly from curiosity and partly as a method of deflecting *his* question. The practical side of me remained skeptical despite his being nothing short of kind since coming across me. In the very last place I should be.

"Same as you." He signaled the bartender for a glass. "I needed to get away from the petty chatter of the north. All they've been talking about for weeks is . . ." He trailed off, a horror-struck expression taking over his handsome features.

"Me? Dusk? If I murdered a Fate?" I finished for him with a knowing scoff. He sighed heavily, an answer if I ever heard one.

Like I'd done moments before, he placed a gentle hand on my arm. "I don't believe a word they say," he affirmed, his voice drenched with conviction. "You were in the wrong place at the wrong time, Wren. I hate that you've been through so much over these last months. I know we don't know each other that well, but I can't help but feel a kinship," he added with a rueful smile.

His sympathy was a balm I hadn't realized I needed. I still didn't know if the police considered me a true threat; I hadn't the nerve to ask Father. Maybe, in truth, I hadn't asked because I didn't wish to hear the answer.

The bartender chose that moment to bring us our ales—mine obviously some time after I'd asked for it, though I thanked him before grabbing the bubbling amber and lifting it to my mouth. Sucking in a collected breath, I took my very first sip of ale.

What? Ladies were never allowed anything but lemonade or champagne. I was breaking all the rules, so why not another?

Everett, who'd been watching my reaction intently, chuckled, the sound deep and comforting. "Your face says it all," he remarked.

My nose wrinkled and my brows dragged together, the unusual flavor assaulting my senses in an intense way. The bubbles didn't help.

"That obvious?" I choked out, putting the glass back on the bar. I'd have to deliberate whether I wanted another sip.

"You get used to it." His eyes dazzled as he tried and failed to repress his smirk.

"I hope so. It tastes like bitter spices and musk." I giggled for the first time in weeks when he snorted, the sound so unlike a well-bred gentleman.

Yet when he took another sip, I matched his movements. *Hmm.* Not nearly as bad the second go-round. I took a few more gulps, enjoying how my belly warmed, and emptied the glass to the half-way point.

Everett shook his head. "You are more fun than I suspected, Lady Hayes. And quite . . . adventurous."

"Excuse me?" I teased, setting down my drink. Some of the liquid sloshed over the rim. "That sounds like you didn't believe me fun at all."

His cheeks reddened. Again. "Shi—sorry, that's not what I meant." He lowered his head, a wayward blond strand dipping into his eyes. "I meant it as a compliment. You always stood out to me. You know that."

"Because I'm a bore at parties?" I supplied, smirking.

"No. Believe me, there are others who are exceedingly boring, and you are anything but. As I told you at the ball, I admired how you shone even when trying to keep yourself hidden. An impossibility, I might add." He glanced down at his drink, hiding his grin. "You take in all of society with such a serious face, and I wonder what goes through your head. If your thoughts are like mine."

Fates, I hadn't realized I came across that way. It wasn't like I despised everyone in society. If someone enjoyed a ball, then I applauded them. Hell, I was jealous. Everett didn't realize I stared because I wanted to fit in and hoped that if I observed people well enough, then perhaps some of their behavior would rub off on me.

"I am not thinking about anything serious, I promise," I said. "I just . . . I don't always enjoy the stimulation. It's loud, even when it's quiet, if that makes any sense at all."

"The judging, you mean?" Everett supplied, the side of his muscular thigh brushing my own. His heat seeped through my dress, and Fates above, my body reacted, tingles shooting down my back. I suppressed a shudder. What on earth was wrong with me? "It could be pin-drop silent in a ballroom, and you'd practically make out every single thought," he added, peering off to the side. "So maybe I do know what you mean. People expect a lot from me, especially my father. I suppose we both have a lot riding on us."

Everett Sinclair surprised me. By being here, by his genuine concern. By the way he studied me at balls, silent yet understanding. I'd believed all the suitors to be boring, pompous asses. Everett intrigued me so much that I had forgotten all about my mission and why I shouldn't be wasting time speaking with him.

I cleared my throat, my palms growing clammy. Nerves. Everett had made me nervous. I blamed that dazzling smile. It was lethal.

"I need to use the ladies' room," I rushed to say. "Are you aware of where I may find it?"

"In the far-right corner from the stage," he directed. "But you better come back, else I'll have to finish your ale."

I narrowed my eyes. "Try it and find out what happens."

He held up his hands. "Fine, but no more threats. I have a sensitive constitution."

I couldn't help beaming as I slipped off the stool and charted my way back and to the right. The modest ladies' room needed a good scrubbing, the lock barely affixed to the wall, but I hurried and made do. As I washed my hands, I studied the woman in the mottled mirror. A glow brightened her cheeks, and her lips weren't pinched. Even the worry lines on my forehead had smoothed. I looked different. *Alive.*

After drying my hands, I exited the room and shut the door—

Only to walk directly into a solid wall.

No, not a wall. Muscle.

"Miss me, sunshine?"

Chapter Eleven

Damien

"Damien."

Her voice was whisper soft, laced with shock. Her cheeks, which had held a delectable hue of red to them, went white as bone, the sight of me wreaking havoc. I clenched my teeth as her shoulders tensed in my presence; like she found my very existence bothersome.

Same, sunshine.

"I see that you're enjoying yourself slumming it in the Void," I said, my tone cold, harsh. I'd observed her from the main room the second she entered the bar. I'd planned to make my way over, but then the fucking lord I'd stolen that watch from came sauntering to her side and took a seat like he owned the place. He caused her to laugh—several times—her vexingly beautiful face lighting up the entire space. It made my blood boil; they were in *my* bar. My side of town.

With my usual seat taken, I crept back to my corner and seethed, arms crossed, glaring daggers into the lord's skull. The bastard had never been here before—and I would know—making me suspect that either he'd followed her or they had come together. All of it was suspicious.

When she snuck off to the ladies' room, I made my move.

I hadn't realized how close Wren and I stood in the narrow hall until her chest brushed against my own, her breathing uneven. A bolt of electricity shot down my front whenever her soft curves grazed me. If she noticed, she didn't let on. Those turquoise eyes hardened at the corners as she tilted her chin to meet mine, all bravado, all fake. A smile crept to my lips at the realization, and I stared down at her, enjoying the difference in our heights immensely.

I could tell it vexed her.

"I'm not *slumming it,*" she seethed. "I came here to find *you,* if you must know. Not that I wanted to."

I rested my hand on the wall above her head, leaning forward. "Oh, you came to find me, eh? I'm flattered."

The noise she made was nothing short of a growl. "I . . . I need help. And you're just the devious kind of man who can deliver."

"I prefer *clever.* Or *creative, sly, resourceful—*"

"Damien."

"Yes, sunshine?"

"Shut up, please."

I arched a brow. "So bossy. Here I thought you were a well-bred lady. Suppose I was wrong. Sneaking out to bars with men unescorted." I faked a gasp. "Scandalous."

I moved closer, my chest now fully pressed to hers. Through her simple dress, I made out the heavy thumps of her heartbeat, of her . . .

Those curves of hers were just as I remembered from the other night.

I expected her to move or shove me away like trash, but she didn't, her attention locked on my eyes. Eyes most people tended not to look into for too long due to their unusualness, how they appeared "like an oncoming storm," as Ruby lovingly put it. Yet they didn't seem to bother Wren.

"You don't know me, *thief*," she remarked coolly, adopting some of that earlier coldness I'd seen her wear back at the guard station. "I'm here to offer you a job."

"*Hmm.* A job? And *I* am the one you came to?" To mask my surprise, I lifted my hand, snagging one of the loose curls that had slipped from her updo. Twirling the silken strand, I kept my eyes on her, waiting for her to squirm. To my shock, she remained in place, stubbornly refusing to show any sign of discomfort.

She tapped her damn toe as if my presence bored her, but her right eye gave her away when it twitched, just once, and a smirk spread across my face. I grudgingly released her too soft hair.

"Well?" she demanded when I didn't speak. "I'll pay. A bonus would be you *not* having to rob anyone. Must be rare for you."

I laughed. I'd make her work for this mysterious request. Even if I needed her, too.

My grin grew absolutely wicked when I asked, "What do you require of me? Bored with the usual lords? You know, I typically don't offer such . . . *services*."

She smacked my arm. "I'm not asking *that* of you, you cretin." The tips of her ears turned a delicious shade of red.

"No?" My voice retained innocence as I cocked my head. "I assumed, seeing as you seemed to enjoy having me on top of you the other evening."

Oh. I'd pushed the right button.

The red that had rushed to her cheeks traveled beneath the neckline of her dress. I wished to capture the moment—of her clenched fists and determined stare, how she didn't pull away from me, no matter how much she might hate me.

"Enough," she said through her teeth. "If you want a job that pays, tell me or I'll find someone more capable."

More capable. As if she could find someone as capable as me . . . who *wouldn't* rob her blind. Or worse.

She placed her hands on my chest as if to push me away. That wouldn't do. Grasping both her wrists, I held her to me, a thrill shooting down my spine when I leaned inches from her pouty mouth.

"I never said I wouldn't help," I argued, inhaling her every exhale. "I just might want something in return." When her eyes widened, I hastily added, "A *favor,* and not the kind your wicked little mind is thinking of."

"I—I wasn't thinking *that,*" she enunciated, clearly thinking of exactly the dark things I accused her of. "You would be the last person on earth I'd ever want."

Like *I* would want her. A pretentious know-it-all who hadn't a clue about life. Ridiculous.

"Good to know we're on the same page." I raised a finger and trailed it down her cheek, feeling her burning skin just to provoke. "Go on then, sunshine. Tell me what it is that only a, what was it you called me? A *devious* man like me can offer?"

My curiosity gnawed at me, my little prey growing all the more interesting. She had guts, coming to the Void. And to the Broken Wing, of all places, I'd give her that. Wren must want something badly enough to leave her rich town house and well-manicured streets.

Our hearts thudded against each other, my own pulse surprisingly quick. Ever since I'd been tossed into her life, I felt like something inside me had awoken. Like a slumbering bear emerging from years of sleep.

The thrill of the chase. It had to be.

"I won't tell you here," she said quietly. "There's too many people." Her eyes scanned the empty hall before moving to the main room. "And don't be such a bastard about it. If you agree, we work together as equals. No more of . . . this." She peered between us, to where we were connected. *Too close.* Even so, Wren made no indication that my closeness bothered her. Well, aside from those rosy cheeks. Her delectable tell.

Fates. Riling her up was too easy.

Too *fun.*

I raised my head far enough to appraise her. "Fine. But word of advice? Coming here with *him* was a very bad decision. I can practically smell the arrogance from a mile away. He'll be a target for any cocky drunkard who wants to put a northerner in his place."

He'd tried to dress like he belonged, but anyone with sense could see otherwise. When he hadn't been speaking with Wren, he'd been too busy downing a beer and studying the tavern, his condescending face twisting. Of course, he flipped on the charm like a switch with her. People like him were actors on a stage, and Wren was naïve enough to fall for the act. Not surprising.

She believed herself tough, while she continued to see the best in people. A shame, really.

A finger pressed into my chest, startling me. "You've been watching me," Wren accused—*correctly*—doing her very best to sound intimidating. Such an adorable yet incompetent attempt.

"Obviously." I shrugged, pressing deeper into that little finger of hers. "You were practically begging to be robbed." *Again.*

"You would be the expert," she snipped.

My smile blossomed. I captured the finger she used to poke into my flesh and wrapped my own fingers around it. She gave it a fruitless tug, and the frustration wrinkling her pert nose caused my chest to swell. Slipping one hand around her waist, the other pressing into the small of her back, I dragged her firmly against me, her lush body molding to the hardness of my muscles.

Heat filled me but I tamped it down, or tried to. But when she let out a gasp of surprise, that heat grew into something devious. Something I *didn't* want. Not with her. I merely liked to play—a lion toying with his food before a meal.

Dropping my head, I whispered into her ear. "Go home before you get yourself killed, sunshine," I warned, thrilled by the ensuing shudder I felt go through her. "Your tenderhearted lord won't be able to protect you here."

I still required answers from her, mainly a list of possible attendees and other suspects who could've stolen her locket the night of the ball. Once I found it and returned it to Wren, surely things would return to normal, and my gift wouldn't continue to fail me. I held on to that sliver of hope with both hands. Her locket was not worth my own magic.

In the meantime, Lord Pompous would wind up getting them both robbed or beaten. The image of someone hurting her flashed in my mind, and I ground my teeth.

"He's doing just fine," Wren breathed, her voice a little rougher. Raspier.

I pulled back, studying her face in the way I knew she hated.

"What are you trying to say?"

"Isn't it obvious?" I asked. The hand grasping her hip tightened and she let out a deep sound that ignited the cursed spark in my chest. "A few friends of mine already had eyes on you, but with me present, they wouldn't mess with you. I've already done you several favors, and you hadn't a clue. You were under my protection the whole time."

It was true. Sandy and her drunk of a husband, Maurice, had been deliberating the best way to corner the pair before I shut that down. Bella and Lonnie, too.

Wren bit her cheek, considering. Meanwhile, my traitorous eyes dropped to her lips, taking in the fullness of them, the natural pink shade they held. Why did the woman I robbed have to look like *that*? If she weren't some spoiled noble, I'd seduce her and purge her from my system. As it was, there'd be no chance in the underworld of that happening.

Besides, something told me once wouldn't be enough. I liked sweet things.

Bad thought. I was getting off track.

"Take my offer," she demanded, her breasts pushing against me, turning my brain all hazy again. She exhaled unevenly, more noticeable than before, her body slightly trembling against mine.

That trembling didn't stem from fear, but rather, sheer determination.

"Again, shocked to see that the princess of Ward One is so bossy." I sighed, dropping my hand from her waist and giving her as much room as the hallway allowed. I watched as she nearly stumbled backward in her haste to be rid of me, but she quickly righted herself, her expression turning cold once more.

I rolled my eyes at the display.

"Name a price. And a *reasonable* one," she added. "I'll give you the details when it's decided."

I pretended to consider, narrowing my eyes. I couldn't let her know how desperately I wanted her help as well. She would have easy access to all the guests who attended the event.

"Three pieces of silver for every day my services are requested."

An unintelligible noise slipped from between her lips. "One piece of silver. At *most*."

I scoffed, crossing both arms. "Sunshine, you can't afford me, then."

"How many times do I have to tell you not to call me that?" Her lips thinned into a straight line.

I laughed. "But you're so nice and bright. Always a ray of light,"

I teased, gently flicking her nose. "The nickname suits you far too well for me to stop."

She glowered. "If you're going to be an ass, then I'm leaving. I knew I never should've come here."

She started to slip around me.

I shot my arm out, blocking her in as I leaned close. "Two pieces."

She crossed her arms, grinding her teeth so hard I feared she'd crack her jaw. "One."

"Damn, you're stubborn, aren't you?" I groaned, aware that I couldn't let her walk—even if I wasn't sure why the hell she needed *me*. All right, truth be told, I had an *inkling*. "Fine, one piece of silver," I ground out, hating to give in easily. She called my bluff, and my desperation to find her locket and restore my own power rioted against her slipping away. Pride be damned.

Wren beamed, her glower turning into a victorious grin, all of her teeth on display as she silently boasted.

"You can stop smiling like that," I grumbled.

"So I can't smile now?" she asked innocently. "It wouldn't hurt you to smile every now and again instead of acting all grumpy and tough all the time."

"Grumpy?"

"Most definitely," she chirped, apparently having regained her confidence. "You and your stormy eyes and scowling face are the epitome of the word."

How rich that she made assumptions about me.

"Oh, no. I don't like that face. It's much worse," she murmured, likely reading my look of sheer exasperation.

"Good." I went to her ear again, making sure my stubbled jaw rubbed against her smooth skin. "Now be the proper lady that you are and scurry home. I'll meet you at your house tomorrow at noon."

A hand fisted my shirt, and I pulled back a little to lock eyes. "You don't tell me what to do, Damien," she bristled, my name sounding like a curse. "This is to be a partnership. And I'll go home *after* I've finished my drink." As if she was just remembering she'd ditched her fancy lord back at the bar, her face paled. "Tomorrow. Don't be late. Oh, and we'll talk about your *favor* then too."

My mouth opened, but I never got a chance to reply. The ward princess slipped beneath my arm and practically sprinted around the corner and out of sight.

She's a means to an end. A way to fix your *mistake.*

It still pissed me off when I rounded the corner and found her and her precious lord slipping out the door, his arm possessively around her waist. I didn't understand what drew me to the woman, but it had to simply be the mystery of the locket. All right, and perhaps a *little bit* of attraction, which could be controlled. Stifled. I planned to stifle the hell out of it.

When the time came, I would be waiting, and then Wren Hayes would lead me to the locket and all would be well. Then I'd never have to see her again.

Chapter Twelve

Wren

The three Fates have been known to interfere
from time to time with mortals. It is best not to gain
their attention; it can be both a blessing and a curse.
—*Origin of the Fates,* Chapter Three

Everett had hailed me a carriage after we departed the pub yesterday. He'd been nothing less than courteous, as always, and asked if he'd see me at the next ball, to be held at the Hockleys' estate. I promised him his well-earned dance.

Now the new day had arrived, and while timid morning light peeked through the window, my pulse pounded in my throat in anticipation.

Damien. The conniving bastard had tried to extort *three* pieces of silver for his assistance, *while* asking for a favor. The absolute gall.

I'd been heated, my hands curled together to keep from clawing his eyes out, but my indecision had been an act—my walking away. There wasn't another option, and for a second there, I didn't think he'd relent. Just as my legs had started to tremble, he'd opened that cursed mouth and accepted the price before I'd fully turned around. One silver went a long way, and I'd have to sneak into Father's room to steal more than my allowance allowed. Breaking the rules ate away at my already frayed nerves, but this hunt was necessary. Especially since Damien was the only thief I knew who *might* know where my gift could be found—or the only person who fit the description Dusk had left. It wasn't like I entertained many cunning or deceitful criminals.

Dusk wished to expose something big, and never in my life had a mission been so vital. If only I knew what she wanted to show me . . .

Not like she was coming out of hiding anytime soon. It wasn't as if she were dead—all of the realm would feel the impact. If three Fates didn't reside on their thrones, magic would die.

So there was still hope.

I huffed, rolling over in bed. The blankets were far too warm, and I kicked them off, Damien's face hovering before my eyes. Fates, his audacity in that hallway. How he'd closed in, his lips brushing my skin, his finger on my cheek . . . Damien had twisted my insides with a mixture of anger and something else. Something foreign that frightened and excited me at once. Sparring with him had been entertaining. A rush.

Particularly when I'd won.

A cool head. That was what I required.

Which would be damn near impossible around him.

Damien had the vexing gift of bringing out my worst traits, and I had a feeling they'd come out with a vengeance now that I'd be spending time with him, hunting down Dusk's magic. *Unwillingly*, that was. But who else did I know that I trusted? I couldn't very well ask Everett, or for that matter, my parents. Callie, I could rely upon, but I wished to leave her out of this mess.

Damien was the safe choice. The obnoxiously grating safe choice. I could leave him behind without a backward glance when I'd accomplished the mission.

I groaned into my pillow. Today, I'd have to admit why I'd hired him. My nerves were unraveling as I even thought about disclosing that I lacked a gift. Like he would have the upper hand and berate me, as he enjoyed doing. Calling me spoiled. A princess. Naïve.

People might see me and think of me as some ignorant princess without a thought in her head—and sometimes, I *made* them believe that. It was easier to hide if they assumed I was a boring young lady who cared for nothing but ribbons. It gave me safety. When you allowed people to truly see you, they had the power to destroy you.

I just had to keep up those invisible walls, strong and unyielding.

If anyone was aware of the thieves of Andalay—and if people were stealing magic—Damien would be. Which compelled me to pull myself together, after spending another hour in bed staring at my ceiling.

A gentle knock roused me from my thoughts.

I jolted up in bed at the same moment Father's voice drifted through the crack in the door. "Wren?" he asked, sounding smaller than I'd ever heard.

"Come in!" I swept the unruly blankets over myself before quickly running my hands through my tangled hair.

Father wore a navy suit today with satin lapels, his hair perfectly combed to the side, his features soft and movements almost hesitant as he approached. I frowned at the image. He was never hesitant.

I moved aside when he shuffled over and took a seat at the foot of the bed. With a deep sigh, he spoke.

"I know I've been hard on you."

The words felt too loud, my thundering pulse drowned out by the uncharacteristic declaration.

"You've always been a good daughter," he said, his stare turning to the open window, avoiding mine. "I understand why you'd wish to seek the Fates, why you'd think it was some mistake. Hell, I would as well." He briefly shut his eyes. I gripped the sheets in my fists, breath stilled. I thought of the night I'd overheard him and Callie arguing. When he'd all but called me a disappointment. That word alone had gutted me.

Father opened his eyes and locked them on me, his stare serious. "But you must know it's time to stop. Stop going to the palace. Stop asking around. Stop sulking in your room." Like the ever-changing winds, his expression shifted, his brows knitting together and his lips curving downward. "Sometimes, life isn't fair, but we deal with it without making a fuss. And right now, you need to do exactly that."

A spark of anger ignited at his command.

"I've tried, but—"

"No, Wren." He cut me off with an abrupt wave of his hand. "There are things you can't possibly comprehend. Maybe one day you'll learn, but until then, I need you to stay out of the mouths of gossips. It harms not only me, but this entire realm."

How did my misfortune hurt the *realm*? I opened my mouth, prepared to protest once more, but his scowl silenced me. He wouldn't hear me anyway. When had he stopped listening? I couldn't pinpoint an exact moment, but somewhere along the way, he'd given up on me.

"Oh, and don't make Callie feel bad about her position," he added, standing and smoothing out the wrinkles in his pants. "We all know she won't get anywhere near becoming a ward leader, but let her hope. She has too sensitive a disposition."

I clenched the sheets so hard my knuckles turned white. Anger seeped into my blood, hot and scorching, the casual way he spoke about my sister and her imminent failure too much to bear. But he didn't see my eyes narrow or lips thin. He was halfway out the door. Already mentally gone.

"Be good," he said over his shoulder, the latch clicking into place a moment later.

Be good.

Let her hope.

Sensitive disposition.

All demeaning words dripping with a disdain he'd allowed to blossom over the last few years. He didn't believe women capable of such high roles, that much was clear. And here I'd thought he actually aimed to boost his daughter to a position of power. To show all the other women of the realm that we were just as capable as the men who'd once belittled us.

I glared at the place he'd occupied, my rage twisting like a trapped beast in a cage.

Father wanted me to stay out of his way? I'd gladly do so, but no way in hell would I do anything but make Callie feel like the cunning and capable powerhouse she would be.

One day our world would change, and all it took to start a revolution was one person.

After everyone but Sarah had left, leaving the house blissfully quiet, I snuck down the stairs and to the kitchen for a cup of tea. Mug in hand, I sipped the peppermint blend, my senses heightening as the caffeine entered my system.

Noon would arrive shortly.

I glanced down at my nightdress and robe, a grumble of annoyance deep in my throat. Damien promised he'd arrive at my home. The fact that he knew where I lived should anger me, but I wasn't surprised he could locate me. Cameron Hayes wasn't exactly a quiet member of society. Besides, I had other things on my mind aside from Damien's ability to find me.

Namely my father being a prick for even uttering such blasphemy.

Fates, I had to settle my nerves if I would be any use today.

Or I could turn all my irritation on Damien. Yes. A much better plan.

An hour before our meeting, I chose to don a simple pastel-pink dress with lacy sleeves and a flowy skirt fashioned of gauze over a silk slip. It was two years out of fashion, but I preferred the freedom of not physically hauling my heavy skirts with each step, and besides, I wasn't about to change my love of pretty things for the likes of him. Using a yellow silken ribbon to pull half my hair back, I dabbed on some rouge and ran some shimmer over my lids. Some armor wasn't always as obvious, and I wore mine now.

Sarah bustled around the kitchen, organizing dinner for that evening. She was an unsmiling woman in her forties whose glowers could skewer a person alive. I chose to avoid her whenever possible.

"Any lunch, miss?" she asked, not needing to look up from her task to sense my presence.

"I'm fine, thank you." Sarah humphed in disapproval but continued working.

"I'm going to the market to pick up fresh duck, your father's favorite. He told me he expected you at dinner this evening," Sarah said, slamming another cabinet closed before marking something on a notepad with a thin piece of charcoal.

Lovely. A sweet family meal filled with saccharine threats and falsehoods.

"Oh, and your mother had a last-minute invitation to Lady Castleton's home. She's there now." Sarah paused her work. "Second time this week, actually. Your mother's been a busy woman. She only just had lunch with Lady Lovett the other day, and she spent hours there. Glad she's coming back to her old self, at least."

Mother hadn't been socially active in years, but in the past months she'd visited the homes of the lords nonstop. I hardly saw her at home, and when she returned, she barely had enough energy to trudge into the house, her stare unfocused and dark circles blooming below her eyes.

Her absence, however, meant one less person to worry about if Damien actually showed his face—but a silver piece was a silver piece and turning it down would just be plain foolish.

"Thank you for telling me," I replied, inspecting my hands, which had turned clammy. My nerves continuously betrayed me, and I wiped the moisture off on my skirts when Sarah turned her back.

Whirling around, she grabbed her wooden basket and appraised me, her brown eyes narrowed. "I'd suggest keeping home, miss," she said firmly. "The lord and lady were on edge this morning. More guards are on their posts because of Dusk."

I forced a small smile and nodded. "Of course."

Fates, my heartbeat pounded, so loudly she must hear it. Lying had never come easy to me, but lately, I'd been frighteningly decent at it. With each lie, it felt like another brick dropped onto my shoulders.

Sarah tsked before walking by, her wool skirts swaying with her hips. The front door opened and shut seconds later.

She was gone. Everyone was gone.

Wandering into the parlor, I observed the face of the grandfather clock, counting the seconds ticking away. Five minutes until noon.

I paced back and forth, just as I had on my birthday. This time, it had nothing to do with elated anticipation.

That thief better keep his word or I'll go back to the Void and find him myself.

Then what? Threaten him? I scoffed, laughing at myself. At the absurdity of my threat and the notion of getting a man like Damien to do anything he didn't wish to do.

"What's so funny, sunshine?"

I jumped, a small shriek leaving my lips before I could swallow it.

Spinning in place, I found the man in question leaning against the door to the parlor, arms crossed and expression bored. He lifted a hand and picked at his nails, his black hair falling into his eyes. I wished to fling one of the many throw pillows littering the room at his face.

"How the hell did you get in?" I said through gritted teeth, squashing down the urge to yell.

Damien pushed off the doorframe and strolled into the space. He wore a black, fitted long-sleeved shirt today, a couple of copper buttons at the top undone and the sleeves rolled to his elbows. That dark hair of his refused to be tamed, sweeping back into his cold eyes, which gleamed as he took me in.

I realized I held my hand to my chest from my earlier fright. I shoved it down to my side.

"I'm so glad you're happy to see me, too," he drawled, moving about the parlor, his lean fingers trailing over the fine furniture as if he owned it. The closer he drew, the more my pulse fluttered at my neck and the more uneven my footing felt. Like I'd topple over at any moment. An absurdity, as Damien was just a man and a heathen at that. I shouldn't fear him. Straightening my shoulders, I cleared my throat when he nearly sent a glass figurine of a dancer toppling off a pedestal. Mother would've had his head.

"Can you keep your hands to yourself for five minutes?"

He looked up, a smirk forming. "Funny. Usually I'm asked to do the opposite. Shame."

I rolled my eyes. He was baiting me, and I wouldn't fall for any tricks. "Yes, yes. I'm sure you have *droves* of men and women just waiting to warm your bed. They're probably fighting outside your room as we speak."

Arrogant prick.

"You'd be surprised." He grinned, all teeth. He ceased his wandering, easily moving to stand before me. His towering physique irritated me as always, and I tilted my chin to meet him.

"I think you're all talk and no action," I said calmly, silently clapping myself on the back for sounding somewhat poised. "If you manage to aid me in my quest, then maybe I'll begin to believe a word that comes out of your lying mouth. I asked you here out of necessity, remember, not because I *wished* to engage with you any more than I already have."

He cocked his head, his smile downright wicked. "Oh, I have full confidence that I can help you, Wren," he said, and damn it, the sound of my name on his lips sent a shiver straight through me. "And I don't think you hate me as much as you claim. There are plenty of other . . . *qualified* individuals you could have asked."

I faked a wide grin. "Shame I don't know anyone other than

you. If you'd like, you could provide me with a list and we can part ways."

His lips twitched at that. "If you wish to actually be robbed of what you seek, then sure, I can give you some names. But I prefer the silver you offer to whatever trinket you're looking for."

Trinket. Ha. He hadn't a clue what Dusk said about my missing gift. It was far more important than he could possibly fathom.

My hands curled into fists as we stared at each other silently. I despised him, hated all his bluster and teasing. His incessant need to be a bastard just for the sake of it. Yet . . . I couldn't deny I found him attractive. The man had a handsome face—sharp cheekbones, a regal nose, and a darkness that would lure anyone with eyes. It made it difficult to keep the scowl on my face, but by the grace of the Fates, I did.

I'd read enough novels to discern the difference between love and lust, and I remained confident that I was experiencing the latter now. The ladies and gentlemen of society got themselves confused about the emotion all the time, and sadly, once they were married off, they found that the thrill of it vanished.

I wouldn't fall victim to his looks.

I had a mission from a *Fate.*

"As fun as this is, would you take a seat so we may discuss what I require?" I asked politely, shoving down the pesky little thoughts of his full lips as they curved upward, his dimples popping up on either cheek.

"You sound so formal," he mused. "After you stabbed me, I believed we were on friendlier terms."

I didn't tell him I'd armed myself today with my letter opener shoved between my breasts.

Just in case.

"If I didn't know better, I'd believe you enjoyed being stabbed." I stared at the spot where the weapon had pierced his skin, my eyes lingering on how his shirt left nothing to the imagination. He was lean but toned, his abdomen—

"Eyes up here." Damien tsked, sliding a finger beneath my chin and shocking me at how quickly he moved. He lifted my face, forcing me to bear witness to the sheer confidence brightening his features. "No blush today?" he asked, his blasted finger still touching me. If I removed it, then he'd have won. "I'm hurt."

Thank all the Fates that my body had cooperated with me just that once. My stomach, on the other hand, twisted in turmoil, all knotted and cold. Good for me that he couldn't see beneath my skin.

Damien mercifully lifted his chin, glancing around the room, though he didn't release me. "Curious," he murmured. "I wonder how much of you is in this parlor. In this home."

"Excuse me?" His finger traced upward, causing an involuntary shiver.

"It's dark, little color. Timeless, yes, but you . . . I don't see a trace of you in here." His gaze locked on mine. "You're all color. This is more like a tomb. Or maybe it's more like your father?"

I bit the inside of my cheek to keep from snapping. Father . . . I felt protective of him. *Still.* Even after he'd hurt me this morning. He'd always been my blind spot, his imperfections difficult for me to conceive.

"Yes . . ." Damien clucked his tongue. "This isn't you at all, sunshine. I wonder how a rose blossomed in such a cold place."

He compared me to a rose—a compliment. Yet it didn't feel like one, not with how scathing his tone had turned.

Odd, that I didn't feel like that derision was directed at me.

"Enough, Damien," I ground out, tone icy. "I'd prefer to skip all of your crude innuendoes and horrendous comparisons to flowers and tombs. The sooner we get this over with, the better for us both."

Damien's smile slipped from his mouth, and damn me, I mourned it. Now he just looked like his typical indignant and broody self.

"Fine." He dropped his finger and strode over to the sofa, where he made a show of taking a seat. "But you're no fun."

I sighed, the urge to pull at my hair strong. Working with him would be torturous.

After I sat on the opposite sofa, as far from the man as possible, I righted my skirts and froze. My mouth opened, but I'd lost the words.

Or the nerve.

Damien lifted a dark brow. ". . . Yes?"

"I—I need you to find something for me." My statement was clipped, soft.

He leaned back, making himself right at home, arms slung over the sides of the sofa. "What kind of something?" he asked without inflection, for once serious.

"My gift was stolen." The words rushed out of me. "Someone took it the night of my birthday, and I have it on good authority that it should've been delivered by a hound. That there'd been an error."

Damien remained damnably stoic. "What kind of authority?"

I couldn't answer that. Dusk's final letter had been hastily written in secret. She wanted to reveal a truth about our society, and I couldn't just involve Damien. I felt protective of the mysterious Fate, which was odd, given I'd never met her before. Yet there was a pull in my belly whenever I envisioned her.

She chose me.

Maybe that reason alone had me on the defensive.

"Just trust me," I said, adjusting in my seat, suddenly filled with nervous energy. "I need to locate the person who stole my gift from the hound and retrieve what is rightfully mine."

I'd deduced the time of the theft that night—when the black hound had been sent to make the delivery.

A rare thing, the theft of a gift, but once the object fell into the hands of another, the power transferred. Perhaps that was why the Fates decreed it pertinent to keep their tokens of magic on our person at all times.

Silence stretched between us, long and heavy, and utterly nerve-wracking.

As I couldn't appear anything but put together in his presence, I kept my eyes on his, and in turn he never wavered, both of us locked in place. Trapped in each other's orbits.

We played a game, he and I—neither of us would win, but it would be played to exhaustion nevertheless.

After what felt like several torturous minutes, Damien sat up in his seat. The smile had vanished from his face; no dimples or mischievous grins. His eyes grew so impossibly dark, they resembled a cold winter sea.

"Do you have suspects?"

"No," I replied stiffly. "Most everyone I socialize with has a gift already, and the rare few without one are typically sent away to the countryside by their parents. I assumed—"

"You assumed it was someone from the Void?"

I flinched in my seat, his harsh tone like a slap.

"I didn't say that, Damien, only that I don't believe it's someone I'm familiar with."

His shoulders grew taut, the muscles flexing beneath the thin material. "Your birthday was when?"

"March eleventh."

He rubbed at his sharp chin, his thumb meticulously swiping back and forth. When he didn't open his mouth, I found him handsome. Maybe I should alert him to this fact when he went home to deal with his oh-so-many lovers.

"I'll look into the usual suspects back south," Damien said, unaware of my fervent attention. "In the meantime, you should really consider someone who might've been at the last ball you attended. Someone closer to home. You'd be surprised how many enemies one might have wearing smiles but holding knives behind their backs."

I frowned at the thought. Closer to home, as in a noble? Since a few children of the upper class hadn't received gifts in the past, it was a possible option. Some remained in Andalay, having convinced their parents to allow them to stay, even with the ensuing scandal. But who would dare? Unfortunately for me, and Damien, I'd been so secluded that I couldn't identify more than a quarter of the nobility. At parties, my instructions were to remain silent unless spoken to, and I'd occasionally dance with a partner who'd mumble about the weather or some other trivial matter that bored me half to death.

I bit my lip. I could be acquainted with the perpetrator, but did I truly *know* them? We all wore masks in our society, and someone I assumed to be harmless could be a wolf in sheep's clothing.

"Agreed," I eventually whispered before tacking on, "And we're going to the Void together when we search. You said *you* will look into the people in the south, but I wish to accompany you. It is my gift at stake, after all."

He barked out a laugh. "You barely made it out yesterday. I spied about five thieves ready to rob you," he added in a lower tone. It sounded angry. "You have no idea what you're dealing with."

"Then show me."

"No."

I shot to my feet. "I'm not utterly helpless, even if you like to believe otherwise, and I can't sit idly by. I'm going wherever you go."

Damien's jaw feathered. "Then I get to do the same," he replied, surprising me.

"Meaning?"

"Meaning I expect to be at your side at your lavish ward parties, balls, whatever you call them." He waved his hand like he batted away a pesky fly. "As we said, it could be someone on this side of Andalay."

"How the hell would I be able to get you an invitation?"

His smirk returned. "You insisted you weren't helpless. Prove it."

Oh, Fates. I'm going to murder him.

Chapter Thirteen

Wren

For thousands of years, the Fates have delivered gifts.
Detailed accounts must be maintained, safely kept
under lock and key. No two gifts are exactly alike, even if they
possess similar qualities. Such precision takes
excessive effort on behalf of our almighty deities.
—*Origin of the Fates,* Chapter Eight

Apparently, the first stop we'd make today was in the north. Damien insisted that since he'd already traveled here and was worn down from a night out—likely from drinking himself under a table or gallivanting with one of his numerous lovers—we should start close to my home before entertaining the notion of going to the Void. I bit my tongue; he acted as if he knew exactly what he searched for and how to go about it, and I *had* paid him for his experience.

Smacking him would accomplish nothing. Unfortunately.

"We're going to start with the younger nobles. The ones whose magic isn't all that powerful, and the nobles who never received a gift," he declared, striding paces ahead of me.

"There's only a handful of those who never got one," I said. "Should be an easy search."

"Hope so, for your sake," he quipped, and I stuck my tongue out at his back.

"I saw that," he said without turning.

I slowed, frowning. "Did not."

"Just keep your tongue in your mouth, Lady Hayes. So unbecoming," he teased, the wind carrying his words to my red ears.

Lucky guess from a lucky bastard.

I tucked my cloak's hood over my head and continued seething. All I could do was pray no one recognized me, let alone believed I was traveling with the cocky thief strutting down Lorndale Avenue. Office suites occupied this section; a few lawyers, accountants, and even a matchmaker and a social organizer inhabited the pearl-colored stone buildings. Elegant snowy steps led to each dwelling, an intricate fence forged of iron blocking them from the street.

People went about their business during this bustling time, mostly men in their posh suits and bowler hats, leaving their wives at home or at tea. As if they could manage a business better than a *helpless* woman. I scoffed. Most of the women I knew were far more fearsome than any of the men, and much more cunning.

My thoughts went to Callie. She'd better get a seat. She deserved one, regardless of what Father or the other misogynistic lords believed.

"Where are we going?" I whisper-hissed when Damien made a sharp left. He guided us into a narrow alley lined with trash. Overflowing filth seeped out from the containers, and I wrinkled my nose.

Not the most hygienic place to begin our search—

A hand seized my wrist and tugged me deeper into the darkness before spinning me around.

"Stop doing that!" I demanded, my vision settling.

"What?" Damien asked, his hand still wrapped around my wrist.

"Grabbing my arm, my wrist, my hand." I shook my arm to make my point. "Oh, and whirling me around like a puppet on a string."

"So dramatic, sunshine."

"So *irritating.*"

Damien peered around us to make sure no one heard me before leaning down. "Whatever insanity you feel, I assure you, what you make me feel is ten times worse."

My lips parted in shock. I'd done nothing but slow him down at the ball when he *stole* Everett's watch. Aside from that, he had no reason to hate me, yet he kept prodding me. Kept battling.

"It's not my fault you insist upon being uncivil."

"But it is your fault that you open that mouth of yours."

I slapped him, the sound echoing in the alley as all the air deserted my lungs in shock. It was a weak hit, but Damien slowly turned back to me, his eyes depthless voids. He appeared a killer at that moment, a monster hiding beneath human skin.

"Trying to intimidate me with your scowls won't work," I

said, heat entering my cheeks. "And never, never, insult me like that again."

I had enough self-respect to cease working with him altogether.

"You're so easy to intimidate," he taunted, that cold mask of his glued to his face. "So easy to rile up. No wonder your gift was stolen. You're the perfect little mark."

Damn him.

This time when I went to slap him, his hand reached out and snagged my wrist. I hissed like a trapped animal.

Damien shook his head. "That wasn't very ladylike of you. But then again, ladies don't curse, drink, or *stab* people."

"You deserved it," I argued, barely keeping my wits about me. "I have a mind to do it again—"

A familiar voice sounded from our left. Ignoring Damien and his attempts to piss me off—attempts he was succeeding at—I peeked from the corner of my eye, finding the worst thing imaginable. One of my father's most trusted advisors stood at the mouth of the alleyway. He'd recognize me in a heartbeat.

"Shit."

"Another curse. I should start counting them." Damien tsked. When I didn't answer, he sobered. "What is it?"

The man—Lord Beaufort, I believed—had yet to move, standing alongside another businessman from Ward One. If he only looked to his right . . .

"That man. You know him." Damien fit the pieces together. I nodded wordlessly. If he discovered me, I'd get worse than a two-week sentence.

Damien leaned in closer just as Lord Beaufort shifted toward the alleyway, turning as if I'd called his name aloud. Any second now, he'd spot me.

"Sunshine?" I peered up at Damien, his eyes softer than before. Perhaps he understood the gravity of the situation. Saw the sheer terror in my eyes. "Do you trust me?"

"No," I replied truthfully.

He sighed heavily. "Probably a good thing, but do you trust me to keep you hidden?"

Damien was in it for the silver. A man wouldn't let harm come to the person providing him with coin, right?

"Y-yes."

"Smack me again if you need to."

Damien's body shifted around mine before I could ask why he'd said those words. His arm rested casually above my head, blocking out the alley's entrance. Slowly, so very slowly, he leaned forward, his eyes morphing into endless depths of deep winter. It was like looking into a snowstorm for too long and losing yourself entirely to the lethal haze.

I gasped when his lips touched my neck. Lighter than I imagined, sweeter, they traveled gently up the column of my throat. I couldn't have repressed the shudder if I'd tried. Damien sucked on the sensitive skin just below my ear, his tongue darting out to taste me. I bit my tongue, failing to swallow the escaping moan.

I felt him freeze before a low noise left his own throat, like he was surprised by his actions, or . . . or perhaps what those actions elicited. Large hands grabbed my hips, guiding me closer to his firm body, further into the sensation of free-falling. The heat of him radiated through his clothing, my own fire burning whether I wished it or not. The flimsy barriers separating us weren't enough to dispel the blaze burning across my flesh, consuming me as his lips grazed my skin, as he seemed to breathe me in. My scent. My essence. My very soul.

"Damien . . ." I spoke his name, both shock and a plea.

This was dangerous. And so, so incredibly wrong.

"Tell me to stop and I will," he murmured against my neck.

"I—"

I couldn't. I knew this was an act, a way to hide me from view with his body shielding mine, but the sensations swirling throughout my core were foreign and intoxicating. And *he* was the cause.

I nearly forgot about Lord Beaufort. How could I remember when Damien inched down, placing tender, almost adoring kisses along my collarbone, his lips treacherously close to the tops of my breasts? My body trembled, the rise and fall of my chest turning erratic.

"Fates," he muttered, and his grasp on my hips tightened.

His entire body remained stiff, like he fought to keep those hands from moving anywhere else. Yet his mouth . . .

I shuddered when he nipped at my jaw before soothing it with his tongue, his hot breath fanning across my cheeks, becoming the air in my lungs.

This was Damien. A thief. A man I didn't even like.

Why, then, did I feel as if the mere touch of him could set me alight?

"Damn it, Wren," he growled against the corner of my mouth—not quite a kiss, never fully taking me. He sounded angry. Like the fault lay with me.

Was I affecting him as he did me—

A piercing *bang,* like a clattering of metal striking the ground, burst from beyond the alley.

We yanked apart at the same time, stunned. His expression one of confusion. Mine likely matched.

Numbly, I looked to my left, finding Lord Beaufort and his acquaintance gone.

I touched my sensitive neck with my fingers, speechless for the first time since meeting the thief.

I had enjoyed that. Far too much.

Damien shoved back and ran an agitated hand through his hair. He didn't meet my gaze, and I couldn't meet his. What had been meant to be a way to hide me from the lord had turned into . . . *that.*

Whatever *it* had been shouldn't have felt that good.

"Sorry about that," Damien said. He plastered a smirk on his lips, the cocky one he wore to tease me, to hide from me, I realized. "At least it worked."

I stood there, unable to process for a moment. "Y-yes, it did."

Damien clapped his hands, averting his stare. "Lovely. Thanks for being a good sport. Very good acting, by the way."

My blood turned hot. "A good sport?" I scoffed. "*You* seemed to enjoy yourself."

His smirk dipped just slightly. "I think fast, Wren. You should know that about me." He winked, and I curled my fingers so that I didn't finally, *finally* allow myself to wrap my hands around his neck. Whatever foolish thoughts had raced through my mind when his lips had marked my skin, vanished.

"Now, hopefully no more of that," I said primly. "We just need to be more careful."

A moment of madness. That was all it had been.

"Agreed," he answered quickly, his tone haughty. Like he'd done *me* a huge favor. Like touching me had been a curse he'd gallantly accepted. "We won't speak of it again." He peered just above my eyes, not into them.

Coward.

"Of course not." I smoothed down my skirts, angrier with myself than with him.

"You're welcome, by the way."

"Welcome?"

"I hear it's polite to thank someone when they save you." He cocked a brow, his typical arrogance entering his tone. Gone was the frantic boy who'd turned my world on its head. I wasn't sure I liked the way he gazed upon me now. "I have a feeling you need a lot of saving, Wren."

I had to clench my teeth to keep myself from slapping him. Again.

"Last time I had to defend myself, I had you right where I wanted you. And you *bled* for me, Damien." Best he recall who'd gotten the upper hand in that fight—not mentioning the watch he'd still managed to steal, however.

"I *let* you win," he all but growled, moving into my space again. "I may not be one of your self-important gentlemen, but I'm not about to hurt someone half my damned size."

"Keep telling yourself that," I snarled, right before tapping him on the nose. He wrinkled it and backed away, eyes narrowed into slits.

"As much as I enjoy this back-and-forth, we have a job to do," he said, his hand at the nape of his neck, tugging at the small strands. "You ready to stop being a thorn in my side?"

"You ready to stop being one in mine?"

He threw his hands up in exasperation. "Ridiculous." Storming out of the alley, he forced me to find my footing and follow. The thief practically ran.

True, our bantering could be considered childish, but our goal was far more important than deciding who annoyed who more.

Damien and I were oil and water.

I slowed my steps, confusion dawning. I didn't know why we were even here, because Mr. Secretive didn't like to share. My temper prickled a little at that. It was my fault, truthfully; I'd blindly gone along without asking questions.

"Are you going to tell me where we're going?" I asked, my mind a tangled mess of unwanted thoughts. I could hardly focus, and I stumbled a little, trying to keep up.

Damien peered over his shoulder, his stare less sharp. Less heated. "We're going to the Registry of Magical Gifts."

I'd asked Father to check there to see if my name had been written in one of the thousands of stored records. He claimed it hadn't been.

"We're about to find out who needs power most. Someone your age who has ambition without the means," Damien whispered, his gaze cold and tone somehow icier than before. Not raspy and deep as it had been a minute ago. "We need to weed out the weakest among you in the higher circles, and then we do a little bit of . . . research."

I cursed the three Fates as I trailed him—

Him and the mistake that had happened in that alley.

One I'd never repeat.

Chapter Fourteen

Damien

What in the underworld had I been thinking?

Answer: I hadn't been. I'd just reacted when Wren's face flushed and fear entered her unfairly enticing eyes. When she looked to *me* of all people for help.

My insides were fire, and my brain . . . well, it ceased to work. I'd meant to pull her into that alley and demand she stop with her questions and trust me—even if I currently *was* attempting to deceive her—when her father's friend inconveniently materialized.

If that man had found her out, with *me,* she would've been on lockdown for a decade, along with her connections. So I did the one thing that would have the uptight lord hurriedly glancing the other way should he spot two people in an alley across the street from the Registry of Magical Gifts—

I *touched* her. Kissed her jaw, her throat, her collarbone. Acted as a lover.

And I liked it far too much.

Damn it.

I compelled myself to march across the pristine bricks of the business district of Andalay, not stealing a peek to see if the ward princess kept up or not. Judging by the occasional indignant huffs, I had yet to lose her.

Was I entirely convinced that my mirror's power waned because I'd stolen Wren's gift? No. But it remained the most logical and impeccably timed answer. Being low on magic was like being low on oxygen; if my magic continued to flicker and weaken, how would I keep myself off the streets? I had no skills aside from unburdening a man of his wallet, and no one would hire me knowing my background, not even in the Void. Cap might, but I didn't want to take advantage of him. I already stayed beneath his roof, and for a fraction of the price he'd normally charge.

I had to stick to the plan. My future depended on it—and I wasn't just referring to my time in the south.

The sunny day was busy, and we had to push past several well-dressed gentlemen, their fine suits pressed and bowler hats gleaming brilliantly enough to blind. I wondered if they could handle a day without their pretentious armor.

My steps weighed heavier the closer we neared, the distraction of the city no match for the images swirling through my thoughts against my will.

My mind was a traitor. One with terrible timing.

I blinked, a flash of the alley causing my core to heat.

Wren's silky skin. Her tiny moan. The way she'd pushed her

body into mine. Fates, I'd had the idiotic craving to do more than kiss up her neck. I'd wished to see what the princess tasted like. To see if her lips were as soft as they appeared.

You're attracted to her. It will fade.

Attraction always did. It was a fickle thing; there one moment, and easily dismissed. I rarely grew attached, and while this new . . . obsession had to do strictly with the locket and the mystery surrounding her, it was a nuisance.

Sadly for me, this wasn't the first time I had pictured Wren Hayes.

There'd been a few lonely nights after the ball; the first being when she stabbed me. In my head, she'd been underneath me once again, but this time, she was free of her voluminous ball gown. That fire of hers hadn't been anger, but need, a longing for *me*. I might be a thief, but there were certain *activities* I did enjoy—but with Wren . . .

She likely never had such an experience, and if she had—

Why did that thought bother me? Of her with someone else?

It shouldn't; I firmly believed the old ways were archaic, and that society ladies shouldn't have to hide their urges and desires. If men were free to act on theirs, why couldn't women?

"Damien?"

I jerked to a stop, lost to my deviant mind. I hadn't realized where we stood.

A drink would be needed after this nightmare, along with some very welcoming company, and then I'd forget all about the spoiled blond and her delicious curves. Even as I thought of other women, a sour taste entered my mouth.

Wren eyed me skeptically, her short stature taking nothing away from her intensity. I loathed that look. It made me feel small and queasy. Inspected, like an insect under a microscope.

Yes, lean into that.

I felt better after embracing what she represented.

"How are we planning on doing this?" she asked, her emotions, like when she'd been interrogated, wiped from her face. So different from the alley and her wide eyes and parted lips. Maybe she had the makings of a decent criminal after all.

"We don't have the right to request private information," I mused aloud, touching my fingers to my mirror, hidden in my pocket. "That means we have to sneak in. You're the distraction if my magic . . . runs out." Yeah, I had yet to deliver the news of my fading power.

I doubted she would enjoy the reason.

"Me? Why do *I* need to be the distraction? And magic running out?" Her forehead creased. "I've never heard of such a thing."

"You're the distraction because you're a well-bred lady they'll think is harmless," I supplied, taking in her simple but luxurious dress. It fit her form nicely, the silken material hidden beneath the gauze custom-made for her delicate skin.

"You didn't answer my other question, Damien."

Wren crossed her arms, drawing more attention to her chest. I tilted my head. "See? Anyone manning the front desk will be too distracted to notice me if I need help getting out." She lifted her eyebrow so high, it was impressively close to her hairline. I groaned. "Fine. My damned mirror has been on the fritz lately, so you may have to step up if it weakens. And don't ask me *why,* because I don't know either." We both knew there were no reports where a gift's power faded. This was entirely new.

Silence stretched as she pondered.

"I hate that you got a gift, even if it doesn't last long," she eventually mumbled. "Such a waste."

"Not when I'm hungry," I retorted, and her face visibly fell.

Her lips parted as she likely prepared to spew something sympathetic or demeaning, but I turned for the steps and headed on. Wren had no idea what true life was like, I reminded myself. If I'd grown up the way she had, perhaps I would be just as clueless. There still might be a chance for her to learn, though. She didn't seem as arrogant as her peers. Aside from her general animosity toward me. I hadn't exactly helped change her opinion.

I took out my mirror and flipped open the lid just as Wren opened the front door, ensuring that anyone inside the lobby would see only her. My shoulders instantly relaxed as a buzz of energy washed over, my power rendering me invisible. My favorite state.

Wren slowed her walk, turning her steps into delicate little whispers across the marble flooring. Her eyes widened as if she were lost, and all the tension clinging to her features from earlier vanished.

"Hello, miss," a young man seated at a dark wooden desk greeted her. Finely groomed, he ran his hand down his pressed suit, even if there wasn't a wrinkle in sight. "How can I be of assistance?"

A choked sobbing noise sounded in the back of her throat. "I . . . I was hoping you could help," she pleaded, a hint of a tremble in her voice. I almost paused to applaud the act. "I was never given a gift, you see, and I—I wanted to find out if that's e-ever happened before."

The young man's expression morphed into one of pity, his stare raking over the mess Wren had fashioned herself into. "Oh, my." He stood just as she let tears slip free. I suspected he had no idea what to do, his hands moving in the air around her body but not aware of how to comfort.

I swallowed my snort and left Wren to her theatrics. How she'd turned on the charm—or rather, the act of damsel in distress—had been inspiring. Who knew she could be so . . .

Much like me.

Devious.

A grin broadened my face as I slipped down the hall and toward the back of the building. Birth years plated in gold hung above each door I passed, and I made my way to the one containing numbers belonging to two decades prior. I suspected the thief would be young. If someone older had wished to steal magic, they'd have done it by now, not wasted power when they could've had it in their prime. That caused me to believe the culprit from the ball had to be somewhere between eighteen and thirty.

Creeping into the marked room, I nearly groaned aloud. The low-lit space with towering racks overflowed with a ridiculous amount of paperwork; rows and rows of boxes filled with thousands of names. This could take forever.

All right, where to start—

Oh.

I frowned, my eye catching a single box on the middle shelf labeled with the years I had in mind.

It's right there.

Cautiously, I approached the box like a live serpent set to strike. Lifting the lid, I skimmed the pages with the pads of my fingers, finding hundreds of documents tabbed neatly for my perusal by year and last name. They were even color-coded, a few red tabs poking up to indicate those who hadn't received gifts.

It seemed . . . too easy. In my line of business, easy meant trouble.

My fingers had only grazed the first sheet when I noticed my hand. It had begun to waver, my fingers going in and out of sight. *Shite.*

It had been strong the last time I used it—well, when I'd been close to Wren.

Close to her.

I cursed. Did she somehow strengthen it? It didn't matter now—I had to get out of here before someone arrested me.

I hadn't planned on stealing the whole box, but desperate times and all that. Besides, Wren could create a commotion so the guard didn't see a floating box exiting the building. I bet they were already getting along, the man too overwhelmed by her tears to notice much else.

Grabbing it with both hands, I hauled it to my hip and pried open the door. The buzzing in my veins hummed like a mosquito; louder when I remained entirely invisible, and softer when my body showed itself. I had maybe a minute.

The door had just shut when two figures stalked down the hall intersecting mine. I held my breath, thankful their focus remained ahead. It was when I glimpsed the backs of their heads that I nearly dropped the damn box.

Hayes. He spoke with some lord I didn't recognize, which wasn't a surprise seeing as I wasn't exactly part of their society.

They paused before an unmarked door lacking a fancy golden plaque or any signage at all. I leaned around the corner, clearly visible by this point.

"I will uphold his end of the deal," the other man muttered, clearly irritated. "We've all had trouble." He ran a hand through his graying hair, looking at anything but his companion. Sweat beaded across his brow.

Hayes sighed heavily. "No excuses," he said, motioning to the open door. The lord glared before they each vanished inside. "We can't afford another error. Not with so much on the damned line. You of all people should know how serious this is. If we don't make it appear seamless, it all goes to hell, and then we'll be hanging on the palace walls. So get your act together, and uphold your end."

What was Hayes doing here of all places?

I stood there holding a stolen box of records, praying that Wren continued to work her magic. I continued to wait until the two bastards eventually exited the room three minutes later. And then I carefully set down the box and, on silent feet, trailed after. Not once did they look over their shoulders, their heavy boots echoing in the hall as they made their way to the back exit—which was odd all by itself and required a very exclusive key I had no hope of replicating.

Either way, their lack of awareness granted me a chance to catch the door to the chamber they'd been talking in before it clicked into place and locked.

A relieved exhale left me when I slipped inside.

A larger space, not unlike the last. Boxes occupied every square inch, some of the papers slipping free of the lids. I didn't have time to waste. Wren would need to charm the pants off the assistant to get me out of here, so I had to be quick in my perusal.

Low-turned gas lamps hung from silver brackets, illuminating the space in an ethereal light. The air itself smelled different from in the other space, more like peppermint and some other scent I couldn't name. Colder, too, I thought, rubbing my hands to keep the chill at bay.

Grabbing the closest box, I flipped the lid and peered inside. The papers were organized by names and dates, though these weren't dated too far back. Pinching a sheet, I slid it out and held it to the light as a prickling feeling slithered down my spine.

Matilda Canmore.

I knew that name from somewhere, didn't I?

I stared at her name, the odd prickling growing worse the longer I looked.

Wait—

My thumb and forefinger gripped the page so hard I feared I'd ruin it. Matilda Canmore. The laundry worker who had been missing for months now. Clipped to the page was a black-and-white photo. Her eyes shut, her face pale.

Almost as if she were dead.

My breathing picked up as I scanned the page, my hands slick with sweat.

Matilda Canmore

Age: 21

Occupation: Laundry worker

Death Date: January 23

Notes: Matilda had little to no effect, and was therefore replaced by another. She lasted three minutes before succumbing to death. Barely anything of importance extracted.

A bright light blinded me seconds before an image flashed before my eyes. I bit my tongue at the assault, even as the light softened, allowing me to see a woman I'd never met. Her face contorted with agony, her shouts mumbled pleas. Fuck, her screams rang in my ears, so loudly, I feared I'd burst an eardrum.

I managed to open my eyes.

The cold gray room greeted me; the woman and her shouts absent.

Even the ringing in my ears had faded.

Whatever I'd just experienced had to be a result of lack of sleep or the sheer fact that I had snuck into this building and could be arrested at any moment. That, and I stared at a dead woman.

Still, my hands shook. My vision blurred. I didn't understand what I read. What Matilda had to do with Cameron Hayes's interest in this room. No idea what the notes meant, or why they'd taken the time to record and photograph her.

I took another page.

> Henry Windsor
>
> Age: 24
>
> Occupation: Butcher's assistant
>
> Death Date: February 10
>
> Notes: Extremely agitated individual. Needed to be sedated. Successful procedure—three years divided.
>
> Died five minutes after extraction.

Just as a man's blond head and young face took form behind my eyes, a door slammed in the hall, making me jump. Sweat trickled down my brow, a droplet landing on the closed eyes of Henry, his body rigid and lifeless.

Dead.

He was dead.

I glanced up. If this box matched the others—filled with missing people from the Void . . .

Voices mingled together and a hoarse laugh filtered down the hallway. I ground my teeth and tucked the two pages behind the back of my shirt and into my waistband. Since my mirror ceased working, I was extra careful peeking out into the corridor once the noise faded. No one lingered.

Even as I ran the same way I'd come, I felt the sudden urge to return to that horrid room. To study every single photograph and read the cruel "notes" posted at the bottom of the page. A single page worth an entire life.

Three years, Henry's file had read. *Successful procedure.*

What the fuck were they doing to those people?

I'd returned to the Gifts section, only to discover my box missing. Some poor worker likely placed it back inside, safe and sound. I didn't have time to grab it again. Not with Wren still out there.

If she hadn't abandoned me yet.

Then laughter echoed, addictive and cheery, from beyond the double doors leading to the lobby, and I knew she hadn't. A foreign wave of relief cooled my insides. I'd taken longer than expected, yet Wren had made do, sticking to her promise.

I leaned against the door and peeked through a small gap. A pleasant buzz shot through me, and I looked down, finding my hands gradually vanishing from sight. The invisibility trailed up my arms and continued, until eventually, my body disappeared.

Maybe I'd been right about the closeness to her being connected to my mirror—which would prove to be an utter pain in the ass.

Nevertheless, she stayed, doing her best to seduce the sweating front desk attendant, his cheeks rosy with shyness. She leaned toward him, her hand on his chest as she laughed at something he must've said. It couldn't have been *that* funny, but she acted like it had been hilarious.

Invisible to everyone, including her, I was struck in the gut when she shifted her chin ever so slightly, and for just an instant, it felt like our eyes met, her stare directly locking onto mine as if drawn to me. She shook her head and returned to the man, drawing his focus to the far end of the lobby, where water and tea were laid out on an elegant mahogany console.

Of course, he busied himself pouring her a cup of tea, and she angled her body so he wouldn't see me should I reappear.

Somehow, she'd sensed me.

When I pushed on the front doors, eliciting a creak, Wren giggled, masking the sound and allowing me my escape.

Fresh air blasted across my damp face, the chill like a slap. I debated bolting and making a run for the Void without telling her what I'd seen. She might go running back to her father and tell him everything. She might turn me in.

But . . . fuck me. My gut wasn't screaming at me to run. It didn't beg me to leave her without a trace. Something deep, *deep* down told me she wasn't like her parents.

Wren was rare. And maybe rare was exactly what I needed in order to get to the truth.

I'd trust my instincts; instincts that had more to do with a *feeling.* Because back in that alleyway, her scent had jogged an old, nearly forgotten memory, the threads unraveling until I put all the pieces together.

The fact remained, no matter if I told Wren or not—while I'd failed to get the names I needed, I uncovered something else.

Something people had been killed over.

Something *I* might be killed over.

Chapter Fifteen

Wren

It is said that the Fates are sisters, though they have never confirmed this. All they have confirmed is that they were born together and if the time comes, they will leave this realm together.

—*Origin of the Fates*, Chapter Three

If I'd been made to flirt with the attendant for one more minute I would've lost my mind.

Thank the Fates Damien arrived at the doors when he did. The attendant had brought up the titillating subject of which of Andalay's finest restaurants were the best, and I suspected he was working his way to asking if I'd like to join him for a meal.

Which might've been awkward, as *No* would have been my answer.

As he talked, icy shivers of awareness raced down my back. It had been hair-raising knowing Damien was there, standing just out of sight, invisible. Those chills spread from my shoulders to the tips of my fingers, the fine hair on my arms raised. It might have been mere chance that I glanced over at the doors when I did, sensing a presence. Sensing him. His weight. It sounded silly even thinking about it, trying to explain how I felt his spirit surround me like a shawl, my pulse hammering as it often did when he stood feet away.

From the corner of my eye, the double doors opened a smidge, just enough for a body to slip through before they closed. Damien and the burden of his spirit vanished, leaving me bereft. I prayed he'd gotten whatever he sought in the back rooms.

After making an excuse about the time and missing an appointment at the modiste with my sister, I scurried away, leaving the attendant with two cups of steaming tea. I felt guilty for leading him on and abandoning him. Fates, I hadn't even remembered his name, but there were bigger things at hand.

Pushing the doors open, I smiled as the crisp breeze grazed my cheeks, the colder air welcome after being cooped up in the stuffy lobby. Practically skipping down the steps in my haste to catch up to the thief, I avoided the stares of some serious-looking businessmen grumbling about taxes. Eyes set on the alley we'd found refuge in before, I lowered my chin and shot across the street, doing my best *not* to recall how Damien had touched me so tenderly. Where I *let* him touch me.

No. It was a means to an end. To save yourself from being recognized.

I nodded to myself like a fool, yet the notion brought me a semblance of comfort. Damien was appealing because he didn't speak to me like any gentleman I'd met. It was the newness of it all, meeting someone who didn't play a game to win my favor—and in turn, my father's.

A hand snagged my forearm and spun me around. I startled before taking in Damien's smirking face, his body covered in shadows. It made his expression all the more sinister.

"You just never learn," I griped, eyeing my wrist before pulling away. "I hate surprises." I had ever since Callie started planning my birthdays, going to extremes to catch me off guard. Callie would smile her Cheshire cat grin and force me to socialize with the ladies she'd gathered. I didn't mind the sweet cakes, however. Those, she could continue to provide.

"Not my fault you're so easily startled." Damien shrugged, but I noted that while he smiled, his eyes were dull. Less intense, that playful spark gone.

"I'm not easily startled, you were just lurking in the shadows like a wraith."

"*Lurking?*" He scoffed at the word. "I don't lurk. I'm just more aware of my surroundings and would prefer not to be seen."

I didn't say he was right. That *I* should be more aware as well. I'd die on a metaphorical sword before I allowed him to wrench the words *You're right* from my lips.

I could murder him later. Besides, there were too many witnesses.

"Agree to disagree," I said, hurrying to ask, "What did you find?" I rubbed at my exposed skin, the air growing bitter. "Flirting with that attendant took considerable effort. He enjoys speaking about his *immense* appreciation for model ships." I recalled my straining smile as I'd listened to him go into *extensive* detail about his hobby.

"Oof. Sounds like a charmer," Damien said, scanning the busy street. "But you'll have to be a little patient, sunshine. I'll show you my finds somewhere safe." He gnawed at his cheek as if considering, his stare piercing me like a blade. Seconds ticked by before he said, "We'll go to my place. No one will bother us there." My muscles locked up at the mention of his place—wherever that was. Alone. With him. Unaware of my apprehension, he continued. "I bet any person who sees us is wondering what Cameron Hayes's daughter is doing talking to me in some dank alley, and attention is the last thing we need. Make your decision."

He was right. Still, the idea of going back to his room . . .

You've got your weapon. You've got your wits. I'd shown him in the Lovetts' garden that I wasn't one to be trifled with. I could handle this trivial detour.

"Fine," I relented. "Lead the way."

Damien held none of the airs of a gentleman. He didn't lift an elbow to escort me or place his hand on the small of my back to guide me through the congested areas. I faced his back, his muscular build moving with ease through the throngs of people going about their day. To anyone else, we might not appear to be together at all. Which worked well in our favor, whether or not his lack of concern secretly chafed.

Or you're upset because he effortlessly brushed you aside after he touched you. He had no idea that the moment had been foreign to me; he'd been the first to touch me in that way. Ever.

The first to make me *feel* things I hadn't before—not that I *wanted* to feel anything at all with anyone. It was a bonus that he was a criminal.

Just my luck.

I bit the inside of my cheek, dispelling the notions of *feelings* and other ridiculous things from my brain immediately. I was Wren Hayes, and once I got my magic, I'd leave this place. I'd explore the continent. Go to the west and see the palace and the king and queen. I would live life the way *I* desired, and I planned on remedying years of repression. Even if I had to do so by running away from my family.

Life was too short to stay in one place.

Before long, the hordes of people dispersed, the cobblestones beneath my shoes growing worn. We stood at the invisible line separating the northern and southern sides, the plumes of gray smoke akin to storm clouds warning others not to pass.

Damien slowed his walk, adopting a casual gait, the Void stretching on either side like an open mouth swallowing him. My boot scraped the back of his heel, his body acting as a human shield. He shot me a look over his shoulder but continued onward, the muscles in his neck stiff.

"Stay close to me," Damien whispered into the wind. He sounded almost . . . worried.

I shivered, pulling my cloak tighter against me. Keeping my focus on Damien and his ominous words, I didn't argue with him, not when I could practically feel the heat of eyes on me. People could spot an outsider easily, and my pulse thudded in my throat.

A shrill whistle sounded, and without thought, I lifted my head to look.

I shouldn't have.

"Whatcha doin' over on this side of the city?" a man cooed, his hooded eyes narrowed on me. "Not that I mind." He laughed, elbowing his three mates. He wore the garb of a dockworker and grasped a half-empty bottle of what I assumed to be liquor.

"Maybe she's looking for some trouble," a second one added, stepping forward, his towering height and strapping physique causing my insides to knot up. My grip on my cloak had turned my knuckles white.

The way his stare roamed the parts of my body not covered by the cloak sent alarm bells ringing in my head. I immediately stepped closer to Damien, my body brushing his back. I resisted grasping his arm.

Damien slowed to a stop as they continued whistling and shouting lewd terms and seedy promises that reeked of threat.

A chill blasted through the air when Damien turned his head, focusing his attention on the men. All I could see was his profile, but his features darkened into something I didn't recognize, something dangerous. This time, I *did* grab his arm.

"The only *trouble* she's looking for is me," Damien announced loudly, confidently, scanning the group. His voice held notes of warning, and I leaned into him farther, my body taut enough to snap. "I'd suggest you remember that."

I swallowed thickly at his declaration, at the way his words had become weapons all by themselves. So sharp. Cutting.

The leader of the group peered more closely at him before a

look of recognition softened his cruel lips. He held up his hands in a placating manner. "Oh, it's *you*!" He grinned. "Sorry, Ghost. Didn't realize she was your girl."

Your girl.

Absolutely not. But I wasn't about to correct him.

Damien nodded stiffly in reply. Tugging me against his solid chest, he slung an arm around my waist. His fingers dug into my dress, showing the nerves he tried to disguise with his scowl.

"Ghost?" I whispered, but he just rolled his eyes, continuing our walk. I stumbled a few times, my footing unsteady after the encounter. Damien simply paused until I regained my balance, surprisingly patient.

That hand. It burned through the flimsy fabric, his long, lean fingers pressing into me whenever a lecherous gaze descended upon me. We were as close as we'd been in the alley, though his hold on me remained unyielding, like he feared I'd drift away should he loosen his grip.

I couldn't see Damien's face, not unless I chose to turn and watch him—which I didn't—but whatever the offenders saw had them quickly averting their eyes. As much as I hated to admit it, the act made me feel safe . . . and another word I wouldn't name.

That was when it hit me—

People *respected* Damien.

He might not be as robust or as muscled as some of the men we passed, nor was he as rugged, but they looked at him like he belonged. A man with some sway here.

"Almost there," Damien rasped in my ear, his voice deep.

The low growl of his words suggested his mood continued to be cross.

I frowned, too overstimulated by his hand, the crowd, and my new surroundings to understand why he spoke so harshly even after we avoided a confrontation. Perhaps he didn't want his "investment" to get hurt.

My lips parted when we rounded a slight corner and found ourselves right outside the tavern I'd visited on my first trip here. The Broken Wing Tavern.

"Why are we going in here?" I asked as he held open the door for me. When I paused, he made a hurried hand motion, gesturing me inside. He didn't answer in the rowdy tavern until we reached a narrow hall at the opposite end of the bar. A rope blocked access with a sign reading NO ENTRY.

Damien stepped over the rope and surprisingly helped me over as well, his fingers wrapped around my hand like a vise. Once I'd landed on my feet, that hand of his returned to my waist, though there was no one here to witness us.

I was too distracted to care—at the very end of the hall lay a stairwell that could've been born of my worst nightmares. No gas lamps bracketed the walls, and the shadows clung to every inch of the claustrophobic space.

"I live upstairs," he said. His fingers roamed lower, now resting above my hip. An unexpected thrill shot through me. The first word that came to mind was *forbidden*. The second word I didn't wish to ruminate over.

"Scared of the dark, sunshine?" Damien teased, giving my hip a squeeze. I wondered if he goaded me on purpose, to thrust me from my cage of nerves.

Heat seared within, and I choked on air like a fool. "Um, no," I managed. "I'm just not a fan of being led up a creepy staircase above a bar with a man who is a known criminal."

Now I turned to him and smiled sweetly, trying to regain the upper hand and maintain a façade of nonchalance as his hand fell. Fates, I hoped it worked.

Damien rolled his eyes and put his palm on the small of my back, gently ushering me forward. "Says the girl who was straddling said criminal not too long ago." I opened my mouth to protest, but he cut me off. "Oh, and drinking like a fish at the very same establishment with another man." We began the climb and he faked a gasp. "Such a scandal would ensue should anyone find out."

I must've come to my damned senses, because I elbowed him in the side, eliciting an *oof.* He stumbled, his hand leaving my back. I should've done that ages ago.

"You know you have a very punchable face," I snipped, recognizing a threat when I heard one. "Has anyone ever told you that?"

"Quite often," he replied, not missing a beat.

Ruby had admitted her urge to smack him. I wondered where she was. Another person on my side would settle my nerves.

Damien's steps were sure and steady as he climbed, and I gritted my teeth, forced to follow his lead. At the landing he spun around, blocking me on the final step and nearly sending me tumbling backward and to my death.

I made a low sound in my throat before grabbing onto the wall for support.

"I never bring anyone here," he admitted, all playfulness gone. "Not that I imagine you will, but I'd appreciate it if you kept its location to yourself."

I nearly laughed. "Shame. I'd hoped to tell the ladies at tea all about my tryst with the mysterious thief, and how we were *alone* in his room. Now whatever will we discuss?"

His eyes narrowed, but he moved aside so I could join him.

"You'll probably turn to the exhilarating topic of ribbons or nobles you fancy," he mused. "Or which new dresses you want commissioned." An indignant scoff left his lips. "I bet the dress you're wearing now costs more than four months' rent."

I gazed down at myself, thinking of the simple garment beneath my cloak. Indeed, it was produced of fine material, commissioned for when I was supposed to appear "modest," as Father put it. I considered it plain, but I never reflected upon how expensive it had been. How that money I carelessly tossed over might feed or house a family for weeks. Months, as Damien claimed.

My lips didn't open to form a clever retort. There was none.

Damien didn't linger long after delivering his cutting, yet true, remark. He marched down a narrow hall and to the last door on the right. Slipping a hand beneath the collar of his shirt, he yanked off a key tied around his neck and unlocked his door.

I strayed, mainly because I felt rotten for being inconsiderate. I hadn't meant to sound so indifferent. Ignorant, really. But . . . I was.

"You coming?" he barked, motioning to the open room with his chin.

Swallowing the burgeoning guilt, I strode down the remaining stretch of hallway and over his threshold.

All assumptions vanished at the sight of his home.

A thin mattress lay upon the rotting hardwood floors beside a cracked window, a chipped dresser with three drawers in reach of the bed. The walls, which might've been white once, now were the shade of fresh mold. The walls themselves didn't hold portraits or mirrors or anything else. Except . . .

I strode deeper into the small space, the floorboards creaking beneath my shoes. I heard a small hiss from Damien when one of the boards shifted.

A hand enclosed my arm as he led me closer to the window, to his bed. "It's not what you're used to, I'm sure," he said, trying to mock but failing to hide how his voice cracked.

I looked around with care, noticing a single tacked-up postcard hanging adjacent to the window. The western coast. A place consisting of farms and endless emerald fields. The realm where the king and queen lived, though they were merely foot soldiers to the Fates. The photograph showed a rustic barn beside a two-story home, cows and sheep grazing in the yard. Stark red letters rolled over the paper: *Welcome to Hazel Glen!*

Did Damien originally hail from there?

I went to inspect it further, but Damien put a hand out before me.

"It's just a postcard, sunshine. Not a clue about my mysterious past, if that's what you're thinking."

I found his clouded eyes, his stare somewhat sheepish. "Then why is it hanging up?" I asked delicately, my instincts telling me it wasn't anything to tease him about.

"Just a dream is all," he replied with a sigh. "Once I get enough coin, I'm out of here. Out to the west where I can purchase my own farm. A place all my own where the air doesn't reek of gunpowder or smoke."

I supposed possibilities were always more alluring than reality—when something is intangible, we don't have the chance yet to break it. This dream of his was his spark of hope, what kept him going. Living each day to fight for freedom. It held much more significance than he let on.

Knowing Damien would clam up if I pushed too hard, I eased into the conversation while slipping free of my cloak and draping it across the mattress. "A farm? I didn't peg you as a farmer. Spending all day covered in the earth, living a simple life."

He shrugged a shoulder before plopping down on the bed, lying on his back. "It's decent money, and I'd get to live alone. No one to pester me"—he shot me a look as if I were the cause of all said pestering—"and it would be beautiful. Built with my own hands."

Easing closer, I joined him on the bed, stiffly lowering myself. With care, and maintaining an appropriate distance, I awkwardly shifted until I lay beside him, my hair fanning across his mattress. I inhaled, taking in hints of leather and spice.

Damien wasn't stealing to purchase material objects. Ironically, he stole to live a criminal-free life. I couldn't wrap my head around it. Even picturing him out in the fields with his tanned skin, worn boots, and soil-streaked trousers felt out of place. Not that I minded . . . Not that imagining him basking in the sunlight and fresh breeze caused my insides to flip.

"Shocked you so much that you're speechless?" He huffed next to me. "I might have to try that again sometime." But his tone was playful, and I turned my head, surprised to see that his face hovered inches away.

"Very funny." I poked at his chest. "But I think it's an admirable dream. I was just taken off guard is all. You don't tend to open up much," I added with a forced lilt. Damien kept his cards close to his chest.

He rolled his head back and stared at the ceiling. "Opening up leads to questions, and questions lead to trouble. Or people who will exploit you. Once they have something of value to hold over you, they won't waste a second to use it."

Such a miserable way to look at things.

"I'm glad you told me," I whispered, shocked by how much I meant it. My head grew fuzzy, a peculiar sense of accomplishment warming my insides.

He continued to stare at the ceiling. "You have no one to tell," he replied easily, though it sounded like a lie, his voice soft and uncertain. It wasn't meant to be cruel, just a fact.

"True. But even if I did, I never would." Regardless of my feelings for Damien and his . . . profession, I would never use his words against him, especially because that dream of his seemed to be the one thing he deemed worthy enough to pin on his wall. A silent hope. I nudged him in his arm and shot him a meaningful look, making certain he glimpsed the sincerity in my eyes. "I hope you achieve it one day, Damien. We all deserve the chance at finding our peace."

I didn't know him as well as I thought. Yes, he'd taken Everett's watch and was a general pain, but I hadn't considered what his dreams might be, or how he ended up as a thief, alone and without a family. If he had one, surely there would've been mention of them. I kept my mouth shut, not bringing up that topic no matter how much I wanted to.

The thick column of his neck bobbed. "Same, sunshine." He rolled his eyes. "Even Ruby doesn't know. She'd laugh her arse off if she did. *Me,* a farmer." Damien sighed, rubbing a hand over his face as if embarrassed. I swore I glimpsed a hint of red on his cheeks.

"I like her," I said decidedly. "Maybe you should tell her. You seem to be quite close."

Being alone, repressing your true self as he did . . . my heart twinged with sympathy. I couldn't help it.

"Don't even get me started," Damien smirked, and I smiled in return, taken aback by how genuine he looked. "I will never properly introduce the two of you. I may be a thief, but I'm no fool. You'd gang up on me in a heartbeat."

While Ruby aided Damien in general depravity, it would be nice to have someone else to team up with me when Damien and his ego got in the way of common sense. I grinned just as Damien shot me a knowing look.

"See?" He chuckled, a lightness I'd not seen illuminating his features. "You and her would send me to an early grave."

"Scared?" I teased.

"Of course I am." The other corner of his lip lifted, turning his smirk into a full grin. Fates, when he did that . . . my heart skipped a few beats. "Two powerful women sicced on little old me? Anyone would be afraid. *And* you have a weapon."

"A letter opener!" I shoved at his chest, and a deep noise of discomfort left him.

"And apparently a decent arm." He rubbed at his side, making a show of it. "Where did you learn that? Etiquette lessons?"

"All I learned from those were which fork I shouldn't stab someone with during the salad course."

His eyes gleamed with mischief, and I felt my own smile broaden.

"You and household items make a dangerous combination. Almost admirable."

"One must be prepared," I said, attempting to tease back, but it came out more somber than I'd planned.

His lips twitched slightly, losing some of the joy. "I imagine the lords you deal with aren't exactly humble. Must think they're owed whatever they like."

I swallowed thickly. He was right—they acted as if ladies were the entertainment and we should keep our mouths shut and accept their actions, however unwelcome.

As if he sensed my distress, Damien lifted his hand, like he planned to reach for me, maybe hold my hand in his, but at the last moment, he let it drop. "I hope you never had to go through that," he murmured, gaze narrowing. He seemed protective then, the concern in his voice like a soothing balm to my ears.

"We all have our troubles," I said instead. The truth was, I *had* encountered men who'd ignored proper behavior. Who had placed their hands on me when no one was looking. It was the reason I carried my letter opener.

Silence filled the room, heavy and tense. Damien looked away, back to the ceiling, an unreadable expression twisting his face. Deep in thought, he didn't notice as I observed the steady rise and fall of his chest, how while he appeared at peace, the arms crossed behind his head tensed.

Time passed, and I delighted when the muscles in his arms relaxed, his lashes fluttering. The thief was surprisingly at ease with me. In his bed. His room. His private space.

Why that thought made me forget all his earlier teasing was a mystery. Or maybe it wasn't at all.

When his eyes shut entirely, his breathing too close to sleep, I tapped his chin. "No time to fall asleep," I said quietly. "You haven't told me what you found that had us rushing here in such a hurry."

Damien craned his neck, his eyes opening to greet me. For a moment I was startled by how handsome he was, devoid of a scowl. His face free of creases and exasperated lines. His eyes soft. I brushed my hair behind my ear, my throat tightening as I looked just above those haunting eyes of his.

"Well?" I pressed.

He sighed. "It's not good."

"I suspected that."

"No." He groaned as he sat up, wiping the exhaustion from his eyes. I followed suit, my back ramrod straight. Untucking his shirt, he yanked out two pieces of paper shoved into the back of his trousers. With his chin lowered, he handed them over. "Look for yourself."

I scanned the first page, taking in the stark black-and-white photograph and the odd notes. It was short and confusing, and I had no idea what it meant . . . other than something was very wrong.

"The missing people from the Void," he supplied. "Both of these people have been missing for months, and there's an *entire room* with more papers like these. I always assumed people just got sick of the place and left, but . . ."

"There's another reason," I finished, inspecting the papers in a new light.

"Your father was there." I flinched. "And some lord I didn't recognize," Damien cautioned. "They went into that room, which is why I followed. I'd been searching the records of magical gifts given to the northerners when I got sidetracked."

A low droning sounded in my ears.

"My father?"

My own father had been found in a room filled with these horrid papers. Bile rose as my stomach churned, the small room suddenly too small, too claustrophobic. The walls closed in, the image of my father hovering before my mind like a taunt.

All his secrets.

All his power.

And he was involved. Involved with whatever had killed these people. Or, at least, he was aware of it.

I hadn't known about the missing people in the Void, but now that I did, and with these documents in my hand . . .

I couldn't help but picture my father as he once was. Holding me in his lap as he read the Sunday paper. Teaching me to hunt, scooping me onto his shoulders when I killed my first duck. Running through the house, chasing after me and Callie, his booming voice making us giggle.

How could *that* man have changed so drastically?

I was in shock. No, denial.

Not that I didn't believe Damien, but to accept that my father was involved sickened me to the point that I held my stomach, nausea threatening to send me hurtling across the mattress to retch.

"If these are being recorded, then someone from the Registry of Magical Gifts is required to be there to witness it," I mused aloud, dazed. "And based on these recordings and photos, why do I get the feeling these poor souls didn't leave Andalay of their own accord?"

It was a silly thought. Obviously they hadn't left of their own accord.

I anxiously scratched at my nose, willing away the shivers that wracked my spine. My father's being complicit in these crimes twisted my world. Flipped it upside down in a way I didn't know how to process.

His late-night meetings. All the secrecy around his job. His sour mood.

Cameron Hayes was not known as a warm man, but he looked like a shadow of his former self. An imposter wearing the skin of a man I had loved. Maybe that person was gone forever. Maybe I just grasped at straws, hoping against all hope to be wrong. Who in their right mind would wish for their parent to be a villain?

"That's why I took the papers. As proof." Damien held out his hand, and I placed them in his palm. "People don't care much when we go missing," he added, shyly peeking up at me.

He'd just told me a perilous secret that I could use to hurt him. Have my *father* use to hurt him.

He trusted me.

I cleared my throat, swallowing my emotions. Not an easy feat.

"Which would make the southern people perfect for what? Experiments?" I wondered aloud, silently aghast to think it might be true. "Were they being tested with something classified, and that's why the experimenters recorded the time they lasted until death? This is serious, Damien." Much bigger than my gift. Much bigger than whatever someone stole from *him* at the ball. My world tilted again; pictures of those two dead faces hovering in my mind's eye like ghosts.

I felt like I was on the verge of fainting, black spots clouding the edges of my vision.

Damien's arms grabbed my shoulders. "Easy there, sunshine," he whispered, carefully turning me to face him. "We'll figure it out." His brows pinched together like he couldn't believe what he'd offered. It wasn't what we originally agreed upon, and he'd just promised his commitment to solve this. With me.

"These are your people. *My* people too, really. Aurilia shouldn't be turning its back like it does." I ran my fingers through my hair and tugged at the roots. "And I'm part of the problem. My own flesh and blood could be doing this. Helping *kill* people." Fates, I could hardly get that word out. It tasted sour, and more bile rose. I cradled my head in my palms, my elbows propped on my knees. I dug the sharp points into the flesh, the slight pain grounding me. "People need to know. There are some from society who'd care, who could help. We just need to show them."

No matter if it ruined my family in the process.

Damien hummed deep in his throat. "I hate to say this, but they really just wouldn't care."

I rose. "They have to! These are people our age! Or damn well near to it. Why wouldn't they care if people are being *abducted* and having Fates know what done to them? Hell, *I* care. There have to be more. Maybe the younger nobles who aren't under their parents' thumbs."

My stomach roiled again, and I feared I'd end up retching all over Damien's bed. It was a fifty-fifty chance at this point.

Damien inspected me, his stare a mixture of confusion and a hint of irritation. "You really do live in a bubble, don't you?" he asked, and it felt like a punch to the gut. "I keep forgetting who you really are, and that's on me." He abruptly stood. My mouth fell open as he ventured to the window, avoiding me.

"I—"

My words caught in my throat. His accusation had been correct. I hadn't known about any of this. But . . .

"I'm sorry," I said, so softly it surprised me when he canted his head my way. "There's nothing I can say but that I'm sorry for my ignorance, for ignoring things right in front of me. But I plan on doing better. I *will* do better." Yes. I'd enlist Callie's help once I got home, and ask if she could provide me with any information. From there, I'd go to Father himself. I might be some naïve noble who'd lived in a luxurious bubble, hidden from the atrocities of the world, but the bubble had just burst. Now I couldn't ignore the outside world. If I did, I'd be just as horrid as the people who actively sought to use those without gifts to their advantage.

I didn't wish to be a person devoid of basic humanity. That was no life. Not one worth living, anyway.

"You're sorry?" Damien repeated, stepping away from the window and to the bed. He hovered over me, a looming giant. "Why?"

It was only a question, but a heaviness burdened each single word.

I tilted my chin, desperately wanting him to understand. "I'm sorry because I allowed myself to be blind when I had the choice to do otherwise. I'm sorry for being a part of a society that uses people when they're desperate. That forces them to remain desperate. Afraid. Hungry." I thought of the too-thin people of the south. The children running in the streets, begging for coin. They hadn't put themselves in that position. The politicians and leaders of the north had made it impossible for them to support themselves properly. They enjoyed the near-free labor too much. It padded their own pockets.

It provided *me* with a home. Gowns. A full dinner table.

And you never wanted to question it.

I hadn't. Fuck me, I hadn't. Not until those faces became real.

I supposed seeing them in black and white, knowing their *names,* and reading their last moments written on paper like an afterthought, finally pushed me over the edge. How could I ignore Elizabeth and Henry? Both young and hopeful and killed without remorse? At home, I'd told myself the south was just where the workers lived. I told myself they were fine. They weren't slowly dying from hunger. I told myself so many things so I didn't have to face reality.

The fire sparked inside my chest. I wasn't ignorant enough to assume that I alone could help. I needed a horde of witnesses. Of people from the south and north. Lords and ladies themselves, to stand up to whoever preyed on the innocent. I just had to figure out the identity of our foe.

Damien hadn't budged an inch, his heavy gaze like fire on my skin. I shrank in on myself. The last thing I desired was for him to think I apologized out of pity. I wanted him to understand that I didn't agree with the injustices that occurred.

I stood, shifting around his body, trying to get him to look at me.

I'd struck a chord inside him, and I feared he would continue to see me as a pompous highborn until I showed him I cared. And I did care. My body blazed with anger, burning my skin and undoubtedly turning it a shade of red.

I realized that only action mattered. Talk was easy; it didn't take anything from you.

We'd solve both mysteries while adhering to the original plan. I might not survive it all, but I'd die inside if I didn't *try.*

Clearing my throat, I said, "There's a ball this Friday night. I'll bet the person you're looking for—that we *both* may be looking for—could be attending." It would be too simple if the thieves were one and the same, but a girl could hope. "Please meet me in two days at the tailor. I'll cover the cost of your suit and you'll blend right in. People won't ask much if you tell them a simple backstory." I already had one planned out, the gears in my head spinning.

Silence reigned, making my skin itchy. I ached for him to turn around. To grunt. To speak. To do something.

Finally, "I'll be there," he muttered, giving me his back.

I nodded, even if he couldn't see. "It's the one at the intersection of Serende and Whisperwood Drive."

He nodded.

That was all I received before opening his door and slipping out into the hall.

I'd opened up some box I shouldn't have, and I feared I'd ruined our partnership. Which was tenuous at best.

Now I wasn't even sure he planned on coming at all.

Chapter Sixteen

Damien

I checked the floorboard after she left.

Wren had been close to shifting it out of place, her slightly heeled shoe pressing into just the right spot. Panic had surged, and I'd grabbed her arm and moved her closer to my damned bed before she could realize what she inadvertently stood upon.

Sure, it was where I kept all my coins when I left the Void, but there were also some other trinkets I hadn't been able to part with over the years; a—now empty—wallet from a high-ranking official I loathed, a black gemstone that had been found beside me when I'd been left at the orphanage, and a single yellow ribbon.

I moved aside the board, careful when I reached inside. The ribbon was silk and smelled like citrus, the color still so bright after all these years. It'd also been my first theft.

I'd been eight, all hands and no subtlety, but my belly rumbled from the lack of food, and I knew the orphanage wouldn't feed us that night. So I snuck into the northern side of town, desperate and half delirious.

Everyone had been dressed finely, out to worship the Fate, Day. It had been so crowded, I blended in, barely anyone peering down at a boy eyeing the cart selling fresh pastries. The owner wasn't looking, his attention on his patrons, and I'd been prepared to make my move. But just before I snagged a chocolate tart, a lilting voice interrupted.

"Hungry?"

I'd turned around, facing a young girl with her blond hair braided down her back. She wore a ridiculous hat that covered most of her upper face, but her smile had been warm, if shy.

I didn't take charity, and I immediately frowned, ready to bolt, but the audacious girl snagged my hand in hers like she'd done it thousands of times and led me to the cart, fumbling behind her. I blamed my lack of strength on the dizziness.

"Two chocolate tarts, please," she said to the baker, offering two copper coins. He grinned down at her and then shifted my way, that smile morphing into a frown. When he passed her the treats, the girl led me from the crowd and I was helpless but to follow, the smell of that delicious pastry overriding good sense.

"Here." She handed me the wrapped pastry once we reached a less bustling part of the celebration. "It's my favorite too."

I snatched the pastry as if she'd take it back. I think I ate it right in front of her in seconds, not ashamed of my haste. It was the best thing I'd ever tasted.

She ate slowly, watching me the entire time from beneath the rim of her woven hat, which was decorated with an abundance of pink and yellow ribbons tied into bows. Just as I finished, prepared to take off without a thank-you to the girl, a gust of wind stole her hat, sending it soaring into the air and across the street. Without hesitation, I shot off after it, sidestepping the baker's patrons and their nasty looks.

When I picked up the delicate thing, covered in stunning adornments and reeking of wealth, my hands twitched. The girl had given me a smile and a pastry. Two things that would make me grin for weeks—not that I showed my joy in public.

With nimble fingers, I snagged one of the yellow ribbons and tugged, breaking the knot tying it in place. I shoved it in my pocket before returning to her, the girl standing in the same place, trusting I'd come back.

My heart had pounded loudly and my nerves were so frayed that I barely glanced at her as she took the wayward hat in her hands. I'd never stolen before, even something small, and guilt ate away at my insides.

"Thank you," she said. "Mother would've killed me if I lost this."

By the time I glanced up, the hat shielded her eyes again. I wished I'd seen all of her.

I grunted in reply, not trusting my voice. I had to run, get out of there before they *threw* me back into the Void. I'd caught too many looks of suspicion. In fact, a broad-shouldered man wearing the nicest tweed suit, and a woman with long blond hair were headed our way. The girl seemed to sense them and turned, shouting and waving. I knew they were her parents, and by the way the man glared at me, he didn't wish for his precious daughter to speak to someone like me.

With her back turned, I ran, shoving through the people mindlessly celebrating and indulging in sweets, not stopping until I made it back to the Void.

It was only today, when I'd seen that yellow ribbon in her hair, that the pieces of memory came back into focus. The girl had smelled like fresh citrus and notes of vanilla.

The same notes I'd detected on Wren when I'd gotten close to her in the alleyway.

Folding the ribbon, I placed it back inside the empty space and tugged the board over my treasures.

Without a doubt, I knew Wren had been that girl who'd shown me kindness.

And she'd also been my first theft.

Apparently, I hadn't stopped taking from her.

"Let me get this straight." Ruby sat beside me at Cap's bar, swishing ale in her glass as she appraised me. "You and the ward princess went on some covert mission to break into the Registry of Magical Gifts, *and* you found a secret room full of records about the missing people from the Void?"

"Yes," I grumbled, snagging my whiskey glass and taking a generous sip. It *was* after twelve.

"And she came with you?"

I frowned. "Yes. I thought we covered that. I originally planned to get information on the high-society members without gifts. She was going to pick through suspects afterward." If anyone would know of these upper-class frauds, it would be her.

Ruby cocked a black brow. "Then you brought her *here.* To the Void. To your *room.*" It wasn't a question.

Hell, even Ruby had never been inside my private space. The small room wasn't much to look at, and the only thing worthy of hanging didn't cost anything—that stupid postcard I'd found at the orphanage as a child. It was just a place to sleep.

Liar.

In all my years, I'd never permitted anyone to enter. Never allowed anyone to see where I rested my head and lowered my guard. My safe place, however barren, belonged to me.

Now it smelled like citrus and vanilla.

Like her.

Ruby rolled her eyes and placed her glass on the bar. Facing me, she said, "Damien. I know you—well, as much as you let anyone know you—and you look miserable. And I don't think it's because of the documents you found. *That* information you shared immediately. I had to practically threaten you to squeeze out Wren's assistance." She placed a hand on my shoulder. I repressed the desire to fling it off. It was a comforting gesture, something most people would embrace, yet I loathed being touched, always had. But again, there had been one exception . . . "I just don't get why you didn't go yourself and then show her the findings," Ruby continued, unaware of my roaming thoughts. That damned ribbon hidden beneath my floorboard tugged at me, and I had the idiotic urge to take it out again today before meeting my friend.

It didn't change anything.

"I brought her as a distraction in case anything went wrong," I said, and lucky for me, she'd been quite the distraction. Maybe *too* much, judging by how the attendant had trailed after her like a lost pup. The grip on my glass tightened.

"But you have a gift—"

I silenced her with a finger to her lips. "Discretion isn't your strong suit." She'd been about to shout for all the Void to hear that I had magic. I'd be a dead man walking.

But Ruby wasn't familiar with my mirror's failures of late. How it seemed to work only in Wren's presence. I wouldn't open up and reveal that flaw. Ruby kept my secret all these many years—my gift itself—and I should be able to tell her of its flaws, but my lips refused to release the truth.

She took another few gulps of her drink before signaling Cap for another. Ruby could drink grown men under the table. "I think there's something you're not telling me," she accused. "You're more"—she motioned at me—"broody and sullen than normal. Which is saying a lot."

"I'm a ray of sunshine," I muttered. Which was a mistake. *Sunshine.*

I'd been pissed when Wren apologized for not knowing how bad it got in the south. How earnest she'd sounded. People tended to feel bad right before forgetting about it entirely, and I bet she'd do the same. I didn't need some highborn lady sweeping in like a savior for my people. But she had the means to at least *ask* her father, I thought. Though if it hadn't been for her gift being stolen, she would've gone on with her life as normal. Totally oblivious and uncaring.

"There you go again." Ruby carved through my muddled reflections like a blade. She released a whine. "Just tell me."

"No."

"You're the worst."

"And you're a busybody," I grumbled, finishing my drink.

How would I work with Wren after yesterday? Was she genuine? And if so, could I forgive her ignorance? Her father played a large part in this somehow, and I hesitated to think she'd stand up to him. Blood was blood, and while she'd acted horrified to learn he'd been in that room filled with documents of the dead, she could easily slip back into a state of denial. The worst part was, I trusted her, and I'd done it too easily.

"You get grumpy when you keep things from me," Ruby insisted, her voice turning chipper. "I've always told you, it's not good to bottle that stuff up, yet here you are, moody and broody, and 'Don't bother me, I'm dangerous and mysterious.'" She mirrored my expression, even going so far as to slump in her seat and glumly sip her ale.

"There are people *dying,* Ruby," I said firmly, locking eyes. "I'd stop worrying about me and focus on that."

She winced. "I know, Damien, I *am* paying attention." She collapsed against the bar with a groan. "I'm just trying to lighten the mood. I hate seeing you this way. Try as you might, I've known you for too many years for you to hide. I know all your moves."

I stiffened. I never got used to how openly she showed her emotions.

"I'm fine, really, Ruby," I promised, more tenderly this time. It took effort. "But if you could do your *thing* around the Void, the whole 'nice and friendly' act you play so well, and find out more about the missing people, and where they were before they vanished, that would help. I'll even split what Wren's paying me."

Ruby gasped in mock shock. "You? *Offering* to split? Something is definitely wrong with you."

Again, she wasn't mistaken.

"As much fun as this has been, I have things to do." I could only handle so much prying. "I'll see you."

She snatched my arm before I left. "At the ball, right?" A light entered her eyes. "I planned on going, and I *may* have snagged an invitation from an attendee. We did well last time, and I figured I'd give it another go. See what I can manage."

"Just blend in," I pleaded. "One of these days you're going to get caught."

She dropped her hand and smirked. "Not if they can't catch me first."

Images of Ruby in the cells made my heart race. I couldn't live with myself if she got caught, even if I had nothing to do with her arrest. And the things they'd do to her . . . We might not be the kind of friends who embraced and spoke of feelings—on my part, anyway—but she did mean something to me. Ruby and Cap were all I had.

I walked away, leaving her and her feigned sense of invincibility at the bar.

Fates, she was lucky she hadn't been arrested already. If the guards caught her for stealing from the north, she'd be more than interrogated. They tended to just toss us in jail and let us rot until we were a pile of bones and ash. As a child, I'd spotted more than one dead body in those cells, and I hadn't even gotten as far as the mines where they sent most of the prisoners.

I didn't need someone to look out for. I had enough on my plate keeping myself out of jail.

I made my way up the stairs and slammed the door to my room, locking it behind me. Immediately, my eyes skipped to the postcard Wren had studied yesterday. She couldn't picture me as a farmer, she'd said. What she didn't realize was that I didn't choose *this* life. No one did.

In my far-fetched dreams, I was a farmer, alone on my land. *My* land. Watching the sun set with my hands covered in earth. If I shut my eyes, I almost imagined the fresh breeze and the smell of the orange trees I'd plant. Oranges were rare in the Void, but they were abundant in the deep west.

People weren't always what they appeared. A lesson I'd learned the hard way in this place. I certainly wasn't. Until I saved enough, I would have to remain the Ghost; not letting my guard down, and collecting as much dirt as possible on anyone who might be a threat. It worked as a decent way to protect myself and keep up a particular image. Like yesterday when those bastards accosted Wren with lewd eyes and vulgar remarks.

My blood boiled at the memory. I'd nearly lost my control right then and there.

With a frustrated groan, I lay down on my bed, tugging the

worn blanket to my waist, my arms propped beneath my head. The water stain on the ceiling always reminded me of a squished frog. A lovely image to have right before I shut my eyes.

The day after tomorrow, Wren expected me at the tailor. Expected to dress me for some high-society event. Make me "fit in." Yes, I required such luxurious garments for the mission, and I knew the tailor had been a way for her to offer an olive branch. Her gifting me with a disguise so I could conduct some research on the younger attendants without gifts. We were nowhere near finding out who stole the locket, and somehow, my insides churned, as if time were running out. Not that I could explain why.

I showed up. As promised.

Really, I should be angry with myself for following her directions like a trained pet, but I couldn't turn down the opportunity. Especially since I'd failed to retrieve names from the Registry. All I'd amassed was more fucking trouble on my plate with a side of a guilty conscience. It was a wonder I still had one of those.

As I entered the ivy-covered brick shop off some fancy avenue—dressed in my black waiter's attire—I shoved the mystery of that sterile room and the missing people of the Void to the side. I'd focus on that once we were done. In many ways, I shouldn't care. It didn't affect *me*. Yet . . .

Fuck. Was I getting sentimental like Ruby? She could've rubbed off on me.

A bell rang as I pushed open the door, and I was met by five pairs of eyes. Men wearing suits crafted of fine wool and striped linen paused their perusal of the tailor's bolts of cloth and gawked, a few snickering as they took in my wrinkled suit, which likely had been made of some horrendous fabric that offended their delicate senses.

I refrained from rolling my eyes and doing what I did best: steal from their pockets and wipe those sneers away.

Instead, I strolled into the room like I owned it, a smirk plastered on my face. What they couldn't see, they wouldn't know. And I'd been pretending since I knew how to walk.

"There you are!"

Wren popped out from behind a rack of colorful bow ties, a sunshine grin in a shop full of gloomy grimaces. I paused as I took her in, watching the way her blue dress swished about her as she bounded for me. It was a simple design, her dress, just like most of what she wore, and yet whatever she placed on her body gave off an air of elegance. I noticed that she always sported a surprise of tulle or pearl buttons somewhere. Something intimately *her,* to stand out.

I frowned. Perhaps coming here had been a mistake. My mind currently hovered on the subject of ladies' *fashion.*

"I'm surprised you made it," she said breathlessly, as if she'd been running. When I didn't answer, she prompted, "Damien?"

I cleared my throat and took a small step back. I didn't belong here, and Wren wasn't my friend—nor was she my *anything.* This was business. "I want to get into this ball, yeah? Then I have to look the part."

It was curt. To the point. Effective.

No need for a mess. Not when I had to achieve my goal and get my mirror working again. If only Wren's blasted locket weren't tied to me. With my photograph to boot. Damn it, if that wasn't some cruel joke from the Fates I didn't know what was.

That sunny smile of hers dipped at the sides, and my throat constricted. "Well, I'm glad you're here, regardless." Her jaw clenched, but she turned on a heel and headed for the back of the shop, her hips swaying with confidence—real or feigned, it was difficult to tell. I trailed behind, making a point to meet every haughty stare as I passed.

"Here's the man I told you about," Wren proclaimed once we'd entered the last room of the shop. Not that I was an expert, but this appeared to be where the fittings took place, a fancy wooden platform set up before a floor-length mirror.

A middle-aged man with a graying mustache that swooped up on each side of his face stood tall in the center, his simple white shirtsleeves rolled up. I froze when he regarded me with steely blue eyes, his focus straying from my head to my boots in a nearly clinical fashion.

"Bring out the suits I've selected," he called to no one in particular. "As I told Lady Wren here, we'll have to make quick adjustments to suits I've already created."

A cart whirled by, pushed by a younger gentleman with beads of sweat staining his forehead. "Here, Mr. Byrne." He stood beside the tailor, his lean figure a tad too skinny for the suit he currently wore. I couldn't place him, but I made out a hint of his accent, which hailed from the south. An image across my mind, there and gone in a flash—of the young assistant on a cold table, eyes shut and blood seeping from his lips.

I tore my gaze from him. Since discovering that room at the Registry, I swore my nightmares were seeping into the daytime.

The assistant appeared perfectly fine, eager, if anything, to be here. He was one of the lucky ones who'd gotten work outside the Void, and the fact that this tailor hired him made me feel a tad more at ease. Still, I wished I could rid myself of the haunting image of his face, cold and lifeless.

A hanger scraping metal stole my attention.

"Good, good." Mr. Byrne snagged a simple black suit from a rack and held it up to me, one eye open and one closed. I swallowed thickly, suddenly feeling out of place. Well, it hadn't been *sudden*. I was an outcast in the northern district, after all.

"This one. Brightens the darkness of his eyes," he announced. To me, he said, "Undress to your underthings. You may fold your . . . *clothing* on one of the benches in the changing rooms." I didn't miss the distaste in his voice as he commented on my attire. Nor his raised brow. I supposed his generosity ended at cheap suits.

Wren stood off to the side, silent for once. When I stole a peek, she made a point to concentrate on the tailor. She'd stiffened since my arrival. Since I snapped at her.

I slipped into one of the two changing rooms and undressed, forgoing folding my wrinkled suit altogether. If I hadn't needed to get into the ball, I wouldn't choose to go through this hell. I despised shopping of any kind, and my three shirts and the two pairs of trousers I owned were enough for me.

When I exited, I was fully prepared to be met with more scornful faces, but I saw only one face, and it stole the very air from my lungs.

Wren was bathed in the trickle of light cascading from a high window, the sunlight grazing each delicate feature and highlighting her in golden brilliance that rivaled her smile. I sucked in a sharp inhale, taken aback by how wide her eyes grew, how her breathing stuttered as if she was surprised by my appearance. Pleasantly so, if I had to guess.

Something twinged inside my chest, not painful, more like a warm squeeze. I hadn't experienced it before.

It wasn't until her turquoise eyes traveled *down* that her face blossomed in red. I wore my underthings; that was all, and the simple black underwear did nothing to hide my bare chest.

Wren's eyes trailed across my skin, her path leaving each inch of me burning. When she reached the dusting of hair at my abdomen, leading down past where the fabric hid, she visibly swallowed.

Her reactions to me . . . they screwed with my head. Because it couldn't be attraction she felt, not the genuine kind. And me; I thought her stunning standing in the gilded room, a creature born from a daydream. But her beauty and wits, which often drove me mad, couldn't be enough for anything *more.*

She's a ward princess. A silly, ignorant girl. Someone I detested. The reminder left a sour taste on my tongue.

"Oh. *Oh.* I should probably leave," Wren hurried to say, clearly flustered. "I t-trust you have it in hand, Mr. Byrne."

When she picked up her skirts, her face flushed and eyes avoidant, my heart pounded, that same odd sensation worming its way under my skin. Was it panic? Something else entirely?

"No."

All eyes snapped to me. *Shite. I'd said it out loud.* "I—I need your expert eye," I mumbled before I could take back the words. An excuse. A cowardly one.

I didn't wish for her to leave. These were all strangers.

Another excuse. Seemed like I had plenty of those these days.

A whimper-like whine left her throat but she nodded, scooting to the far back of the room like the shadows would swallow her up. Even from there, I noticed how that telltale blush of hers traveled down her neckline. Fates, she would never survive a poker game. I opened my mouth, about to tease her, but promptly shut it. I'd made myself a promise.

All I had to do was picture my little secret—my farm. My freedom. A *true* future.

My muscles loosened and I relaxed. The tailor's assistant didn't wait to grab hold of my arms and place me on the small platform before the mirror. Now that I stood a good two feet taller than everyone else, all the tension rolled back up my spine, my muscles taut.

"Relax," Mr. Byrne demanded, and I flinched like a schoolboy being scolded. "This won't take long at all. Just a few adjustments." He peered up at me, though the expression he wore wasn't unkind. "Lucky you have a woman who won't take no for an answer. She wouldn't leave my shop until I agreed to the fitting."

My gaze darted to Wren, who pretended that a nearby silken tie was the most interesting thing in the world. She could've just bought me a ready-made suit, but she'd fought for me to stand here, to have something created just for me.

"I can only imagine it's a wondrous occasion," Mr. Byrne mused, his pins nearly poking me as he worked. "You two make a beautiful pair as well." He spoke that last part so quietly, I was certain only I heard. I didn't correct him. My lips had forgotten how to move.

I felt like a bastard, standing up on that pedestal.

Tonight I'd be among the enemy.

And my guide? A woman I'd betrayed. One I loathed and desired in equal measure.

I might be confident, but I wasn't a fool.

I was screwed.

Chapter Seventeen

Wren

If a gift is lost, it can be used by another. The Fates are adamant that only the deserving keep their gifts close to their hearts.
—*Aurilian History of Magical Objects,* Chapter Seventeen

Mother allowed Callie to select my gown that evening.

My older sister stood behind me at the vanity brushing my blond waves. She tsked whenever she struck a tangle. She stayed quiet, likely waiting for me to initiate the conversation. These past weeks had been challenging, and Callie, thanks to her gift, had a tendency to understand when to prod and when to leave well enough alone. Judging by her harsh strokes, she struggled to keep her thoughts tethered.

"Callie?" I finally called, my throat like sandpaper.

A flare of warmth entered me like the heat of the sun on a summer's day. Her magic. Sometimes when she wasn't paying attention, it seeped out of her. Right now, elation filled the room.

"Yes?" she asked, meeting my eyes in the oval mirror before us. Hers gleamed.

I couldn't recall the last time we had an interlude to ourselves like this, and I missed her.

"Does Father ever go to the Registry of Magical Gifts when you accompany him to work?"

The corners of her mouth turned down, and the warmth I'd felt earlier vanished. "Why would we go there? Father deals with the law, not gifts." She continued with my hair, her nimble fingers working the strands into some half-up, half-down design.

I had to ask. Had to know if Callie was aware of the missing people. If she knew . . . it would devastate me. "You go everywhere with him. Follow his every step."

"And?" Callie braided two sections of my hair and clipped them together with an onyx claw studded with diamonds. One of my favorites. The finishing touch consisted of a petite red rose she tucked into one of the braids, the petals lush and bright.

"And . . . I always feel like he's doing more for the ward than he lets on, and when I didn't receive my gift, I assumed he'd try whatever he could to find the cause," I suggested carefully.

Callie made a low humming sound. "I mean, he and I did go to the Registry after your birthday, but . . ."

"You found nothing," I supplied.

Callie nodded solemnly. In the mirror, I watched as she briefly shut her eyes, her jaw tight with tension. "I didn't want to tell you," she admitted. "Your name wasn't there. Which was odd, actually."

"Why?"

She paused her movements, eyes on mine in the mirror. "Even

if someone in the north doesn't receive a gift, their name is recorded, and it states they never received one. You *should* be in there regardless. It's almost like someone . . ."

"Someone what?" I nudged.

"Like someone removed the page." She groaned. "Look. I don't know what I'm saying. Don't listen to me. My specialty lies with taxes, accounting, and shipment scheduling. Things like magic rarely cross my desk."

"Do they cross Father's?"

"Occasionally," she said, frowning at a particularly stubborn strand that wouldn't stay in place. "But only high-priority cases, and even those are rare. The Fates mainly deal with problems themselves, meaning he gets the leftover work."

So he didn't *just* run the ward. What kind of *leftover* work did they assign him? I wanted to push, but I had to act at least somewhat levelheaded. If Callie found out about my investigating, she might tell Father for my "safety," and I'd never uncover the truth. Fates, I wished I could talk to her.

I forced myself to look at my lap and asked instead, "What happens to those like me who don't get a gift? I know of a few lords and ladies, but has anyone ever succeeded in their ventures without the Fates' blessing?"

When Callie gnawed on her lower lip, I got my answer.

"I see," I said. "I bet they were disappointed. Same as me." I should have felt awful for manipulating my sister, but vital questions had yet to be answered.

"The Hockleys' older son was pissed," Callie remarked dryly. "I also know the Simmonses' child left for the west last year when she didn't receive hers. The girl was about to set the realm aflame by the look in her eye. I hear she's married now to some obscenely rich businessman, which is what she always wanted." Callie shrugged.

That counted Lady Simmons out. "The Hockleys' son?" I asked. "He still here?" If he remained, there was a chance I'd see him at the ball.

"So many questions tonight, little bird." Callie tapped me on the head. "You're going to be just fine, I promise! Do you honestly think I'd allow you to be anything but spectacular once I take over a ward seat?" She cocked her head and made a smug face. "You yourself told me I'd get one. Not many people believe in me, but you do. It means more than you know."

My heart fell into my stomach. Should I tell her? Ask about that eerie room with records full of missing people? About Father's involvement?

"Besides," she continued, "Father is teaching me everything he knows, and while he isn't the most honorable man at times"—she made a face, her nose scrunched—"I've learned a lot."

I froze, seconds from spilling my secrets.

"You'll get a seat," I said, smiling. She was too close to Father. Too close to thinking her dreams were coming true to see reason. "I just worry. About you, me, Father." The words were stiff. "Hell, even Mother has been out more than usual. She's always off by the time I wake."

Callie waved a hand. "She has her new horseback riding lessons, and then she has her tea sessions. As far as Father and I are concerned, I'm managing, but he's, well, he's acting off lately. Probably due to stress. The usual. Especially since he's stayed up late writing letter after letter to appeal to the other leaders to fix the wage decreases. Riots will start in the street if he doesn't get his way, and then the Fates will be pissed."

"But with his pen, he will." He could convince anyone with it.

She snorted. "That's why half the lords don't even open his letters. Smart, really."

True. If I got a letter from the notorious Cameron Hayes, I wouldn't touch it with a ten-foot pole.

"When I fight my way to Father's seat, I won't allow anyone to walk over me," Callie said. She beamed, her reflection in the mirror like a ray of sunshine. "I will make certain things are fair between the two halves of our city. I won't even have to use my influence to do it. Just good old-fashioned politics." She tapped the side of her head and winked.

We might be sisters, but we were crafted of different materials. She wished to conquer and battle her way to becoming a politician. I, on the other hand, had dreams to travel—or, as I was discovering, a desire to escape. Lately, those dreams seemed inconsequential in comparison to what I'd seen and learned.

How could I travel without a care and live my life in bliss when I had *some* power to do the right thing and speak up? Open up the eyes of some old friends who would eventually become ward leaders themselves. Sure, most had strayed from me now, but I'd pick out the few who would listen. Those who weren't as invested in petty society gossip. Tonight, I'd make a mental list.

Everett could be on that list. He was kind, too kind, probably, for society. But if Everett rose up, spoke to the other heirs waiting to take their parents' titles, we might have a chance.

Thoughts of traveling shifted in my mind's eye, turning to new dreams. Ones that actually mattered in the grand scheme of things. I was no politician, but I'd find my own way to help.

Callie swiped some lip stain over my lips; a pretty, darker shade of red Mother would flinch at.

It matched my dress perfectly.

"Thank you," I said, pushing my chair back to stand. The voluminous tulle blossomed from my form like a flower, the vibrant crimson bottom a contrast to the midnight-black top: a silken corset—and one that left my shoulders bare. I winked at Callie. "I'll have to grab a shawl so Mother won't see until it's too late."

"Want me to boost your confidence?" She tugged on one of her earrings, an impish light in her stare.

"I think I'll be all right. No magic for me tonight."

She nudged my shoulder. "Well, either way, I love being a bad influence on you." She snagged my arm and forced me into a hug. Briefly stunned, I returned the gesture. She didn't embrace often. "I'm just glad I'm here with you. Able to see you grow," she whispered into my ear. "You're turning into a woman I admire, and even though I can't get the image of you wading in the muck when we were children, trying to catch frogs, out of my mind"—she chuckled at the memory—"I'm still proud."

My heart skipped several beats. In many ways, Callie had acted as more of a mother figure than our own mother. She'd taught me how to dress. How to dance. How to navigate the reality of society with grace. And when I first bled, she tucked me into bed with a hot-water bottle and a stack of novels.

"Ready?" she asked, releasing me.

When I took her in, I realized how lucky I was to have someone like her. Not many people did. I would do everything in my power to protect her when I eventually revealed the truth. Even if it broke our family in two—and *me* in the process.

"As ready as I'll ever be."

I captured more eyes than I anticipated.

Having received a brusque comment from Mother after I ditched my shawl in the carriage, I made my way past the people I'd known most of my life. All the ladies and lords who peered down their noses at me but smiled at Father. Even at Callie. I held my head high and embraced the shock of it all.

The glowers weren't nearly as venomous as before, but I could tell that their judgment held them back from approaching.

They could call me what they wanted. I'd never been shy about what I wore or about my body. Why should I be? Sure, I wasn't built like my mother, nor was I as graceful, but I adored my curves, and tonight, I let them show.

The Hockleys had decorated the ballroom in their four-story mansion with an abundance of violet, gray, and black flowers. I bet most of them had been magicked to retain their unusual color. Silver accents and mirrors of every shape and size hung from the gray brocade walls, and the reflection of the crystal chandelier shimmered upon each surface.

It was a wonderland. Elegant and ethereal. I smiled as I picked up an empty crystal flute, about to head to a decadent champagne fountain, when a dashing dark blond man with tawny skin stole my attention. Sporting a red velvet suit and skillfully mussed hair, he radiated the kind of effortless style I worked painstakingly hard to attain. He looked vaguely familiar, around my age, but I couldn't place him.

"Allow me," he offered, knocking a gold signet ring engraved with the letter *H* in fancy script on the top of the glass. Immediately champagne filled the glass, the bubbles stopping just short of overflowing.

"Thank you," I replied, thinking of his gift and wondering if it was similar to my old friend Danielle's and her ability to replenish.

Reading my expression, he said, "It fills your glass or plate with what you desire most." He cocked his blond head, his eyes a darker shade of honey gold. "Apparently that was champagne. Oh, and lovely to see you again, Wren."

"Do we know each other?" I asked, taking a hesitant sip of my drink. It was delectable and *had* been exactly what I'd craved.

He placed a hand to his chest in mock affront. "Really, I'm wounded! I'm the notoriously handsome younger son of the manor." He waved his hand around him. "Lord Grayson Hockley at your service. Or Grayson, but just for you."

The younger Hockley. So Adrian, the giftless boy Callie mentioned earlier had to be here somewhere . . .

"I shouldn't have forgotten," I replied, unable to keep the smile from my lips. "How foolish of me."

This close, I analyzed his face; his sharp jawline and regal nose. He wore kohl beneath his eyes, bringing out their striking shade, and his lids shimmered with flecks of gold. I'd seen him at parties before, but not many. We might have danced once when I first had been permitted to attend balls, though all the faces blurred together.

Grayson scoffed. "Well, the eligible bachelors and bachelorettes tonight better not forget. I've been off my game as of late."

Already looking for a suitor. Or maybe his parents were forcing it on him.

"I have a feeling you'll find it again tonight." I nudged his elbow and he smiled, his easygoing energy welcome.

"Maybe you can be my wingwoman. I like your style. Brave and bold. And of course, daring enough to start some gossip." He eyed my dress and its low neckline with a smirk.

I instantly liked him.

"Gotta lean into the gossip when I'm at the center of it." Might as well give 'em a show.

"Ah, yes. No gift." Grayson shook his head. "My older brother has the same issue."

My muscles tensed. "Your older brother. What was his name again?" I asked innocently.

"Adrian," Grayson replied. "He's up sulking in his room. He's in poor form tonight, as usual." He snatched his own empty glass and filled it with a deep amber liquor, his ring pressed to the crystal. "I swear, I assumed things were turning around just last week when he told me he might have found a way to earn a gift—like that's even possible—but then he marched to his room and refuses to come out."

A way to "earn" a gift.

Finally, a genuine name to add to a list of suspects.

"Why do you think things were turning around?" I pressed.

Grayson shrugged. "He just came home one night like his old self, telling the family he'd do better. That he had a new business venture and some nonsense with a powerful member of society."

Business venture? "What kind of—"

"Son!" A voice cut me off. I turned at the same time as Grayson, met by Lord Stuart Hockley's reddened face. He'd indulged already, his words slow and slightly slurred as he said, "I still need to introduce you to a few more suitors. They've been waiting all night!"

The older man didn't notice me, or chose not to, which was fine by me.

Before Grayson was carted off by his father, he shot me a wink. "Let me charm some pants off, and then save me a dance, Hayes."

"Of course," I said, returning his wink. Grayson appeared harmless. A little cocky in his demeanor, but that was about all. His brother, on the other hand . . . yes. I remembered Adrian, had at least seen him when we were younger. Fates, now that I recalled it, he had been sort of insufferable; boasting about his birthday and how many women would come flocking his way once he received his gift.

But it never came. Since the Hockleys were powerful and hid much using Lady Hockley's rare gift of distraction, most people moved on quickly. I envied her and her gift. She could turn the conversation by touching the golden hairpin she wore in her hair.

I finished my glass with a few unladylike gulps. Liquid courage—I demanded it in abundance now that no one stood at my side. Eyes practically burned into my skin, and although Callie had selected a gown I would've picked myself, I suddenly questioned my choice when scrutiny followed me like a curse.

A band struck up a slow tune, couples aiming for the dance floor in the center of the space. Floating silver mirrors on all sides produced a mind-bending sight.

Scanning the lively room, I spotted Cecile, Lilly, and Danielle all grouped together, whispering behind cupped hands. They wore varying shades of pastel satin tonight as if they'd planned it together. A part of me missed that, even if I knew they weren't true friends. It made my heart ache, an emptiness forming in my chest. As before, Danielle peeked up at me, a sad expression contorting her lips before she turned her cheek.

Would I ever be able to truly trust again? If I somehow got my gift back, I'd remember how callous those ladies had been once I wasn't seen as useful to them.

A gentle hand grazed the back of mine.

I expected to see Damien's sullen face and stormy eyes, but Everett Sinclair greeted me.

He made a fine sight, I couldn't deny it, what with his charcoal woolen suit and freshly shaved face. It showed off his square jawline and impressive cheekbones. And his smile . . . he beamed at the sight of me, his eyes swiftly turning hooded as he took in the rest of my outfit. When he eventually met my stare, the tops of his ears had reddened.

"You look stunning," he managed, clearing his throat. "You always do, Wren."

The admission forced my smile to grow. I often wore what people would consider scandalous dresses, and this gown was no different.

"I remember owing you a dance," I said, placing my empty champagne glass on the nearest table.

He straightened and ran a hand through his blond hair. "I believe you do. Although if you're not in the mood—"

"Hush, Everett," I admonished, playfully shaking my head. "It's the least I can do, and besides, I want to."

While my mother had been a renowned dancer in her time due to her magicked shoes, I didn't own her effortless grace. But it never stopped me from enjoying myself, and I took to the floor whenever I could. Everett lifted his arm for me to grasp, and I felt *normal* for the first time in weeks. A little like my old self.

Silently, he led the way, carefully steering us past a woman snapping her bare fingers and lighting a cigar. The flame sparked before she shook away the magic, and puffs of heavy smoke saturated the air.

Another man chose the time to use his power to impress his much younger dance partner. I watched in awe as he lifted her with ease and twirled her midair before catching her again without a single bead of sweat.

Everett's hand slid to my waist as a new song played, and I

raised one hand to his strong shoulders and placed the other in his hand. I thanked the Fates I'd worn gloves, because my palms were clammy. Nerves . . . around Everett, no less. How interesting.

But they weren't the same as the nerves I got around a certain other person with gray eyes and a permanent scowl. I hated to admit that.

We started our dance, Everett unusually silent as he carefully spun me before bringing me back into the safety of his arms, but never to his chest or close enough to feel the heat of him. My skirts swished against the parquet floor, and I knew my cheeks were rosy by the time the song ended.

"Do you think they'd notice if we danced once more?" Everett asked, leaning to whisper into my ear. Now I felt his heat. The way his breath tickled my skin. It elicited a shiver, and I glanced up, looking at Everett from a different angle. Maybe he wasn't so uptight after all.

"Let them notice," I said conspiratorially. One glass of champagne and a risqué dress had turned me into a new person. One I quite liked.

Everett had no qualms about another dance, and a devilish smile lifted his lips. "So, Lady Hayes," he began as the music flowed around us. "I wanted to see if you had any interest in horses."

"Horses?" I repeated.

Everett swallowed thickly. "What I mean to say, not so eloquently, is if you had an interest in riding? I hope to have a companion one of these days on my rides."

Oh.

"I enjoy riding," I answered, completing another spin without falling on my face. My liquid courage appeared to be wearing off. Another drink would be a necessity.

"Good," he said, his eyes sparkling. "Perhaps this upcoming week then, if it suits your schedule." Like I had one of those to keep now that society had deemed me a pariah.

"I'd like that."

We completed a few more steps, his hand securely on my waist, the feel of his fingers gripping me causing my head to spin with confusion.

But it was simple—this. Him.

When the song slowed, coming to an end, Everett neared, closing the small distance between us. I lifted my head, our lips inches apart.

"I rather enjoyed that," he murmured softly, like a secret. "I know I'm not daring or bold, but I can't stop myself from at least trying around you. In fact, even being in your presence makes me want to damn the rules and ask for another dance—"

A shadow loomed over us before a deep voice interrupted Everett's speech.

"I think I'd like to cut in now."

Chapter Eighteen

Damien

They looked like they'd been about to kiss.

Her lips had parted less than an inch from his, her eyes peering up in a question. And the way he gazed at her, like a man who wished to devour her alive—

I'd spent the past twenty minutes on the sidelines, eavesdropping on various conversations—most centering around the still-missing Dusk—when the hairs on the back of my neck rose. When I turned, drawn by some invisible hand, I saw *that* look on his face. How his expression evolved from innocence to something more.

I loathed it.

Before I could stop myself, I was moving.

The spineless bastard reeled as I brusquely cut in, his jaw clenching at my interruption. One I *shouldn't* be making. A slight furrow grew between the lord's brows as he gave me a rough once-over. Something akin to recognition flashed in his stare, there and gone in a blink. Though he'd only seen me disguised as a waiter, and even then, he hadn't paid attention to the "help."

"Ah, this is . . ." Wren stepped back, dropping Everett's hand as if it were on fire. She motioned to me and said, "This is Lord Ca-Cassington's son from up in the Far North. He's on a visit to see Andalay." I watched the delicate bob of her throat, her teeth tugging on her bottom lip with nerves.

Bet she hadn't expected me to interrupt their far too cozy dance.

Surprise.

"Thanks for the introduction, Lady Wren," I said with a smirk, careful to mask my accent. Fates, it took effort. "I'm not a well-known face around here."

My eyes wandered to that damned lip she kept tugging. She had to be doing that on purpose; driving me mad. Taunting me.

A beast had overtaken my body when Everett put his hands on her. It had yet to leave.

And it was hungry.

As if she realized where I strayed, she released her bottom lip and smoothed her features. Her eyes grew sharper, her posture straighter. My sunshine pulled herself together with a single blink, donning her mask with ease.

"I hear the duke never leaves the far north," Everett interjected, forcing me to look away from Wren. Everett's eyes narrowed as he sized me up. "Nor do his sons."

I had to refrain from rolling my eyes. The only information I held on the lord currently staring holes into my skin had to do with those glasses of his he kept tucked away. They calculated numbers or accounts or something special that made him popular. And a very rich man.

I returned his appraisal with equal venom. Wren could do much better.

"Well, *I* left the north," I snapped, much more sharply than intended. "I was growing tired of all the snow." I waved an idle hand as if the conversation bored me. Which it did. "Time for a change of scenery." My focus centered on Wren as I spoke—mainly to piss off Everett.

Wren's eyes, which had been dulled yet serene while dancing with Everett, blazed, the flecks in her irises morphing into golden fire. A warning to play nice. *Cute.* Didn't she know I thrived on living on the edge? Her caution made me all the more reckless.

I winked at Wren when a new song played. Physically sliding between Lord Pompous and her, I grabbed hold of her gloved hand. I didn't give a shite if he remained standing behind us like a fool. Her soft gasp had been worth it.

Wren peered over my shoulder, practically bouncing on her toes, as I angled my body, hiding Everett's departure. When I was certain he'd slunk off in defeat, I released the tension in my shoulders, my feet moving us along the dance floor.

"What are you thinking?" Wren demanded, all of her previous charm gone. Red danced over her cheeks, the rouge painted there making her skin blaze as if on fire. I liked this version of her better. Not the mask she wore—it was a bore, and Wren's brazenness ignited my own flames. "You can't antagonize people like that," she scolded, "and Everett is actually nice."

"Nice?" I snorted, my free hand moving to her waist. "He's putting on an act to get beneath your skirts. You're welcome for the heads-up, by the way."

"He's . . . he's not trying to do that." Wren skewered me with another burning glower. "Some people are simply kind without wanting something in return. He's had the opportunity to charm me when no one could bear witness, and he was nothing but a gentleman. Maybe you wouldn't understand that."

They'd been alone together.

That thought by itself made my throat tight.

"Oh, little naïve Wren," I forced out, attempting to sound unbothered. "Seriously. How would you survive on your own?"

I was being an arse, I knew this, but screw it. She couldn't walk around with blinders on for her entire life. She'd get hurt. I wasn't sure when the idea of Wren coming into harm's way had begun to bother me, but thinking of her hurt or heartbroken now . . . it pissed me the hell off.

Was she already heartbroken over her father? Fates, I hadn't actually asked.

I didn't know what it was like to have parents of my own, but it must've gutted her. Yet I hadn't considered the inner turmoil she battled; loving someone even if they were a villain.

"I don't want to fight with you now, Damien. There's too many people staring. All because of your little, and quite unnecessary, show," she muttered, her feet moving in sync with mine. The dance was thankfully a simple one I could keep up with, and most couples simply swayed to the lulling melody.

"Fine. We won't fight." I tugged her closer and a whisper of a gasp left her. I liked that sound, so I inched her forward again. Her lips parted as mere centimeters separated us. A scandal, surely.

When she leaned back, I watched as she removed a single red rose from her braided crown of blond hair. Watching with rapt attention, I froze as she tucked the flower inside my jacket's breast pocket.

"Much better," she said, almost to herself.

My throat worked, the flower seeming to weigh a thousand pounds and yet lighter than a feather with each breath.

"How do you know how to dance?" she asked, drawing my attention from her small gift.

"Ruby taught me," I said, moving into place, the rose's sweet scent wafting to my nose. My friend had relented after I nagged her for most of yesterday. The hours spent stepping on her toes hadn't pleased her.

"Oh, and I have a name for our list," I added as the seconds ticked by—us embracing, a tender hold with our arms wrapped around each other. We weren't pressed together in some alley, and for some reason, this felt . . . it felt intimate. Raw. Not me. "Elizabeth Saridon ring a bell?" I asked, my throat suddenly dry. The words came out like I'd swallowed dust, and I silently cursed when beads of sweat slid down my spine.

I was off my damned game.

Wren's lips twisted and her gaze strayed while she pondered.

"Lizzy. Yes, Lizzy Saridon." Her attention circled back to me. "She's older than me and Callie. I hadn't considered her in years before all of this."

I huffed. "Well, she's been surrounded this evening by so-called friends flaunting their gifts, and one of them made a comment about how they should play nice, seeing as 'Lizzy here doesn't have one.'" I almost stopped in my tracks when I'd passed by that backstabbing group of friends. Judging from the look on Lizzy's face, she hadn't appreciated the companionship.

These people might be wealthy and powerful, but they could be just as cruel as those in the Void. More so, even. At least my people had the respect to say what they meant without feigned niceties.

"She might be a suspect," Wren mused. "Her family isn't well known, as Lizzy lives in Ward Five. While I never pegged her as someone with aspirations, all these years of being overlooked could've sparked something. A need for revenge." Wren made a deep sound of frustration. "Did she appear *off*? I mean, how are we to know how our perpetrator would act in public? Her grief could be an act. Or she may be using that as a façade."

My hand lowered farther on Wren's waist, but she was too busy rambling about Lizzy.

Fates damn her for wearing this dress. She embodied the image of a siren. A vixen. Sin itself. My fingers dug into her lush hips, yearning to explore lower, my fingers toying with the many satin ties at her back, untying them in my mind.

The whiskey I'd had on the way over here had *not* been a good idea.

"Wait!" Her entire face brightened. "I have a suspect too! Adrian Hockley. He never got his gift either. Apparently he was furious. Still is." Now *her* fingers dug into my shoulder. Excitement caused her reaction, her face aglow with delight.

She looked too beautiful. It hurt, a physical ache taking

residence in my chest. Looking at Wren Hayes was akin to looking at the sun for too long. Both brilliant and blinding.

Where the hell is all this coming from, you sap?

"Anyone else attend these balls who doesn't have a gift?" I asked through my teeth as she inadvertently leaned against my chest. I felt every breath she took. Each exhale.

Why did she have to meld her body against me like this? Press her head beside my thundering heart as if she felt safe right there in my arms? Didn't she know I was the predator? She should be shoving me away, not holding me.

I couldn't recall the last time someone had held me.

"Hmm, maybe Olivia Waterstone," Wren pondered, having no clue as to the havoc she wreaked upon me. I took in a deep inhale, trying to calm myself and see reason, but I scented something soft and floral. A new perfume she wore. The seductive smell invaded my nose, making me lightheaded as heat coiled in my belly.

Once more, she had no hint as to what devious things went on in my head.

"But Olivia is married off with five children and never gave the impression she cared. Lizzy, too, seems well-off," Wren continued. "She's neck-deep in riches, and her husband is a viscount or something. He travels a lot so she lives with her parents at the moment, but they plan to move west. The viscount knows the king and queen personally."

Ah, the famous King and Queen of Aurilia. Of course, they resided in the western region, away from the Fates and *their* palace. I bet they were jealous. They were nothing but old ornaments of the past in a run-down castle, from what I'd heard. All they did was go on parades and perform works of charity. I suspected the Fates would've done away with them long ago if the royal family held any ambition whatsoever.

"You sure she's not hiding anything?" I asked, turning to the side to avoid that delectable scent. It didn't work.

Wren suddenly twirled, forcing me to go along with the motion. I barely pulled her back before she tumbled. Ruby and her dance lessons were failing me. To be fair, she hadn't much time to teach me.

Winded, Wren said, "No, I think she's in the clear, but we keep searching. Already we have two names." Her chin canted and her bewitching eyes held me fast as a small smile lifted her lips. "By the way, you look rather handsome tonight. Who knew you cleaned up so well?"

Such a simple statement. My body didn't agree.

A silent curse rang through me as she openly admired my attire, her eyes finally landing back on my face with a brilliant gleam. All I'd done was wear the damned suit and slick back my dark hair.

"It's nothing," I managed to grit out. "Thanks for the suit."

"It's not the suit," she said quietly. "I mean, it fits well, but you seem confident. That's all."

I'd die before I admitted the garment *did* bring out a certain sense of self-assurance. Like none of these bastards could touch me. To them, I was a visiting noble—if Everett spread the word, which I doubted.

I smirked at her compliments, returning to one of my favorite games to play with my little princess. "Am I making you flustered, sunshine?"

She missed a step, but I caught her, a small laugh leaving me when I took in her pursed lips. "Flustered?" she repeated as if it were ridiculous. "Why would I be?"

"Because you're squeezing the life out of my hand at the moment."

Her attention fell to where she held me in a viselike grip. I hardly felt my fingers, but I instantly regretted telling her. She dropped her hand immediately.

"I'm so sorry," she said, brows pulling together. "It—it must've been the excitement of uncovering suspects."

"Of course."

Wren put more distance between us. I found I had to stop myself from chasing after her. "We should grab a drink and peruse the room," she remarked stiffly, her mouth thin, tugging down at the sides. "Three suspects aren't enough. Well, two, seeing as Olivia doesn't attend balls or events, and she wasn't at the last gathering."

She started for the drinks station and I followed, watching how her delicate dress swayed against the polished flooring. Wren was a vision tonight, I could admit it. Half the eyes in the room homed in on her, and not because of any gossip regarding her gift. Men's and women's eyes lingered on her voluptuous form, not bothering to be subtle in showing their appreciation.

I quickened my pace and curved my body around hers, glowering at a young man staring straight at her chest.

"Your daring outfit is causing a lot of . . . distraction," I mumbled.

Wren picked up two glasses. The liquid inside shone blue, and I made a face. What drink was *blue*?

"Are you going to be like my mother, Damien?" She lifted a threatening brow. "I wear what I like. Not my problem if people stare."

She was right. It wasn't her problem—or *mine*—and I admired how she wore what she wished. Then why did I feel like a bastard who wanted to grab a damn shawl and toss it over her shoulders?

"I think we should sneak upstairs and check out Adrian Hockley's rooms." Wren took a sip, briefly closing her eyes at whatever flavor danced on her tongue. "Wait. Seriously," she sighed, "try this."

Fine. I took the other glass from her hand and tested the drink.

Shite. It *was* good. Like blueberries with a hint of raspberry.

"Damien?" I tore myself from the drink and followed Wren's pointed stare. She gazed steadily at her father and Lord Hockley, who were making their way out of the ballroom. The latter trudged behind Hayes, his already red cheeks nearly purple. They vanished a moment later.

"You thinking what I am?" she asked.

"Oh, you know it, sunshine."

Chapter Nineteen

Damien

We crept up the stairs, keeping a decent distance between us and Wren's father and Hockley. By the time they reached the third floor, both men slowed, and Hockley motioned to a door off the landing. Reaching into his pocket, he retrieved a bronze key.

I grabbed my pocket mirror. I had to get in through that door before it closed.

"I'll tell you what they say," I told Wren, but before I dashed up the final steps, she snagged my hand.

"No, we go together," she insisted, fingers tightening.

A protest sat at the tip of my tongue just as a buzz droned in my ears, tingles racing down my arm. Those tingles reached my fingertips and then continued . . . to *her.*

What—

Wren's confused face was the last thing I saw before she disappeared.

Her fingers, gripping me like a vise, dug into my skin, on the verge of pain. A small whimper of surprise filled the air, yet she didn't release me.

We were both invisible, both using my power at the same time. Which, as far as I knew, hadn't been done before. Only a single person used a gift at one time, never two, but here we stood, two ghosts on the landing, *sharing* magic.

A palm thrust into my side, followed by a near-silent *"Move"* breathed into my ear.

Stunned, I reacted to her command while marveling at her composure, seconds after disappearing into thin air. Fates knew, the first time I used my mirror, I'd tossed the damned thing like it was a curse.

With her holding on, I led the way forward as Hockley shoved open the door. It banged forcefully against the wall, and I noted several dents marking the paint. Hayes entered first, as expected, then his host. Wren abruptly yanked on my hand, pushing us into the room before the door swung shut.

I said a silent curse, still not understanding how the hell Wren had managed to vanish along with me, how she could *steal* some of my magic for herself when really, I should be the only one able to use it. Not that we could discuss it now.

While I couldn't see Wren or whatever expression she wore, I sensed her fear weighing the air. How her body drifted to mine, pushing against my side. How it trembled.

This was all new to her. To *me.*

But . . . the photograph in the locket. Our odd connection. How her close presence bolstered my magic—

It made sense that she of all people might be able to harness my gift.

I shook my head in disbelief, reminding myself to focus on the scene happening in the study with two of the most powerful lords in the realm. When Hockley began to anxiously pace, I hauled Wren to the corner and behind a bulky armchair, careful not to break contact. I didn't trust my magic to hold, and in case it gave out, we could at the very least hide behind the furniture. I instinctively looked to where Wren should be, careful to move her so she didn't brush against the chair. Once situated in front of me, her fingers lost some of their stiffness, and some feeling worked its way back into my arm. The girl had a strong grip.

"How many times do I have to tell you that you're late?" Hayes asked with an exasperated sigh, hands behind his back, his stance casual. Cameron Hayes cut an imposing figure, and I didn't blame Hockley when he turned, his eyes widening and desperate.

"You told me Day said I had another week."

"That *was* a week ago," Hayes replied, shaking his head as if in pity. "She already gave you a warning. One I'm sure your son might hate you for, but if she's not satisfied . . ." He left the threat hanging, and Hockley swallowed thickly. "We all must do our part, old friend, or everything stops. You know what's at stake. If we don't appease Day, she won't waste a second to ruin everything."

A warning. Hockley's son Adrian hadn't been given a gift. Was that the warning Hayes referred to? And what exactly was at stake for these men?

Hockley retained his seat as the influential leader of Ward Two.

Every year he grew richer while others were left in squalor, and his many businesses flourished. Thus far, no bad luck had touched him, yet here he stood, being threatened with retribution by a Fate.

So many questions bubbled to mind, and Wren must have felt the same way, because I heard the slight sound of hitched breathing. She backed up against my chest, and I wrapped my arm around her. Her body trembled, and I feared her knees would buckle.

I ground my teeth, understanding exactly what she was thinking. She couldn't break down now. If she believed she hadn't received a gift because her father had angered an immortal, then she might do something rash. Her fingers on my arm were loosening, almost to the point of letting go entirely.

I had to act. For both our sakes.

Pulling her around with my arm, I backed her against the wall, hoping the solidness of it grounded her. With as much gentleness as I could muster, I intertwined our fingers and placed her hands above her head as her chest heaved, the smallest whine escaping. My chest pressed against hers, practically holding her upright as she tried to catch her breath. This must be torture for her—hearing her father speak this way. Hearing that he might be why her dreams had fallen through.

"I need to tell Day something," Hayes continued. "I'm visiting her tonight. Tomorrow . . . tomorrow we both know where I'm headed, and consequences will be doled out as well. We have to time this perfectly."

He was visiting Day and then what? Seeing another Fate? Where did he plan on going?

"Tell Day . . . tell her I'll be ready by tomorrow," Hockley muttered, his words frantic. I couldn't see him due to my position, but it didn't matter. Footsteps were already heading for the door.

"You best not disappoint me again," Hayes warned. "Next time, it might be you who suffers."

I made out the *click* of the door as it opened and closed, and then more of Hockley's incessant pacing. Wren flinched when items clattered to the floor, the man wreaking havoc on his study.

Bringing my lips to where her ear should be, I whispered, "Almost there, sunshine. Breathe for me."

No gap remained between us, my head a mere inch away. I could feel her warm exhale fan across my lips. I closed my eyes as I leaned forward, grateful when I felt the soft brush of her cheek meeting my stubbled one. I murmured into her ear, telling her it would be over soon, but her frantic heartbeat pounded wildly against my chest.

I wished I could see her . . .

Hockley continued his rampage, the crashing of furniture being flipped causing my own heart to beat faster. We had to leave. *Now.* But we couldn't very well open the door and depart without notice. Even in Hockley's inebriated state, he'd see a door swing open by itself.

"Breathe, sweetheart," I soothed, my lips moving to her ear once more. A sharp ache pierced me. I wanted to release Wren and scream at Hockley for frightening her into this state, for unleashing his vicious temper. When Hockley tossed something made of glass and I pushed deeper against Wren, she did something that utterly surprised me—

Lips brushed my neck.

I went utterly still, overstimulated by the chaos in the room and the chaos Wren had wrought on my body with one press of her lips.

I swore I heard her say my name as she moved upward, grazing my jaw, so soft, so sweet. My insides were molten, and I had to swallow a groan when her mouth continued its slow perusal. She felt so damned good . . . too good.

"Wren." I said her name like a whisper of a plea, a shiver wracking my frame. Her response was another kiss, this one placed dangerously close to my mouth. My heartbeat galloped in my chest, every muscle tensing as I held back, as I let her take charge. I didn't know what was real and what was a distraction. If she'd kissed me to calm her nerves, or if . . . *If.*

I should've remained frozen in place. I should have done so many things besides what I planned to do.

Fuck me. I was damning myself and I didn't care.

When Wren Hayes, daughter of my enemy and Ward One princess, released a soft *"Please"* I lost whatever control I possessed.

Straining from the effort to remain silent, I swept my lips along her jaw, making my way to her cheek with tender kisses that were unlike me. Another glass ornament shattered behind us, masking my muffled groan as I tasted her skin, scenting her signature citrus hiding beneath her floral perfume, that intoxicating smell that clung to her hair. I moved her wrists to one hand as the other inched down, my mouth gliding across her cheeks, her nose, her chin. Everywhere and anywhere I could reach.

Cursed Fates, did I like it. Liked how she stopped shaking and curved into me. With my eyes still closed, I saw her as perfectly as I had when I kissed her neck in that alley.

I made a point to avoid her lips. To avoid the one place my mind begged me to go. Instead, I paid attention to the delicate curve of neck, her collarbone, moving down to where the tempting neckline of her dress began. I didn't go farther, but she arched into me, and only I heard her hum of approval. Only I could make out the way her hips moved in sync with my own.

We were trapped, and yet I'd never felt so fucking free.

The door slammed shut.

Wren released her breath, the air ghosting against my cheek, but she didn't move. Didn't try to pull away. In this in-between place where we were quite literally invisible, she surprised me once again.

Wren fused her lips to mine.

I groaned, deep and full of need. Her lips were supple and sweet and fucking delicious. My skin burned and my head swam. No way could I cease this madness. Not when Wren parted for me, allowing me to slip inside and taste her and the remnants of our drinks of blueberries and raspberries.

We didn't speak. Why ruin this? In my delusional state, I told myself this wasn't real.

So I acted like it wasn't.

I tightened my hold on her hands and invaded her mouth,

stealing her air, using it as my own. She sighed, the raspy noise going right to my center as that fire became an inferno. Somewhere along the way, our kisses turned needier, my teeth grazing her bottom lip. Nipping at it. Sucking it. I rumbled with approval when she returned the favor.

She pulled away, just for an instant, but a part of me died, the coldness like a knife to an already opened wound. I started to protest, but her lips traveled down my neck. Sucked on the skin. *Marked me.*

I cursed aloud.

My sunshine had transformed into something dangerous. Something that could ruin me. In all my years, I'd never had this intense a reaction. I thought I had, but no. Never like *this*. I existed on a whole new plane, kissing Wren Hayes. Feeling her hips buck against mine while she swirled her tongue, matching me move for move. Overpowering me with nothing more than her addictive kiss.

I felt like I'd lost my mind as she moved up and down, her teeth scraping my sensitive flesh, her pouty lips soothing any bite she made.

This had been bound to happen; this pull of ours too strong. But it was just that—a pull. A connection. An attraction.

For Fates' sake, she danced in Everett's arms not more than fifteen minutes ago, giving *him* her radiant smile. Holding on to him like he could be her rock.

I'd forgotten everything tonight. Forgotten who I was. Who *she* was.

My body tensed. Was I the boy she toyed with before moving on to someone of her own station? The dalliance she could think on years from now and laugh about?

"Damien?" Her voice filled the air, and my name came out breathless, so full of want and desire, it physically hurt, the ache in my chest throbbing.

I . . . I liked her. And the one thing I'd learned the hard way in the Void was that attachments could break you in the end. Especially with her; a lady who lived an entirely different life. Realization struck me. Hard.

We'd never work.

"It's time to go," I said stiffly, abruptly lowering her hands. Still entwined with her out of my gift's necessity, I gently urged her invisible body forward and around the chair. She didn't say another word, and I wondered what went on in her mind. If it was just as chaotic as mine.

I didn't let go of her until we slipped through the door and left it unlocked behind us. Didn't let go until shadows swarmed us on the stairwell.

When we broke apart, I swore a great shudder shook the very floor beneath my feet.

Slowly, she took shape—her gown, her hair, that face that could destroy me with one coy smirk. Now it was blotched in red and marred with confusion.

We should talk about what had just transpired, but talking would lead to things I didn't want to know.

"We break into Lizzy's home tomorrow," I said, not meeting

her eye. I knew we should try to inspect Adrian Hockley's room, but he was inside it, so that would be something I'd do alone. Once I got away from her. She just had to believe I'd left the ball.

I couldn't stand one more moment in her presence.

Lies. It was all a fantasy. A fiction. A dalliance she partook in before leaving me cold. I knew better than this.

"Damien, please. We need—"

I grabbed my mirror and stepped back, fading from her sight. The smell of the rose in my pocket overwhelmed, and I grasped the short stem, rolling it between my fingers. The bud slipped, falling to the floor.

Wren didn't move for a good many seconds, but when she did, a lone tear slid down her cheek as her eyes drifted to the rose.

Eyes glassy, she passed me, her chest inches away, her body near enough to grab and swing her back into my arms. But I didn't.

"I hate you, Damien."

Hell, I hated myself, too.

I stared at her retreating back, cursing as I ran a hand through my hair in frustration. Frustration with myself. Clutching the banister, I sucked in a deep breath, preparing to return to the party, invisible to the world. That was when my focus once again landed on the single flower abandoned on the floor.

My mouth fell as the edges of the pristine petals withered, a sickly gray consuming the color like a disease. I watched until no red remained, a scent of smoke replacing the floral. I'd never seen anything like it.

When I reached down to grasp what remained, my fingers swept through ashes, the form of the flower crumbling to nothing.

Dark magic.

Backing away from the remains, I stumbled down the steps, pretending all the while that I didn't smell like smoke. That I hadn't been the cause of the bloom's ruin.

Lies, like dreams, tended to turn into nightmares.

Chapter Twenty

Wren

There have been unique instances when gifts could be shared simultaneously. However, this is so rare that there isn't much research on the matter.
—*Aurilian History of Magical Objects,* Chapter Thirty

He left.

Just like I knew he would.

I had no plans to meet Damien anytime soon. He could sit there in his pub and stew for all I cared.

All right. Perhaps I cared. More than I wanted to, especially when the person in question was an ass. And a liar. And a thief. And a bunch of other things that, combined, drove me insane and turned me into another person entirely. So many more reasons to add to the list of why I despised the thief.

The night after the ball, I curled up in bed and read, trying to lose myself in another world. My mind, on the other hand, had other plans, and I reread the same sentence over and over again.

Damien kissed me back.

There was no denying it. He'd reacted when I pushed up onto my toes and kissed his lips, too overwhelmed by the scene to think about my actions. With his hard body against mine, protecting me, guarding me, I had wanted to *feel* him. There hadn't been much thought other than needing to drown in him before the world swallowed me up.

And Fates, he'd made me feel alive, wholly and dangerously alive, for the first time in my life. Damien destroyed me with his ravenous kisses. With the eager way he'd touched me, his broad hands skimming my figure with care before those fingers dug into my hips and he yielded to temptation. I'd been shocked for just a moment, stunned that he returned my advances with such fervor. And Fates, the low noises of need he'd made sounded like he'd been in pain. Like he'd wanted to give in ages ago.

Then he disappeared.

Having left me shaken, reeling not only from our new discovery, but from what we'd *both* done, he had the audacity to use his gift and vanish.

I groaned now, my book flopping onto my stomach.

Was this all a game to him? If so, I planned on bowing out. He couldn't kiss me and then run like a frightened boy. *He* was the one who'd continued long after Hockley left.

I felt foolish for thinking about Damien when I *should* be focused on my gift. Though, truth be told, the fire to find it had waned, replaced by a new need.

My father was obviously a player in a game I hadn't known existed. Maybe I'd always known he involved himself in less than proper dealings, but this . . . threatening lords and speaking of appeasing Fates—and another powerful entity, it appeared—threw me over the edge.

I tried not to think about it, I really did. Every time I pictured my father's heartless face as he warned Hockley of the consequences, I wanted to curl up into a ball and cry. To mourn the image I'd made of a man who didn't exist.

I felt like I'd just lost a parent.

He obviously knew about Hockley's son and his lack of a gift. Had Father believed the same had occurred with me? That he'd somehow displeased Day and I'd ended up being a casualty? How easily he lied, then, if that was true. Looking right into my eyes and pretending he'd searched the Registry, relaying that I was unblessed. Did it even bother him that he'd hurt his daughter? Could he be *that* cruel to someone he claimed to love?

A knock pounded at my door, jolting me upright.

Callie opened it before I replied, practically falling across my bed in exhaustion, her gray dress wrinkling on the mattress. I could tell she loathed it, her hands running down the skirts with a frown. She wore it to appease the leaders of the wards, as if they'd look at her like she was an imbecile merely for wearing pink.

Those bastards probably would.

"Why, yes, sister, do come in," I said, my words dry. My feigned teasing fell flat, my heart not in the right shape for me to converse with anyone at the moment, even her.

Callie rolled over and opened one eye. "I think our father is trying to kill me." She sighed and placed a hand over her eyes. "A ridiculous number of shipments are arriving, and apparently I'm the only one who can keep track of them."

I sat up straighter. "What kind of shipments?" Could this be related to last night's conversation?

"Oh, just everything," Callie hedged, twirling a strand of long black hair around her finger. "I catalog the crates and shipping containers, but they've been arriving erratically lately, and not all of them belong to Father. Meaning he's pawning me off to his friends for free labor."

"He doesn't pay you *at all,*" I remarked wryly, suddenly realizing how ridiculous that was, considering her workload.

"No," she admitted. She angled herself until she perched on her elbows and faced me, her hands cradling her face. Dark circles painted the skin beneath her eyes. She truly was beyond overworked.

"Why do you still go, then?" I asked cautiously. "Do you really think they're changing their minds about women in power?" I certainly hoped so, but seeing Callie so defeated—

It made me angry. Protective.

"I go because one day they will." One side of her mouth lifted in a somber smile. "You know better than anyone how fickle these people are. How they view women." I watched the bob of her throat as she swallowed down her emotion. She never cried, but I understood her well enough to recognize when the urge struck her. "I want power, Wren, for both of us. I want to be better than Father. Stronger and more influential. I just want to *do* better than him. Fates know he's not the most trustworthy man." She lightly smacked her forehead. "It's all a dream, right?"

I shook my head and reached for her, my hands curling around her upper arms.

"No. You have always been the ambitious one in the family, and I think that's a good thing. It doesn't hurt that you're *somewhat* clever." I gave her a playful grin, some of my earlier tension waning. "Don't give up so easily." If she did, then they'd win. And with Callie on the inside, she might uncover what Father planned and *do* something.

"I won't," she promised, averting her gaze. "I just wish it didn't always come at some sort of price." I hurried to ask more, but Callie lifted herself up, readying to leave. "I need to sleep before I fall face-first down the stairs." She shot me a smirk at the threshold of my room.

"Callie?" I called out before she shut my door. She hesitated. "Why won't Father work with the other ward leaders to help the Void? It's still Aurilia. I just don't understand."

Damien and Ruby floated across my vision. The Void and the children begging for food, the smoke clogging the streets, making it nearly impossible to breathe. I wasn't certain why I even asked. If Father was involved with unsavory dealings, why would he care?

Callie took a step back into the room and leaned on the wall, her expression somber. "He needs them where they are, Wren," she said softly, briefly shutting her eyes. "A week ago, I learned *he* was responsible for the failure of the proposed bills to remedy conditions. I found out only when I overheard him speaking with Lord Lovett and Hockley, and"—she swallowed thickly, averting her eyes—"I didn't want to say anything to you because I'm a coward, and to be honest, I didn't want to think him capable of such cruelty."

It was as if I'd been dealt a blow to my chest as I stared at my sister, her eyes shining with what looked like unshed tears. She held them in for me.

"Why stay?" I asked, my throat so tight it was surprising anything made it out at all.

"Because if I leave, no one will be there to watch him should he decide to do something worse."

This was the moment. I had to tell Callie about what Damien and I overheard. She had access where I didn't.

"Listen, Callie," I began slowly, my head spinning. "Last night I saw something, and I think you should know. Maybe you can investigate." She cocked her head, brows pinched in worry. "I saw Father—"

"Callie!"

We both jumped as the man in question called out for her, his voice booming as it rang through the halls.

"I need you in my office. Now!" he ordered, causing Callie to flinch slightly. She shot me an apologetic look, and I swore that true fear washed over her features before she composed herself, morphing into a woman constructed of stone.

"I have to go. He's been more demanding as of late," she whispered. "But tell me more about what you found out. *Please,*" she added before hastily running from my room and to the study. I heard her frantic steps in the hall.

I cursed aloud with no one there to scold me.

Callie wanted to fight her way to the top, tooth and nail, and she was my sister—the same one who'd mended broken birds' wings when we were younger and had stood up to Father when she knew he was wrong on a subject. I envied her bravery.

If anyone would help me, it would be her. Yet I never would get the chance to tell her with Father breathing down her neck. They were always together, his watchful eye on her like an invisible noose.

Maybe it was best to wait until I understood the whole picture. *Then* I'd tell her, even if I had to wake her in the middle of the night. The promise bolstered me, and for the first time in days, a weight lifted as I knew I'd soon have my sister on our side.

As the hour was late, I couldn't do anything now. Tomorrow promised a new day with new chances to hunt for the truth of Father's threats, but I'd have to force my brain to relax and sleep if I was to be of any use.

Grabbing my book, I once again attempted to read the paragraph I'd left off at, trying three more times before I finally fell into its rhythm. It was a tale of the Fates, and how Day had saved the first princess of the realm in the west from a terrible monster. According to legend, the monster had taken the girl, prepared to devour her whole and consume her royal blood. Day had dashed onto the scene like the beacon of light she was known as, and using her powers, she had vanquished the monster.

I'd read this story before, but that had been ages ago.

> *A beastly thing, with elongated teeth and resembling both a bear and a griffin, the creature was ten times the immortal's size. All hope seemed lost, yet the young Fate faced the being with hope in her gaze and the soul of a warrior in her blood. When she opened her eyes, they were so stormy, they sparked like black ice. As she trained them on the creature, light shot from her irises, burning brilliantly and searing the monster alive. The once-great beast turned into a pile of ashes. The princess, who'd been hiding in the corner, ran to embrace Day, and within her arms, Day radiated pure joy—a perfect reflection of the princess. She held tight to the girl, even when her sister and fellow Fate, Dusk, materialized, her raven hair floating around her form as if a great wind trailed her everywhere. She swept the ashes into her floor-length cloak, the animal and its soul gone forever to the underworld. Dusk vanished, leaving behind a simple token for the princess and all she'd been through. A gift, some might say.*
>
> *The princess reached down, picking up and donning the simple necklace Dusk had left behind. Around her neck, magic flared to life, and the princess was bestowed a great power that many coveted.*

My eyes snagged on one particular passage.

When she opened her eyes, they were so stormy, they sparked like black ice.

While Day was golden-haired, her eyes, unlike her sisters', were cold and gray. Dawn's were a calming coral, and Dusk possessed eyes the shade of a deep blue, much like the last light before the setting sun.

Damien's eyes were unlike anything I'd ever seen before . . . impossibly dark gray and stormy.

Perhaps similar to black ice. Like Day's.

I reread the passage, only to notice something else.

Every other book in my modest library depicted Day as the Fate who had created the first gift. The story was the same—about the princess and her monster—but this one . . . I flipped the cover over, inspecting its design. I didn't recall purchasing it. I'd merely grabbed it at random from my shelf earlier. But its leather cover, a beautiful deep blue and embossed with a single gold star, was new to me. Running my fingertip over the cover, I jerked back when a light shock pricked me.

It appeared like any other book, and yet . . . I brought it closer to my eyes, flipping it this way and that. My heart thudded when a pressed red poppy fell out from between the pages.

My hand shook as I took the poppy flower and rubbed my thumb over its velvety surface, my thoughts roaming back to that day in Dusk's garden.

I frowned, hunching over the book, curious about its origins. Father wouldn't have purchased it for me, let alone Mother. And Callie was far too busy to shop.

Where did you come from?

A soft *clack* sounded against glass. I dropped the red petal, watching as it fluttered to the bed.

Another *clack*.

Easing out of bed, I padded to my window just as the third *clack* struck the glass.

I nearly jumped out of my skin at the face staring back at me.

Yanking up the window, I snapped, "What are you doing here?"

Damien's hand gripped the branch of the tree closest to my room, leaning to the side as his left foot found purchase on a lower branch. Somehow, he made the pose appear effortless.

"We agreed to meet," he gritted through his teeth. Damien was far from thrilled, by the looks of it. "We planned to break into Lizzy's home and do some investigating." He shifted his foot on the trunk of the tree, adjusting. "Now you've made me climb a damned tree and I'm probably coated in sap—"

I shoved the window closed.

"Wren!" My name came out muffled, but Damien's cold features flared to life. His eyes sparked with irritation, his forehead creasing in confusion.

Good.

I shook my head and crossed my arms. If he was anywhere near as cunning as he believed, he'd figure it out.

He kept shouting my name, forgetting that my parents and sister were at home. Fool.

I yanked the curtains together and shut out his face altogether. There. Much better.

"Wren! Open up!" he continued. "Stop being stubborn."

My blood boiled. Crossing the room to my bed, I whipped my blankets up and climbed inside, rolling over so I faced the door rather than the blasted window he tapped at.

Stubborn. No. I was done with games.

Hell, maybe I didn't need *him* anymore.

The prick showed up again the following evening, his pebbles striking my window with more force than necessary. I glowered before shutting the curtains, and he again called my name, the sound muffled by the glass.

This time, he was more persistent, going so far as to try to swing himself to the windowsill and close the gap between the house and the tree. I knew this because I heard a rather ominous *thump* before a crude curse.

I turned off my light and pretended to sleep.

The next morning—after trying and failing to pick the lock on Father's study—I received a letter from Lord Everett. The fine paper and elegant script stared back at me, the words bringing a much-needed lightness into my chest. Everett asked if I'd join him for a ride at his estate just outside the city in a few days' time.

Such an uncomplicated request.

After days of Sarah watching my every move, making it all but impossible to leave the house, and with my attempts to break into the study a failure, the letter was surprisingly welcome.

Maybe clearing my head would be a good thing, and then I could focus.

I'd never planned to marry—I *still* didn't—but I enjoyed Everett's company. It helped that he was handsome, the admiration in his eyes when he looked at me like a warm blanket on a cold night.

The more time I spent in his company, the less I saw him as the stiff gentleman I'd originally pegged him as, and perhaps he might understand and accept my unwillingness to marry. He could want the same things I did—adventure and independence. It wouldn't be terrible to have a companion if I ever left Andalay.

I replied an hour later, accepting.

Afterward, I wandered about the house, empty aside from a busy Sarah in the kitchen, and inspected my parents' room. Neat and orderly, it was clearly designed by Mother, what with all the golden and rosy accents. A copious number of pillows lay across the bed, the two nightstands occupied by matching mother-of-pearl gas lamps.

Rummaging through their drawers, mainly Father's, I found nothing but neatly folded clothing. Even the socks were laid out to perfection. The massive closet beside their bathroom provided nothing either—mainly filled with Mother's luxurious gowns and Father's pressed suits. Peering up at a shelf lining the closet, I found old sketches Father had crafted, chiefly scenic landscapes and drawings of strangers in the park. I hadn't seen the artistic side of him, but holding his artwork, which had been shoved so carelessly inside the closet, weighed on my chest. I couldn't deceive myself any longer, and seeing the love he'd put into these drawings pained me. Placing them neatly back where I found them, I continued my search, bypassing Mother's newest pink boots, her fashionable heels, and a silk shawl I yearned to borrow.

In a box shoved in the corner, I uncovered Mother's magicked shoes. She hadn't worn them this season, which I found odd. It was the first time she hadn't. I peeled open the lid of the box and carefully pushed aside the delicate wrapping paper. Simple and crafted of a vivid blue that shone black in some lighting, they were stunning—the matching satin ties meant to wind up her calves were the purest silk that slipped between my curious fingertips.

For a moment, I pictured her last performance. I'd been young at the time, but I recalled her innate elegance commanding the stage, the light shining directly on her ethereal form. My throat grew tight as I repacked the shoes, realizing the last time I'd seen my mother genuinely smile had been on that night.

Even with a gift from the Fates, her joy hadn't lasted.

She'd shoved her gift carelessly in a box and out of sight. Like she didn't care. Or like her cares went elsewhere, namely toward impressing the nobles with her grand teatimes and luncheons. Her busy schedule had increased, if such a thing were possible, and she rarely came home until after I'd already gone to sleep. Not that Father said anything of it.

The remainder of the day passed with me trying to pick the lock on Father's study, a futile attempt that made me want to simply hack through the wooden door with the axe from the garden. Defeated for now, I wandered back to my room in time for the front door to swing open.

Mother entered, her long pink skirts sweeping over the floorboards.

I froze as if I'd been caught. "Mother?" I hadn't expected her home so early.

Her head lifted, finally locking on me. "Oh, Wren," she said, her voice like a melody. Light and carefree—which didn't describe her in the least. "I'm just stopping by for a bit. Forgot something I needed to bring to Lady Dudley."

She breezed past me on graceful feet, but I kept up, trailing at her back. "I haven't seen you in days," I called out, stumbling to keep up with her long strides. "Not even at dinner."

Mother didn't pause as she ascended the stairs. "I've been busy, little bird. Lots to do in order to raise our family's name out of the mud."

I paused for just a second, knowing full well she referred to my cursed birthday.

Mother walked to her room, ignoring me entirely. When she reached the door, she all but slammed it in my face.

The lock sounded a moment later.

That familiar ache throbbed as I stood there, staring at the closed door. Tears gathered in my eyes, ones I desperately wanted to shed but wouldn't. I should be used to her curt behavior by now, but it never ceased to sting.

Ten minutes passed while I remained there like some pathetic pup, wishing she'd come out and show an ounce of affection. But she never did.

Swallowing the hurt, the pain of her indifference, I snuck to my room and shut the door before leaning against its back. Sliding down, I had no choice but to give in when one single tear escaped. It slid down my cheek and onto my dress, wetting the fine fabric. I watched the wet spot until it dried, not moving even when Father and Callie arrived home, Father's boisterous voice wafting up the stairs as he asked Sarah what she'd made for dinner.

Why was I surprised? I was a foolish girl who continuously allowed these people to hurt me. Again and again and again. The walls surrounding my heart rose, and I shut my eyes, imagining building the fortress stone by stone until no more tears fell.

I only deserted my room to attend dinner, a requirement. Blessedly, it stayed a noiseless one. I didn't even try to catch Callie's eye. So much went on inside my own head that if I looked at her, I feared my carefully constructed walls would crumble.

With a full belly, I performed my nightly ritual and read in bed, moving on to the next story in the mysterious little blue book. No more petals fell from its pages, but I chose a story about Dusk and her Realm of the Unknown. The passage mentioned the reapers at her disposal—people who were born with the ability to sense when someone would soon pass, *and* what would occur afterward. According to the story, the reapers' talent only surfaced when they encountered a loss so tragic, it burst free from their souls, rendering them reapers and servants to Dusk as she guided souls to the underworld.

A small picture had been sketched on one page: a woman rising from a burned building, remnants of what had to be a house fire beneath her feet. A shadowy figure hovered behind, arms outstretched as if about to hug the woman. With my nose practically pressing into the page, I studied the drawing, the hairs on my arms rising. The fire had wiped away her home, yet three items lay untouched in the rubble: a pair of shoes, the laces spared from the flames; a plain goblet; and a necklace, the pendant a simple oval shape.

My focus continued to land on the necklace, my heart thudding in my ears as every other noise faded.

I wasn't certain how long I stared, but the thudding in my ears lessened until I heard it—

A *clack* against my window.

I groaned and set the book on my bed, still opened to the page. Ripping the covers back, I headed to where Damien glared at me through the glass.

This time, I opened it a fraction, just enough so he didn't have to yell.

"I'm done," I told him stiffly. "I'll send payment to the Broken Wing."

I was preparing to shut the window when he called my name, his hoarse voice cracking at the end. It made me pause, against my better judgment.

"I feel bad, all right?" he ground out, his tone not helping his case. "I . . . I shouldn't have left after that. I should've stayed, but you have to understand, we come from very different worlds."

It sounded like he'd rehearsed his paltry speech.

I laughed, outright laughed in his face. "You *felt bad,*" I repeated incredulously. I didn't even touch on the "different worlds" admission. I shook my head. A heaviness settled over me, my feet sticking to the floor as if unable to move and shut him out even though his words pricked. I was no one to be pitied.

"It's not like I didn't *want* to, Wren. Actually, I was shocked by how much I did," he said, lower this time. He couldn't meet my eyes. "But it can't happen—"

"You and I are done. Done working together. Done speaking. I asked you to help me with a simple job, yes, but somewhere along the way you and I both know something out of our control happened. You walked away *twice,* uncaring how I might be affected. You're selfish," I all but spat. "And I've realized I don't need you to figure out the truth. I have a plan of my own. One that doesn't involve you."

I couldn't allow his ever-shifting feelings to affect me. I had to uncover a mystery much bigger than us.

"Wren, you're going to get hurt," he grumbled, his brows pushing together. "You can't possibly think you can go out alone. You'll be found out in minutes."

I stood there, my heart thumping madly against my ribs while heat blossomed on both cheeks. "You may think me incompetent, Damien. Weak. Afraid. A lost ward princess. But I'm so much more than anyone has ever given me credit for. Myself included."

I'd never been given the chance to find out for myself. To know that I could accomplish a feat aside from teatime and plastering on a fake face for society. Enough was enough. No more sulking. No more staying locked behind the doors of my home. The time had arrived to discover who Wren Hayes truly was.

"I didn't mean it like that," Damien protested, nearly losing his footing and sliding down the rough bark of the tree. "I just know you don't understand—"

The slam of the window shut him up.

I prayed he'd seen the fire in my eyes. That he understood how much of an ass he'd been. But in the end, did it matter?

Damien's eyes pleaded with mine through the glass, his lips parting as if he wished to speak. Likely to spew more excuses. Yet it was the way he reached for the window that caused a pang of sorrow so deep and cutting to slice through my heart that I stumbled back a step.

He mouthed my name. I ignored it.

I wouldn't fall for those pleading eyes or the way he appeared on the verge of breaking. I would wipe Damien from my life.

I would be the one to find out why my gift had been taken and why the people of the Void were going missing.

Alone.

Chapter Twenty-One

Damien

She shut me out. Again.

Not that I didn't fucking deserve it.

Like the fool I'd become, I'd gone to her window the past three nights hoping she'd eventually let me in and talk. Thinking that if I plied her with empathetic words, she'd forgive me. Hell, I *expected* her to.

Sadly, she remained steadfast in her hatred for me.

That first time in the alley—when I'd kissed up and down her neck, secretly relishing her scent, her taste—had been a ruse, even if my head swam whenever I returned to the stolen moment. The second time . . . even if she'd initiated a hesitant kiss, the rest was all me. I'd leapt at the chance she provided, indulging in what had been building in my core for weeks.

A want.

A need.

An *obsession.*

Once I'd left her on those stairs—her crestfallen face haunting me with each blink—I'd spent that night wandering the party, invisible to all and learning nothing but how ignorant and careless I'd been. I hadn't thought of the flower or the ash it had become, and I threw myself into investigating.

The attendants' drivel about the trouble they'd be in should magic vanish was damn near impossible to stomach. They didn't care that Dusk was still missing, they just knew that their power would be gone should the immortal somehow die. And Fates, when they smugly showcased their gifts, half drunk and cackling, all I wanted was to return to the strong-willed blonde who worked some sort of dark magic on me. The same one who'd brought this *mess* of fucking emotions to the forefront.

It was her fault.

Even my mirror liked her; it had never shared its power with anyone else. The significance of it—well, I wasn't sure what it meant. I wasn't sure I *wanted* to know. It only worked to tie us closer together.

Nothing enduring could ever happen between us, but I'd gone ahead and acted on what I wanted anyway, devouring her and that smart mouth that had made me feel more alive than I had in years. All of our bickering had ended with a moment of vulnerability, a combustion that I'd mistaken for hatred. Or wished was hatred.

I *hurt* her when I ran away. When I played the coward and used my power to vanish before I could say or do anything I'd later regret.

Because I *would* regret it.

Attachment will only get you hurt. Or killed.

Then why had I gone to her window three times like a lost pup? Why did she suddenly fill my thoughts first thing upon waking? When I closed my eyes at night?

She was still the daughter of a man I loathed, a possible murderer and a crime lord, for Fates' sake. She was still a sheltered ward princess. But Wren herself, down to her bare bones . . . she was more than the titles I'd given her. Well, *sunshine* fit her well.

Brave. Confident. Daring. Still a know-it-all. Those all worked too.

She could be naïve, but she *wanted* to learn. Wanted to help her city. The problem was, she felt powerless. I sensed her defenses drop whenever her shoulders slumped in raw defeat as she spoke about the Void or even her father. Little did she know, her empathy, her *trying* to right this wrong, was the first step.

The attraction I'd assumed would go away hadn't—it had *grown*. I *liked* the princess in the tower. A disaster waiting to happen—I was no fabled knight in shining armor.

I was the thief that had ruined her life.

Ruby would be laughing her arse off if she knew what ran through my thoughts like a plague.

Speaking of Ruby . . .

She should've been here by now. It was nearly midnight, and I called in a favor she owed. If I was to get the locket back to Wren and restore my magic, it was time to go back to the beginning—to uncover the original buyer. It should've occurred to me sooner, even if the person cloaked themselves in secrecy and shadow. For all I knew, they'd been at the ball the other night. Their carriage was nice enough to fit in on the northern side of Andalay. Unfortunately for me, they'd never showed their face, just their bodyguard when we first met to agree to the terms. And their carriage? When I scoured the houses in the north, not a hint of it could be found.

So when I stumbled upon that very carriage—with its silver handles and blue curtains—sitting right out front of the Broken Wing Tavern like a wrapped present, I sent a ruddy-cheeked messenger boy to fetch Ruby. For all I knew, the buyer or his assistant recognized me, but they wouldn't recognize Ruby. As much as I wanted to go barreling into the tavern and demand answers, I was forced to wait in tense silence outside in the alley, which reeked of Cap's unpopular fish stew; no surprise there.

Anxiety dug its claws in, my teeth grinding together whenever someone exited. Whoever the buyer was, I needed them to stay put.

"You're really abusing your nickname, you know," came a raspy voice from just behind me.

I reared back, bumping into a solid body. Ruby's laughter floated like smoke in the alley, and the tips of my ears grew hot. "Maybe *you* should be the one nicknamed the Ghost. Fates, Ruby."

Maneuvering around me, she stared up through her thick lashes. "What was so important that you had to send a messenger to come and get little old me?"

I could tell she was delighted nonetheless. Ruby lived for the days when I cashed in on a favor. Or maybe my cynicism was at play, and she actually enjoyed my company. I didn't exactly despise hers.

I nearly snorted aloud at the idea.

"See that carriage over there?" I tilted my chin to the side, where the finely carved wood stood in stark contrast to the rest of the wagons parked on the street. Distinct sky-blue velvet curtains with silver trim had been pulled back, but as long as I'd been watching, no one had exited. Only a burly bodyguard with a low hood covering his face stood sentinel, his muscled form leaning against the door. Probably the same bodyguard I'd encountered. I turned to Ruby. "That was the carriage belonging to the original buyer for Wren's locket. I know he'll recognize me if I go inside, so . . ."

She placed both hands on her narrow hips and skewered me with daggers in her brown eyes. "You're going to have me go inside and check it out, aren't you? See if I notice anything unusual?" Not the daring adventure she probably imagined I'd planned.

I gifted her a toothy grin, a smile many had called handsome. It didn't work on her. Fates knew I was far from her type.

"Stop making that face," she said. "You look like you have a stomachache." I glared back. It *did not*. Or I didn't think it did. "Such a pain in my arse, Damien." With a huff, she lifted her long cherry skirts and stormed inside the tavern, her dark brown curls loose around her tonight, the gas lamps shining on every strand and making them glow.

Ruby loved to play spy, so I gathered that her little act had been just that. Besides, she liked Wren—hell, she wanted to get to know her more, and she'd made it obvious she wasn't pleased that I stole Wren's gift. Long ago, Ruby and I had promised we'd only steal from those who abused power or could afford to lose a copper or two. A pang of guilt clenched my chest. I had failed to keep that promise.

Slouching farther against the wall, I observed the drunken men and women who entered and exited the tavern. All harmless, all out for a fun night when the burden of living became heavy. While entertaining to watch, I became restless, pacing the small alley until I stubbed my toe against a bin, sending the top clattering loudly to the ground. So much for subtlety.

My nickname was a joke tonight.

Twenty excruciating minutes passed before a slinky silhouette graced the entrance of the alley.

"Well?" I asked Ruby. "Did you get a good look at them?"

It would have been easy to pick out a newcomer among the regulars. Just as I spied Everett that day when he visited the tavern. While he'd done his best to dress down, the materials he wore were far too rich for anyone who lived in the Void.

Ruby crossed her arms as she sauntered closer. "There was no one there who looked out of place," she admitted crossly. She hated to lose. "I don't know why the carriage is parked here, but no one suspicious is inside. Or anyone I didn't recognize."

I grumbled a curse before scrubbing a hand over my face. "That makes no sense. The buyer's carriage is *right there.* Meaning they're here. Or somewhere near."

Ruby shrugged. "Don't know what to tell you, but seems like your luck ran out." She whipped out an ancient timepiece and checked its polished surface. "Shite. I'm late. I told Annie I'd be at her place by now, and I was late the last time." Her eyes lifted to mine, narrowing. "If you just cost me a fun night, it'll be me who haunts you," she threatened before shooting me a crude middle finger and skipping away. "Next time pick a more fun favor."

I prepared a clever retort, but the same needling sensation I'd been experiencing stole my breath. As I stared at Ruby's back, nausea churned and slick sweat slithered down my back. Ruby's face popped into my thoughts like a vision; her inquisitive brown eyes were closed, her lips unsmiling. She lay still on a metal table. The same table I'd seen that tailor's assistant on.

Fuck, I had to be losing my mind. Imagining the worst possible scenarios. Losing Ruby . . . the very idea had to be my own fear rushing to the surface. A hellish trick my mind played.

When was the last time I'd truly gotten a decent night's rest? What else could explain why I'd been the victim of these sporadic hallucinations?

I released a frustrated groan and faced the filthy, mud-streaked wall of the alley. Resting my forearm against the cool brick, I silently seethed, focusing on the task at hand. I just needed to track down the buyer. So damned simple, and yet they remained elusive. If they weren't inside the tavern, they had to be close—unless the carriage functioned as a distraction. The question was, had it been a distraction for *me*? I *had* reneged on our deal in the end.

Before I had the chance to exit onto the street, the distinct *squelch* of steel meeting flesh greeted my ears.

A few seconds elapsed before the pain followed.

Fates. A burning sensation shot across the left side of my upper chest and down my back and torso like a venomous snake bite. I let out a low and anguished noise deep in my throat as my vision blurred and blackened, the edges tapering into slits.

Copper filled the air, and if the pain wasn't clue enough, the smell was.

Stabbed. Someone had *stabbed* me.

I dropped to my knees with a painful jolt, my hands grasping the grimy black stones by my boots. I tried to turn my head, to see who'd attacked, but my body didn't seem to be working. Nothing was working.

A shadowy figure draped in a dark cloak stepped around me, his size imposing—tall and built of hard muscle. He must've turned around, because for a split second, I swore I glimpsed a spark of blue eyes in the shine of the nearby gas lamps.

I ground my teeth and attempted to ease myself up, my hand grazing the alley's wall. My knees nearly buckled with the effort. The man . . . why did he seem familiar? If I could trust my sight at all with the way the damned world continued to tilt.

He hadn't even used magic, just what I assumed to be a fucking knife . . . in my back.

How poetic.

A second later, reins flicked and a horse's whinny echoed down the street.

I staggered forward, the world and the night slanting like a twisted carnival mirror.

Excruciating agony drowned out every logical thought of survival. It dug its pointed claws into my bones and squeezed, sucking the very life from my flesh. Never had I experienced such pain. Such a feeling of helplessness. *Fear.*

A pattering sounded behind me, and I reached around with a groan. Darkness coating my fingers. So. Much. Blood.

Delirious and defeated, I took one more step before my knees lost the battle and gave out.

The last image I saw was of myself—

On a metal table, dissected and beaten, eyes wide open in horror.

Chapter Twenty-Two

Wren

Day is known for her ambition; Dawn, her gentle strength; and Dusk . . . she is often mistaken for death itself.

—*Origin of the Fates,* Chapter Fifteen

Damien leaned over me, his dark hair falling into his face. We lay upon supple green grass, the breeze tickling the orange trees in the distance.

"What are you thinking, sunshine?" he murmured in my ear, sparking my nerves. He pulled back and studied my face, a great grin brightening his handsome features. "And a blush? Is that for me?"

"So cocky," I managed. My thoughts had strayed to a somewhat . . . risqué place.

"You wouldn't like me any other way," he said, shifting so his elbows rested on either side of my head. He teased me with his proximity. With how his body draped over mine. Fates, I could feel every hard ridge of him, every sinewy muscle.

I reached up and flicked his nose, startling him. "Bring down the ego a peg, and we'll see."

"You little liar." He shifted, tugging me with him as he spun onto his back, forcing my legs to fall on either side of him. From this angle, I saw the golden light of the sun cascade over his softened features. His easy smile. The one he gave only me.

"Says the thief."

*"*Former *thief," he amended with a scoff. "Or am I not as appealing now that I'm a hardworking man?" He angled his chin behind us, to where our home sat. A modest thing constructed of wood and painted a pastel blue—at my request.*

I shook my head. "No. You did it. And I"—I paused for dramatic effect—"I found out just how much I enjoy toying with Hazel Glen's politicians. Who'd have thought I'd like to argue so much?"

He laughed, so deep and full it warmed my chest. My heart. My soul. "Oh, sunshine. You surprise me every day."

"Good." I leaned down, my lips inches from his. "I have to keep you on your toes."

A clattering rang from far away, forcing my head up. "What was that?"

Damien shrugged. "Don't know or care." His arms ran up my thighs, his touch like fire. He settled on the small of my waist. "I just want you to come back here."

The noise came again, louder this time.

"No, I heard—"

I jolted up in bed, a flush on my face and my heart pounding. I'd dreamt of the bastard. Imagined a life *together.* My face scrunched as I silently admonished myself—that was never the plan. I had to continuously remind myself of this. Whether it was with him or another, I wouldn't tie myself to someone else forever. They'd only take advantage. Trap me.

Just a silly dream.

Something struck the window hard enough that a small crack formed. I lurched from bed, ignoring the way the tree's limbs cast eerie shadows on the walls.

Yanking up the window, I stared out into the dimness, my eyesight adjusting. "I swear, Damien, if you ever come back—"

My mouth shut.

Sure enough, Damien hung from the tree with one hand, his footing unsteady on the branch beneath his boots. His eyes were shut, his shirt stained black at his shoulder. Fates, he appeared half awake.

"Damien?" Dread constricted my throat, his name coming out distorted.

Something bad had happened. His face . . . it was too pale, even in the moonlight.

I leaned over when he didn't reply, the top half of my body dangling from the window. Grasping his face, I forced him to look up, giving him a small shake when he didn't stir.

I cursed. That same dark color slicked his cheeks, his forehead, his lips.

"Come inside," I coaxed, my blood pounding, my instincts rearing up in alarm to protect him. To get him off that damned tree before his grip loosened and he fell. Anxiety, like insects, swarmed the inside of my stomach, and I had to remind myself several times to breathe.

"Damien, I need you to help me." He mumbled something

incoherent but managed to look at the window. "There's a small ledge below," I instructed quickly, praying he didn't let go of the trunk. "I'm going to pull you, and your feet are going to aim for that ledge. Look down. Find it."

An odd panic shook my voice. I watched as he angled his head to the ledge, which was just wide enough for him to rest the tip of his boots.

"Count to three with me, Damien." He slowly, too slowly, found my eyes. "We can do it. You just have to trust me. Jump when I say, all right?"

I had no idea what I was doing or whether I could support most of his weight. All I understood was that he would bleed out in front of me if I did nothing. The darkness smelled of copper, the scent of it permeating my senses. "Damien."

He locked eyes, holding firm as he nodded. "F-fine," he muttered. "Don't d-drop me, sunshine."

"I won't," I assured him, even if I wasn't confident in that promise. "Now. *One.*" I grabbed his hand, my other one resting close to his hand that clutched the tree trunk. "*Two.*" I let out a steady exhale. There wasn't time to question this. "*Three!*" With every ounce of strength I possessed, I yanked him forward, and Damien did his best to lunge toward my window. I groaned when he struck the side, only one boot managing to catch the ledge. My grip was the lone thing keeping him from tumbling backward.

"Wren," he murmured, his head lolling. "*Please.*"

My grip on him loosened, his hands clammy and cold. So very cold. I dug my bare heels into the wooden planks at my feet, cursing like I never had before as I awkwardly lugged him closer.

In his state, I was going to have to take over almost entirely.

Wishing I possessed the gift of strength, I bit my cheek and pulled, hauling his limp body through my window, ignoring his small whimpers of pain when he grazed the sill.

Damien and I fell to the floor at the same time—me, sweaty and on my back, and him sprawled face down across the boards, unmoving.

I didn't waver.

Lighting the lamp beside my bed, I brought it to him and inspected him. He wore trousers and a stark white shirt, though blood stained most of it and the material had been brutally ripped at his left shoulder. Leaping up, I raced to my desk and snagged a pair of sewing scissors. Back at his side, I slashed through the fabric, tearing it from his body with shaking hands.

Scraps lay around me in a pile, revealing his torn flesh.

I was no expert or healer, but someone had *stabbed* him. Blood trickled from the wound, which required stitches, and it coated most of his back. Based on the way the front of his shirt had looked, I assumed the weapon had run right through him.

Should I go get help? Find a doctor? Wake Callie?

I wanted to cry. Wanted to scream. Punch something.

I was out of my depth here, and he'd die if I sat and watched him fade away as pain shook him. Terror raced into my veins, constricting my breathing. I had to get help.

I rose, but Damien weakly lifted his head, his hand seizing my wrist with more force than I believed him capable of. He avoided my gaze when he spoke, his eyes still shut. "Only y-you, Wren. Don't . . . n-no one else."

He didn't want me to involve anyone. No matter how desperately I yearned to wake someone and have them assess his state, to free my hands of the burden of possibly losing him because I wasn't capable enough. He swayed, barely keeping his head up as his eyes peeled open. They bored into mine with such intensity, such conviction, that I nodded in assent.

Gently, I dropped his hand and padded outside my room. The hall was clear, Damien's arrival not having woken anyone. As quickly as possible, I slipped down the stairs and to the parlor. There I found Father's liquor. Back upstairs, bottle in hand, I stopped at the linen closet and grabbed a handful of the old towels Sarah used when she cleaned. Ones that wouldn't be missed. Below those shelves, she kept some spare sheets. I took them too.

Supplies in hand, I scrambled back to my room, locked the door, and placed the items on the floor before taking my sewing kit from my desk. An uneasy calm overtook me, my mind homing in on his wound and pushing the rest of the world away.

He wasn't going to die.

He *couldn't.*

I wasn't sure when Damien and his moodiness had gotten beneath my skin, but he was there, steadfast and refusing to release me. Something about him forever drew me to him, and while we bickered and fought, he'd been the one to help me on my quest. Even if he required a few pieces of silver. Something in the back of my mind told me he would help me now without the coin. I wanted to believe that.

Adjusting my measly instruments, I shoved down the panic rising in my throat like bile. It was either hesitate or take action, and

I'd hesitated most of my life. My eyes prickled as I assessed the ruined mess of skin. The attacker appeared to have come at him from behind, aiming for his heart. Fortunately, they had terrible aim. Or Damien had shifted at the last second. Either way, he got lucky.

Pouring water onto a towel from the pitcher on my nightstand, I cleaned around the wound as quickly as possible. Next I drenched a fresh cloth with the liquor. Damien hissed when I gingerly cleansed the open gash, his eyes briefly opening before fluttering shut. *Fuck*. The earlier panic overrode everything now, and I could no longer shove down my emotions. Frantically, I poured the bottle directly on his wound. Damien didn't wake this time. He must've passed out from the pain.

I was a terrible nurse.

Threading my needle, I began my clumsy stitches, having never done this before. I winced when the needle pierced his skin, and cursed the entire time, loathing the grunts of pain he unconsciously released whenever the sharp needle pierced him. Far from the best, due to my trembling limbs and heavy breathing, the stitches were at least tight enough to stop the flow of blood.

I hoped.

It took time, sweat beading on my brow, my hands slick and clammy, but I finished his back. Another splash of liquor, and then I ripped at one of the old sheets, forming strips. I positioned the makeshift wrappings as I used both hands to turn him over, exhausted, my muscles aching.

Damien flopped on his back with a *thump,* and I grimaced.

Repeating the process with his chest, I cleaned the wound before stitching where the tip of the blade had come through. My hands had steadied, thankfully, but the rest of me shivered violently as a few tears slipped free from my eyes. Damn me and my inconvenient emotions.

"Sunshine," he muttered, his voice soft, an agonized whimper.

"I'm right here," I said, more tears falling down my cheeks. His plea sent a shot of adrenaline pumping through my veins.

"I'm going to fix you up, Damien. We're almost done," I coaxed, but he didn't reply. Just mumbled incoherently.

Once his chest was disinfected and stitched, I used a large portion of the ripped sheet and wound it tightly around his upper shoulder and torso, grateful that the knife hadn't struck anything vital. I grunted, my body blanketed in sweat as I moved him, but he must've passed out again.

He'd better fucking wake up.

Already, he looked better, at least from the outside. I had no doubt he'd lost blood on his way here. Which I didn't understand. Why not go to the bar? To the bartender who rented him his room? Rather, he'd come across the city. To *me*.

I sat back on my heels for a moment, the fatigue weighting my arms. My white nightdress clung to me, all sticky and red, and I bet I had streaks of blood on my face. Before I tended to myself, I laid down a thick blanket I found in the closet and an extra pillow. I wouldn't be physically able to haul him into bed after what I'd just done, but I hated the idea of him sprawled on the floor.

Slipping both hands under his arms, I gradually pulled him over to the pallet, mindful of his new stitches. He groaned, which I took as a good sign, when I arranged his body on the padded blanket. Lifting his head, I slid the pillow below and pushed his dark, sweat-soaked hair from his pale brow.

Wetting another scrap of cloth, I dabbed at his face, cleaning some blood from his hard features, which were rigid even in his sleep. The cloth stained instantly, and I soaked the cloth with fresh water before wiping it across his muscular arms. My eyes were traitors, wishing to linger on his impressive form, and the heat in my cheeks slid down my neck.

Not the time, Wren. Fates.

At long last, hours after he'd arrived and tumbled into my room, I cleaned myself. I threw away the nightdress in the bin beneath my sink, hidden by other rubbish, and washed as best I could without waking the house by running a bath. The pipes in this old house were noisy.

Slipping on a fresh nightdress, I wandered back to his side. Without thinking—because I wasn't really thinking at the moment—I went to my knees beside Damien.

I shouldn't lie down beside him. Shouldn't be wearing just my nightdress, pressing myself against his bare torso. But *should* had always been a suggestion.

Unable to think of sleeping in my bed in case he needed me sometime during the night, I curled up around him, one of my hands pressed against his chest. Right over his heart.

Damien had come to me when he needed help. Not his best friend or Cap. He dragged himself across town to my window.

And that knowledge twisted something within me. Changed something.

I held him close, ignoring his feverish skin and instead feeling the beating of his heart beneath my palm.

He's alive. Still alive.

It didn't matter that I was still furious with him, or that he'd hurt me. We could talk about that tomorrow. Right now, all I cared about was that his heart continued to beat. That he hadn't left this world. Left me.

"Wr-Wren," he murmured in lucid sleep, his head lolling to the side, close to mine. "You're h-here."

"I'm here," I replied. My heart tugged at the sound of his desperate voice, and I leaned closer, not an inch separating our bodies.

Damien's hand fumbled around as if searching for mine. I clasped it, intertwining our fingers over his chest. His grip strengthened as he begged, "Don't l-leave, s-sunshine."

"I won't," I promised, squeezing his fingers in assurance. "I'll be beside you all night."

He hummed, eyes still closed. "I th-think I like the s-sound of that." His face turned to nuzzle my hair, and my heart fluttered as he took in an audible inhale. "You s-smell like my f-favorite," he whispered. "I love how you s-smell. How you t-taste."

Heat burned my cheeks. He was delirious. Still, I couldn't find the words to reply. To relay what he'd done to my insides with words alone.

"I wish you knew the real m-me," he said, his nose grazing mine. "But then I . . . I would dull your shine."

I shook my head, even if he couldn't see. "No, you wouldn't, Damien," I said firmly. "I want to know the real you, too. You just don't let me see inside."

He played the role of nonchalant thief. Of a criminal with a cocky swagger. But ever since I'd glimpsed that postcard—or maybe before—I knew there was so much more he hid beneath his practiced exterior.

Another hum, and then, "I think I've always l-liked you, Wren. Even wh-when I hated you." He let out a weak laugh. "You remind m-me of safety. L-light. Hope."

I wanted to pry, to ask him his innermost thoughts while he was in such a state. But I wouldn't take advantage. Even if it killed me.

"I think I like you, too, Damien," I said instead. "Even when I hate you."

Tilting my head, I found a soft smile on his lips—a smile I'd put there. With the little strength he had left, Damien slipped his arm around my body and pulled me in so my head rested on the uninjured side of his chest. Skin to skin, my ear listening to the steady pounding beneath it, I smiled, too.

"Good night, thief."

Damien ran his hand down my arm, sending tingles racing and goose bumps rising. "Night, sunshine. D-dream of me."

Chapter Twenty-Three

Damien

Something soft tickled my nose.

My eyes fluttered, working hard to open. It felt like they'd been glued shut. I twisted slightly, attempting to rouse feeling back into my limbs, but all that did was send excruciating pain sprinting down my shoulder and torso.

What happened?

A flash of an image before I passed out—of me on one of those metal tables, a sheet drawn up to my neck, my face cold and lifeless. It had been the final thing I'd seen before darkness ate me up.

I wished it had been the first time I'd seen such a thing, but there'd been those waking nightmares. Seeing people of the Void, visions of them in similar states. And then I'd envisioned myself, dead and gone.

Something was happening to me, and not due to my mirror and its fluctuating magic. I just didn't understand it yet.

It took several minutes to garner the courage to peel my eyes open, and I instantly debated shutting them when harsh early-morning sunshine struck my senses.

Too bright.

A little sigh that didn't belong to me came from my right. Every muscle tensed—the ones that weren't *already* tense.

Biting my cheek, focusing on the slight pain, I turned my head, knowing deep down what I'd find but terrified to look.

Wren.

Her body was flush against mine, her hand wrapped around my very bare waist, her fingers digging into my skin like she held on to me for dear life. Faint exhales left her slightly parted lips, her stunning face serene in deep sleep.

At first there was confusion. So much of it that my vision tilted and black spots hovered at the corners. Then, traces of memories; dark alleys, pain, walking, mostly stumbling, to the northern end.

That hooded figure, the one I'd first met with when arranging the theft, and then again last night leaning against the carriage. He *stabbed* me in the back. There'd been darkness for a time after I fell, but as if it were a dream, I'd pictured myself going to a place where I felt safe.

Yet it had been no dream. Now I lay in a goddess's arms.

Carefully peering down at my body, I took in the wrapped linen binding my wound. With my stiff neck I couldn't examine it properly, but no blood seeped through the cloth. I wondered if she'd stitched me up.

I glanced at the sleeping woman beside me. Dark circles painted the sensitive skin below each eye, her blond hair a tangled mess. I grimaced when I spotted red flakes coating some strands. *My* blood.

I'd come here—instead of the pub. Instead of stumbling to Ruby's little flat. I'd stumbled all the way to the north end and managed to fucking scale a tree. Or I thought I had.

It was a miracle I'd made it so far without bleeding out.

Memories of Wren's distraught face hovered in my mind. A soft lamp illuminated her determined features as she threaded a needle. The next memory showed her dabbing liquor onto a shredded piece of linen.

My head pulsed with a nasty headache, my every inch heavy. Even with the pain, even after the attack, I had felt safe. Hell, I had trusted her with my life. Trusted her with so much more than I realized.

As if sensing my eyes upon her, Wren stirred. Her eyes opened a second later, the turquoise in them piercing as she stared unabashedly into my eyes' dark glacial depths. It had always made my heart beat faster when she did that—looked into my eyes when no one else dared to. I'd heard the whispers, starting at the orphanage; it had been the reason the other children hadn't wanted to play with me. They averted their stares to avoid the coldness in my eyes. The "death," as some claimed.

"You're alive," Wren said, her voice raspy from sleep.

"So it seems." My voice wasn't much better. "Did . . . did you do all this?" I asked, nodding at the linen. Her taking care of me and cleaning me up. I suddenly felt vulnerable, like she'd seen too much, seen my weakness. Had I said anything to her? Said something I couldn't take back?

Why did it feel like I had?

She adjusted herself, though she didn't go far, her body remaining glued to my side. Heat coiled in my belly at the way she melded herself to fit all of my sharp angles. Perhaps she was too exhausted to realize our positions, but even in my state, I focused on nothing else. Not the throbbing ache in my shoulder or the welcoming need for revenge. It was only her and the fire she sparked. Only her and the sunshine.

"You scared me, Damien," she admitted, turning to look at my shoulder. "It was bad. The wound . . ." She let out a heavy sigh. "I thought I would lose you come morning."

My first instinct was to ask why she cared. Old habits, I supposed. I disregarded that instinct, though it took effort to say the next words, even if I meant them.

"Thank you, Wren," I said, the rawness of my gratitude seeping from every syllable. "I think you saved my life. Even if you probably hate me."

As predicted, Wren's cheeks turned a light shade of pink. Her blush would forever give her away, and I kind of liked that idea. Of knowing and seeing how I affected her.

"You hurt me, Damien, but not enough for me to want to see you killed," she said quietly. "You kissed me back in that study, and then you *left* . . . you just left after what we shared. Was it just a distraction for you?"

She laid herself bare before me, her eyes wide and waiting. Vulnerable.

Did I open up? Allow her the chance to stab me with words just as thoroughly as the hooded man had with his blade?

She waited, the air growing thick with tension.

"No," I said, breaking the silence. "It wasn't just a distraction." I couldn't force out any more words. Not all that I wanted to say. The confession lodged in my throat, all the admissions I desired to speak trapped by years of training myself to protect myself.

She nodded like she understood. Or maybe she knew I wasn't capable of more. "Nothing feels simple now."

"It doesn't," I admitted.

She didn't know what to say and neither did I. Her full lips pressed together, eyes lingering on my wound as I yearned to see what went on in her head. When she withdrew her arm from my torso, I nearly groaned, and not from pain. I liked the feel of her weight there. Liked waking up with her tangled around me. Far too much.

It was the first time I'd lain beside another.

"Sorry," she said at my wince. She scooted away and I hated it. "I tend to move in my sleep."

"Why didn't you sleep in your bed?" I asked, switching topics like a coward. I grimaced when I lifted my hand to tip her chin so she'd look at me. Worth the pain.

"I didn't want you to sleep alone," she admitted. "And I feared—"

"I'd die in my sleep?" I supplied, granting her a lopsided grin I knew she loved.

Wren shut her eyes and shook her head, likely resisting the urge to smack me for my lighthearted tone in such a serious situation.

"I'm all right, sunshine," I coaxed, wanting that smile to show again. "Thankfully the prick missed my heart, but I'm still alive because of you."

The blood loss alone would've done me in.

"Why did you come here instead of the pub?" she asked, gnawing at the inside of her cheek.

I squeezed my eyes shut as I answered. Damn me, honesty was *hard*. "I don't remember much. Just walking."

But I *did* know. Even if I wasn't ready to admit it.

"It's not like it's the first time someone tried to stab me," I joked, though she didn't smile. "If people get a hint that you've got coin, they'll attack. That's why I had to install four locks on my door above the pub. Cap insisted after I got my arse beaten three years ago by four thugs. They took my coins and vanished. *After* they messed up my pretty face."

"I hate when you joke like that," she said, her stare turning hard. "I hate when you use humor to hide every true emotion you have." Her forehead creased as her voice rose slightly. "It's infuriating."

I frowned, eyeing the woman staring at me. She'd tucked both hands beneath her chin, her body separated from mine by mere inches.

There was fear there, her gaze a mixture of simmering anger and concern. Because of it, I forced myself to say something true, just for her.

"If I couldn't laugh about it, then I'd just succumb to the misery." I turned to scrutinize the ceiling. "I don't like what I do, Wren, but it's necessary, and because of it, I make a lot of enemies. Some who'd kill me on the spot if they knew I had a gift from the Fates. Only Ruby knows." And Wren.

"You don't trust easily. I get that," she mused. "I wouldn't either.

Your life . . . I know I have no right to say anything, but I wish you didn't have to go through all that pain."

Something foreign stabbed at my heart. "We all face our own troubles. But surviving can be easy. Surviving is an instinct. Actually living . . . that's freedom. Which is why I want to go to the west, where the Fates are far away and I'd get to spend my days surrounded by open skies. No one would know of my gift or hunt me for coin. No one would call me the Ghost or admire me for thievery. I'd get to start again." A rebirth I desperately wanted.

Wren stayed silent for a few moments, and a twinge of anxiety shot through me. Had I revealed too much? Showed her I wasn't the man she believed I was—strong and uncaring? Someone who'd get the job done?

"I wish I knew what I wanted, like you," she confessed. I faced her, my neck aching as I turned. Her eyes had a faraway quality to them. "Sometimes I pretend I'll leave here and explore. I used to tell myself all the time that once I got my gift, I'd leave. I think now I'm using its absence as an excuse to stay. Even knowing that my father isn't who he claimed to be." Her throat bobbed with emotion. "It's so hard to make myself picture him as the villain. But . . . after the other night, hearing how callous and cruel he sounded . . ." She trailed off, her eyes watery.

"It must be hard. Seeing your parent as they actually are. Not the person you once respected."

Her stare landed on me, searing me in place. "I know you hate him. Most people do, but I truly convinced myself he wanted to help the people in the south and did business with the lords to get it done, even if they weren't honest men. I was a damned fool." She hid behind a hand, shaking her head. "Fates, I only saw what I wanted."

With great effort, I clutched her chin between my thumb and forefinger. "You are no fool, Wren Hayes. And you aren't weak for wanting to see the good in him. Kindness, while deadly where I'm from, is a gift. One people shouldn't sneer at. It's more precious than any coin, and not many I know have the capacity to carry it."

People would have you believe it was a fault to show emotion and kindness. Like you were somehow less than, less strong or powerful. I had been a victim of that belief, but looking at her now, totally exposed and open to me—fuck, it twisted my stomach and my mind. Made me experience a sense of lightness. *Relief.*

"Well." She cleared her throat. "I will take that as the biggest compliment coming from you." Wren's lips tugged up at the sides, and the sight of it was akin to balm.

"Just don't tell anyone," I whispered. "I have a reputation to hold up, and all."

Her lips quirked further. "You know I'm still mad at you, Damien, but you have the annoying ability to make me forget all that."

"Probably didn't hurt I showed up half dead," I added with a smirk.

"That definitely helped."

"Lovely. I'll just have to nearly die for you to forgive me," I said.

She shook her head. "I never said I forgave you. Just that you make it hard to be mad at you."

I didn't have the courage to bring up what we both were thinking of: the kiss. Me, leaving her afterward. It was all too confusing. *Complicated*—and I'd never done complicated.

"I'll gladly take your anger," I insisted softly. "As long as you always open your window."

Hell, I didn't know what I was saying. I blamed the blood loss. Nevertheless, they felt true, all of my admissions. I knew at that moment an irrevocable shift had occurred. One I wasn't sure I could fix.

Before she replied, knuckles rapped on her door.

"Wren? Why is your door locked?"

"Damn it." Wren shot up. "Callie."

The older sister. I'd spotted her leaving with their father a few times. She seemed nice enough, but I wondered if she was aware of her father's dealings or if Wren had told her.

"I'm getting dressed!" Wren called out.

Silence, and then, "All right, just wanted to say good morning before I left."

"Love you!" Wren shouted again, sounding all sorts of frantic. I smiled at how flustered her voice became, how she anxiously smoothed her dark golden hair, which stuck out every which way.

"Love you, too." Footsteps thudded in the hall before Wren exhaled. She grabbed her face and buried herself in her hands.

"Thank the Fates I had the decent sense to lock the door last night. I was half delirious." She laughed, though it was brittle.

"Imagine the scandal," I murmured in a haughty tone. "You, on the floor with a known criminal."

She moved to smack my shoulder before she stopped, remembering my wound. "Good thing you're injured," she muttered, narrowing her gaze. "But yes, it *would* be a scandal. And only because you're half naked, not because of who you are. Though, all right, the criminal aspect doesn't help." She nibbled on her bottom lip, flustered, and I couldn't look away. Fates, I wanted to do the same, to take that bottom lip between my teeth.

This injury dulled all my good sense.

"You're going to need to rest some more," she said decidedly, analyzing me in an almost clinical way. "You'll sleep in my bed and I'll stay here too. I'm great at feigning sickness to get out of things. Not that I have much to do since I've become society's newest pariah. It's actually been nice," she said with a smirk.

An odd sensation slithered into my chest. I couldn't name it, but it felt both pleasant and frightening.

"Quite rebellious," I said quickly, spurning the sensations rioting inside my body. She rolled her eyes and stood.

Wren smoothed down her nightdress before her lips parted, like she only now realized how little she wore. "I need to change." Her chest heaved beneath the thin cotton, and the light streaming from the window outlined the perfect shape of her beneath the fabric. I shut my eyes, willing my body to cooperate, willing myself not to think about how delectable she appeared. How that little glimpse forced me to shift to the side.

She made a mad scramble for the bathroom, the clanking of pipes coming soon after.

I smacked myself in the face before remembering my

injury. But the pain worked to dull some of the lingering heat. A *little*.

I'd never shared that much. At least not in the way I had with her. That knowledge told me I was in trouble.

The villain never got the princess in stories. And I certainly was the villain in her story—she just didn't know it yet.

While Wren took her bath, I struggled to my feet and found a pen and paper on her desk.

Meet me tonight outside at midnight.
Going to explore Lizzy's home.

I paused, pen in hand. It felt too stiff after what happened, so I added two more words that still didn't measure up to what she'd done for me.

She might not understand how difficult this was for me, how allowing someone to take care of me protested against everything I'd been taught. All I could do was add the most sincere words I held in my heart.

Thank you.

Leaving the note on her bed, I snuck out into the hall and found her father's room. Snagging a shirt, I tugged it on, ignoring how my body protested. Avoiding the cook proved more difficult, but I managed after she dropped her basket of fresh vegetables and cursed up a storm.

I slipped through the front door and shuffled down the street.

Wren had wanted me to stay. Told me I needed rest and that I'd spend the day in her bed.

The problem was that if I stayed, I knew I wouldn't want to leave.

Chapter Twenty-Four

Wren

Before Andalay in all its splendor was built, the Fates wandered aimlessly across Aurilia. They were known to choose their lovers without care, and had no qualms about their fascination with mortals. Yet none could ever interest them long enough to stay, and only once had a Fate been tempted.

—*Origin of the Fates,* Chapter Three

The thief left a note.

A *note.*

I saved his damned life and he placed a crinkled piece of paper on my bed in reply. Yes, he'd *thanked* me, but the entirety of the letter consisted of three. Short. Sentences.

I ripped it in half and tossed it in the bin beside my desk, feeling like I was the one with the stab wound.

I . . . I had shared secret pieces of myself with him, and he'd told me things that changed everything. All the frustrating attraction I'd felt had morphed into something greater in the span of a single confession.

Maybe he really doesn't remember, I thought, but even then, a *note*? I'd just finished telling him to stay in bed and rest, and I'd turned my back for one second and he'd left.

My damp hair dripped on the robe I'd put on, making me shiver. My room felt empty now, cold. I glanced at the blanket and pillow on the floor. Tucked under the bed were the bloodied rags I'd have to dispose of later, discreetly, along with my bloodied nightdress, before Sarah came around and cleaned.

But their presence meant Damien had come to me. Had chosen me to help him. Had opened up. He couldn't just allow himself to sit still and accept that people cared about him. Instead, he'd done what he did best—he'd run. Logically, I guessed it had everything to do with his upbringing and living the way he did, but that didn't make it hurt any less.

Prick.

I kicked half-heartedly at the pillow on the floor, wishing it were something harder. Something I could break. Like Damien's nose.

How reckless was I? I didn't wish to be with Damien, nor he with me. The anger I felt was likely due to feeling rejected. Yes, the more I ruminated on it, the more sense it made. I had a whole life ahead of me, and I planned on meeting others who'd catch my eye. I would go riding with Everett, and when all of this mess with Damien and the mysterious disappearances was over, I might just leave as I'd originally planned. Aurilia was a vast kingdom with so much to see. So many people to . . . *meet.*

I smiled then, picturing the wide-open future.

Damien could be a friend if things turned out all right. Or maybe I would forget all about him once I abandoned this city and my old life.

I'd make friends of my own choosing—friends who wouldn't stab me in the back in a time of need. Maybe some like Ruby. I liked her, even if we'd only met for the briefest of moments. She'd left an impression, and I enjoyed how welcoming and easy she'd acted around me.

The truth was, I didn't know who I was. Where I fit in. What I would do with my life.

I perched on the windowsill, gazing out to the garden and the wilting roses. Mother would be furious, even if the weather had been turning colder. She tended to toss out blame to others whenever possible. I found it unfathomable that I came from her womb. Or that Father had *any* hand in my creation.

I gazed upon the garden for a good long while, feeling sorry for myself and taking a few minutes to let that pity consume me and my ever-changing emotions. It felt good to relinquish myself to the shame and hurt and drown in it . . . but flashes of those horrid photos Damien showed me kept interrupting.

It wasn't all about me. Maybe I *was* selfish. I believed, in a way, most people were. But people could change, right?

When a knock came on my door, I started.

"Miss," Sarah grumbled behind the wood. "It appears that you have a visitor."

I expected Everett.

Instead, the handsome god that was Grayson Hockley stood in the parlor, his hands tucked stiffly behind his back. He wore a fine suit of forest-green satin, standing out from the rest of the boring black suits most wore, his dark blond hair—which contained hints of gold in this light—slicked back from his face. However, a lone curl refused to be tamed and slid into deep brown eyes outlined in a thick black. I'd believed them more honey in appearance, but that might have been due to the way they sparkled so brilliantly at the ball.

"Well, this is a surprise," I welcomed him, striding into the room.

I'd changed into a simple pink dress with pearl buttons, though my hair refused to fully dry. Not much I could do about that.

Grayson bowed, his smiling mouth forcing a genuine grin to my face. I found something about his presence comforting, almost as if he had the same soothing influence as my sister.

"Hayes!" he boomed, surprising me with his exuberance. "You left the ball early. Thought I scared you off."

I shook my head. "Of course not. I'm just not a fan of all the . . ."

"Beauty? The refinement? The carefully selected design scheme?"

I blanched at his devious grin. "You *designed* the ball?" He nodded, those eyes brightening once more as a mischievous look forced a smile to my lips.

"Surprised?" he asked, flourishing a hand before him.

"Actually, no. You have great taste in general," I said, admiring his suit further. Even his cuff links were silver skulls, the eyes a sparkling red.

“I know,” he replied with a wink. “And to think none of my family has the trait. Such a shame. One of these days I’m going to beg to redo the entire house. It’s centuries in the past.” He clapped his hands. “But I didn’t come here to speak about how amazing I look, though I’m up for that discussion at a different time.”

“Happy to accommodate whenever the need arises.” I laughed, though it came out more as a snort, which seemed to please him further. “I am, however, eager to hear why the sudden visit? Not that I don’t welcome it.”

I nodded to the closest leather chair, and he obliged, crossing his legs and angling his chin to the chair across from him. I took the hint and sat, fluffing out my skirt.

“Lucky for me, I happened to meet someone wearing a scandalous red dress who intrigued me. Someone interesting who didn’t care what everyone else thought.” Grayson eyed me from head to toe, a serious look slowly washing over his earlier gleam.

I huffed before I could contain myself. “Then you made a mistake. I’m far from intriguing, and I *do* care what people think. I just enjoy pretending I don’t.” And that was the truth. In my mind, interesting people captured attention and didn’t have to fake confidence.

Once I stilled, curling my fingers to keep from nervously adjusting my skirt, he shot me a dry look. “You must work on your self-confidence, dear,” he said. “Not only did you hold your head up when everyone and their mother talked about you after . . . well, after you didn’t receive a gift, but then you showed up in the most beautifully wicked dress I’ve ever seen. So yes, I’d say you piqued my interest. I’d judged you far too quickly in the past, believing you shared the opinions of those who surrounded you. When they abandoned you for the pettiest of reasons, you continue to hold your chin up and smile. Not many I know can live in this world of judgment and swim through such murky waters with grace."

I was too stunned to speak. No one besides Callie had ever said such things. Made me out to be anything other than boring. Complacent.

"There was no other choice," I said with a shrug. "They abandoned me in the end, but to be honest, it showed me they were never true friends." He nodded as if he understood. "Besides, as far as my gowns go, I like fashion. It's armor, a way to show them all I'll never change simply because of a single night."

Grayson beamed and adjusted his own suit. "I understand all too well, Wren."

"Hiding away would only make the snakes come out and bite. I'd have been devoured by now if I'd done so." I sat forward in my seat. "If I may be bold, I believe you aren't like many of the nobles I've encountered, at least not the ones my father allows me to engage with. Not only did your welcome appear genuine, but you speak so brazenly. Bluntly. A trait I admire."

A dark blush entered Grayson's tawny cheeks before he cleared his throat. "I'm not always bold; sometimes I wish I were more so. But you inspired me. I suppose I visited because—"

The rattling of the tea cart interrupted him. A frowning Sarah pushed the cart into the parlor, her jaw clenched. She left without a word.

Charming. As always.

I nodded my head to the tiered cart. "Want a cup?"

He wrinkled his nose. "Not of that. Hold on."

Grayson grabbed an empty cup and shut his eyes. I watched in wonder as he tapped his golden signet ring on the porcelain and the cup filled with amber liquid.

"Impressive, though I expected nothing less," I teased. "Do you have enough energy to muster some for me?"

"I'd hoped you would say that." He snagged a fresh cup and tapped his ring on the side. Instead of dusky liquor, a pale pink drink sloshed against the sides. He chuckled. "You *really* do love pink."

"Always have, always will," I said. "What's inside?"

He sniffed the drink. "I'm guessing something entirely you. Here, try it."

Taking the cup in my hand, I lifted it to my mouth and sipped. The moment the drink splashed across my tongue I nearly groaned, shutting my eyes and falling into the delightful strawberry lemonade with a splash of clear liquor.

"Perfect." I cradled it like the porcelain might float away. The heat from the alcohol warmed my belly, and I sighed in appreciation.

When I finally opened my eyes, Grayson's had dimmed. He shifted in his seat and rested his elbows on his knees.

Something was amiss. He'd come here for more than teasing and drinks.

"Wren? I have another motive for coming here," he said, as if reading my thoughts. "Even if I do plan to get to know you regardless." A boyish smile spread.

"What is it?" I set down the delectable drink and copied his pose.

"I saw you coming down from my father's study," he began, and I went stiff, my pulse quick at my neck. "I don't really know how to begin this, so screw it." He studied the room, likely to make sure Sarah wasn't hovering nearby. "I have a suspicion you were looking for something in there, something confidential, and so am I. Ever since this year started, my father has been . . . angrier than usual. Hell, he was so stressed this morning, he left his study unlocked, allowing me to check his books." He reached into his suit pocket and retrieved a scrap of paper. "I found this."

Ice slithered down my spine when he handed it to me.

I anxiously smoothed out the paper on my thigh and took a closer look.

Fifty more souls and your debt is paid.

A signature lined the bottom, faded, but clear to me.

Cameron Hayes

I glanced at Grayson while he rubbed at his face, his eyes on the paper. "I'm not the only one who knows about your arrest and attempted visit with Dusk, but I keep feeling as if you're looking into something important. You and that handsome man *claiming* to be a lord." He arched a brow. "The one I had never seen before in my life."

I silently cursed. "Damien is the son of—"

Grayson held up a hand. "I'll stop you right there. I know those boys personally, and while I appreciated the ruse, *Damien* isn't one of them. Not that I care. I just thought since you were obviously going out of your way to hide him and your . . . extracurricular activities, then maybe you were someone I could trust. Fates know, there aren't many in society, and I'm taking a huge risk by doing this." He spoke gently, a quiver of real fear shaking his voice.

I trusted no one. That was what I told myself. I hardly trusted Damien with the mission. But that was his fault.

Here Grayson was, freely giving me secrets after one meeting and a gut suspicion. How could someone ever be that confident? That certain? I envied that.

"Wren, I understand that you may be hesitant to share, but I suspect my father is into some crooked business. Business I want no part of. Since Adrian didn't receive a gift, all of the estate and my father's work would go to me, and if he's up to something unseemly, I need to know about it." He shut his eyes. "I just want answers as to why he's always going to the docks at midnight, or having late-night meetings in his office. To add to it, the wording of that note . . . it's wrong. *Souls?* What does that even mean?"

"When is he going to the docks next?" I asked in a hushed voice.

Grayson's eyes sparked to life. "Two days. I overheard him yelling at Mother. She's been upset that he's been out of the house so much." He rolled his eyes. "Not that she hasn't been busy. Always going to tea with the other lords' wives. It's been excessive of late."

Just like Mother . . .

"Then we go there and find out for ourselves." The words were out of my mouth before I could think better of it. "I—you're right. I, too, think the lords and ladies of society are up to something." He visibly relaxed at my admission. "You're not alone, Grayson." I reached for his hand and he wrapped his lean fingers around mine. A sigh born of exhaustion and relief escaped, the tightness of his shoulders visibly relaxing.

"You have no idea how much this means to me," he rasped. "I was afraid to speak with anyone but you since I spotted you at the ball, sneaking up to the study. I had been tempted to befriend you before, after the Lovetts' first ball, but I was confident you might be just the person who could help. Besides, as I've told you, I have good taste." His lips tugged up in a smile. "Thank you."

I could've been making the biggest mistake of my life, but for some inane reason, I *did* trust him. Or I was reckless and Damien would be furious.

Speaking of Damien . . .

Lizzy's house still had to be dealt with, and while Damien had snuck away, he expected me to meet him. I was tempted to ignore him and stay in, but as much as I loathed it, his *specialty* would be needed.

Tonight, we were breaking into a lord's home.

Chapter Twenty-Five

Wren

The Fates are the oldest creatures ever to have walked our world. They are the beginning, the middle, and the end of all, created by the magic of the earth itself.
—*Origin of the Fates*, Chapter Thirteen

I wasn't pleased when Damien showed up, and he instantly grimaced upon seeing whatever uneasy emotion lay on my face.

"You feeling better?" I said through gritted teeth.

I hated that I asked it. *He* should be the one falling to his feet thanking me. I smoothed down my only black skirt and anxiously pulled at the too-high neckline. I wasn't a fan of being choked by clothing.

Alas, breaking into a lord's home required stealth.

He nodded stiffly and finally said, "Yes, thanks to you." He ran a hand through his hair. "I . . . are you upset with me?"

I rolled my eyes. "If you have to ask that question, then you're not as clever as I assumed." Turning on a heel, I started for Lizzy's town house. It would be a twenty-minute walk. I didn't rejoice in that fact.

"Wren, slow down!"

I didn't. He could catch up.

"Wren, I shouldn't have left, all right?" he said panting behind me. "I just . . ."

I whirled on him. "You just *what*?"

"I thought you'd want me to leave," he replied, but I didn't believe it to be the truth for a second.

"Liar."

I spun around, ignoring his calls. When he eventually caught up, he panted between pleas. In a petty way, it was nice to see him in such a disorderly state. Not his typical arrogant self.

"All right, fine. Listen. I left because staying would mean something important," he managed. "And I—"

"You act tough, but you're just as frightened as the rest of us. So save it or grow up."

Maybe we shouldn't have crossed that line to begin with. Maybe it *was* mere attraction.

Damien remained silent for ten minutes, trailing behind me. The cocky thief didn't have a snappy comment for once. Disappointment filled me.

The bending streets of Ward Two were twisting and uphill, and I, too, found myself winded minutes away from Lizzy's house. I only knew its location because Father had stopped there once to drop a memo off for her father.

Looking back now, maybe it had been a threat.

Fingers wrapped around my arm, slowing me. "I can't believe I'm saying this, but I don't like the idea of you hating me." Damien's nostrils flared when I turned, giving him my best glare. "Seriously, it's messing with my head." He made a low grumbling sound in his throat, like he had any right to be irritated. All of this was his doing.

"Damien?"

"Yes, sunshine?"

"Do me a favor and keep quiet." I snatched my arm back, his stunned gasp faint.

"I'm apologizing," he said, striding to keep pace. I wondered if his wound pained him.

"Is that supposed to absolve your actions?" I stopped, turning to look him over. Dark circles shone prominently beneath the light of a street lamp. He was refusing to let himself rest and heal. "This whole thing"—I motioned between us—"was a mistake. We both know it."

His hand shot out and cupped my cheek, a determined glint in his eyes. "A mistake? So you weren't the one grabbing onto my shirt and raking your hands in my hair? You didn't murmur my name or kiss me like you'd die if you didn't? That was all in my head, right?"

"Why are you arguing with *me* about this?" I asked, stunned. "You're the one who's pushed me away saying it was a 'mistake' first. It's not even like we know each other all that well."

He dropped his hand and stepped back. "Then we will."

"Oh, it's decided, then?" I placed both hands on my hips. The nerve of him.

But Damien merely smirked that irritating smirk I hated and sidestepped me, hands in his pockets like he didn't have a care in the world.

"Coming?" he asked over his shoulder as I stood there fuming. Beads of sweat trickled down my temple, and I felt the heat of rage burn my skin.

I didn't answer him when I set off for Lizzy's, choosing to mutter curses beneath my breath.

The cocky bastard. I wasn't in the mood to be nice. I'd been nice my entire life, and I wanted to let myself feel that gloriously hot anger boiling my blood.

I wanted *him* to simmer tonight, but he'd turned the tables.

Ignore him, I told myself, shoving down my anger, the taste of it bitter on my tongue.

At Lizzy's front porch, I paused.

"What are you waiting for?" Damien asked at my side, still infuriatingly calm.

"You're the thief," I whisper-hissed, motioning wildly at the door. "Go pick the lock or something."

"Demanding tonight," he muttered before heading around back.

Don't smack him don't smack him don't smack him.

My fists clenched. The idea was far too tempting.

Lizzy, like most in the north, lived in a spacious town house with a small garden in the front and a larger one in the back. The impressive three-story brick home had an intricate front gate designed to resemble tangled vines. I eyed the arched windows; they would likely be our way in if Damien failed.

When we reached the back gate, it was no surprise to find it locked.

Damien inspected the lock and took a small black satchel from his jacket pocket. He let out a small noise of pain when he knelt and began to work, poking and prodding with long, thin metal instruments. He held back the agony he must be feeling; stab wounds didn't typically heal overnight. Still, he didn't miss a beat, and I observed him intensely, studying his every move. I secretly wanted him to show me how to do this sometime. If I watched closely enough, perhaps I could get into Father's study.

When the lock clicked, he swung the gate open and waved me through. I bit my tongue before I could say anything snippy—only because he was still hurting—and headed toward the rear entrance to the house. It felt like everything and anything would set me off tonight.

The back door was thankfully unlocked.

"They think they're invincible," Damien chuckled. "I may have to scour—"

I cut him off with a stern look. "Don't even think about it." Lifting my finger, I warned, "No stealing."

Returning to the door, I eased it open, careful not to make a noise. The house was silent, not a voice or creak to be heard. Entering through the kitchen, I maneuvered around the cook's workspace and into the dining room, which connected to the parlor. Lizzy's parents had atrocious taste—everything had been decorated in ruby and gold and some form of brocade. If the lights had been on, I might've been blinded by it all.

In the foyer, a curving black staircase led up to the bedrooms, and, presumably, to Lord Saridon's study. Damien's hand fell on my shoulder midway through the climb. I wanted to shove it off to make a point, but my damned body wouldn't listen.

"Want to split up?" he asked. "I'll check on the woman's room, and you can check out the father's study, seeing as you'd probably know where the lords like to keep all the good stuff."

"Yes, I'm such an expert," I said, a bite to my tone.

"Damn, sunshine, you really are going to kill me, aren't you?"

"Just don't turn your back on me," I threatened. I reached the landing and eyed the hall. "Lizzy is an only child. Her room should be down that hall," I instructed, pointing to the smaller of the corridors. The other would bring him to the primary suite.

Damien nodded and crept away, leaving me to explore. On the opposite side of the stairs a door framed in more gold glimmered in greeting. It had to be Lord Saridon's study. I tried the handle, only to discover that it was locked.

Of course. And we'd just split up. I shook my head, wanting to smack myself.

Now I'd have to wait for Damien to return from his own sleuthing. Two people messing around in Lizzy's bedroom would cause too much noise.

Yet another reason for me to learn how to pick my own damn locks in the future.

I swore I leaned against the wall for a solid twenty minutes before Damien's silhouette emerged from the corridor. When he got within reach, I noticed his empty hands.

"Any luck on your end?" he asked.

"It's locked," I admitted, raising a brow at him. "I couldn't start."

"Mmm, probably should've thought about that." He knelt and pulled out his tools. "By the way, Lizzy snores. Loudly. Like, earth-shattering snores."

I nudged him with my boot. "Be nice." Inwardly I scolded myself for repressing the chuckle I'd swallowed.

"I'm just saying. We could've both gone in there and thrown a party, and I doubt she'd have woken up."

I released an exasperated sigh. "Focus." The longer we were here, the greater the chance we'd get caught. How would I explain breaking and entering to Lord Saridon, let alone my father? Damien would probably sprint and leave me here anyway. Yet . . . even after sneaking out of *my* room, I somehow didn't believe he'd abandon me. "Also." I nudged his boot. "You're teaching me that when we get a chance."

Damien's lips curled slightly. "Would you forgive me if I did?"

I glared down at him, wishing I hated how handsome his profile appeared, even as he was slouched and breaking into a locked room. I planned to say *No,* but instead a feeble "Maybe" escaped.

"I'll take a maybe from you, Wren," he said, pausing to lift his chin. We locked eyes, his gray ones seeming to ask something of me. To *take* something.

"What? You're looking at me oddly." I ran a hand through my hair self-consciously.

"Because you drive me mad sometimes," he murmured, still smiling.

"Good." I squatted down to his level, our lips inches apart. "I like driving you mad."

It seemed only fair.

His warm breath fanned across my cheeks, the scent of him—spice and leather—wafting to my nose. So close, one tiny little move would send our lips colliding.

"Such a naughty mind," Damien said, cocking his head. "If I didn't know any better, I'd think you were trying to seduce me."

I huffed. "I wouldn't need to *try,* Damien."

He shut his eyes when his name rolled off my tongue. "Stop distracting me," he begged. "It's cruel."

And just because he'd angered me this morning, I leaned over, running my lips against the sensitive skin of his neck until I reached his ear. He groaned.

Making sure my lips brushed against him, I murmured, "Then you shouldn't have run away."

I jerked back abruptly, satisfied when he let out a needy growl, his shoulders slouched.

"Cruel. Just like I said."

"Open the door, Damien, and then you can complain."

He mumbled an incoherent word before looking back to his work. All the while, I fought to keep a smile from creeping over my face. I enjoyed tormenting him. Just a little.

A *click* sounded. "Finally." Damien nudged the door open and motioned me through. Stepping around him, I entered, Damien and our squabble put aside. We had a vital mission.

Aiming straight for the desk, I rifled through all the usual places. I rapped gently on the bottoms of the drawers to discern whether a secret layer hid below. Nothing. All of Lord Saridon's neatly stacked notes pertained to the family business of textiles and the shipments coming into port.

Damien busied himself by scouring the cabinet beside the liquor cart. He opened it—likely with his lockpick set—to reveal more ledgers. He sat down in a wingback chair and flipped through some, creases marking his forehead. I smiled at serious Damien, how full his lips looked, the way his eyes narrowed in concentration. The small tics in his sharp jaw when he flipped a page—

Focus, Wren. Ogle the thief later.

All right. If I were a corrupt politician trying to hide something, where would I conceal it?

The details of the study were difficult to see in the dark, but I pushed and prodded the golden frames displaying dull forest scenes and other landscapes, hoping to find a safe. With nothing to show for that effort, I moved on to the life-sized *tiger* Lord Saridon had commissioned in gold. Unsurprisingly, it was pure metal, not a seam in sight in which to hide anything. The man sure liked his gold.

Wait. He works in textiles.

I got on my hands and knees, inspecting the round rug beside the twin set of chairs; a place for smoking cigars and probably discussing how best to screw over an opponent. A table sat in the middle with a crystal ashtray etched with the lord's initials in fancy script. Feeling around the table's sides, I rounded the rug, searching for tears or lumps.

Sweating now, I aimed for the larger rug beneath his desk. Crawling to it, I did the same as before, feeling for anything that might act as a hiding place. The corners came up empty, but . . .

"Damien."

There was a shuffle of footsteps, and then he crouched beside me. Near the window, away from foot traffic, I spotted a sliver of a cut in the fabric. An incision I now noted had tiny stitches on the side.

"Knife?" I held my palm open without looking at him.

"Where's your letter opener?"

"I left it at home so I wasn't tempted to kill you," I replied sweetly. A grumble came before he placed the handle of a blade gently in my palm. Getting as close to the sewn area as possible, I took the knife to the threads. Damien kept the weapon sharp, and the threads ripped apart without fuss. "I may keep this," I threatened, but he snatched it away before I could hide it.

"Rude."

Slipping my fingers between the top and bottom of the split rug, I felt around. I was half terrified something might bite me, like a spider with a penchant for sleeping in rugs, when I latched onto something.

Paper.

"*Yes,*" I said, satisfied by my own cunning. Damien didn't seem to appreciate it.

Pulling out my findings, I laid a dark folder on the carpet.

Moonlight streamed through the window, granting enough light to see, but only barely. I squinted at the words on the first page.

"Shite." Damien inched forward. "This is part of a ledger and an official grievance. Lord Saridon made a claim that he lost his shipment at sea."

I flipped to the next page. A black-and-white photograph.

It depicted crates being removed from Saridon's ship, and stamped on the bottom of the photograph was a date. A date that matched the ledger entry claiming he'd never received the wares.

I turned to the next page, curious, but it had nothing to do with his business.

You have failed to deliver the requested amount. Consequences are forthcoming. Do not make the same mistake again.

C.H.

Below, ink splattered the page, and I noticed what looked like a few tearstains marring the paper.

Cameron Hayes. Again. I doubted he'd been the one crying, though.

"My father used his pen for this." The words sounded like they didn't come from my mouth. They were almost an echo. His pen always left ink blots behind. Like it couldn't contain all of its magic and begged to burst free.

"Wren." Damien's hand gripped my arm as I swayed. First, Grayson and his note, and then this? The consequences had to do with Lizzy being denied a gift, I knew it. The timing matched.

My father had blackmailed Lord Saridon and then taken away the chance for his daughter to receive her gift from the Fates.

"Wren," Damien said, more loudly this time. "We need to leave."

I wanted to rip apart the paper and set it aflame. It was yet more proof of my ignorance. I lived with the man, for Fates' sake. I should've known. Should've—

Damien snatched the papers and shoved them into his back pocket. We needed evidence, and this was only the beginning.

"You didn't know," he coaxed, heaving me to my feet. "I know you didn't."

My lips were frozen as Damien led us out of the study and back down the stairs. In what felt like a blink, we stood outside, the fresh air doing nothing to dispel the horror seeping into my pores.

"Come on, almost there." Damien guided me through the back gate and onto the street. We'd done it, made it out without detection, but somehow, even after seeing Grayson's earlier note, my world tilted on its axis. That photograph and note had been undeniable proof that Father was the ringmaster. A master manipulator. And worse . . . a possible *murderer.*

"I feel like I can't do this anymore." It was all too real; seeing the threat in his signature scrawl, watching as he paraded about the city, terrorizing lords to do his bidding. For *souls.* It made me want to retch into the nearest potted plant.

"Hey." Snapping sounded by my face, and seconds later Damien's finger and thumb grabbed my chin, forcing me to look at him. "You're just in shock. No one wants to know their parent is—"

"Evil?" I finished. "Fates, I told myself I'd come to terms with it, but after each new shred of evidence and hearing him with Lord Hockley the other night, I just— It's just too much. I feel like it's rushing in on all sides at the same time and I hate that this is the truth." I shook my head. It felt heavy, fuzzy. "I chose to ignore any signs. And there *were* signs well before this. Well before my birthday."

Flashes of Father leaving the house at all hours of the night. Him in his study, yelling at me to leave whenever he used that pen. The people he associated with. How those people hunched in on themselves at times, yet seemed eager to do his bidding.

I'd told myself it had been respect. That he had to be commanding to get things done safely in the ward. To keep us all safe.

What a pretty little lie I'd spun.

"You are not your father," Damien argued forcefully. "The mind is funny. It can make you ignore what's right in front of your face in order to protect you." His gaze seared into mine, something obscure flashing across his already dim eyes. "All I'm saying is, don't beat yourself up. I believe you. I might not have originally, but now that I *know* you, there's not a single doubt in my head that you were unaware."

A tear slipped free and I hastily wiped at it. I wanted to let it all out, but not in front of Damien. When the second tear slipped free, I realized it was too late.

Arms banded around me, holding me close. "It's all right," Damien whispered into my hair as I wept. His hold was firm and tight despite his wound, and it was everything I needed to keep me from falling to my knees. I didn't even have the energy to be mad at him anymore. "We can fix this, sunshine."

My life had been a lie.

"I hate this." I sniffled, my tears wetting Damien's shirt. "And if you tease me later—"

"I won't." He brushed my hair gently aside. I didn't think he did gentle. "Right now, in this moment, let it all come out. Be mad. Be angry. Hurt. Sad. Whatever you need to be in order to pick yourself up again. Because you *will* have to pick yourself up when the time comes to end this thing. It's either you choose defeat, or willingly accept the pain and make it a part of you. Only then can you bottle it up and do what's necessary."

Without moving from his chest, I asked, "Is that what you did?"

His heart thudded beneath my ear, my simple question wreaking havoc.

"I did when I left the orphanage."

My arms were around him. I didn't remember putting them there, but I found myself hugging him tighter, careful to keep clear of his left shoulder.

"They kicked us out at sixteen, and well, I didn't have a skill to my name," he confessed with a brittle laugh. "I mean, I was good with sleight of hand, a bunch of us boys playing cards and such. So stealing had always been easy. It began with food, to feed myself and a couple of the others who went without because days would pass before they fed us. Sometimes, I didn't get so lucky."

"How did you continue?" I asked, unable to imagine such hopelessness.

He cleared his throat, silent for a moment as he contemplated.

"Someone abandoned me at the orphanage as a baby, with nothing. And because of that, I was treated like nothing. Being the spiteful person I am, I wanted to prove them all wrong. Buy my farm, own land. I want to show them that just because I came from nothing didn't mean I would turn into it."

I peered up at him, his face inches from mine. "You aren't nothing, Damien."

One side of his mouth quirked. "I won't be."

"No. You aren't *now.*" He truly deemed himself as nothing. I could see it. No wonder he'd left this morning.

Here I was, falling back into his orbit when he had the ability to shatter me should I fall entirely. The kind of breaking that left a person beyond repair. But he held me as I sobbed over a falsehood of a life. He had agreed to help me with my quest—though his motives hadn't been altogether altruistic at the beginning—and he had come to trust me enough that *I* was the person he crawled to after getting stabbed.

Damien enraged me at times. Like how he couldn't open up and admit out loud that there was something between us. Something that could be real. Other times, he surprised me, allowed me a glimpse into his true self.

If only he showed me that self more often.

"One day I want to hear about your farm," I said, lightening the tension in the air. "I want to hear all about the man you want to be. Can you do that?"

"Yeah, sunshine. I think I can." He slipped his arm around me, but his body was tenser than before.

When we reached the garden behind my house, he paused. "Here." Slipping a hand into his jacket, he all but shoved a thin book into my hands. "Get lost a little." He smirked before walking backward, practically disappearing into the darkness.

I glanced down.

Flowers and Their Meanings: Volume One.

My heart skipped a beat, warmth replacing the icy cold of betrayal.

"You better not have stolen this!" I called out to the shadows.

I swore I heard a chuckle in the night.

Chapter Twenty-Six

Wren

When a gift is not given, it is a sign that the person of age isn't competent enough to handle the weight of magic.
—*Aurilian History of Magical Objects,* Chapter Four

I didn't want to pretend. To smile and play the perfect lady on my outing with Everett. Hell, I'd completely forgotten about it until Sarah announced I had a visitor, her lips curling downward. I swore, that woman was always in a sour mood.

Then again, I wasn't in the best mood either.

After last night, witnessing the photographic proof that my father was connected not only to *blackmail* but also to Lizzy and possibly Adrian not getting their gifts, I'd been left empty. And I had the niggling suspicion that those crimes were just the beginning of what we'd find.

When Father said goodbye to me this morning, I couldn't meet his eyes.

"What's wrong, little bird?" he'd asked, his mustache crinkling. He set his briefcase on a chair, his initials gleaming in gold on the foreign leather.

"Nothing, Father," I replied, too afraid to say anything else that might give away my nerves.

His forehead creased. "You look pale. Have you been outside at all this week?"

I wanted to laugh in his face. He had no idea what I'd been up to.

"Yes," I replied, my grin straining. I could feel my lips tremble. "I probably will spend today in the park as well. No need to worry."

Laughable. It was laughable that he worried about me when my misery was his fault. I could no longer discern whether he truly cared or if it was an act.

"Good," he replied. "I like that you've been keeping busy." He leaned down, meeting me at eye level. "I just can't wait until I get to brighten your spirits. *Everyone's* spirits." His stare drifted to Callie as she descended the stairs.

"What's happening?" I asked, but he held up a hand, silencing me.

"It's a surprise" was all Father said before he swept my sister out the door. She barely had enough time to blow me a kiss over her shoulder, confusion written all over her face at how eagerly Father ushered her to the waiting carriage.

Last night I'd stood outside her door, hand raised and ready to knock. I had let it fall, shuffling back to my room in defeat.

You'll tell her when the time is right, I convinced myself. When I had irrefutable proof in my hands. Well, *more* proof that no one could dispute.

When Everett showed up, finely dressed and handsome as ever, I was half dazed, feeling insensitive because I planned to go out for a fun jaunt at his estate when there were people missing.

But my act had to be maintained. For now.

After gasping and begging him to wait five minutes, I quickly dressed in my riding breeches, black calf leather boots, and a snug-fitting shirt and belt. For once, I didn't add my typical embellishment, my lonely pink and yellow ribbons tucked in my drawer beside the book Damien had gifted me. It had been a shock, his unexpected gift, even if he *had* stolen it. Did it make me a horrid person that I was still touched by the gesture?

With a sigh, I took in my reflection. My clothes and expression were dark, like my mood.

Not that Everett wouldn't be decent company, and maybe a distraction from the thief was welcome.

Walking downstairs, I found Everett in the parlor sipping the fancy western tea Sarah had brought out. The woman loved her damn tea.

"Morning!" I exclaimed, feigning cheery and bright-eyed. Based on his raised brows, I didn't think my act had worked. He appeared more alarmed than anything.

"Sleep well?" he asked, setting down his cup. Like me, he was outfitted in riding gear. He was kind enough not to mention my earlier state, my hair sticking out and face red after I'd fallen asleep on the blue leather book of lore I'd been reading.

I forced a smile. "I did. Just feeling a little off this morning."

"Well, I hope to change that," he confessed with a grin, his handsome face illuminating the cold room. Extending an arm, he waited for me to take it. When I did, his smile lit up the entire room. "I can't wait for you to meet Mayberry. She's my favorite horse, but today, I imagined that you could ride her. Maybe get to know her in case you ever decide to ride again. All I want is for you to be comfortable."

I caught his meaning. He expected more engagements like this one. The way he spoke with such assurance sent shivers down my arms until goose bumps rose.

Just get through today. Come nighttime, I had a date.

We headed for the door, Everett opening it for me and ushering me out into the fresh air. The streets were busy today, everyone parading about in their newest dresses or suits, the sky bright and blue and sunny. The perfect weather for a walk to the shops or a ride.

"Thank you for today, Everett," I made myself say, trying to be polite. "And for sharing your horse. I'm sure she's beautiful."

"That she is. She's known for her speed, and I think you'll enjoy keeping up with her." He chuckled as he gracefully led me down the steps and to his waiting carriage. His hand was warm and steady when he lifted me inside, and my lips tugged up as I settled myself. Everett didn't propose to loan me some mare months away from pasture, believing me some fragile creature. I liked that he sensed I'd enjoy the speed and exhilaration.

He might not be the one who'd tie me down with a marriage contract, but I had a notion that he saw me much more clearly than most people. I should at least try to see him in the same light. If he showed me that I could trust him, then somewhere down the line he might be useful to expose the crimes of my father and his lackeys.

I had to recruit as many members of high society as possible.

The carriage took off, and Everett and I eased into a relaxed conversation. The muscles of my shoulders gradually loosened as we discussed our plans for Solstice, which was still ages away. We both agreed it to be the best time of year: the snow that coated Andalay and the lights that were strung up and painted everything in a magical glow.

When we arrived at his estate—an hour's ride away—the time seemed to have flown. I grinned as the carriage jerked to a halt, thinking of how Everett had asked all about me. Not idle conversation, but questions about my hobbies. What made me smile. What my ideal future looked like. Whether I desired to travel, and if so, where?

I didn't ask him nearly enough about himself, but he didn't appear to mind, leaning in close to capture each of my answers. He made me feel seen. Heard.

"Welcome to my home," he announced, helping me down the carriage steps. I peered up, my mouth falling open in wonder as I took in the grand estate. Four levels of imported stone greeted me, dark green ivy climbing up every inch. Wide-open windows welcomed the sun inside, and the front door was entirely comprised of clear glass, as if visitors were always welcome. I was about to compliment him when I noticed the gardenia bushes bordering the house.

"Those are Callie's and my favorites. Well, aside from roses,"

I said, dropping his arm and racing to the closest bush. Cupping one of the sweet-smelling blooms in my hand, I inhaled, instantly pacified, steadier. I wished Mother would let me plant them in our garden, but she refused, claiming they were too "overpowering." I disagreed but hadn't the energy to argue with her about flowers of all things.

"They were my late mother's favorite as well." Everett stood tall beside me, clearly proud. He glanced at the bush, a faint smile ghosting his lips. "She planted them everywhere on the estate."

I'd heard that his mother died when he was younger, just a boy, really. I stood, brushing at my skirts nervously. "I wish I could've met her."

"She was a spirited woman," he said, motioning me toward the entrance. "Father liked to try to rein her in, though." He spoke that last part with a hint of distaste.

I sensed that the rumors had been correct; Everett and his father didn't get along.

Lord Arthur Sinclair evaded society, even when invited to every ball his son attended. The man was a mystery, and I'd never seen him in person. The Sinclairs were renowned for their wealth and their noble heritage, Everett's father a duke. Meaning that one day, Everett would inherit the title and all this land.

Hopefully, he would do better than his father.

The double doors opened, revealing two women with welcoming smiles.

"I'm so happy you're home, Rett," said the first one, an older woman with vivid snowy hair and a crooked smile. She tugged him inside, and shockingly, embraced him on the spot. Everett hugged her just as fiercely.

Rett? I lowered my chin, smiling at the nickname.

"Haven't I told you not to call me that, Evelyn?" he replied playfully. Pulling back, he took in the second woman. She was younger, perhaps ten years older than me, with haunting blue eyes and blond hair tied in a strict bun. "And wonderful to see you, Miss Ava. Hope your mother here hasn't caused you too much trouble."

I stood there, watching the interaction with fascination. Most lords didn't treat their staff kindly, let alone hug them. It spoke well of Everett's nature.

Was I a fool for not truly considering him and his courtship? I had all these grand ideas, but could they actually become reality? Maybe Everett wouldn't mind my traveling, maybe—

No. I stopped myself right there. Perhaps I stopped because Damien's face invaded my thoughts, or maybe I daydreamed about a safer life given my father's heinous dealings. It had to be the latter.

"Oh, this is Lady Wren Hayes!" Everett exclaimed, shaking his head. "Excuse my poor manners. She and I will be riding today."

I took a step into the foyer, both mother and daughter beaming at me.

"Well, aren't you just as stunning as Everett said," Evelyn remarked. She looked at Everett knowingly, and he grunted in embarrassment, the tips of his ears reddening. "Don't mess it up, boy." I laughed when she gently smacked his side.

"Trying not to," he murmured, avoiding my eyes.

"Go on, then," Evelyn said, waving us ahead. "Don't let us get in the way. But do call if you need anything!"

Everett nodded his thanks and once again took my hand. "This way. The place can be a maze." He led me beyond the breathtaking foyer and the double staircase, the rich wood carved with intricate gardenia blooms. The style of the home was open, showcasing the gilded furniture, cream accents, and expensive paintings. A few portraits hung on the wall leading to the parlor, and I took in Arthur Sinclair's and Everett's portraits side by side. In the painting, clearly made when he was a younger man, Arthur had severe, sharp features, his reddish-blond hair gleaming. He didn't smile, his lips thin and turned down at the sides. Next to him rested a petite woman I suspected was the late Emily Sinclair. Unlike her son, she had long chestnut hair and green eyes, but it was her smile that illuminated her features. Much like his.

"I'm sparing you from a tour," Everett said. "Unless you'd like one, that is? I just thought you'd like to ride first. You have this look on your face that can only be remedied by one thing."

I didn't want a tour, he was right. I wished to be atop Mayberry, feeling the wind in my hair and allowing myself to float away into the sensation of flying. My heart leapt, skipping a beat as I looked Everett's way. He truly did his best to understand me.

"Astute observation." I squeezed his arm in encouragement as he brought us to a set of doors leading to a grand porch. In the distance, I spotted the stables, the echoing whinnies music to my ears.

What caught my attention was his garden.

Iridescent cerulean blooms mingled with gardenias, along with pastel pinks and warm, honeyed yellows. They shimmered in the sun, each petal dazzling as if light were trapped inside. It was a wild, untamed garden cut by a single path of stone steps that guided one to the stables . . . and I couldn't peel myself away.

"It's stunning," I mustered, tempted to reach out and pluck a blue flower with a golden center. Specks of glittering dust dotted the middle, but the wind picked up the motes and dispersed them into the breeze.

Everett came up beside me. I'd drifted down the porch steps and to the first row of flowers as if lured by a spell.

"They were my mother's gift," he explained. "Her gloves created these." He gazed across the sea of magic, his sea-blue eyes glistening. "My earliest memories are being out here with her, planting. She adored her flowers, spoke to them like children." He laughed, a heartbreaking smile on his lips. "Mother was patient, a trait I need to learn to channel more. She used to tell me that nothing of beauty is easily won. It takes time, and if you're patient and take a step back, you might be fortunate enough to watch magic take shape before your eyes." Everett glanced at me, a mischievous glint in his eyes. "Just don't blink."

"She sounded wise," I said gently, praying he wasn't insinuating that he was trying to win *me*. He merely nodded, his attention glued to her blooms, wonder softening the hard ridges of his face. "Did you continue her work?" There were so many flowers. I felt as if it would take decades to build such a scene stolen from a fairy tale.

"I'm the only one who uses her gift. Her gloves. She secretly gave them to me before she passed." He studied his shoes. "I wish I had more time to get out here, though."

I bit my lip in thought. Typically, when someone passed away, it was customary to bury them with their gift. I'd never heard someone admit that they used another's magic.

"Come," he said, shaking his head as if dispelling old memories. "I promised you a day of riding."

Mayberry was just as fast as Everett claimed.

I clutched her silken black mane, her matching coat shimmering in the sun. Grinning from ear to ear, we stormed across wide meadows of wildflowers.

Everett drifted behind; his mare, a stunning chestnut thoroughbred, couldn't keep up.

I lifted my hands in the air and shut my eyes. My body flew, the world ceased to exist, and I relished the euphoric thrill shoving my heart into my stomach with each gallop. *This* was freedom. Open spaces and clear skies. Air that smelled of musky woods and earth. And the mare beneath me that granted me the gift of flight.

I didn't wish to slow, to open my eyes and ruin the illusion. Sitting up in the saddle—straddling the beast—I rose, silently daring myself to let go.

"Wren!"

A grumble worked up my throat as I forced my eyes open and peered behind me. Everett's mare reared back on her hind legs, the panic in Everett's blue eyes soon matching my own. With a curse, I slowed and yanked on the reins, spinning Mayberry around.

Everett's horse whinnied, doing her best to unseat him. He gripped her tight with his muscled thighs, but he was no match for her strength and determination to be free. Something must've spooked her.

In horror, I watched as he fell backward, slipping from his saddle and dropping onto his back. The horse took off, dashing away from her rider and into the woods.

"Everett!" I screamed, angling close before hopping off Mayberry. "Are you all right?"

He groaned at the question, attempting to push himself into a seated position. I crouched down and braced him, my hand wrapping around his thick biceps. He had a dazed look, his gaze unfocused as he stared straight ahead, his usually impeccable hair falling across his eyes.

"I-I'm fine," he murmured, shaking himself. I watched the column of his throat as he swallowed hard, his attention drifting to where his horse had bolted.

"Let's get you up," I said, trying to haul him by the arm. "We can take—"

Everett froze midway to standing, his focus locked on something ahead.

I followed his line of sight, all the way to—

His glasses. The ones the Fates had gifted him.

They now lay broken and shattered feet away, likely having fallen from his jacket pocket and then having been trampled upon.

Gifts from the Fates *didn't break.*

They didn't shatter. Bend. Fracture.

Everett slid from my grasp, his legs unsteady as he darted for the ruined glasses. "They're all right," he said quickly, as if I hadn't borne witness to their destruction. "I'll clean them up when we get back. Just a little dirt. Nothing to worry about."

His ramblings didn't help his case.

"Everett," I began, but he held up a hand, stopping me.

"I told you they're fine."

"But they're not." I snagged Mayberry's reins and quickened my pace as Everett took off in the direction of his estate. "They were broken, and we both know a gift from the Fates can't be broken."

So what were they? What was he hiding?

Everett whirled on me so quickly I stumbled. The expression on his face was one of fear mixed with a tinge of rage. My breath caught; I felt hesitant around him for the very first time. I'd never seen him look at me this way.

"You don't know anything, Wren," he snapped, his tone icy. "You don't know what you saw."

Like hell I didn't.

"I don't need you to tell me what I did or didn't see," I returned, proud that my voice held steady. "You're hiding something. It's obvious. And the fact that you're so defensive tells me—"

"Tells you *what*?" he countered, his shoulders straightening and making him appear larger than life. The grimace painting his features marred his handsomeness, destroying the gentle quality I'd seen moments before.

"Everett, you don't need to be upset. I won't tell anyone." It was a whisper, and not because I was frightened. I understood exactly how he felt. But to pretend . . .

Because that was what he'd done. Those glasses were *fake*. He'd worn them with feigned pride, allowing society to believe him blessed.

He just wanted to be accepted. I could understand that. But his anger twisted my gut, a prickly feeling causing me to shiver.

Everett paused to run a rough hand through his mussed hair and shut his eyes. The curse that fell from his lips was coarse, as were the four after it.

"I've always been good with numbers," he said so quietly that the wind nearly stole the words. "Then my birthday came and my father . . . Oh, my father wasn't pleased, but he didn't look surprised, either."

Everett turned, giving me his profile. From this angle, his nose reminded me of Damien's; regal, with a slight bump in the middle, like he'd gotten into a fight. Maybe Everett's time at the rowdy southern pub hadn't been his first.

Everett took in a deep breath. "Lord Sinclair never loses," he muttered. "He expects his son to be no different. Which was why I found it odd that he didn't seethe or scream. He barely even looked at me. That was, until weeks later, when he employed *other* methods to defuse his anger."

I flinched. Did Lord Arthur Sinclair physically hurt his son? By the way Everett shriveled in on himself, his shoulders now hunching, I suspected as much, and while I didn't know the duke personally, powerful men had a tendency to harm when they lost control. That harm, though, frequently happened behind closed doors.

I placed my hand on Everett's shoulder, my fingers slightly trembling. He winced, but he didn't move away. "You have my word. I won't speak of it. *Ever.*"

I swore he leaned back against me, his muscles relaxing while he welcomed the gentle hand on him. The urge to embrace him beckoned, but it didn't feel *right*.

"Thank you" was all he said. He gazed over the meadow, his back to me, the wind whipping at us as it whistled in our ears. Time seemed to stop, to freeze, as he all but admitted he didn't have a gift. That like Lizzy and Adrian—and me—he, too, had been deprived of magic.

Did that put Everett on the list of suspects? Was he capable of stealing my gift for himself and putting on this act of courtship? I wanted to believe him innocent, but . . . most people looked out for themselves.

I eyed the house, far off in the distance. Maybe I should meet Arthur Sinclair myself.

Chapter Twenty-Seven

Wren

What makes a Fate? Scholars have long debated this mystery, and while the Fates themselves have claimed divine destiny, skeptics refuse to give up the search for a solid answer.

—Pages found in the banned book *Questioning Fate* by Alexandra Collette, Andalay historian, location unknown

I never did get the chance to see Lord Sinclair. After Everett and I rode back to his home in unbearable silence, he all but whisked me to his carriage with hardly a word.

He'd been ashamed, and I understood, but if anyone would sympathize with what he'd gone through, it would be me. Or maybe I was just lucky to have someone like my sister who cared enough to listen and talk without judgment. Everett didn't have any siblings, and if his father abused him . . .

Everett's not wanting a heart-to-heart would be understandable.

I'd keep his secret nevertheless, even from . . . even from Damien. He'd been the first person I'd thought of running off to tell. In fact, Damien tended to cross my mind more and more lately, even over trivial things *barely* related to the case. Shame prickled underneath my skin, and I brushed aside the thought. I could keep *one* secret. It didn't mean Everett was our culprit, and I liked to think my word meant something.

When I arrived home and after my parents had retired for the evening, I hunted Callie down.

She lay across her bed, a few open ledgers spread across her fluffy violet blanket. Twirling a pink fountain pen in her hand, she rested on her stomach, bare feet in the air and kicking casually back and forth. I smiled. She looked like she had five years ago—before my partner in crime had endured Father's tutelage.

"Yes, sister?" she asked in a teasing tone, not glancing over her shoulder. Fates, she had the uncanny ability to know when I was sneaking up on her. Maybe she sensed my emotions radiating from my damned pores.

"Do you or Father ever deal with Lord Arthur Sinclair?" I asked, leaning against her doorframe.

She paused, twirling her pen, to sneak a peek at me, the space between her eyes pinched. "That old bag? *Ugh*. He's the worst. Why?"

"Why is he the worst?" I continued, pulse pounding at my throat.

"He stays to himself mostly, thank the Fates, but whenever Father and I have to go to his estate for business, he's a real . . . pleasure."

"Do you think he abuses his son?"

I got straight to the point. No child should suffer a parent's abuse, and my hands clenched as I thought of Everett cowering while his own father swung at him.

Callie frowned, her pretty features fraught. "I mean, I haven't heard any gossip, but . . ."

I walked deeper into the room. "But what?"

"But there was some talk a couple of years ago that Arthur hit his late wife. She died when his son was younger, so my memory could be foggy, but I wouldn't exactly put it past him. He has a well-known temper. Father even had a bruise once from where Arthur threw a paperweight at his shoulder during an official vote."

I sucked in a sharp breath, hating that I hadn't tried harder to talk more with Everett before he rushed me out through his gates. He could be the victim of abuse. Then again, hounding him when he didn't feel comfortable wasn't ideal either.

"Why are you asking about him?" Callie dropped her pen on the biggest ledger and twisted herself to an upright position.

"I saw Everett today. He just seemed off when we brought up his father," I lied. Well, half lied.

Callie nodded like she understood. "You like him," she said confidently and with far too much pleasure. If she read my emotions, she'd know I *did* like him, I just wasn't certain which kind of *like.* Everett had grown on me easily enough, but my heart didn't pound like a madwoman's at the mere sight of him. It was a gentle beat, sure and steady. The problem was, I wasn't certain I liked the steadiness of it all. "Just be careful, little bird," Callie warned. "A romantic entanglement with him would mean dealing with his father, and while I like Everett as a man, I'd be wary."

"I will." I stepped back, itching to get away from the topic of courtship. "Night, Callie."

"Night," she called as I left her room.

I walked to my own room and shut the door with a deep sigh. A few hours remained until Grayson and I were to meet to follow his father to the docks.

The idea felt thrilling at the time, but now, after today—

I was drained. Mentally, emotionally. I stared at my reflection in the floor-length mirror opposite me, noting the dark circles below each eye and the limpness of my hair. Even my skin looked pallid. Pinching my cheeks, I roused some color, but it wasn't enough to dispel that haunting version of me.

Before I turned eighteen, Callie had often teased me about being a bundle of energy. How I'd bounce off the walls whenever a ball was planned and think for days about what to wear. How excited I grew at the prospect of the quarterly festival days in the town market, where I'd buy silks and ribbons and all manner of frivolous things.

I'd been the younger, lively sister who'd thought only about herself.

After my eyes had opened, after misfortune had befallen *me,* that had all changed. Funny how that worked. You're blind to the unpleasant things in life when you're happy. Like other people's pain was nonexistent as long as you were smiling.

I plopped onto my bed, eyes on the ceiling. I might not enjoy my reflection, but I was glad I wasn't that girl anymore—or was trying not to be. She'd been self-centered and delusional.

I'd trade dark circles for clarity any day.

Hopefully tonight would provide some.

At ten-thirty, I pulled on the dreariest dress I owned—a lapis blue number with long sleeves and a higher neckline. Taming my hair, I pinned it up into a tight bun so the cloak I stole from Mother's closet would easily slip over. Mine was caked in grime, and Sarah had insisted it be cleaned.

In case anyone lingered by the front entrance, I chose to use the garden. Grayson told me he'd meet me a block away to avoid suspicion.

My hands dug into the cloak's pockets as I walked, the night too quiet, the air stagnant. My fingers curled around something hard. Removing my hand from the deep pocket, I squinted beneath a streetlamp at the black card I grasped.

The Black Dahlia.

I blinked in confusion at the golden script, noting that the address lay *south.* There was no other hint as to what the establishment was, but ice shot down my back. Even if it belonged to someone innocent, my mother was too stuck-up ever to set foot in the south. Or so I believed.

When a horse neighed impatiently nearby, I shoved the card back in her pocket.

Grayson's carriage waited on the other side of the street, a block away, as he'd promised. Lifting my leather-gloved hand, I softly rapped on the door, his hunched-over driver not sparing me a glance. A beat passed before the door swung open, and I hastily climbed inside. Thankfully, it wasn't as ostentatious as his parents' usual transportation; no gold or carved wood in sight.

Grayson dressed the part of a vigilante—though a stylish one, covered in head-to-toe black with crisp button-down and velvet trousers. His leg jostled as he appraised me, his eyes wide enough to reveal the nerves he failed to conceal. "Wren," he murmured, nodding to the opposite seat, his natural charisma nonexistent. I took my place with a nod. We were linked, both of our fathers a part of something we prayed wasn't as terrible as we imagined.

Souls had to mean people.

Like the ones who'd lost their lives in the Void, their black-and-white photographs clipped to a thin sheet of paper, filed away and forgotten beneath a layer of dust.

The face of the man who raised me loomed in my mind.

Aside from blackmail, I suspected my father was involved with those files and the people who had mysteriously gone missing. It was a sickening thought, that he could do worse than steal gifts and blackmail lords, but he'd risen so high in the ranks so quickly, becoming representative of Ward One, and his thirst for more influence might drive him to do nearly anything. Even something as heinous as cold-blooded murder. My heart had started to break when Damien spotted him at the Registry in that cold room. After Grayson's note, it was fully broken. But my feelings couldn't matter anymore. We had to catch him red-handed, dealing with *people,* and bring him to justice so no more were killed. Grayson would make the perfect witness—while some might not believe me due to the ridiculous fact that I was a woman, they wouldn't hesitate to listen to Grayson if he made the claim.

I dug my nails into my palms as I thought about how outrageous our world was. How we pretended to be *civilized* when all we amounted to were bloodthirsty animals.

Grayson wordlessly tapped the roof of the carriage and we started off, for once not making clever remarks or even shamelessly flirting. We sat in uneasy silence for many minutes before he spoke.

"We're just doing some spying," he assured me. Or himself. "No interfering, and we stay as far away from my father as possible."

I nodded in agreement, my stomach twisting. The dress I wore had been a bad choice; the heavy material caused sweat to pool down my back, the feeling of being wrapped in stifling wool making my pulse flutter in distress at my throat.

It didn't ease my mind that I'd left Damien high and dry. He probably would be pissed if he showed up and I was gone on a mission without him, but I'd had no way to get a message to him with Sarah breathing down my neck all day. I should have felt guilty, but the vindictive side of me wished I could be there to see Damien's scowl when he realized I wasn't always waiting at his beck and call.

When we arrived at the docks, Grayson's nervous foot-tapping ceased. Mercifully.

"Ready?" he asked, opening the door. I nodded. Steeling my spine, Grayson exited before offering me a hand. It shook.

I eyed our surroundings.

We were at the docks, sure enough, the sight of the sea and the scent of brine and varnish washing over my senses. To our right, the great import and export ships waited, moored at the dozens of tidy docks spread out like spindly fingers reaching into the ocean.

Grayson had the good idea to hide the carriage behind the port master's office, and we moved around to the edge of the central walkway.

His father's ships were closer to the end, but I heard shouts ringing in the air. Peering into the night, I glimpsed men and women lifting crates with ropes and pulleys, hauling them off the ship and onto a rolling device secured to the dock. Stamped on the black container was a hatchet and moon symbol. The Hockley emblem.

"Let's move closer." I nudged Grayson.

He stood frozen. "There's hardly any cover." He was right. Just an open fence separated the docks from the mainland, though I did see some thick reeds we could slink behind.

"We might get a little messy, but aim for those." I pointed at our destination. Grayson cringed. "I'm right here," I assured him, grabbing his hand and squeezing.

I barely knew him, and yet it felt like we'd been friends for years. I supposed some people were like that—forging a connection that tied them together, making everything feel effortless.

Or I felt that way because we were in the same horrid predicament. Pain made for an easy bond.

"Together," Grayson said with a sigh.

With his hand in mine, we started to creep along the fence when an irritated voice rang out.

"Did you forget someone, sunshine?"

Chapter Twenty-Eight

Damien

It took effort, but eventually, I managed to pry my eyes away from their intertwined hands.

Wren had planned to leave me waiting all night while she gallivanted around the docks with this *stranger.* Who now held on to her like *I* was the outsider.

"Who is he?" I demanded, my voice deep. I sounded pissed, there was no disguising it. Wren and I had worked together this entire time without anyone else involved, and now? She stood there hand in hand with some unfamiliar noble. One who wasn't hard on the eyes, I could admit. He looked like a bronzed statue, his dark brown eyes appearing outlined in kohl. The perfect rake whom every eligible man or woman would fall for.

My hands clenched into fists the longer I looked at him. At *her.*

By some stroke of luck, I'd arrived at her town house early and watched the whole thing play out—her sneaking through the garden before getting into his carriage without a care in the world. I'd planned to knock on her window, hoping she was game to break into the Registry, but she had other plans.

I think I blacked out when I used my last remaining coin to tail them in a hired carriage idling on the main avenue. Throughout the drive, I seethed; angry at myself for feeling angry, and angry that that I allowed myself to be entirely consumed by that anger.

Wren was infuriating. She'd patched me up and slept beside me all through the night, her soft skin and that damned citrus scent of hers invading my thoughts. Sure, I'd been the one to leave, that morning, but . . . But I didn't think she would go running off with some other man the second I was away.

This was new to me.

Another reason I never did *feelings*.

It was arrogant of me to assume she'd be at home, ready for me to knock on her window. Hell, it made me a self-centered prick. The awareness didn't make the heat in my chest simmer down, however. Just picturing her next to him fueled the flames, and I imagined her off on some midnight tryst. She never spoke of suitors, but she could very well be hiding them from me.

How many suckers did she have at her beck and call besides me? Did she smile at them in the same way, looking at them like a goddess fallen from the heavens? Did she smack them when they said something stupid? I wondered if she told them all of her darkest secrets and hopes. Her dreams of traveling.

Fuck. I shouldn't have been thinking that way, but I couldn't help it. Aside from Ruby, I hadn't allowed anyone else in my life, and the woman I stole from had become—

Something.

Something *more.*

Before we reached the docks, I hopped out and hunted down a messenger on his way into the city. After I bribed the messenger with a week's worth of Cap's drinks on the house—a promise I wasn't sure I could uphold—he took off for the tavern. I imagined Ruby would receive the message soon. Backup might be needed.

"Wren?" I demanded when she sat there, watching me, that defiant little chin lifting. I had the urge to grab it, to yank her lips to mine and—

She released a weary sigh, yet she didn't falter or stumble. "This is Grayson."

Grayson. Such a nice name for an arrogant bastard.

"And?" I prowled closer, inspecting the highborn man with distaste. When he smiled in reply, my hatred for him swelled.

"*And* he brought me a clue I couldn't ignore," Wren said. "He suspects his father and mine are meeting here tonight. There's a new 'shipment.' "

Her face relayed no emotion, not like earlier when I'd watched her take his hand, soothing and comforting him.

Shite. Jealousy was not a good look on me. And I felt it in spades.

That unbidden fire burned like an inferno, the kind that felt like more than mere jealousy. An emotion I couldn't, *no,* wouldn't name. I hadn't even felt like this when she'd danced with Everett. I knew her well enough by now to know she wasn't interested in him.

Which you shouldn't care about . . . but do anyway.

Screw my thoughts.

"You trust him? How long have you known him?" I asked, daring to step closer. Why did Wren have to keep attracting untrustworthy strays? First Everett, then this smiling fool. Grayson could very well be working with his father and luring her into a trap.

All right. The irony wasn't lost on me. I'd deceived her first, but I was rectifying it, so it didn't count.

"Just . . . just trust me for once," she said. "We have to know what's in the shipping containers."

I ground my teeth. I'd like a word with her afterward about the danger of befriending strangers and following them to shady places in the middle of the night, but for now, I let it go. Call me a bastard, but I didn't want her dead. "Fine," I bit out. "But we wait for Ruby. I sent word for her to come."

At the mention of Ruby, Wren's face instantly brightened, and damn it, I'd never been more envious of my friend than at that moment.

"At least someone with sense will be here," she said, one corner of her lips curling upward into a smirk.

The little vixen was goading me.

I took the bait.

"Someone with sense, eh?" I ran my eyes down her form, a chuckle leaving me. "You could be dead right this minute—"

"I'm right here, you know," Grayson interrupted. "And don't worry, I don't plan on murdering anyone tonight."

Funny.

"You just like to lure women to the shadiest parts of town without hired muscle in the middle of the night, then?"

He had no idea what could've happened if some of the dockside boys had found them.

Wren dropped his hand for a moment, and they exchanged a look. He nodded.

Great, now they were communicating telepathically.

Bounding up to me, she snatched my hand and all but lugged me aside, away from the prying ears of Grayson.

"Damien." She practically growled my name, her blue eyes storms of fury. "What is it with you tonight?"

I took her by the shoulders, my fingers digging through the material of her dress. Why couldn't she understand that she'd put herself in danger?

"Whenever you come to the Void, tell me," I begged. "You could've been hurt, and—"

"You always leave before plans can be made," she said. "One moment you run hot, the next, you're ice-cold, afraid of even looking me in the eyes. Get yourself together."

I jerked back, her passion a surprise. An adorable one.

"Besides," she continued, "I don't have to alert you every time I leave the house."

Unable to stop myself, or simply unwilling, I took her defiant chin between my fingers and angled it, my eyes immediately glued to her lips.

"You infuriate me, Wren Hayes."

"And you drive me mad."

My fingers twitched as I ran my thumb across her lower lip. When they parted I knew with complete certainty that I'd done the one thing I promised I'd never do—

I'd fallen for a mark.

Or *was* falling.

Leaning down, I whispered against her mouth, barely a kiss, more like a warning. "Whenever you're concerned, it's my business."

She exhaled, allowing me to taste traces of peppermint and something distinctly her. The memory of her kiss seared across my mind like a brand.

"Are you *my* business?" she asked, breathless.

"From day one," came my answer, quick and truthful. "Or maybe when you stabbed me. That's when . . ."

"When *what*?" We were centimeters from touching, from giving in to what had been building like a storm.

"When I . . ." *When I wanted you,* I wished to say. That was when she became real. My ward princess. A spot of sunshine in the abyss of my life.

"You can't even say it, can you?" Her eyes narrowed, and I swore I glimpsed tears lining them in the dimness. "You can never just say how you feel. You're too much of a fucking coward to—"

I yanked her forward and kissed her.

She whimpered in surprise, but her body fused to mine, those delectable curves all but begging for my hands. Since we weren't alone and I couldn't indulge in my baser instincts, no matter how much my body ached, I pressed my lips against hers and stole her breath instead. I ran my tongue across the seam of her mouth before invading it, before tangling my tongue with hers. She moaned softly, and that damned sound, it made it near impossible to pull back. But now wasn't the time. Or place.

Breaking away with a curse, I held her to me. "I'm sorry I ran," I admitted. "I would've spent all day with you. Would've loved it. I . . . you make me think of things I shouldn't. Impossible things that will only bring disaster in the end. You and I both know it."

We were a tragedy waiting to happen, and I'd become a glutton for punishment.

"I want to know these impossible things you speak of." She rocked forward to nip at my bottom lip. "You should know by now that I'm not one to care what society thinks of me. I do what I want, and will continue to do so. And you, Damien, have driven me mad since the moment I laid eyes upon you. You've enraged me. Comforted me. Made me question if I was going crazy too."

"Same, sunshine," I said, my hand curving around her hip. "I'm not used to the feeling. It's . . . grating."

"Get used to it," she demanded. "Because I won't wait for you to decide."

With that, she pulled free of my hold and strode back to Grayson, his attention diverted to the ships. When he cleared his throat awkwardly, Wren took his hand in hers *again* and whispered in his ear. He visibly relaxed, and turning to her, he smiled.

He was lucky I didn't wipe that smile off his face. Tonight, at least.

I stood behind them in brooding silence as the invisible clock ticked. We were all on edge, the noble glancing anxiously over his shoulder while Wren fidgeted from foot to foot. Maybe she was eager to begin. Usually, I could sit still easily enough—it was useful for my gift, after all—but I scanned the night as if it were my job, analyzing each and every movement like a threat. This part of town was the worst place imaginable for us to be, but it was shockingly quiet, like even the lowliest of criminals knew to stay away.

When Ruby eventually strolled down the docks with a bounce in her step, the three of us let out a collective sigh. She'd take my side over a noble's, surely, and I felt more confident now should this Lord Grayson pull any tricks.

"Wren!" Ruby immediately ran to wrap her arms around her. Wren startled, but she dropped Grayson's hand and returned Ruby's unexpected embrace. Ruby was touchy, and she showed her emotions without care. Living like that in the Void, it was surprising she wasn't dead already.

Showing emotions is what she *wants from* you, I thought with a grimace.

Baby steps.

"I'm glad to see you again," Wren said brightly. There was a teasing quality to her voice, her eyes twinkling.

I loved how we *both* had relieved Wren's precious lord of his watch, and yet I was the only one paying the price for it. Figured.

Ruby grinned wide. "Same, princess. I asked to join you and Damien on your secret mission ages ago, but he was being greedy and told me no."

Traitor.

"I didn't want too many people involved," I replied, glaring at my friend when Wren craned her neck at me, an eyebrow raised in question.

"Too late now," Ruby mocked, stepping to my side before she nudged me. I grunted in pain, my body still sore. Hell, *sore* was an understatement. My wound was healing better than expected, but streaks of blood continued to stain the bandages, and while anyone with a lick of common sense would rest, I'd never felt more on edge.

"Who's this handsome man?" Ruby ran her eyes over Grayson with interest. If she hadn't preferred women, I'd have been worried.

He wasn't *that* handsome.

Grayson made his introductions and explained the situation while Wren caught my stare, giving what she might believe to be a look of warning to behave.

My sunshine considered herself frightening. It was almost cute—if I hadn't been so furious that she'd put herself at risk.

Was I being irrational? Territorial? Insane? All yes. But after the other night, well, maybe before then, I'd grown protective. And our kiss just now? It cemented things in my caveman brain.

She wanted me to make up my mind? I had, and now she'd probably regret asking.

"Let's go, then," I muttered, stepping between Grayson and Wren. I snagged her hand and ignored her grumbling protests. It wasn't lost on me that Ruby let out a tiny gasp of surprise at the display.

"You're injured," Wren said. "Take it easy."

As if my earlier rage had made me forget the pain, it now reared its ugly head. My damned shoulder ached, but I didn't care. Besides, I'd survived far worse.

"I'm not leaving," I said, gripping her hand tighter. "Besides, I have a dagger. Not a letter opener on me."

She scoffed. "It worked well enough last time."

With her safely in my hold, I led the way to where the workers were unloading the crates. Motioning to the group, I urged everyone to drop to their knees and keep low behind the reeds. I didn't release Wren.

"This one's heavy as shit, boss!" someone called, kicking at the side of a crate. The ship it sat beside belonged to Hockley, his logo of a hatchet framed by a crescent moon painted on its side. He trafficked mostly in carpentry, delivering wood and construction supplies.

Wren startled when two shadowy figures seemed to materialize from the darkness. One of the men snapped his fingers, and a flicker of light illuminated his face, a small flame cradled in his palm.

Hockley and his silver handheld lighter. He could summon deadly flames to his bare hands whenever he wished as long as his gift remained on his person—something that could prove useful in a fight or as protection.

The second man, I recognized from his overconfident gait alone. As Hockley's enviable gift shone on the man beside him, I instantly curved myself around Wren. I grimaced when her entire body stiffened.

Cameron Hayes and Stuart Hockley sauntered down the dock and to the crate, dressed in their finest suits.

Stuart tapped a shiny black cane against the side, and I swore I heard muffled screams. The older man smiled.

"It should be heavy," he boomed. "I paid plenty for the cargo."

"Then everyone will be pleased," Cameron replied, stiff-backed and emotionless. "Especially since it's *late*. Next shipment better be double and ready to split. We can't have any suspicion set on us yet. Things need to seem like business as usual."

They were hiding something from the Fates. It sounded like they were tricking them with double shipments. So where did the overflow go?

Hockley's victorious face fell, but rather than take it out on Cameron, he kicked the side of the crate once more. "Load it up!" he boomed to his men. "We have a schedule to keep. Bring the rest as quickly as possible." The flame in his palm danced in warning, angry reds and burnt oranges sparking.

His workers rushed into action, pushing the crate to the walkway, where a wagon waited. They surrounded the crate, a few boasting weapons.

"Open it up and put them inside," Hockley instructed.

I held my breath as they pried open the door with crowbars. I suspected what lay inside. But seeing it? Seeing the dirtied *people* stolen from their homes walk out in a frightened daze and onto the wagon made it all too real. Something I couldn't ignore.

People. They were delivering people. Men. Women. *Children.*

"Souls," Grayson whispered. "He really meant it." Wren

reached out for him with her free hand, comforting him regardless of the tears in her eyes. I ground my teeth but returned my gaze to the men.

"We need to follow them," Ruby said to Grayson. "We'll take that fancy carriage of yours and confirm the delivery location."

For once she wasn't smiling. In fact, I'd never seen her look so murderous.

Grayson stood, taking Wren with him before I could secure my hold. Together, they led the way back to the carriage, and I seethed—both at the sight before me and at Cameron fucking Hayes.

That room with all the documents and photographs of dead bodies. The shipment of living people. Those missing from the Void. He was the cause. No. The *ringleader.*

"Wren didn't know," came Ruby's tranquil voice. She incorrectly guessed that my furious mood was directed at Wren.

Wren couldn't possibly have known—she was the embodiment of sunshine. The light I dreamed would one day shine on the fields of my farm. Maybe that was why I'd taken to calling her that. Ever since I'd laid eyes upon her, my cold black heart had warmed, and while the ice thawed, her brilliance wormed its way under my skin, marking me. Sometimes I loathed it, but most of the time I craved the heat she exuded when she took me in, truly looking into the depths of my eyes and not flinching. It was like a high, a drug no one could replicate.

Of course, she hadn't had the heart to suspect her father of something so cruel until she'd seen the proof with her own eyes. And because I understood her, I realized how her heart must be breaking—even as she walked side by side with her newest stray.

Wren might think herself weak and naïve, and sure, she *could* be naïve, but she was far from weak. Many would shatter on the spot in a similar situation, yet here she stood, tall and unyielding.

The cursed fire in my chest flared to life as I resisted the urge to hold her. Comfort her. Tend to her like she'd done me. But she and Grayson had reached the carriage and it was too late.

"Where's your driver?" Wren asked with a frown, peering around the carriage. The driver's seat lay empty, and not a sign of the hunched-over man I'd spotted earlier could be found lingering close by.

Grayson swore, swiping at his hair. "I have no idea. He's usually a footman, and I bribed him to take me here tonight. He hasn't been on my father's payroll for long."

"Great, now we have to make a run for it, and the only thing I despise more than running is cake with fruit in it," Ruby grumbled. "That's not cake. It's a trick."

"Enough about cake," I groaned, shooting Ruby a withering look. She rolled her eyes. "We need to leave. Now." I turned to Grayson. "You all right to walk, pretty boy?"

He beamed. "Good to know you find me pretty. But yes, I'm perfectly fine, regardless of my life being flipped on its head."

I wanted to rile him, but he just smiled, either genuinely charmed or playing a part superbly. When his right eye twitched, I suspected the latter. "All right. We head to Cap's, and then—"

An explosion shook the ground, sending me to my knees. The others collapsed, yelps of pain following the impact.

Smoke flared from the docks we'd just left, the scent of char clogging my nostrils. There was another smell there, something almost sickly . . . *floral.* I twisted my head, taking in the plumes of smoke wafting from the ships.

It would be a nightmare tomorrow.

"Everyone all right?" Grayson shouted, his arm around Ruby and Wren protectively.

"No injuries here," Wren murmured, Ruby nodding beside her.

I shot to my feet and offered Ruby a hand before lifting Wren. When she started to pull her hand away, I grasped it, not letting go as I scanned the darkness. I'd have to inspect her later to make certain she hadn't been lying about injuries.

"Someone bombed the docks."

"Obviously," Ruby retorted. "Your impressive deductive skills are at it again."

I glowered. "I wasn't finished. Someone bombed the docks, likely knowing what the lords were up to. Question is, are they competitors or friends?" Shouting erupted from the site of the explosion. "I'm going to go check it out," I told the others. Pulling Wren close, I whispered in her ear, "Stay close to Ruby, and whatever you do, please don't leave Cap's for any reason."

Her hand shoved against my chest. "I'm coming with you," she said. "You don't get to decide—"

Vicious light blinded me as I dropped to the ground once more, Wren's hand in mine. The second explosion was ten times as deafening, a thunderous boom that rattled my teeth. I recalled very little other than crawling over Wren's prone body. Could hardly see anything as that light flared and sparked.

In the wake of it all, debris plummeted from the sky, raining down upon us like snowflakes. Ashes coated my skin, the combined smell of char and flowers making it difficult to fill my lungs. The air buzzed, quivering from the aftershocks, but it felt like more than that . . . like how I felt after using my mirror.

Magic.

Someone had used magic.

Below me, Wren shifted, her ragged breaths compelling me to move so I wasn't crushing her. But she was safe, no visible signs of harm. I, on the other hand, had unquestionably reopened a stitch. *Fuck,* my shoulder screamed with each movement. "That was too close for my liking," she said, voice raspy.

I peered through the thick smog, swallowing the agony I wouldn't let show. There, one hundred feet away, stood what remained of the port master's office.

"They aimed for the office where they keep all the shipping schedules," I managed, my own throat like sandpaper. "Ruby? Grayson?"

This time, Ruby had used her body as a shield for the noble. She popped her head up, face streaked with dark gray and sporting a line of blood that trickled from a small cut on her temple. "We're fine. Again."

"That's our cue to run." I snatched Wren's hand and we got to our feet, Ruby and Grayson at our heels. Taking off for the Void, I didn't chance a peek behind me as we raced from the chaos at our backs.

It wasn't until we nearly reached the main avenue bordering the waterfront and warehouses that I spotted him—

A hooded figure bolted from the direction of the docks, his features masked but his gait anxious.

It was *him*. I felt it in my soul.

Gently pushing Wren into Ruby's arms, I yelled, "Stay here!" before sprinting after the stranger. Each time my feet struck the pavement, a wave of pain shot down my torso.

My gut screamed to let it go, but that man, his build, how he moved . . . it was familiar.

I reflected on the night I first arranged to meet with the buyer. To the cloaked man the buyer had sent out, his face hidden by shadows as we negotiated the deal to steal Wren's gift. Then there'd been the night of the stabbing.

Perhaps I was delirious and running on literal fumes, but there was a chance they were the same person.

He could've set off the bombs.

But why? Who did he work for? Because he was undoubtedly some lackey. The real leader hid themselves and sent others to do their dirty work. It could all be a ploy Cameron had laid out to claim innocence should the Fates decide his shipments weren't enough. Or the man answered to a noble who was pissed they hadn't received a gift.

Hell, I didn't know what to believe.

The man could've bombed the docks to *save* the people, for all I knew. That sounded far-fetched, but he *had* aimed for the empty boats. He could be a rebel.

That thought was all I required to shoot out into the Void and trail him, swerving around the people who'd come out of their homes after the explosion, their mouths gaping and eyes wide when they took in the distant docks.

The man left a scent in his wake, no matter how easily he maneuvered around the inhabitants. *Gardenias.* Yes, I recognized the flower because Wren loved them and I paid attention. Mostly.

I silently cursed as I shoulder-bumped a man, sending him to the ground. I didn't apologize. There was only the hunt, and I had my prey in sight.

When the cloaked man entered the Black Dahlia, I slowed.

A brothel. And a place renowned for people stepping inside and never leaving. At least not intact.

I flipped open my mirror and walked undetected past the man guarding the door, each footfall like a drumbeat of death in my ears.

Wren was going to kill me.

The Black Dahlia was one of a kind.

None of the other establishments of the night compared to the luxurious feel of the two-story building lavished in gold and plush black velvet. An onyx chandelier fashioned to resemble a skull dangled from the ceiling, a few shards of bone hanging from wires. Gas lamps lit the place just enough to see where you were putting your feet, but it maintained a dim and eerie atmosphere. Intended, of course.

Local crime bosses sprawled out in front-row seats before a

slick black stage engraved with the lounge's namesake flower, the men and the women who accompanied these patrons hanging off them like decorations. I recognized a few of the crime bosses—I'd been asked a handful of times to join and swear allegiance to a group, what with my notorious nickname and all. I steered clear of them as best I could, but it didn't stop their lackeys from seeking me out.

Nimble waiters scurried about the room, accustomed to the darkness. The women wore black corsets and scandalously short skirts, and the men's chests were bare above fine brocade trousers that hung low on their hips. They smiled as they handed out drinks from golden trays, beaming at the crowd, which murmured in anticipation of a burlesque show readying to begin.

But I wasn't here to catch a show.

Closing my eyes, I caught the whiff of gardenia to my left, my prey within reach. Angling around a waitress, invisible to the patrons and performers—and the brutal-looking security guards—I stepped beyond two towering men in pressed suits standing in front of a long hallway.

The scent continued past them, the murky hall lined with several shut doors. Each handle was crafted into a skull, and I ground my teeth, knowing exactly what went on behind them.

The Black Dahlia was popular with the Void's underbelly for a reason.

At the end, a single doorway stood out from the rest. Its knob wasn't a skull, but a golden raven. Ethereal light shone down upon it, even without gas lamps illuminating the dim corridor. Almost like it was magicked.

I got to the door, preparing to press my ear against the wood and listen in on any conversation I might overhear, when I noticed it was ajar.

My heart galloped in my chest, my body giving a flicker, showing a hazy outline of my form. Wren must be too far away—

Yet I couldn't leave yet. I'd come so far.

Peering into the narrow opening, I studied the room. Although it was decorated like the rest of the Black Dahlia, traces of polished gold and silver illuminated the room, and the three gas lamps hanging from the walls made it easier to spot the hooded man's broad back. He stood before a seated figure, both of them shielded behind a carved screen made of black wood.

"They hit the boat."

My blood turned to ice. Who was *they*? And that voice . . . I fucking *knew* that voice.

There came a tapping noise like fingernails beating an agitated rhythm against a glass table.

Unsure if my invisibility would hold should I inch deeper into the space, I didn't so much as move a muscle.

"That's . . . unfortunate," came another slightly familiar voice. A woman's. "I'm disappointed. The thief have anything to do with it?"

"Not to my knowledge."

The woman sighed. "Then he doesn't know everything just yet."

"No." The man's head hung impossibly low. "Tonight was a failure, but I will do better."

A scoff, and then, "You best. That was the last shipment I'll have to split. The next will come to me and me alone. I've worked too hard to keep a low profile for you to go and mess everything up with carelessness. We're so close, they won't know what hit them." A pause, and then, "You, out of everyone, should know what it's like to be born without power. Going so far as to fake it. My gift has proven just as useless over time. But the moment is coming. *My* moment. I'm done hiding behind a man."

"I understand. I want that for you as well. For us." He mumbled something unintelligible, and I strained to make out the words, to no avail.

"Yes. And you'll get your little treats at the end of it all, which makes everything that much sweeter. That, and the whole city will be turned on its head."

"I promise. You'll get your souls, mistress."

I watched as he knelt at her feet. Just the barest hint of luxurious pink leather shone, her matching heeled boots peeking out from beneath the material.

She muttered something too low for me to hear, and then he stood, his back stiff as he turned, heading my way.

I shoved against the wall, breathing hard.

"Oh, and Everett?" The woman's dulcet voice wafted to my ears. "I know he's your brother, even if by half, but take care of the stony-eyed thief. We can't afford any more problems."

Chapter Twenty-Nine

Wren

I don't believe the Fates are natural.
They are no divine deities. Not the gods we should worship.
They are the monsters in the dark.
—Pages found in the banned book *Questioning Fate*
by Alexandra Collette, Andalay historian, location unknown

The thief abandoned us on the streets, running Fates knew where.

Memories of the night he'd crawled to my house, half alive, haunted me. I wrung my hands, imagining all of the horrible things that could happen. If that man attacked again. Or if Damien was being led into a trap with more assailants. Or—

The thought of him hurt, bleeding out on the streets, *alone*—it drove me insane. I should've run after him, but he'd been too quick. I regretted not at least trying.

Damien would follow *me*.

"Hey," Ruby said, grabbing one of my hands. "Damien does that sometimes. I promise you, he's fine. He won't engage with the man unless he has a plan, which is why he's one of the Void's best thieves. Most people are reckless. He isn't."

She let go of my hand, gifting me with a reassuring smile. I returned the gesture, watching as she half skipped, half walked away. Not even the explosions had been capable of wiping away her exuberance. Dried blood covered one side of her face, but it made her look all the more fierce.

I rubbed my temples. Not worrying was easier said than done. I'd specifically told him to stay put.

My thoughts careened to a halt. *I* had gone with Grayson without him. Unfortunately, I couldn't admonish Damien without being a damned hypocrite myself.

Grayson had just looked so broken, and he trusted me. I'd thought I was doing the right thing by keeping Damien out of our plans, if only to gain Grayson's trust and information.

What we'd discovered . . .

Both our fathers were monsters.

The man who'd held me in his arms and read me fairy tales as a child had unloaded *people* ready for slaughter from a shipping container not a half hour ago. Apparently the inhabitants of the Void weren't sufficient, and whoever they delivered those poor souls to would probably request more.

I'd suspected for some time who they were intended for, much as I'd protested. The very notion argued against everything I believed. But I couldn't ignore the evidence, and that room at the Registry building had been damning.

But why? If the Fates were all-powerful, then why did they need souls?

I trailed after a defeated Grayson and Ruby, thinking of Dusk and her letter. She'd wanted me to find my gift and prevent something awful from transpiring. She'd *known*. Meaning . . .

My father and the other lords were working with one of the other Fates, if not both Day and Dawn.

I had a hard time believing the Fates worked alone—they never left their palace. And unless those souls were intended for some other deity I'd never heard about, the three women who ruled Andalay were murderers and liars.

My mind reeled, a headache forming. The civilians of Andalay had to know the truth: that the people they worshipped could be masquerading as deities when they were nothing but criminals.

I flinched when Grayson nudged my shoulder. "So . . ." He grimaced. "Our parents are evil. I mean, I always assumed as much, but to see it in action. It changes everything." He let out an audible exhale. "I don't know what to do with myself." Grayson intertwined our fingers, and I could practically feel his exhaustion seeping into my bones. "But I'm glad I know," he said, his voice hardening. "Together, we can do something about it. Right?"

He wanted me to have the answers. *I* wanted to have the answers.

"How? How are we going to do something?" I asked, my voice breaking at the end. "We don't have solid proof as to what the souls are used for. We have nothing but speculation. Yes, there's evidence of their deaths, but why? Why them? What is the need?" I practically shouted, and a few heads turned my way. I didn't care.

Grayson's grip on my hand tightened. "Hey. Take a breath," he soothed. "We don't have to solve this all right this second. We have people we can trust now, and I know it's not a lot, but we can bring in more. Build a group who can expose the truth. I doubt every citizen would be fine living with blood on their hands."

I hoped he was right. There had to be some, even in the north, who'd rebel against killing innocents.

The building tears I'd been working to hold back almost spilled, regardless of Grayson's support. "I have no magic, and Ruby and Damien might not want to endanger themselves," I whispered so she didn't hear. "Damien said he was in, but . . ." Damien wanted his dream. What if this got too dangerous and he skipped town? What if—

"They'll stay," Grayson said assuredly, and I envied his easy confidence. He should be shaken, and in some ways he was—his jaw clenched, shoulders stiffened—but he remained solid as marble. "They came here tonight and they aren't running. Well, Damien *did* run, but I think that was to tail a suspect," he amended. He rubbed at his eyes with his free hand, exhausted. Perhaps I'd been wrong, because the veneer of calm he wore slowly disintegrated before my eyes.

I felt the same.

We trudged toward the boundary separating the two sides of Andalay, Grayson holding my hand, Ruby gracefully weaving her way through the throngs of gawking onlookers. Fear had breathed life upon the Void, the explosions an invisible arrow aimed at its heart. You could tell by the way no one fully lifted their head or met your stare. It was a tangible thing, this unknown trepidation, and it built like a crescendo.

A hand yanked me to the side and I let out a scream.

"Wren!" Damien enfolded me in his arms, and I flinched, shocked by the act. How he so openly held me. It was new.

It was also comforting. Enough for a few tears to slip down my cheeks.

He drew back an inch to study my face, his eyes colder than before. "You're safe, you're all right." It wasn't a question. Or rather, it felt like him telling *himself* I was fine. The longer he analyzed my face, the softer his own became. He lifted a finger to catch a falling tear, the tenderness in his touch causing me to shiver.

My hands automatically wrapped around his torso, the cold air failing to stave off the heat he emanated. I met his wild gaze with a thumping heart, relieved he wasn't injured.

"What happened? Why did you run?" His lips parted, and he peered over my shoulder, perhaps at Ruby and Grayson. "Damien?" I pressed, my fingers digging into his jacket.

He maneuvered us beyond the masses, moving into a small corner in an empty vendor's stall. He hadn't let go once, and I found that troubling. He'd uncovered something.

"Spill," Ruby said, coming up on my right, arms crossed as Grayson towered behind her.

But Damien's eyes weren't on her. His hand cupped my cheek, the reverence in his stare sending a spark rioting through my chest. "I saw him," he said. "Everett."

"Everett?" I shook my head, not understanding.

"He went to the Black Dahlia and spoke to some woman there. I don't think it was one of the Fates, but . . . it has to do with them. I just don't understand it yet." The wall that had separated us for days had been too heavy to maintain. Looking up at him, I realized that it had been shattered, and the fear creasing the corners of his eyes spoke his truth. The worry, the anxiety, the alarm. There wasn't a single cocky bone in his body as he held me, his chest against mine, our bodies exhaling in perfect rhythm.

"Everett was the one who ran from the docks," he murmured. "But it's odd. The woman spoke to him as if she wasn't working with the lords. Or she was, but . . ." He trailed off, his face pinched. "She spoke of splitting shipments. But the next one wouldn't go to *them,* she said."

Them, as in the Fates.

"This woman wanted souls for *herself.*" I finished his thoughts, a thousand images of the highborn ladies I knew swirling through my head.

I pictured them all now; hiding in their lacy gowns, sipping tea, gossiping while living in luxury. My own mother was one of the most respected ladies in the city, and . . .

No. I was reaching. Thinking that if my father was evil, then Mother had to be as well. Yet the idea wouldn't leave me.

"We need to get the hell out of here," Ruby interjected, the women of the north and their secrets slipping to the back of my mind. "We could be next, and Aurilia is a large kingdom. Maybe we could leave it entirely," she suggested. "I heard the Southern Isles of Marnett to be beautiful."

"You want to leave?" Damien looked at her for the first time. "We've spent our whole lives here, Ruby."

"Yeah, and when have you ever cared about anyone else?" she retorted. "It's been us against the Void. The northerners. I'm tired of fighting."

Damien shook his head. "They're our people. *We* are them. I was hoping to leave this place, I'll admit, but I can't run now, knowing everything I do." He ran a rough hand through his tangled hair. "It'll haunt me. Nothing will make it all right, not even distance."

I analyzed each flicker of emotion on his face, stunned by his fierce protectiveness. There was something he wasn't saying. I glimpsed it in the twitch of his eye. How tightly he gripped me. The frustrated curl of his lips. How he dared a few peeks over his shoulder.

"Damien," I whispered in his ear, on my tiptoes. "What aren't you telling me?"

Grayson and Ruby spoke behind us, something about Grayson wishing to stay and fight and Ruby saying it was a lost cause. As they argued, Damien drew back, his Adam's apple bobbing.

"I think I've gone mad, Wren," he confessed. "I swear I have, but those last words the woman said . . ."

I found myself clutching his shoulders, pushing myself protectively against him. Damien wasn't a soft man by any means, so to have riled him in such a way was unfathomable.

"'*I know he's your brother, even if by half, but take care of the stony-eyed thief. We can't afford any more problems,*' she told Everett," Damien said, glancing down.

Stony-eyed thief. I'd only seen one thief with stony eyes, and they belonged to Damien.

The words hung in the air, suspended in time. I wished I had something better to say, something to take away his frantic look.

I was at a loss for the right words. I didn't think there were any.

"We'll find out, Damien. I promise," I vowed, feeling helpless. It was the same thing we'd been saying for weeks. And with this new revelation? Everything had just gotten messier.

"Why are you so certain?" he shouted. "Everett was there, right before my eyes, kneeling. He could be one of who knows how many who are in on this."

"So you think that you and Everett may be brothers—"

"I don't know what I think!" he said, louder than before. His outburst put an end to Ruby and Grayson's arguing. "But I don't know where I came from. I don't know anything!" He released his grip on me and spun around, his hand threading back in his hair as he drowned in his frustration.

Ruby placed her hand on his shoulder, and Damien faced her. "And the object I have? I don't even have an answer to that! My whole life has been a mystery, and I'm *exhausted*. When I was dropped off at the orphanage, no one knew of my origin. What if I *did* come from the north?" He looked at Ruby and then at me. My throat tightened as I watched him crumble. I wanted to be the one holding him, but he appeared one blink away from bolting.

Ruby shut her eyes. "It's a possibility," she finally admitted. "With your gift, it explains a lot."

Only members of high society and their kin were gifted.

And Damien's mirror tied it all together.

Chapter Thirty

Damien

When I looked back at the Void for the first time since we'd reunited, I spied the smoke originating from the docks. Someone had bombed the ships. Possibly with people still inside. Or maybe it had been a rescue? I had to believe in the second option. Everett had certainly made it clear it hadn't been him or the woman he worked with, after all.

I'd been too focused on chasing Everett and wondering about my birth parents to fully take in the moonlit destruction. Somewhere along the way, I'd felt myself being pulled, a small hand wrapping around my waist. I didn't shake it off. Not *her.*

While a huge part of me wanted nothing more than to bolt to the Broken Wing and drink myself into a stupor, she kept me grounded. Kept me from running.

The worst part of it was that she had no idea of the ghastly truth.

What I had done to her.

How I'd deceived her.

Would she stay after learning the truth? I doubted it. So I held on to her, knowing our time was running out—that my kin were somehow tied to this monstrosity too.

If what I'd heard was true, Everett had a *brother.* One that could be *me.*

And I loathed him. Had hated him from the second I laid eyes upon him, and not simply because he courted Wren, though that didn't help. No, I'd sensed a darkness lurking beneath the blue of his eyes that had put me on edge when I'd relieved him of his wristwatch, posing as a waiter. He'd glanced at me for just a moment, long enough for my skin to crawl.

My companions and I continued walking in silence. All of us deep in thought.

I dared a glance at Wren, noting her attention moving to the people living in the south, the ones without homes. They camped outside alleys or homes, children and elderly alike. That was how it worked—the wealthy kept rising while suffocating the less fortunate. It was a vicious cycle that kept on repeating, and I'd watched several succumb to the hunger, the backbreaking work, the cruelty they experienced each day.

"This needs to end," Wren whispered, quietly enough that I didn't think she intended for me to hear. It was a reflex to slide my own arm around her waist. It felt natural, like we'd done it thousands of times, and my heart didn't thunder in panic. How could it when she looked at me like that, water filling her eyes, staring at me like I was a hero? "We need to do something, Damien."

Change didn't occur overnight. She knew it too. Maybe that was why she slumped in my grip. A throbbing ache pulsed in my shoulder where I'd been stabbed, but I ignored it.

I could run as Ruby suggested, but I suspected my friend would change her mind once the dust settled. She, too, wasn't one to run, and it could've been panic that caused her to act out of character.

"First we focus on the people that were taken," I said solemnly. "We figure out where they were headed. It was Hockley's ship, so he must keep some sort of record hidden in his study."

They'd likely been brought to the palace, but there was also the chance that someone had taken them to our *second* enemy.

By the time we stepped over the boundary separating the Void and the north, all of us shuffled to a halt, beyond tired.

"Still can't believe that my father is such a monster. I mean, I knew he wasn't a good man, never had been, but . . ." Grayson scrubbed a hand over his face. "I don't think I can go back there. Back home."

I looked at him, possibly for the first time without jealousy coursing in my veins. He appeared beaten. Broken.

For a fraction of a second, a mere blink, an image of Grayson with blood pooling from his mouth crossed my thoughts. I squeezed my eyes shut, and when they opened, all traces of red vanished from his lips.

These damned hallucinations. They wouldn't leave me be.

"Stay with me, Gray," Ruby offered. "I have a couch that's uncomfortable as all hell, but we can pile it with blankets."

Grayson craned his neck, a hint of a smile on his face. "Thank you," he said sincerely, eyes creasing. "I'll take you up on that offer."

The fact that he was sickened enough to leave the comforts of his palatial home surprised me, yet warmth spread, a kind of hope, I thought. Grayson was the new generation of lords. He'd take over when his father stepped down.

Perhaps things *could* change in time.

Fuck. Now I sound like Wren. Optimistic and hopeful.

Ruby nodded to me knowingly before leading Grayson away. Wren lifted her hand in farewell, but it was half-hearted.

How could we go up against the lords? And who had bombed the docks? Friend, or foe?

Wren shuffled along with me as I led her to her town house. That trust she placed in me made the guilt weighing on my shoulders unbearable. I should tell her now. Well, not tonight, but soon. Tell her I'd taken her locket.

I would, I decided, once her head cleared and the terror of the evening wore off.

"Stay with me?" she asked outside the entrance of her home. We'd come through the back, her garden free from prying eyes.

"Stay," I echoed, throat tightening.

"I'm here, right here, Damien, and I need you." Wren's eyes pleaded with mine, the unspoken words causing my breath to catch.

What she didn't grasp was how much I needed her, too.

She became utterly still when I kissed her temple. Wordlessly, I held her, rocking slightly, soothing my frayed nerves. *Her* frayed nerves.

She clutched me tighter in reply, nuzzling my hair, my shoulders, my cheek. I felt a hint of wetness touch my skin. To think that just hours ago I'd nearly thrown such a gift away. Believed she would toss me aside once she grew bored of a southerner.

"You say that now, sunshine, but you can leave Andalay if you'd like. You'll be safe from all this."

The thought of her being caught anywhere near another bombing or in the hands of a murderer scared me half to death. And I'd only been frightened once before in my life: the day Cap found me in the snow, half alive and on death's doorstep.

She lifted her chin. "I won't abandon you. Not if you don't lie to me. Not if you *stay*." Wren's smile strained. "Fight with me."

I pictured it then—all of us reclaiming our city. Discovering the connection between the Fates and the mystery woman ordering shipments of people on her own. Flashes of possibility assaulted me, Wren the center of every one of them. Of justice doled out. People saved from a cruel death.

It hurt. Fates, it hurt to see things that might never be. Yet the look she gave me now, wide-eyed and pleading, barred any words of dissent.

"I'll stay, but you may not want me to."

When she ran her palm over my stubbled cheek, I leaned into it, embracing her delicate touch. It was something I'd craved for so damned long: to feel her touch me like this without needing a lie or an excuse.

Tonight, seeing her with Grayson made me realize how selfish and foolish I'd been. How I'd nearly lost her to my own pride and ignorance.

I liked Wren Hayes. My enemy's daughter and princess of Ward

One. I liked her to the point that I woke each morning thinking about when I'd see her again. When she'd yell at me for saying something arrogant. Her small smiles that she tried to hide that were meant just for me.

"You're not leaving my sight, Damien," she said fiercely. "Besides, as much as you vex me sometimes, you make me feel safe." She glanced away. "I really want to feel safe right now."

"I can do that," I promised without thought. If nothing more, I could protect her heart tonight.

It was tomorrow and the days to come that worried me.

Wren led me through her home, hand in mine. I studied the boards on the stairs she avoided, and we crept to her room without making a sound. She shut the door behind her and silently brought me to her bathroom to sit me on the edge of the tub. Since the pipes were old and produced too much noise, she didn't turn them on, but she did dip a washcloth into a basin of fresh water beside the sink.

I gazed up as she approached, stunned by her beauty. Her kindness. My heart swelled as she cleaned my face free of grime, when she checked my stab wound, when she took off my threadbare jacket. In the end, she got down on her knees and took off my shoes. My throat tightened as she peered up at me, and I knew then and there it didn't matter who she was. Goodness couldn't be faked or replicated, not forced. Wren might not have a gift with her now or be influential among her peers, but her empathy set her apart.

"Your turn." I got up and gently lifted her until she'd taken my place on the edge of the tub. Snagging a fresh linen, I went to work, wiping the streaks of grime from her face, making sure I didn't press too hard on her skin. With her face clean, I took in her dress. It didn't appear to have laces or buttons, and I dropped to my knees like she'd done for me, taking off her boots instead. I was surprised by how scuffed they were.

"I go hunting with him sometimes. It seems like it's the only time he's proud of me," she said hoarsely, noticing where my attention strayed. "I like them worn in."

Tonight, she'd found out her father was beyond worse than a simple devil in disguise.

Tonight, I'd found out I had a brother. A family who'd abandoned me.

Tonight, I'd decided I wouldn't run.

"Do you need help undressing?" I asked, eyeing the tiles of the bathroom like they held all the answers we sought.

"Damien," she said, forcing my chin up. She smiled at the tremble in my words, and once more her hand cupped my cheek, cradling it like I was someone precious. I felt weightless, and the sensation sent a spike of fear coursing through me.

Rising, she gave me her back before moving her long hair out of the way. "Can you undo the ties?"

I hadn't realized there were a few ties close to her neck. With hands that shook for an entirely different reason besides fear, I yanked on a bow, watching as the silk slid free. Small loops ringed in metal held the ribbon in place, allowing the user to tighten the garment. I loosened them as well until I slid the fabric away. My fingers grazed her bare shoulder and she shuddered.

"I stole some ointment for you," she admitted. "It was in my father's bathroom. It should help heal your wound faster."

My hands paused their work, not wishing to leave.

"Thank you."

She nodded and turned. "I'll apply it after I change."

I expected her to usher me out the door, but every muscle locked when she pulled the sleeves of her dress from her arms and allowed it to slide down her body.

The world faded. There was just a goddess standing before me in nothing but a see-through chemise. My heart pounded, my eyes roaming her form. Her perfect body of curves and wondrous, supple handfuls. She met my gaze before her hands drifted to my shirt, pausing on the first button.

It was a question.

I'd lose her to the truth. I shouldn't be doing this—

"Damien." Fuck, my name on her lips debilitated me. Froze me in place. I could see nothing but her. "I want to forget tonight. *Please.*"

My heart rate picked up.

"Wren . . ." I pleaded. "You'll regret it."

"I won't. No matter what," she argued. "I know my own mind. Trust that."

I trusted nothing now.

But she stole every ounce of willpower I owned when she rose up on her toes and fused her lips to mine.

Chapter Thirty-One

Wren

Damien took it all away.

His kiss was fire, igniting a spark that turned into a blaze. His hands, which had been so cautious before, roamed freely, my body melting in his hold. I arched my back, desperate and seeking, swimming in the myriad of sensations causing my head to spin.

I traced the seam of his lips with my own, reveling in how a shiver wracked his frame, and how *I* was the cause of his undoing. Taking his bottom lip between my teeth, I gently bit down, eliciting a low rumble of approval from his chest, the addicting sound one I wanted to hear again and again. His hair slid like silk between my fingers, and I grasped the strands, yanking him closer and melding our bodies until not an inch separated us.

This felt more potent than before, than when we were in Hockley's study. This wasn't a kiss hidden behind the mask of a lie—it was honest. Raw and untamed. A collision of two people giving in to what their souls demanded.

Damien took his time sliding the thin chemise off my shoulders. He placed a kiss where each strap had been, torturously moving across my collarbone as he worked the slip down, his callused palms rough on my skin, the sensation heightening every sense I possessed. When he drew back, taking me in fully, heat erupted across my cheeks, his stare storm clouds of need. Like if he didn't touch me, he'd perish.

"You're so beautiful it kills me."

The admission wrecked me.

"Wren." He spoke my name sweetly against my neck, his fingers brushing up and down the sides of my bare arms. "You're better than any gift. Any kind of magic." Those wicked fingers slid up, and he grasped my chin between his thumb and forefinger. Against my lips, he murmured, "It's the kind of magic I don't want to steal." A press of his lips to my jaw. "I only want to revel in it for a while." Another kiss to the corner of my mouth. "To feel all of you."

My hands fell to his torso, running over the bandages on his chest. I expelled a shaking breath at the hard ridges of muscle, the defined abdomen that begged for worship.

"You're beautiful too, Damien," I said, pressing my lips right over his wounded shoulder. I made my way to the other broad shoulder, exploring him, admiring the handsome thief who had made me burn for weeks. But it was more than attraction. Damien had done the impossible—

He'd made me *feel*. He liked the woman I'd locked away, and he desired her now, more than anything.

"Are you certain you're all right?" I asked, forcing myself to look up at him. He was still injured, and tonight had strained him.

Damien didn't deliver a cocky smirk or clever retort. He placed both hands on the sides of my face and brought my lips to his, stealing all the air in my lungs. Minutes passed when I couldn't tell where I ended and he began, his exhales becoming my inhales, giving me life. Eventually I leaned back, gasping.

"I hope that answers your question," he said, features serious. "With you, only you, am I never better."

"Promise?" The idea of him in pain sent an ache throbbing in my chest.

He let out a soft chuckle. "It would hurt more if I walked away. Even though I should." His jaw clenched. "But I can't. I can't turn away, Wren."

"Then don't, thief," I said against his skin.

It was frowned upon in our society to engage in what we prepared to do. I didn't give a shit. I was my own person. My own woman, and while it might not last forever, I wanted Damien more than my next breath.

Damien unbuttoned his trousers at the same time as he peppered my throat with kisses, never once leaving my skin. He was a man bewitched, and I had never felt more powerful being the one who'd entranced him.

I broke our connection, needing to see him. When he stood before me, vulnerable and raw, my knees nearly buckled.

Fates, he was stunning.

He intertwined our fingers before walking backward, carefully leading me into the darkened bedroom. This side of him was tender and soft, yet wild and utterly *him*, and I wished to bask in it forever.

When my back hit the mattress, Damien paused for a moment above me, his forearms braced on the bed on either side of my face. He stared down with hesitation, his eyes narrowing as his mind seemed to race a thousand miles an hour.

"I want you," I said, hoping to assuage any doubts. "Even when you infuriated me, I wanted you." I smiled up at him, watching as his face lost some of its tension. His relieved exhale ghosted against my parted lips.

"You made it very hard not to fall for you, sunshine," he whispered.

Damien shifted on his elbows and a small wince slid over his face.

"Don't worry about me," he said into my ear.

"I can't help it." Somewhere along the way, the thief made it impossible for me not to worry about his welfare. Regardless of how much his smart mouth stoked my temper at times.

"Is it wrong that I like it? That I like you worrying about me?" His head dropped, his jaw taut with tension.

I shook my head, forcing his strong chin up. "Is it wrong that *I* want you to want that?" I asked, chuckling slightly. "You kept pulling away, and when I told myself it was what I needed, no, *wanted*, it stung, because I've never been fully myself around someone the way I am with you."

Damien stroked my cheek as he situated himself. "*You,* Wren Hayes, are the only magic I will bow down to. The only gift I covet," he said. "I'm lucky you see me, too."

I did see him. Every crooked and mismatched part. It made a masterpiece of shades of gray.

"Wren," he murmured reverently just before he slowly pushed forward. My eyes rolled to the back of my head at the onslaught of new sensations. "I've got you," he promised, his tone a soothing melody. "Just hold on to me, sunshine."

I gripped his shoulders, trusting him with every fiber of my being. Something I'd thought impossible when first meeting him. Now . . . now I knew he'd risk his own life for mine. He had when he covered my body during the explosions. He'd done it without thought or hesitation.

Damien moved, setting my world alight. His lips never left mine, his callused hands roaming my body freely, touching places that sent stars shooting across my vision.

"You're perfect," he said. "So perfect."

My fingers wove into his hair, holding him close as he shifted, each movement bringing a wave of pure ecstasy. I couldn't formulate words, could hardly get out anything other than a moan. At the sound of it, Damien's movements quickened, one hand gripping my hip, the other cradling the back of my neck.

I never wanted this moment to end, the closeness of him undoing me.

When the world shattered and remade itself, as I fell to pieces,

Damien held me tight. He shuddered atop me, falling himself seconds later.

For a while we lay there, frozen in time, him surrounding me like a shield. I inhaled his familiar scent as he nuzzled my hair. Eventually, he carefully rolled to the side before curling around me. His hand extended to my cheek, brushing aside the dampened hair on my forehead.

"Wren?" His voice held hints of hoarse worry, but I smiled, turning to him.

"I'm all right, Damien," I promised, concerned that he felt guilty. "I chose this."

It felt that way right then. Like I'd shed my old skin and chose a path of my own making.

Several minutes passed, and his eyes lowered. "Promise you won't shut me out, Wren."

I frowned. "Shouldn't I be the one asking that of *you*?"

But he shook his head. "Just, whatever happens, don't shut me out."

The rawness in his tone broke me. My throat was tight as I made my vow. "I won't shut you out. No matter what."

When he lifted his eyes, they weren't as bright as before. I had a feeling he didn't believe me, and that wouldn't do.

Grabbing his cheeks, I kissed him, cementing my vow. My lips explored his cheeks, his nose, his brow. "Sleep, Damien. And you better not escape in the middle of the night or I'll hunt you down."

"Promise?" He smirked. And my chest fluttered in relief at the sight.

I rolled my eyes and fell into his embrace, my leg falling across his body. "See," I said with a grin, "I got you trapped."

He laughed, and the sound went straight to my core. "You certainly do," he said, sleep coating his words. "I think I rather enjoy being trapped by you. Funny. It feels a lot like freedom."

Chapter Thirty-Two

Wren

Stealing another's gift is punishable by death.
—Aurilian decree

He stayed.

I woke tangled in his hold the following morning, my head resting on his arm, my leg flung over his body. The shy new day slipped through the window, its rays highlighting the form beside mine in shimmering gold.

Damien was so handsome when he slept. His brow smooth, free of worry, his lips slack. Peaceful.

My eyes ran across the expanse of his bare skin, too afraid to run my hands down his muscled chest and wake him. But look I did, and what a glorious sight it was. The muscles of his abdomen were pronounced and hard, and a few scars dotted the flesh, silvery in the light. The sheet spread across his lower half hung low, the defined muscles forming a delectable V that I yearned to trace.

I'd spent the night with a thief. With a man who exasperated me as much as he enthralled me. And I didn't regret a single second of it. There was no remorse as I brushed my eyes over his beauty, memories of last night playing in my mind like my favorite song. He'd been different than what I expected, and a small smile lifted my lips at how he'd worshipped me as I fell to pieces around him.

"Are you going to continue to stare? I do like the attention."

I flinched at the sound of his raspy morning voice, deep and inviting. A lazy smile played on his lips, his usually dark gray eyes bright and welcoming, sparking with silver.

"I wasn't admiring you, you cocky bastard," I said far too quickly, though we both knew it was a lie. "I was analyzing your wound."

"Ah, so you were being considerate," he rumbled, the arm around my body hauling me closer, pressing me tightly to his chest. His fingers dipped below my chin before forcing me to meet his stare. "Will you allow *me* to be just as considerate?" he all but purred, his hand smoothing down my side, grazing over my curves. I shuddered in reply.

I couldn't speak. I'd lost the ability to. He gazed upon me with renewed hunger, fiercer than the night before. In a sudden movement, he slipped from me and shifted toward the end of the bed. I gasped when he ripped off the sheet to expose my naked body.

"Damien!" I whisper-hissed. "I'm cold."

He grinned wickedly. "You won't be for long."

Fates. I'd thought last night was life-altering.

"I need . . ."

"You need what?" he asked, climbing back over me, his hair dipping into his eyes. "Tell me exactly what you want." His fingers leisurely ran up and down my body, lowering until they met my thighs. I think I said his name, but my eyes fell shut when his warm breath tickled my ribs, his mouth lowering slowly down, down, down.

"Damien," I murmured, and he pressed his mouth to my skin, tickling the inside of my thigh. He was dangerously close to setting me alight, and his ensuing chuckle proved he knew what he was doing to me. I hissed when his teeth grazed my delicate skin deliciously, and my fingers raked through his hair. "I need you—"

The door banged open, wood striking the wall. A small scream sounded.

Damien cursed, grabbing the flimsy sheet hanging halfway off the bed and covering us. We turned to the door to find my sister standing at the threshold, her cheeks as red as roses, both of her hands smothering her cries.

"Callie! Please close the door!" I all but yelled, praying she would oblige. Praying no one else would come stumbling down the hall and bear witness to my state. I cursed myself for not locking the damned door, but in all fairness, we'd been in a state of shock, and then . . .

"What on earth are you doing?" Callie asked as she locked us in. "Not that I . . . not that this is wrong, but . . ." She couldn't seem to find the words, her stare flicking between me and Damien, who continued to shield my body with his, even with the sheet. "I just didn't expect this . . ." she finally said, her eyes wide.

I wasn't thrilled that she'd walked right in on me naked beneath Damien, but at least it was her and not Father.

"I didn't expect it either," I admitted, wanting to hide while gripping the sheet for dear life. "But you can't tell anyone, Callie, please. Especially not Father."

Callie's shoulders drooped, her stunned expression softening. "I would never," she said, tone harsh with offense. "Your life is your own. But lock the door next time, Fates, Wren!"

I sighed with relief, though my body was strung tighter than any bow. My sister still stood in front of me and Damien, both of us bare beneath the sheet, tangled in each other.

"All right," I groused, silently communicating with her to leave, my eyes aiming for the door. "I'll lock it after."

Callie sucked in a deep breath. "Oh, yes. Sorry." She smoothed her dress, her movements nervous. "I get the hint, but I came to tell you something important," she said, glancing at the floor and avoiding Damien entirely. He seemed content to pretend she wasn't there either. "Those ledgers I worked on the other night? There are missing containers from almost every ship belonging to a lord. Some go to the palace, and others end up at an address Father blacked out. You asked if there was anything off, and there it is." She waved her hands around. "All right, I'm leaving now—Fates." Callie made it to the door before looking at me. *"Lock it."*

She slipped out into the hall. As Damien rubbed at his face, I sprang out of bed and twisted the lock.

"That was unpleasant," Damien groaned, an arm over his head in shame. "If she'd walked in a few seconds later . . ."

"Yes, I know," I replied, cringing. Heat erupted across the tips of my ears. I sat on the edge of the bed, my heart beating an anxious rhythm.

Aside from the embarrassment of my *sister* walking in on me and Damien—which I might never get over—she added some support to the theory that the shipments were being split and shipped to two different addresses. Meaning we'd been correct to fear the possibility that there were two different enemies at our backs.

"Wren?"

I peered over my shoulder, Damien's face scrunched in uncertainty.

"What is it?" I asked, thinking he was worrying over Callie's words as I was.

His hand reached out for me, only to run gently down my spine. "Do you regret—"

"No," I said. "I don't." He was idiotic even to ask if I regretted our night together. It had been my choice, and one I felt no remorse over. But looking at Damien now, I knew he craved confirmation.

We'd both needed to heal yesterday. After everything we'd seen and been through. But it wasn't why we'd collided. Why we were currently in each other's arms.

Lying back down, I snuggled into his chest, pressing my face into the crook of his neck. "I don't regret a single thing. You weren't absolutely *horrible,* I suppose."

I peeked up with a soft smile and he flicked my nose. "Maddening little thing."

"In fact, I rather hope we can repeat it." I internally cursed at myself as seconds ticked by and silence reigned.

Maybe I shouldn't have said—

His arms wound around me tight. "I don't regret it either," he whispered. "I regret so many other things, but not that. And I certainly would love to repeat it. Next time without any interruptions."

I frowned, thinking about his *other* regrets, but before I could pester him, footsteps echoed from the hall.

"That would be my parents," I said, heart racing. I cursed—a habit I'd quickly been forming thanks to Damien—and dove out of bed. Snatching my dressing gown and flinging it on, I ran a hand through my hair while looking into the mirror attached to my vanity. Just as I thought. The evidence of last night showed everywhere; from my wild hair, to the darkened love bite on my neck, to the glassy look in my eyes.

Rustling came from behind me. Damien yanked on his pants and made quick work of buttoning his shirt. I winced, hating the rush of it, but knowing he couldn't stay. If my parents found him he'd be arrested on the spot.

Damien finished dressing and strolled over to me, an unnamable emotion swirling in his stony eyes. His face, which had been bright and smooth seconds before, was now fraught with strain, and while he promised he didn't regret anything, my eyes weren't deceiving me.

He was hiding something.

"Damien—"

He placed a finger at my lips, his focus on the door. Slowly, he leaned down, his warmth skimming the shell of my ear. "I'll see you tonight, sunshine," he vowed, right before he gave my lobe a nibble that had my toes curling.

When he drew back, that same odd look marred his face, but

he crept backward toward the window. With ease, he lifted the glass and edged onto the sill. I made a face when he lunged for the tree, his injury not hindering his grace.

I held his stare until he broke it and vanished down the trunk.

No matter my joy, I couldn't help but feel like the other shoe was about to drop. That something dire lay on the horizon. That was how life worked, after all.

Or maybe the other shoe had dropped already, and I'd been too busy with Damien to take note.

Either way, I couldn't shake the feeling the rest of the morning.

The more I had time to ruminate over the peculiar feeling, the more restless I became. The house was empty, and like always, I felt akin to some ghost haunting it, pacing back and forth in my room. I had no occupation, no husband, and no *purpose.* It had never been as apparent as it was now.

But that was *before.* Before I learned the truth of the missing people. Of the lords who presided over our city, acting like kings. My father—Fates, my father was the worst among them.

I had a purpose now, and while it could end with my death, I wouldn't stop until we uncovered the truth and helped set things right.

I clenched my hands into fists, pressing the sharp tips of my nails to bite into my palms. The pain distracted me from the blow of my reality, but with Damien gone and the house silent, it wasn't enough. I had to move. To do something.

Walking into Callie's room, I went to her vanity, searching for something to cover up the purplish-pink bruise Damien had left on my neck. I shook my head as I ran my fingers over it, the flashes of memory assaulting me and causing my cheeks to heat. *Again.*

Focus, Wren.

I finally found her powders in her vanity's top drawer and went to work. In the end, it covered most of the mark, but I'd have to wear my hair over that side of my head for the remainder of the day. With a sigh, I shoved her drawer closed, only to hear a clicking noise.

Pulling on the handle of the second drawer, I gazed upon the contents, finding nothing but more makeup and hair clips. It must have been one of them—

I froze.

Underneath a compact mirror, half hidden by accessories, were torn-up pieces of black and gold. Carefully, I extracted the ripped fragments, placing them on the desk. Moving the jagged papers around, I made whole what had once been a small business card.

The Black Dahlia was written in golden script, listing an address and nothing more.

That had been where Damien said he went when he chased after the hooded man—*Everett*—from the docks. Where he heard him talk to a woman who demanded he remove his thief of a *brother* from the equation.

Damien and I hadn't delved into that topic last night. I honestly had been too exhausted to understand or try to broach the subject, and pushing him was the last thing I wanted to do.

But why did Callie have this card at all? Why had she ripped it to shreds?

Another memory flashed.

I'd seen this card before—

Mother's hooded cloak. This card had been buried deep in its pockets.

Standing, I abandoned Callie's room for mine, my thoughts drowned out by a droning in my ears. I felt tingles race up my legs with each step, my thoughts screaming *Danger.*

I didn't think before I donned a simple light pink dress I was able to slip on by myself and placed two long black pins in my hair. Tugging on my boots, I left my home, my feet moving stiffly as I navigated the streets.

I hardly paid attention to the passersby as they debated Dusk's return and "that horrid incident in the south last night." Could hardly see but a few steps in front of me. It was as if I floated down the street, numb and thoughtless, frost cooling my blood.

The Black Dahlia—

A place neither Callie nor Mother would *ever* be caught dead frequenting.

When I made it to the Broken Wing Tavern, Ruby was already at the bar. Well before noon, she didn't hesitate to gulp down a hearty glass of ale. She wasn't alone. Beside her sat Grayson, his shirt as rumpled as his hair. They clinked glasses and whispered to each other before indulging in another drink, acting like old friends.

"Ruby." My voice wasn't my own. It was hard and cutting.

She craned her neck, clumsily twisting my way, along with a very drunk Grayson. They both slouched against the bar for support.

"Wren!" she shouted, only for Grayson to leap to his feet and scoop me into a too-tight hug.

"She lives!" he exclaimed before pinching my cheeks. He tried to take his seat, but he fumbled, nearly missing it entirely if not for Ruby's guidance.

"Wh-what are you doing?" I asked, too tense to take a seat. Hell, I wasn't sure my limbs could contort into a sitting position, with how rigid my muscles were.

"We're forgetting last night," Ruby chirped. "Well, forgetting until we have to remember again." She pouted at Grayson, who took a generous drink. I probably wore a horrified expression, because Ruby added, "It's just one day of rest, Wren. Not like you didn't *forget* in other ways last night." She hiccupped. "I know Damien walked you home." She winked, and for once, I didn't blush at her insinuation.

I didn't have time for this. I'd come here for their help, and now I realized I wouldn't get it—not that I judged them. For Fates' sake, Grayson's life had turned upside down in one night. I understood his turmoil. And Ruby lived in the south, where she could be taken at any moment and killed.

"Do you know where Damien is?" I asked as I peered at the stairs leading to his room.

Ruby shook her head. "He's not there. I already picked the lock and tried to find him."

I hoped he didn't know she'd picked his lock. He would be furious—he was private about his space.

"Do you have any idea where he might've gone?" The ripped pieces of the card I'd taken with me from Callie's dresser were crumpled in my hand, wrapped tight in my clammy palm. Backup would be nice, but it wasn't necessary, and I was too impatient to wait.

Something felt off in the air, and after discovering this card . . .

"He's probably trying to fix his mistake." Ruby rolled her eyes. "He's been mopey ever since he took it."

Grayson swayed and I reached out to keep him from plummeting onto his face. "What mistake?" I asked, panic slithering into my chest like a coiled snake set to strike. "What did he take?"

He was a thief, I knew this. It could be anything.

Ruby put her hand to her lips, eyes widening. "Shite, I wasn't supposed to say anything." She giggled, grabbing Grayson's arm. "He's my new friend. Best wingman ever. Even Annie forgave me when Grayson explained our night!"

I ignored that part and grabbed Ruby's hand. She frowned down at it.

"What mistake did Damien make, Ruby? Tell me."

"So bossy, Wren. I told you. I c-can't." She hiccupped once more, hiding it with her sleeve. "Damien would kill me if I told you. But he's gonna make it right! Don't worry, you'll have your locket back before you know it and then you won't be giftless!"

"Locket?" The room blurred around me, people morphing into distorted shapes of color. That droning returned, growing louder and louder until the beginnings of a headache prickled my brow.

"Ahh, you made me say it." Ruby grimaced, hiding her face in her hands. "He's gonna be so angry with me. Please don't tell him!

We're friends, after all, right?" She beamed at me like she hadn't just upended my world. "I think he cares for you, like really, *really* cares. Which isn't like him. He's never looked at anyone like he does you. It's actually sickening," she said with a laugh.

I whirled around, not interested in how much Damien liked me. How much he cared.

A locket. That was my gift. And Damien had *stolen* it.

Rage burned in my belly, hot and vicious. All this time. All this time he'd lied. He might've lost it, but he stole it in the first place. He took my fucking gift. And now he what? Wanted to get it back to make up for his crimes? No. That wasn't right either. He'd loathed me—or acted like he had—when he claimed something had been taken from him at the Lovetts' party.

And his mirror . . . he talked about his mirror not working lately.

I cursed aloud, the room spinning, drunken revelers dancing like marionettes around me. He'd said it was losing its power. Maybe he thought it was punishment for taking my gift. Maybe that was the entire reason he'd *helped* me.

All of it.

A lie.

"Wren!" Grayson called out when I stormed from the tavern. Ruby shouted my name as well, but screw that. Screw the lies, the betrayal, the secrets.

Screw them all.

Ruby had known too.

Uncrumpling the pieces of the black card in my hand, I read the address.

I marched down the streets of the Void without fear in my heart, my eyes narrowed and my pace determined. I wouldn't stop for the world. Driven by rage, carried on the wings of betrayal, I delved into the boiling sensation of my hurt and allowed it to empower me. And empower me it did.

I was going to the Black Dahlia with or without *him*.

The man who had a chance of breaking my heart.

I vowed he never would get the chance again.

Chapter Thirty-Three

Damien

The trust in her eyes had been too much to bear.

I'd forgotten myself for a moment, caught up in the sunlight possibilities of everything, of *her,* of how she'd felt so perfect curved to the outline of my body, like a puzzle piece that had finally found its partner. For the first time in my life, my heart had shed the bricks I'd built around it, and I happily allowed the destruction to happen.

Then her sister knocked, and reality had struck. *Hard.*

Wren wouldn't forgive me. Ever. Eventually, she'd uncover my treachery and cast me aside as the man who betrayed her in the worst possible way. She'd go on either to roam the world like she wanted, or to marry some lord. One day, I'd be nothing but a bastard she rarely thought about.

I trudged up the hill, the midday sun bearing down on my exposed neck. Droplets of sweat trickled down my back, my black shirt soon clinging to my skin. If I'd realized how far away Everett Sinclair's estate was, I'd have scrounged up a copper and hired a carriage.

All of this heat and the ache in my legs would be worth it—I needed to know what that woman had meant when she said "brother." And the stony eyes. She'd described *me*.

The stony-eyed thief. I scoffed. That was what I amounted to.

My birth parents had been a mystery my whole life, but with Everett in the picture, I was the son of either Emily or Arthur Sinclair. It was likely the latter, as men such as Arthur weren't known for their faithfulness. It had to be the reason I'd been given up. Still, with Sinclair blood in my veins, I'd been handed a gift when others in the Void hadn't.

The possibility of a brother like Everett—a child they kept safe and coddled—boiled my blood. If I focused on my anger well enough, I could almost forget the pang of hurt and blistering envy that threatened to blind me to reason. It sat there, beneath the fury, an ache in my stomach refusing to go away.

So I went home after I left Wren's, dressed, and walked to his estate. I didn't have a plan after that, which wasn't like me, but none of this made any sense. If I had a brother, even a half brother . . . That changed *everything*.

Finally, *finally*, after hours had passed, I crested the neatly trimmed hill of the grand estate. I expected nothing less from Everett and his family—the fine mansion basically a palace of blooming flowers and ivy, the scent of luxury potent upon the breeze. It made my insides tighten. Made that gnawing ache inside me swell.

Standing before the enormous entrance, I stared daggers at the lion knocker, my fingers inches from grazing the gold paint.

You need to know.

If I didn't, I'd always wonder. Always question. The secret of my parents had haunted me like a specter for my entire life. Hell, I didn't have a last name. It was simply Damien. Or the Ghost.

Those were the only names I went by, and they felt so fucking hollow.

I grasped the knocker with clammy hands and pulled it back before letting it drop against the wood with a thunderous *bang*. A sudden gust of wind inched the door open, and I stepped back as the wood creaked, allowing me entry into the house.

No one would be so careless as to leave it open. Not with servants manning the place.

Unease raised the hairs on my arms as I nudged the unlocked door with the toe of my boot. Not a sound could be heard.

Wrong. I didn't need a damned instinct to tell me I should run away.

Too bad I was a masochist.

Slipping inside, I stood within a grand foyer of ostentatious wealth. I'd seen it all before, the lords decorating their homes to reflect their status, and I hardly paid attention to the cream-and-gold décor.

No. My attention drifted to the ground—

Red smudged the shiny white marble flooring.

I grew cold all over, like glacial ice water had been poured over my head. The abrupt boost of adrenaline flourished in my system, my body heating as it readied for a fight. The blood led deeper into the house, splotches of it staining the white stone, marring the otherwise pristine dwelling. Heart thudding in my ears, I stepped around the red, slowly following its trail.

Death. I scented death in the air—and not merely due to the blood. An odd weight settled over my chest, a rotten stench overpowering the floral scent wafting from the vases of gardenias scattered around the house.

My vision twisted, a gray sheen sliding over the color of life. I blinked, but the gray didn't dissipate. The red on the floor, however, shone as brightly as before.

Shutting my eyes, I tried reasoning with myself. Saying that the next time I opened my eyes, the world would be right again. That my recent hallucinations were due to seeing photos of the murdered victims. That the flashes of death surrounding me were nothing more than me projecting my fear.

I opened my eyes.

Gray.

The world was gray and red.

I stumbled back into a china cabinet, the porcelain plates rattling within. Dizziness and nausea combined to form a sickly spell, and I struggled to remain upright.

I didn't dare call out for help—I was, after all, sneaking in. Yet no staff emerged to greet me, and not a single person scurried around an estate. It was too quiet. If I announced my presence, whoever had caused all this gore might decide I looked like their next victim.

Forcing my eyes open, forcing myself to take in the new shade that covered my sight, I breathed deeply, focusing on each inhale, each exhale, centering myself.

Something crashed nearby. Glass breaking.

The jarring noise kept my vision from tilting, which helped. Cautiously, I placed one foot in front of the other, finding my footing again and cursing all the while.

There could be no more denying that something dire was happening to me. Something . . . magical. And not in a good way.

Talk to Everett and get out of here.

I'd find Ruby and we'd go to a healer. Yes, we'd uncover whatever sickness currently seeped into my body.

My boot suddenly slid out from under me, smearing the blood as I stumbled through a hallway, my senses painfully heightened. I swore I could hear every scurrying mouse and ragged exhale. Each tick of the grandfather clock. Everything was too loud, too bright.

I pulled out my dagger, holding it before me while my nerves prickled. The steel made me feel slightly more at ease. *Slightly* being the key word. I was far from fine.

The red trail came to an end on the second floor, in front of a pair of elaborately polished silver doors. One was slanted, somewhat ajar. I barely had enough space to sidle up, my back pressed against the wall behind me, and peek inside.

Get in, get out.

"Son," a garbled voice pleaded, low enough for me to know that whoever spoke rested on death's doorstep. *"Please."*

There was no answer.

"Stop this." A choked noise came, followed by a sputter. "I-I'll give you *a-anything.* I never meant for it to happen to you! I swear! She's manipulating you! A snake, that one, always had been!"

"*You* are the one who deceived me, Father. She's the one trying to make things right. How could you allow your failings to ruin my chance at success? Selfish. All my life you've been a stain on our family name, and how you treated Mother?" A scoff. "I should kill you just for that."

Everett. His voice was unmistakable.

"Is that why you killed them?"

Sweat dripped into my eyes and I wiped a shaking hand across them. Killed who?

"They *watched,*" Everett snarled, more beast than man. "I should've thought about it earlier, how they did nothing, just sat there and allowed her to be beaten and bruised by your hand. I just needed my eyes opened."

"No, you're being manipulated—"

I ground my teeth as the distinctive sound of steel piercing flesh punctured the silence. No more gurgles came. No more pleas.

I smelled it—death—the same as earlier, though it was more potent now. Like I'd inhaled chimney smoke and couldn't expel it from my lungs. My skin prickled, my adrenaline continuing to pump. It was odd, this foreign sensation, this burden that weighed on me, and the way my body responded. The feelings overpowering me weren't born of fear . . . but something I couldn't name.

The gray shrouding my eyes flickered, flashing black before settling once again. I was too far gone to think about my vision anymore, too frenzied to think clearly.

Without opening my mirror, I kicked the door and strode into the bloodstained study.

It was everywhere, the blood. On the lord's desk. His books, his carpet, the furniture. It appeared as though the attacker had severed an artery and tossed him about the room like a rag doll.

"Fuck." I lifted my eyes from the prone body on the floor, his features hidden and his back to me. Arthur Sinclair. My possible father.

Standing before his dead body, holding a glinting knife smothered in blood, was his son, Everett.

"What did you do?" I asked, breathless. So much anger had gone into this rampage of his. So much rage. The room was a testament to it. To Everett's need to cause his father as much pain as possible.

Everett's head slowly swiveled to me, a detached look on his slack face. His blue eyes swirled, the bright color mixing with flashes of white. As if he were in some sort of trance.

"Everett?" His severe posture frightened me, his deadened stare one that sent chills to my very bones. Instead of smoke and rot, I smelled a hint of gardenia again, and mixed together, the two scents nearly had me retching.

I stuttered out his name again, not daring to draw nearer. I repeated it four times before his shoulders slumped. Before his body loosened and his stained blade clattered to the floor, echoing throughout the house. His head shot up, his shocking eyes pinning me in place. The dazed look about them had vanished, and they shone with sharp, fresh terror.

"Wh-what did you do?" he asked, voice trembling. He blinked rapidly, his muscular form shaking. He stumbled back a few steps, almost knocking over a bust of the newly deceased lord.

"Everett," I began, cautiously starting toward him like he were a wounded animal. He lifted his hands before him—they were coated in blood. Some of it dripped onto the parquet floors.

"Stay back!" he screamed, his eyes shifting between me and his dead father. "You'll p-pay for this! You'll d-die for it!"

I froze midstep.

"What are you talking about?" I murmured, shock numbing my limbs, the scene before me one of horror. "I just watched you kill him!"

Everett wasn't listening. He stormed toward me with such tangible ferocity that true fear slithered into my veins. Everett lunged, almost tackling me to the floor before I sidestepped him at the last moment. He rose, not ready to end this fight, but I didn't wish to stick around and figure out what nightmare raced through his head. Clearly, he wasn't in his right mind; his eyes had been clouded and glazed when he murdered his father, his irises nearly white.

"Evy!" he shouted, but no one came. "Ava!"

Silence. More ungodly silence.

"Did you kill them too?" he gasped, tripping backward in alarm. The horror painting his creased features told the truth—that he actually believed he'd played no part in this. That *I* was somehow to blame.

I need to get the hell out of here. Now.

"I just got here, Everett," I coaxed, attempting to calm him down, even when I was rioting on the inside, my stomach tied in painful knots. "I didn't hurt anyone."

My heart plummeted as resolve hardened his gaze. He dove for me and I instinctively reacted, punching him right in his regal nose. Red splattered, adding to the macabre scene, and Everett let out a hiss of pain. He clutched his nose as blood flowed out in a torrent. I didn't wait one more second before bolting through the house of death and gray.

As I turned the corner, I glimpsed the body of a maid, red pooled around her stark white hair like a halo.

Fuck. He'd killed her.

And now he blamed *me*.

"You'll be caught before sundown!" Everett shrieked, his voice hoarse from the blow. "You're a dead man, Damien!"

Chapter Thirty-Four

Wren

The powerful fight and bicker over trinkets. Some even kill—but the records of those crimes have long been sealed by authorities.

No one wants to know the truth of humanity's ruthlessness.

—Pages found in the banned book *Questioning Fate* by Alexandra Collette, Andalay historian, location unknown

I barely recalled the walk to the Black Dahlia. People shoved into me and I faltered but never fell. Some catcalled. Others yelled lewd words. It was obvious that I was an outsider. That I didn't belong.

I didn't belong *anywhere.*

I approached the entrance with silver in my pockets and glowered at the two burly men guarding the two-story black building. Only an embossed crimson dahlia so dark it shone black in the sun hung above the men.

When they made to stop me, I sighed. Every bone in my body

ached. Each step a chore. I didn't care. Not about the fear these men were attempting to radiate. To frighten me. Nothing could frighten me anymore.

Without answering, I shoved a silver coin into each of their meaty hands and nodded once more to the double doors. Without flinching, I waited as they sized me up and inspected the silver I'd given them.

"She must really want trouble." One of the men laughed as he opened the door for me with an exaggerated flourish.

I did want trouble. But first, answers.

The club was all but empty at this time, and the stage was lit by gas lamps, the dais surrounded by black carpet. It rose from the ground floor, glittering with fake gems and plated gold trimming, empty leather chairs set before it, just awaiting a warm body. A few hardy patrons sat off to the side at a winding bar of obsidian, silently drinking from their crystal glasses. The real show wouldn't begin until the sun set, and only the desperate sought out their vices now.

I scanned the room, my eyes reaching the upper floor, enclosed by a golden railing. No stairs could be seen, but that wouldn't be a problem. I aimed away from the bar and farther into the club. Another large man eyed me from head to toe, but he said nothing as I passed, seeking a darkened corner to gather myself. As the shadows enfolded me, my eyes adjusted, and I made out a narrow corridor.

I wasn't Wren Hayes anymore. Not the optimistic, stupidly naïve girl who thought she could mend things. I wasn't anything but a tangible fury that had sunk into my core and spread into my limbs like poison. My mind lacked the capacity to conjure theories about why Mother or Callie had this card. I couldn't even focus on Damien, who I'd spent the night with, who betrayed me from day one. I didn't think about my father or his crimes. I just . . . walked. I walked until the hallway enclosed me, and I took in the many closed doors on either side. At the end, a larger door tempted. I'd nearly made it to the door when stairs beckoned to my left.

I took them up to the second story, the darkness, my friend. A welcome oblivion I desired to sink into. At the landing, I surveyed the slip of a hallway overlooking the first floor. More doors lined it, some shut, some open.

The opened ones revealed matching rooms—a large mattress, onyx sheets, and several candles. I easily guessed what they were used for. I passed them, aiming now for the closed doors. Inside, a faint flutter caused my heart to skip several beats, and a scent wafted to my nose.

Floral and soft. Feminine, yet with a hint of musk.

I chased that smell, more sweat soaking my spine the closer I grew to the source.

The last door, unlike the others, had a knob in the shape of a single flower. The scent I recognized clogged my nostrils, almost making me gag.

My hand trembled as I grasped the flower and turned.

Locked.

It wasn't shocking, but I'd come prepared, and I'd watched Damien closely enough when he broke into Lord Saridon's home.

Kneeling, I plucked the two pins hidden in my tangled hair and went to work. Without Damien's years of experience, feeling around for the mechanism took longer than it should have, and I was surprised no one came upon me.

Nearly thirty minutes of agonizing desperation passed before a telltale *click* greeted my ears. My breath froze in my lungs as I stood. If *I* had been able to pick the lock, it must not be a good one.

Now or never.

I couldn't hold the truth at arm's length any longer. Couldn't hide from it.

I turned the knob and sighed in relief as it twisted. A low groaning sounded as it creaked open, revealing a room painted in soft pinks and black. A blush velvet lounge took up space beside a grand arched window, a desk with pink-accented knobs beside it. The massive four-poster bed dipped in black paint to match the walls stretched out as if in welcome, the covers shining beneath a single lamp bracketed to the left wall. A dresser sat below the lamp, only a brush and bottle of perfume taking up space.

Shutting the door behind me, I absently swept my hand across the dresser, noting the hairs stuck to the bristles. Lifting the perfume to my nose, I sniffed, immediately regretting the action as more of that sickly scent assaulted me, my headache growing worse.

The drawers were filled with fine clothing. Neatly folded trousers, some silky and lacy undergarments, and a drawer devoted to black nightclothes with hints of pink undertones. I abandoned the dresser and located a spacious closet. Inside were a dozen or more dresses, all simple, mainly black with a few pink selections. They were stunning and alluring, and I ran my hand across them, the quality unlike anything I'd ever touched. Below, shoes had been lined up in rows; a few with fashionable heels, mostly tall lace-up boots. My attention snagged on a pair of pink ones. My mother owned a pair like this, I recalled. She'd worn them to tea once. I flipped to a dress hanging to the left, a small red stain marking the pink bodice; the exact one Mother wore to tea with Lady Lovett. So unlike her—the design cheerful, not like her usual attire of deep autumn colors. She'd claimed they suited her hair best.

Shutting the closet door, I wandered to the desk next. Taking a seat in the chair before it, I perused the first drawer. Inside, I discovered not makeup or vanity products, but pens and parchment and ink. The second drawer was larger, filled with black folders. I removed one and gingerly spread it out. Inside, a picture of Lord Lovett stared back at me. He wasn't smiling as he usually did. This was a simple black-and-white photograph attached to the folder with a cheap clip. Beneath his grimacing face, several addresses were listed beside women's names. I scanned the page, noting the ink marks scribbled next to each one. They were dates and times.

I turned to the next page. This one showed another stark photograph of Lord Lovett and a woman who certainly wasn't his wife. He had his arms wrapped around her, the younger woman succumbing to his kiss. My stomach twisted as I eyed page after page of him with different women, all in compromising positions far worse than the first.

Blackmail. Just like Damien and I had uncovered from the rug at Lord Saridon's.

I shut the folder and slid it back in place, my focus on the third and final drawer.

This one had a golden lock in the shape of a broken heart.

Grabbing my pins, I worked at the lock, more sweat trickling down my spine as my nerves frayed, as I fell apart at the truth that would truly and wholly break me.

The *click* came, and I yanked it open.

Necklaces, rings, ribbons, knives, scissors, pins, glasses, and . . .

A locket.

My body hummed in tune with the magic seeping from the drawer, the power of so many gifts together in one place causing bile to rise in my throat. My hands could barely grasp the locket, they shook so hard, but when they did—

I arched back, a spark of light igniting behind my eyes. The draw of the object consumed me, called to me, demanded I place it around my neck. It sang a song only I knew, a melancholy tune that fit with my shattered heart.

After the light faded and I clutched at my stomach, I garnered the strength to pry open the clasp.

I wished I hadn't. Wished I'd been too frightened to break in here. Wished I had left the damned locket shut.

Damien's face stared back at me, his cold eyes ones I'd lost myself in so many times. His hair was styled in the same nonchalantly messy way, the same strands I'd recently run my fingers through. It was him; his picture inside a gift *he* had stolen.

Without thinking, I put it around my neck, the call of it lessening once I fastened the clasp. I grabbed the closed locket in my fist, tears welling in my eyes. Betrayal speared me better than any knife, and Damien's face, his loving words from just last night, looked and sounded more mocking than tender.

I snapped the locket shut and wrapped the pendant in a tight grip, uncaring if I was being rough. All I could think about was—

Everything blinked away. The room, the club, the truth. Blackness engulfed all until a murky figure took shape, wisps of gold dancing at its feet.

No, there were *three* figures, three women, the gold flourishing until it chased away the black. They lounged beside a stream, their gleaming bodies shimmering like the sun. People wearing clothing I didn't recognize drifted over to them, offering them plates of food and drink. They smiled, their grins more haunting than reassuring.

Another flash and the scene melded into another.

A woman with dark hair and olive skin—one of the three I'd seen—carried a bundle in her arms. A cloak hid most of her features as she raced through the streets of the Void. A scream pierced the vision, a baby's cry. The woman glanced down, softly shushing the small child and rubbing its brow. Her steps didn't waver as she sprinted to a stone building with several cracks running up the sides. A worn placard was affixed to the building: ANDALAY HOME FOR BOYS AND GIRLS.

"I'm sorry, little one," she murmured, blue eyes wet with tears that didn't fall. "I can't let them find you. They'll make me kill you." She ran a finger across the babe's cheek. From a new angle, I saw its features with more clarity, gasping as dark, glacial gray eyes stared up at the woman with trust. "One day you'll know when to find me. Just follow the light."

She bent down and set the child on the top step. Rapping loudly on the door, she waited a few heartbeats before scurrying away to a nearby alley, watching as a stern-faced woman appeared and frowned at the wrapped bundle. With a curse, the stranger picked up the now screaming child and slammed the door.

Pain shot across my chest, my skin burning. I felt warmth and wetness slide down my cheeks, but the visions still came, not allowing me to return to my body.

A palace. The ivory palace of the Fates. I moved, seeming to float downward, beneath the building itself. I wanted to scream, wanted to break free of this vision, but it held on tight with claws that left behind invisible scars.

The Fates sat before a long table crafted of stone, two of them smiling as the familiar dark-haired woman frowned. Doors opened in the windowless room, three men wheeling in three carts. Atop each one lay a body. Dead.

The woman in the middle licked her pink lips, her ethereal beauty turning cruel as she grabbed the sides of her chair, nails digging into the wood. *Dawn.* I recognized her from the portraits, and she sat beside . . . she sat beside *Day*—her silver-gray eyes narrowed and focused on the bodies delivered to her feet. The woman who looked away from the dead was Dusk. The very same woman who'd left her child on the steps of an orphanage.

I would've given anything to close my eyes then, to hide from the gruesome attack that ensued, but in this state, I only screamed as the women ripped into the bodies and felt around, the noise of deadened insides squelching.

Day popped up first, her hand filled with a dulled silver light. Opening wide, she placed the orblike object into her mouth and swallowed, a too-wide grin stretching. Her body shook as her skin grew radiant, her sunshine hair more lustrous.

Dawn pulled her silver light next, swallowing greedily, coral eyes shuttering. She, too, transformed, her already stunning features turning lethal.

"Go on," Day urged Dusk. "We won't have more until next week."

Dusk ground her teeth as she rose from her seat and plunged her hand into an older woman's corpse. Her hands wrapped around the same light—a *soul,* I realized.

When she swallowed it, a heartbroken expression crossed her face, even as she, too, became ethereal. Magical.

"We'll need more," Dawn said, slumping in her seat, unaffected by the horrific act she'd committed. "They're wearing off more quickly, and the lords have been behind on their deliveries recently. We're weakening by the second."

"I've scheduled another batch, don't worry, sister," Day cooed, and my insides boiled. "I've arranged a few shipments this time from across the continent to avoid suspicion. No one will suspect anything is amiss in Andalay. Besides, we require the upper-class fools to be happy so they continue giving us what we need." She looked nothing like the spring goddess I'd once adored. Even her outward beauty couldn't disguise her as anything less than a monster.

Faintly, I felt the weight of the locket against my palm. I'd clutched it so hard before, not knowing I would be thrown into this nightmare. As the scene changed, I attempted to pry my fingers from the cold metal, managing to free two.

Almost there.

When the third finger was released, I paused, struck by the sight of Damien. He stood outside my home before using his mirror and vanishing. A moment later, one of the Fates' onyx hounds bounded down the street. I pried a fourth finger free, more warmth covering my cheeks as I watched Damien pry my gift from the dog's mouth. He smiled. A satisfied grin I'd not seen him wear. It sickened me.

When the last finger ripped free, the locket fell, and I slumped backward, falling forward into time.

I couldn't catch my breath, could hardly see in the dim room. All I smelled was that damned floral perfume.

"See anything interesting, little bird?" a voice asked.

I didn't have it in me to turn. I'd known for hours who I'd find.

Chapter Thirty-Five

Damien

I ran to Wren's home first.

Scaling the tree outside her window, I jumped onto her sill and lifted the glass.

An unholy quiet greeted me once inside, and for a moment, I feared the same thing that had overcome Everett manifested here, too. I ran through her room and out into the hall, uncaring if her parents saw me. I had to tell her. Had to warn her. But the house was empty, her parents' room vacant. Aside from her sister's desk having being opened and rifled through, nothing was amiss or out of place.

Racing down the stairs, I almost collided with the cook, a stern scowl on her face.

"Who the hell are you?" she shrieked, snagging the nearest knife.

I didn't answer. I was too busy running through the rest of the empty house and toward the front door, my vision still shrouded with death and gray.

If Wren wasn't here, maybe she'd come to find me. Maybe—

Maybe was all I had to go on.

The Broken Wing was lively, and I found Ruby and Grayson slumped at the bar, both a drink away from falling off their stools.

"Ruby." I grasped her shoulders, staring into her glassy eyes. "Where's Wren?" Fear clutched my throat and squeezed, the unfamiliar sensation nearly making me double over. She was in trouble. I knew it. Could feel it in my bones. Fuck my sight. Fuck being arrested or accused of murder. She was all that mattered.

"Umm." Ruby glanced at Grayson, who hid behind his hands. "She m-might've come here looking for y-you." Each word was slow or slurred, and I shook her gently.

"Where is she?"

Grayson peeked out from behind his hands with a wince. "She ran out of here s-so quickly. But I . . . I don't think she w-went home." He shook his head. "She may have turned right. Yes, she d-definitely turned right instead of l-left."

I cursed. Wren was in the Void, alone, and Ruby was drunk off her arse with her newest friend.

Grayson elbowed Ruby then, his eyes narrowing. "Ruby, maybe you should t-tell him," he intoned with a hint of remorse.

She sighed, running a hand through her curls. "Look, Damien." She couldn't meet my gaze. "I m-might have l-let it s-slip you took her gift."

I yearned to reach out and strangle her, but . . . it was the truth.

It was my own damned fault this had happened, and I should've told Wren about it sooner. Fire burned in my chest, an unbearable ache yawning there. *She knows. She fucking knows.*

"You said she ran out of here?" I asked Grayson, unable to look at Ruby. I was pissed at her, even when I had no right to be.

Grayson nodded. "Yeah. She s-seemed like she w-was in a rush."

I pounded the bar with my fist, causing several patrons to look my way. Even Cap growled at the end of the counter. Screw them all. I shot out of the tavern, my boots pounding the grimy stones. Wren didn't know this place or its dangers, and if someone cornered her—

A longing to scream and yank out my hair made my hands twitch.

I'd come to care about her. Care in a way that could mean something *real.* Hell, I was already there.

I didn't stop running until an insane thought occurred.

Last night she'd seen me race off toward the Black Dahlia. I'd told her what I found. *Who* I found.

Wren wouldn't just sit around and wait. She'd want to investigate, and with that name on her mind, she'd go there alone. Especially since she learned the truth of what I'd done.

Without a second's hesitation, I headed in the direction of the club, hoping to get there before the woman from last night or Everett had the chance to corner her. If they did, I doubted she'd survive the encounter.

Chapter Thirty-Six

Wren

In our history, a mortal has never been known
to wield more than one gift at once—and even that
cost them something more precious than their lives.
—*Aurilian History of Magical Objects,* Chapter Four

"Callie."

My voice sounded broken and sad to my own ears. I swiveled in the chair, watching as my sister closed the door behind her. She wasn't wearing her customary dour clothing that she claimed helped her fit in at the office.

Callie had donned a fine dress, much like the ones I'd spotted in the closet. It was her favorite color, pink—just like mine—tiny blossoms stitched across the skirt, the corset adorned with flowers.

"I knew you were with the wrong crowd, Wren, but I didn't think you'd manage to come here," she said sadly, eyeing the black carpet at her feet.

"You . . ." I couldn't get the words out. They were trapped in my throat, which grew tighter by the second.

"You need to calm down," Callie said, lifting her head.

I silently cursed as she drew her hand to her earrings. Before I could squeak out a protest, her fingers grazed the metal, and a wave of soothing relief washed over me, stealing some of my anxiety. I didn't even have the energy to grind my teeth in frustration. She knew I didn't want her using her powers on me, that I hated being controlled.

"I see you found it," she said coolly, nodding to the locket around my neck.

She drifted closer, and as much as I wished to jump back, to shout and curse at her, I couldn't. The air weighed a thousand pounds, holding me in place.

"That's it," she whispered, close enough to smooth my hair as she loomed over me. "You don't want to hurt me, do you? You're all right. Everything is all right."

The nausea vanished. My headache gone.

Callie smiled, sighing in relief. "I've wanted to tell you for so long, but I was afraid you wouldn't understand."

Somewhere through the haze of forced calm, I recognized the wrongness of this. I gripped that shred of cognizance tight, refusing to release it. I had to remember why I'd come here. To remember the souls, and—

Callie took a seat on her bed. "The Fates aren't divine entities. Just mortals like us who uncovered the secret to eternal life." She shrugged a shoulder. "They feed off souls, and poof"—she snapped her fingers—"years are added and magic at their fingertips. Well, until recently. They've grown weaker, which helps me."

"Why?" I managed, my tongue feeling too big in my mouth. There were so many ways that single word might be construed.

"Because their time is up," Callie answered. "New Fates need to rise, it's just the natural balance of things. And why shouldn't I be able to take one of their spots? Of course, I'd replace the other two seats with those I trust." She gave me a knowing look. "I've worked too hard not to reap the benefits of this backward society, and the old crones refuse to let go when the world is trying to pull them from their thrones. You and I both hate how things are being run, and maybe together, we can actually change things. *Help people.*"

She was delusional if she believed I'd *kill* someone for power, even if she professed she did so for the greater good. Did she know me at all?

"My . . . my necklace," I ground out, despising that I could hardly speak. My head lolled to the side.

"I had to, Wren," Callie confessed gently. "I'll give it back, I swear, but I needed to collect gifts powerful enough to set all of this in motion. At first it was to enchant the palace guards so they'd give me the bodies I could use to feed. Then, after growing my collection"—her eyes fell to the open drawer—"I was able to influence the same men who'd laughed in my face when they learned of my ambitions. Using stolen or lost gifts, I blackmailed them, yes, but they deserved it. They'd already been delivering people to the Fates for centuries."

Lost gifts. Something dark argued that she'd acquired them through less savory means.

"I'm forcing the lords to split their shipments, just so the Fates don't catch on quite yet. I want them weak before I strike." Her eyes sparkled like this was the happiest of days. "Even Father listens to me instead of them now, Wren. Can you believe it? He has to put up an act in the office, but he's fully committed." She laughed, the sound ringing painfully in my head. "With enough gifts at my disposal, he and his precious pen are practically useless. I bet the old man would never have let me shadow him at the office if I hadn't used magic. By the time my magic grew, he didn't even hesitate to bow to the daughter he once deemed worthless."

Father *had* changed his mind last year when he gave Callie a more prominent role. Before, he indulged her dreams, allowing her close, but never close enough to see real power. I thought of his conversation with me recently about Callie's future. Had that been a diversion, a trick Callie set in motion to keep me off her path?

"I have the powerful leaders under my control," Callie said, a small smile lifting one corner of her mouth. "And your necklace, Wren, it's helped so much. Allowed me to uncover the secrets I needed. The darkest ones no one wanted shared. It sped everything up, and for that, I owe you so much."

She reached for me and I flinched. While influenced, my body still recognized danger.

"Everett?" I asked, shrinking back as best I could.

"He was a means to an end." Callie peered to the side. "I promised him a true gift when I take one of the thrones in exchange for his complete loyalty." She tugged on her earrings, the silver hoops shining. "Everett's protected me. And *you,* little bird. He's been in love with you for years, but you've never really noticed him until recently. He's elated."

He . . . he had *agreed* to this? I felt sick, and the second the nausea struck, Callie sent another tranquil wave over me. I loathed it.

"But you don't need to worry about any of this, sister," she said lovingly. "When I rise, so will you. I'll return your gift, and you won't remember any of this foolishness."

Won't remember?

"And that thief . . . well, I'll set Everett on him next. He's anxious to claim his reward." She made a face, scrunching up her features like she did whenever she kept a secret from me. "I *did* promise him something else, but I think you'll find it favorable too! You and he do get along quite well." Her stare fell to me, and nausea churned again in my stomach at her insinuation. I actually might be sick. If I were, I hoped it ruined her perfect dress. "Right now, I sent him to clean up a necessary mess. Some lords don't like to play fair. Then again, the *Fates* don't play fair, either. Dusk had her fun with Lord Sinclair, and that resulted in Everett's criminal half brother, who has a power he has no idea exists. Which is for the best. Few can beat the power of a fully turned reaper."

My lips tried to move, but they were frozen.

Reaper?

Dusk was the Fate who played shepherd to the dead. The one who enclosed them in darkness and safeguarded them. That book I'd read, the mysterious blue one I didn't recognize with its single red poppy, contained stories about her reapers. How they wouldn't turn until they knew true loss, eventually morphing into her aides that guided souls to the underworld.

So Dusk's child . . .

"I say we get this over with and get you home and into bed!" Callie said, feigning cheerfulness. She ignored my pleading eyes, her jaw clenched tightly. It was obvious she'd never wished for me to uncover her secret. She'd have done it all behind my back. "You'll feel so much better soon, I promise. And I can finally take care of you properly. Mother and Father never were proper parents." She rolled her eyes. "Thankfully, Father and all the brutes he works with are all but husks, so I suppose I got our revenge."

I had never really hated Father . . . until I discovered what he'd been up to for years. Had Callie coerced him as punishment for years of holding her back? Did she feel any remorse? Not just about Father, but for the *people* she consumed?

This wasn't the sister I knew and loved. What had the thirst for power done to her? Had the magic she collected slowly corrupted her over time?

Callie's cold fingers grazed my cheeks. They were slick, my tears slipping free even with her gift working hard. She softened at the sight.

"I love you, Wren. Please know this. The time for change has come and we both know it's needed."

Not like this. Not by killing innocents.

"Just close your eyes and let me take care of you—"

The door banged open, the wood splintering as it struck the wall.

"Get the fuck away from her!" Damien stormed into the room, his eyes dangerously glacial. I'd never seen him so unhinged, his upper lip curling into a vicious snarl, reminding me more of a beast than a man.

"Oh, I suppose Everett hasn't had time to collect you after all." Callie dropped her hand from my face and crossed her arms. She was unbothered by Damien, her posture shockingly relaxed, like she'd expected his presence. "Looks like I have to clean up his mess. Again."

Damien wasn't paying her any attention. He stared at me, his eyes imploring, *begging.* Heat traveled through my numbed body, a spark igniting as he whispered my name. The very sight of him broke me.

"I really don't like you," Callie snapped. I sensed the moment she released her power, the magic humming in the air as it beat against Damien's body. I wanted to close my eyes. Even if I was angry with Damien, I couldn't bear to see him hurt. I supposed that would be my downfall—seeing the good in people who didn't deserve it.

"I don't like you, either, so I suppose that makes us even," Damien replied, standing tall. "Let her go." His eyes found mine again, and the warmth I'd felt spread. I shifted in my seat, my sister's power over me weakening. I bit my lip to stifle a groan as I moved, my limbs gradually being freed. Agonizing heartbeats passed before I stood up behind her. Callie's focus lay on Damien, a frustrated scoff escaping her lips as she shot wave after wave of power at him.

It didn't work. Her gift didn't affect him.

Impossible, my brain argued . . . But Callie had called him a reaper. A being belonging to Dusk. His ability to withstand her power could be a testament to his birth mother's magic. Callie had said he didn't know what he was.

"I'm so sorry, Wren. You have no idea how sorry I am." Damien's stare landed briefly on the locket clasped around my neck. "I can't say anything to make it better, and even when I tried to help you, it was for my own selfish purposes. I don't deserve you, I know this, but . . . I want to."

The raw admission fractured something in me. Like a dam, emotions flooded out—hatred, rage, betrayal. And then there was another emotion I didn't want to name. Yet it was that unnamable emotion that allowed me to stumble from the chair and across the room. Damien grabbed me, catching me at the same time Callie reached for my sleeve. I slipped through her fingers with a sigh.

I hated what Damien had done, but he hadn't *murdered* hundreds of innocents. He moved me behind him, using his body as a shield while we slowly backed up, his hand grasping mine tightly whenever I wobbled. The door to freedom was so close, and once we got out, I'd turn my attention to the thief who'd robbed me of more than my gift.

He could apologize for *days,* but what he'd done, how he deceived me—it was a wound I wasn't certain could heal.

Callie shut her eyes as if exasperated. Waves of her influence sifted through the air—but it didn't strike me. It went over my shoulder.

Slowly, I turned.

Everett loomed at the threshold, his white shirt covered in blood, his blue eyes transforming into an almost hazy light blue as he turned them to Damien.

"Hello, brother."

Chapter Thirty-Seven

Damien

No one knows what happens to the children of the Fates.
They've hidden them well, but all the magic
flowing in the Fates' blood leads this scholar to believe
that some of it must flow into the veins of their offspring.
These children can be dangerous indeed.
—Pages found in the banned book *Questioning Fate*
by Alexandra Collette, Andalay historian, location unknown

Everett hovered in the doorway, his bulky physique like a wall of bricks.

I drowned in a murderous wave, my need to destroy him a tangible thing. We were so close to escape, and this *brother* of mine had his eyes set on Wren. *My* Wren.

Losing her, having her learn the truth and look at me with *those* eyes, was like a slap in the face. Yet I'd take a thousand slaps if it meant there was a *chance* she'd forgive me.

"Wren," I warned, trying to shield her with my body from both enemies approaching from each side. "Stay behind me." She scoffed, her fire not put out, regardless of the havoc her sister's influence had wrought. Before she argued, I said, "She can't use her power if I'm *shielding* you. You saw what happened when she tried it on me."

Which had been interesting. Never before had someone attempted to use their power on me, and Callie had failed miserably. I'd search for an explanation once we weren't surrounded by traitors.

But I assumed it had something to do with my changing body. With my eyesight. With the hallucinations. It was all connected.

"Oh." The word slipped out of her, and Wren quickly maneuvered to a better position, her hands pressing flat on my back. We were still trapped, Callie not yet defeated. Because though my body could protect Wren from her sister, Everett stood right behind us, a menacing presence ready to strike and wholly under Callie's control. He wore the same unfocused look he had when he killed his father.

"Callie, let us go," Wren pleaded. "I'm your sister, for Fates' sake!"

I stumbled into Wren as Callie shot another blast of magic. It simply tingled, like an itch, but once more, she couldn't command me.

"I'm *helping* you, Wren," Callie insisted. "That thief is the one who stole your gift in the first place, and you're standing behind him?" Shock filled her voice. "If anything, I got it back for you! I'm merely borrowing it."

"To *kill* people," Wren retorted, dangerously close to exposing herself. I carefully nudged her behind me as Everett sauntered deeper into the room, his usually pristine façade ruined.

"You're so fucking gullible, Wren," Callie bit out, her cool vanishing. She waved her hands at Everett. "Take him and dispose of him already."

I'd been in fights before, but not one with a man in magic's grasp. It didn't help that he was broader and had a good twenty pounds on me.

"Wren," I warned, "run as soon as he attacks."

"I'm not a complete idiot, Damien," she said through her teeth. "Though maybe I am. I trusted *you,* after all." The words were biting, but her eyes were filled with unshed tears.

The growing void in my chest widened. I deserved it. All of her anger. But I'd be damned if I didn't take the chance to make it up to her.

"I'm so sorry, and I'll explain everything once we—"

Everett lunged, cutting me off. The brute barreled into me, knocking Wren to the floor. I winced as a *crack* sounded, a small yelp following.

I'm going to kill him.

Distantly, I saw Callie approach her sister, the humming of her magic aimed at Wren, who lay dazed on the floor.

Pain exploded across my jaw as Everett managed a hit. "Funny how things turn out, *brother,*" he sneered. "I'll get magic and your girl." Black spots filled my already distorted vision, and I swayed to the right, avoiding another hit by inches.

"She'll never be with you," I spat, outraged at the very idea. "You're a killer."

"No, I'm a businessman," Everett corrected. "If I need to kill someone to make a deal, then it has to be done. Besides, she liked me well enough before, and once this is all over, she will again. You're just the bastard born of my father's lust." Everett scoffed. "As if the Fate actually gave a damn about him."

What the hell did that mean?

A Fate? Was my mother a fucking *Fate*?

He lifted his fist, ready to bring it down, when Callie interrupted. "Stop. I want him conscious. I think he should see this part."

The swirl of white in Everett's eyes flashed, and instead of another fist, he grabbed me by the jacket. I went flying forward, only to be yanked back as cold steel pressed against my jugular. "Stay still, *thief*," Everett said, his tone one of outrage. Anger. Callie had been stoking the flames of his rage all this time. He'd turned into a puppet, no soul in him to make his own decisions.

Wren wasn't moving from where she'd fallen, but she eyed her sister warily. I struggled fruitlessly against the beast holding me, but it was no better than trying to escape an iron cage.

"Give me the locket, little bird," Callie coaxed, fingers stroking her earrings. Her other hand grasped something in her pocket, and I wondered if it was another stolen gift. "Wren," Callie pressed harshly, and to my horror, Wren reached around her neck to unclasp the locket.

I screamed Wren's name, but it was no use—she handed it over without a word.

"Good." Callie sighed, briefly squeezing her eyes. "I hate to do this next part, but you won't even remember it, will you?"

I grunted as I elbowed Everett, but whatever adrenaline swam through him acted like a barrier against pain. There was no possible way this man could be my flesh and blood.

Unless Callie is lying . . .

But why would she lie about that? Everett Sinclair and I had different features, but that meant nothing, especially if a Fate was involved.

"Wren! Don't give in!" I shouted as Callie opened the locket. My photo lay inside, but Callie plucked it out and tossed it aside like rubbish. With her eyes shut and the locket in hand, Callie murmured quietly as the room sparked like a storm swirled inside. I sensed the power igniting in the air, a peculiar breeze ruffling the hem of her dress.

Wren screeched, falling onto her back.

The sound of Wren's pain was worse than a dagger to my chest, worse than anything I'd known. And I couldn't move an inch with Everett's influenced arms wrapped around me like a manacle.

On the carpet, Wren's eyes snapped open, and I sucked in a sharp breath. They were white as snow. Her body shook as Callie finished whispering into the locket, as the rush of magic and pain turned the slight breeze into a gust that whipped at every available surface.

My chest constricted when she shut the locket. That *click* echoed like the closing of a coffin, and when Wren's eyes rolled back into her head, she just sat there. Blank. *Unfeeling.*

Callie's demeanor changed like a flip had been switched. Rushing to her sister's side, she eased her up. "Are you all right?" she cooed, helping Wren to her elbows. "You hit your head when you fell."

No. When you *pushed her out of my arms.*

Wren blinked several times, her face relaxing when she recognized Callie. But then it sobered as she took in the rest of the room. "What . . . why am I here?" She cocked her head when her gaze landed on me. "Who's that?"

Me. She meant me.

"Oh, sister, you must've really hurt yourself when you fell." Callie wrapped Wren in her arms. "That *boy,*" she spat, glowering at me, "was the one who shoved you. He tried to rob you and Everett, but thank the Fates, Everett bested him." She gave the bastard holding me a sickeningly sympathetic look. "I ran here as soon as he called for me. I wanted to check on you myself and see this cretin thrown in jail."

I snarled, teeth bared as I landed a hit to Everett's shin. He merely grunted.

Frown lines wrinkled Wren's forehead as she turned, confusion sweeping across her beautiful face as she took me in like a stranger. Which, it appeared I was.

"Wait, Wren," I pleaded, just before Everett struck me where he'd wounded me days ago. I almost dropped to my knees from the sheer agony. "You know me!" I cried, stabbing pain shooting down my torso.

Her stare remained devoid of recognition. Of *anything.*

"I don't . . . I don't know you," she said, seeking her sister for help. "He hurt me? Why are we at this place? In this room?" she asked.

I wanted to pull out my own hair. I'd rather hurt myself than see any harm done to her. I'd throw myself on the flames before they touched her skin. I'd do anything.

Anything.

And it meant *nothing.*

"You insisted on coming with Everett when he inspected this property for a business proposition. This thief just so happened to trail you two," Callie lied, grabbing Wren's hand. Wren swayed on her elbows, her eyelashes fluttering like she'd pass out at any moment.

"Can we leave?" Wren asked, eyeing me, looking upon my face with *fear.* "I—I don't want to be here. I don't know—"

I screamed her name as Callie held her and motioned for Everett to take me out of the room. Callie mouthed two words over her sister's head. Two words that would cement my fate. *Wren's* fate. *Kill him.*

He grunted as he dragged me out, but I dug my heels into the carpet, clawing at his arms. "Wren, you know me. Deep down, you know me, sunshine. *Please.*"

Her body went rigid at the nickname, and for just a second I had hope, but . . . But she just held on to Callie for dear life, still swaying a little from when she'd fallen.

Fuck, I'd kill Everett and Callie both. They hurt her. They'd forced her memories away. Stolen them. Stolen *us.*

Why had I gone to Everett's estate? Why couldn't I have just stayed with Wren, wrapped in her sheets and sunshine? I'd been too afraid to lose her, thinking she could never be mine, that my actions drove her straight here.

You should have told her then, my mind argued, about the locket, about my original intentions. But *should haves* were always thought of after the storm struck. After the devastation.

I held on to the sight of her as long as I could, my eyes not leaving her until Everett yanked me into the corridor. Maybe it was a fire originating from the agony exploding where my heart should lie, or maybe it was destiny finally working on my side, but I grasped Everett's arm. *Hard.*

Smoke clogged my nostrils. Darkness swept over my eyes.

Flashes of mourners surrounding Everett greeted me, a casket being lowered into the earth. I hissed through my teeth as I dug my fingers deeper into Everett's arm, more smoke filling the air.

This hallucination felt stronger, like I stood right before the casket, my feet rooted to the soil. I existed in two places at once, but it didn't frighten me like it should. A sense of elation and peace moved through my veins. Like I'd finally come home.

Everett howled in pain and his hold fell. As his bare skin slipped from mine, the world came back into focus. I sucked in a lungful of air as I staggered backward, away from Everett and the possibility of his demise. He was staggering, trying to stand.

My heart dropped in my chest when I realized what I had to do.

I had to run.

I was no match against them both, and they wouldn't hurt Wren.

They'd manipulate and placate her, but never harm her. Callie was her sister, and Everett—he wanted her with his ring on her finger. But not the *real* her, just the version of her he'd concocted in his mind.

My feet were glued to the floor, sweat dripping down my back. I had seconds to decide, and with Everett regaining focus, I finally accepted how this would end should I attack in my weakened state.

My death wouldn't save Wren.

"I'm coming back for you!" I shouted, hoping Wren heard me, even though I realized I was just a stranger who likely frightened her. Still, I had to maintain some faith or I'd lose what little shred of sanity I possessed.

I'd come back when I was stronger. I'd make certain to get her free of her sister's clutches. And then . . . then I'd make her remember it all. Remember me.

My eyes burned as I took off down the stairs and bolted out the doors of the Black Dahlia and onto the streets. They burned with tears that I refused to let fall—because this wasn't the end.

I'd thought I understood what the Fates had in store for me. A life on the street. A chance to escape and maybe leave for the west. I'd believed that was my destiny.

The truth ran much darker.

I felt it now, that otherworldly darkness. It slithered in my veins, as icy as when I'd dug my fingers into Everett and glimpsed a scene of death.

Magic. The kind that shouldn't be possible.

I was the brother of Everett Sinclair . . . but my mother—Everett had alluded to what she could be, and the time had arrived to finally hunt her down. She owed me a lifetime of answers, and I wouldn't leave this city until I burned its monsters to ash. Even if one of those monsters carried my blood.

I'd find out the truth and *make* Wren remember. I wouldn't stop until she held each stolen midnight we'd spent together in the palms of her hands.

Epilogue

I woke in a bed of silken ivory.

The sheets felt divine on my skin as I rolled over with a contented sigh, reveling in the heavenly sensation. The mattress I lay upon was a cloud. It had to be.

"Darling, are you awake?"

"Hmm," I murmured, eyes still shut. I wanted to sleep for another hour. Or five.

A hand rested atop my arm, warm fingers tracing my exposed flesh. Shivering, I peeled open one eye.

Everett sat beside me on the bed—

Which wasn't my own.

I bolted upward, my head swimming. Where was I? I glanced about the room, noting the creamy colors and fine golden accents. The bed itself took up most of the space, a gorgeous armoire and vanity nestled in the corner. I blinked, the light coming in through the gauzy curtains suddenly too bright. Too much. No, *everything* was too much.

"You hit your head pretty hard," Everett said softly, rubbing my shoulders. "I've been worried sick."

I frowned, reaching for the back of my head, where a steady throbbing radiated. My fingers traced a decent-sized bump, and I winced at the touch.

A flash of a memory struck me—of me in a dark room, lying on the floor. Everett had been there, leaning down to pick me up. The rest was a blur.

"What happened? Why am I here? And *where* is here?" I asked, gazing up at him. He wore only his trousers and a simple button-down, which was halfway open, the top of his muscular chest exposed. Another oddity. But worse than that were the swollen nose and black eye he sported. Had he gotten into a brawl?

Everett's gaze grew clouded. "Wren. You live here," he said, his fingers tracing up to my cheeks. He cupped one, cradling my face as confusion rendered me frozen. "We eloped, remember?" He laughed, shaking his head. "Your father was furious at first, but he's come around—"

The pounding in my ears muffled whatever he said next. As Everett beamed and spoke, his eyes alight with joy, I lifted my left hand.

There, nestled on my finger, shone a bright pink diamond ring surrounded by a gold band.

"No." I cut him off, yanking the covers off the bed and shifting around him and to the floor. "This isn't real."

I'd never get married. Not to him, at least . . .

"Darling." Everett bent toward me, his brows pinched in concern. "You must've really hurt yourself when you fell. The doctor who examined you told me this could happen."

I wrapped my arms around my body, moving to the end of the

room. I wore only a thin nightdress. "What could happen?" I questioned, thinking of how to get the hell out of here.

He sighed and rubbed at his temples. "Memory loss. It can happen with falls like yours. Some cretin from the south knocked you over and you struck your head. He'd been trying to rob us when we visited the site I had my eye on for a new business venture."

"I—I don't remember that," I said, inching toward the door. I needed to find some proper clothes. "The last time we were together, we went riding."

I recalled that day just fine. He'd fallen and broken his glasses. That was when I realized he hadn't received a gift either.

Everett flinched as if he'd been struck. "You don't remember anything else?" he pressed, standing. His hulking frame moved before me, blocking off my only exit.

I'd never been afraid of Everett before, so why was I now? He—he wouldn't be lying, would he?

"Shh." He grasped my shoulders and tugged me into an embrace. Wrapping his arms around my back, he secured me to his hard chest. "It's all right, Wren. I bet your memories will return soon. Just need to give them some time."

Time.

"How long ago was that day?" I mumbled against him. "When we went riding?"

"Well, it wasn't that long ago," he admitted. "But when we returned to the estate, I asked for your hand. When you said yes, you told me your only stipulation was that we do it soon. That you didn't trust your father to say yes."

No, no, no.

None of that made sense.

I tried to shove him away, but he was built like stone; unyielding and firm. I couldn't budge, and a spike of adrenaline had sweat pouring from my brow. "Everett, please," I begged, needing to be free.

Somewhere behind him, I heard the light tread of footsteps. I tried to crane my neck, to see if the person slipping past him would help explain what was happening to me, but then—

A wave of calm washed across me, warm and soft and heady. My shoving ceased and I relaxed, slumping in Everett's arms. He felt nice, too. Strong and safe. Yes, I felt his soothing presence waft off him like the sweetest perfume.

"There you go," he said. "Maybe you just need some more rest."

His dulcet tone had me swaying, suddenly exhausted. Before I knew it, he had swept me from my feet, his arms under my legs while my hands automatically went around his neck.

Placing me on the bed with all the care in the world, he made sure to tuck the covers up to my chin.

"So good, Wren," he praised, and I blushed, feeling heat all over. "You've always made me feel like nothing bad could ever happen. I knew from the moment I saw you that we were alike, and now I'm going to make sure nothing bad ever happens to you again. I promise, little bird." He leaned down and kissed my forehead, his full lips sending shivers down my spine.

Everett grinned, one hand resting on my waist, the other toying with what appeared to be a shiny hoop. An earring, much like Callie's.

"From now on, we aren't alone," he murmured, almost to

himself. "I'm here to take care of you." He lifted himself from the bed, peering at me like I was his greatest treasure. "Sleep, now. I'll check on you soon."

I sighed, about to heed his orders when I glimpsed the flash of a pink skirt from the hall. Somewhere in the back of my mind, that particular shade and material looked familiar.

"Night, darling," Everett said, backing up before shutting the door.

Sleep sounded so nice. And this bed felt so soft. Rolling over, I glanced at the ring shining on my left hand. A rare pink diamond. I frowned for a moment, surprised he selected something so big and ostentatious. So unlike me. But he'd chosen my favorite color, and it was indeed striking.

Everett had told me to sleep. Told me to relax, and miraculously, it worked. I smiled, thinking of Callie's silver earrings. He didn't even have to use magic to soothe me.

Just before I drifted off into a deep sleep, I made out my name. Deep and low and coming from unfamiliar lips. The dream man whispered my name over and over, but he wasn't strong enough to break the spell of exhaustion.

"Sunshine . . ."

Blackness embraced me, and the man's voice faded away.

Acknowledgments

This book began as a whimsical dream that slowly delved into a reality that reflects our own society in many ways. I want to thank those who stand against the injustice we see every night on our television screens. Who march and protest. Who don't sit down and accept the hatred our world is sadly growing too familiar with. This book is for you all. The ones I admire with all my heart.

Stolen Midnights wouldn't have been possible without the support and love of my partner, Joshua, who pushes me to write what matters most to me. You and the children inspire me every day to pick up a pen and create my wildest dreams.

To my agent, Cole Lanahan. Your enduring kindness and unwavering faith have been instrumental in fulfilling this wish of mine. You are empathetic and strong, and you fight every day for not only your clients but what you believe in. You have my immense gratitude and respect.

To my editor, Ali Romig. Thank you for taking a chance on *Stolen Midnights*. Without your guiding hand and your confidence in this story, it wouldn't be what it is today. I cannot express my thanks enough for believing in me, Wren, and Damien.

To my friend Morgan Gauthier, a talented author and an even kinder person. To Elizabeth Trauer and Haley Councillor—both of you had faith in this story when I doubted myself. Thank you.

And to the readers—it is you who I write to, and you who give me the strength to not give up on doing what I love. I thank you all for coming along on this journey with me. I cannot wait for our next adventure together.

About the Author

Katherine Quinn is a fantasy romance author and poet. She graduated from the University of Central Florida with a degree in psychology. She lives in Houston, Texas, with her husband and children.

Her love for writing began after she read her first fantasy series, *Song of the Lioness* by Tamora Pierce. After that, she wanted nothing more than to be a dagger-wielding heroine. Unfortunately, giving a child a dagger is frowned upon, so she settled for writing about daring adventures instead.

Coffee is her true love, and she believes anything can be fixed with Starbucks and dark humor.

katherinequinnauthor.com